In Love
with my
Enemy

Also by A'zayler

Passion of the Streets

No Loyalty (with De'nesha Diamond)

Published by Kensington Publishing Corp.

In Love with my Enemy

A'zayler

Dafina
BOOKS

KENSINGTON PUBLISHING CORP.

www.kensingtonbooks.com

DAFINA BOOKS are published by

Kensington Publishing Corp.
119 West 40th Street
New York, NY 10018

All Kensington titles, imprints, and distributed lines are available at special quantity discounts for bulk purchases for sales promotion, premiums, fund-raising, and educational or institutional use.

Special book excerpts or customized printings can also be created to fit specific needs. For details, write or phone the office of the Kensington Sales Manager: Kensington Publishing Corp., 119 West 40th Street, New York, NY 10018. Attn. Sales Department. Phone: 1-800-221-2647.

Dafina and the Dafina logo Reg. U.S. Pat. & TM Off.

ISBN-13: 978-1-4967-1808-2
ISBN-10: 1-4967-1808-9
First Kensington Trade Paperback Printing: September 2019

ISBN-13: 978-1-4967-1814-3 (ebook)
ISBN-10: 1-4967-1814-3 (ebook)
First Kensington Electronic Edition: September 2019

10 9 8 7 6 5 4 3 2 1

Printed in the United States of America

Prologue

"Hey, Free, make sure you be checking your phone," Echo warned.

"Come on, now. You know me. I don't fuck around when it comes to business."

Echo chuckled. "A'ight, bet. I'm set. I'll meet you at the drop in a few."

"Cool. This it, my nigga. Let's eat."

Echo's laughter filled the phone. "Already," he told him before ending the call.

Jalil Donquez Free—Free to the streets and Don to himself—was a hidden loner with a constant intent to kill and no time for the pleasures of a simple life. With his hood covering his head, he took a deep breath and made his way into the club. It was game time. Since he'd gone through the side exit, he was in his seat and chilling within minutes.

Flashing red and white lights flickered across the room as smoke and music filled the dark atmosphere. Heat radiated from one wall to the other as the floor shook from the bass of the music. Men were everywhere, with a barely dressed woman strewed here and there.

Liquor bottles, red cups, and marijuana-filled blunts that were louder than the music rotated from the mouth of one person to the next as the partygoers interacted vibrantly with one another. Pool tables decorated one corner of the room, while sofas, bar speakers, and a homemade bar occupied the rest.

A parade of nudity filled the gleeful eyes of the many men that enjoyed that type of thing, but not Don. That wasn't something that moved him. The naked women were such an irritant for him that they might as well have been flies circling his food at a barbeque. Unwanted, and just in the fucking way. He liked his women a little more respectable and a lot less social. Hood girls that knew their status without hanging out at every party to let the streets verify it.

Since he hadn't wanted to be there from the beginning, Don sat in a large chair in the corner of the room minding his business, simply observing his surroundings and chilling. Too many people in one room with too much going on wasn't his scene, but for money he'd do what he had to do.

"Why you always looking so mean? You're too handsome for that," an around-the-way girl known as Mocha whispered into his ear as she leaned over the back of the chair he was seated in.

Don looked over his shoulder with an annoyed expression on his face. His brows were furrowed while his mouth held a small frown. He was in no mood to be bothered, and he'd made that very clear from the moment he'd walked through the door. One thing he couldn't stand was a woman that didn't know how to listen. He wasn't the most social person to begin with, but he most definitely hated women with no morals. Specifically, ones like Mocha. She'd do anything for money, no matter how backstabbing or disrespectful it was.

"Care your ass on," Don shooed her away with his fingers.

"Why are you being so mean? You ain't been acting like this."

Don blew out a frustrated breath and ignored her while looking at the screen of his phone. He checked his text messages for the thousandth time, waiting on the message from his friend Echo that would get his night going. His thumb was tapping on his screen when he felt Mocha's hands sliding down the front of his chest. She wasn't given the chance to get much further than his collarbone before Don had a death grip on one of her wrists.

"Bitch, you must want to die."

Mocha sucked her teeth and tried to pull her hand free of his grasp, but it wasn't happening. Don squeezed it a little tighter, even twisting it until she whined in pain.

"When you see me, do your fucking job and keep it moving."

"Let my arm go. I got it."

Don applied a little more pressure, this time twisting it harder to one side. When she yelped and dropped a set of keys into his lap, he finally let her go. With no more words spoken, she walked away nursing her wrist. Don watched her rush to the back corner, where a few niggas he knew from around the hood were sitting.

He pushed the keys into the front pocket of his hoodie as he observed her switch back to where she belonged. Mocha was one woman that did too damn much. It had been a tedious task to be cordial to her during their brief alliance, but he'd done it and he was more than happy that it was finally about to be over.

He wasn't surprised when she sat in the lap of the biggest man in the section, and held her wrist up to his face as if he was going to do something about it. Her thick lips were moving rapidly as she relayed what had just happened. Don watched and waited. Bishop, a well-known pimp, held her wrist and placed a kiss on it as his pudgy fingers rubbed her back.

Like Don knew he would, Bishop looked his way with a grimace. His eyes searched the people around Don until Mocha whispered something in his ear. Finally, Bishop's glare found Don's. Unmoving and unbothered by anything that Bishop could possibly be attempting, Don peered back.

The frown that had been there earlier disappeared and a simple head nod was rendered. Don nodded back before looking away. He hadn't expected anything different. He wasn't to be played with, and even Bishop knew that. He might run them hoes, but he didn't run Don, and that was known.

Back in his element, Don leaned back and checked his phone once more. Still nothing. His irritation grew by the second. It was a little after one in the morning, and his job was scheduled to have been completed by midnight. Don huffed out another ragged breath and stretched his legs in front of him.

His hands were resting across his stomach with intertwined fingers when he heard a loud commotion at the door. Accustomed to staying alert, he sat up with the speed of lightning. His hand went to his back, releasing the large Glock nine that had been secured in the waistband of his jeans. He made sure the silencer was intact before allowing his eyes to scan the crowd where all the noise was coming from.

On his feet, sliding further into the darkness he'd just been occupying, Don waited to see what was happening before making any further moves. The bright red exit sign above his head, leading to the unchained door behind him, was the perfect avenue out, if things blew out of hand. His seat for the night hadn't been by chance; Don was a thinker, and so was Echo, so anything they planned was bound to run smoothly.

In a room full of niggas he knew nothing about, near the exit had been the safest and smartest place to be, for reasons like the one unfolding in front of him. Still unsure of what was going on, or who it was causing the disturbance, Don squinted his eyes trying to see the faces of the yelling men. With the loud music still playing, and the staggering drunk patrons, it wasn't easy to make out the issue, but Don wouldn't relax until it was revealed.

He was squeezing the handle of his gun when he felt his phone vibrating. In a hurry, he pulled it from his pocket and checked the screen. **GO** was the one word message he'd been waiting on all night. With the skill and expertise of a trained shooter, Don raised his nine and aimed it until the red beam attached to it landed on his first target. *Phew . . .* body number one. *Phew . . .* body number two . . . *Phew . . .* Three. He was done.

An uproar of screams and frantic cries sounded throughout the room as Don hit the exit without looking back. There was no need to—his job was done. He'd killed all three people before the first one's body hit the ground. Positive no one had seen or heard him do it, Don trekked down the sidewalk coolly, but with a little more urgency in his step.

The hood to his black hoodie shielded his head as the cool breeze from the night air brushed against his face. His hands were tucked securely in his front pockets as he bent the corner heading for the big black pickup truck parked on the side of the hole-in-the-wall club he'd just been in.

Don looked over his shoulder once to make sure no one was coming, before snatching the keys out and hitting the locks. Once the door was open, he slid in and backed out of the parking space. The block was empty and dark as he cruised down the street. That too was a part of their strategic planning. From the fifth-floor window of the abandoned apartment building to his left, he'd shot out every street light along that block hours prior. The lick he'd just hit had been in the works for weeks and he had one last step to complete before giving himself a pat on the back.

With no outside help, Don and Echo had hopefully set themselves up to become a part of something much larger than themselves. Something that would potentially alleviate his loneliness and repetitive struggling. Echo had his family, so he was good, but Don was alone. Just trying to make it. He'd been living from one dump to the next since turning eighteen four years ago, and had been putting in work ever since.

Nights had been long, with days that were even longer but he'd made it happen. With nothing or nobody outside of Echo, Don was self-made and planned to keep it that way until the day the city covered his corpse with the dark dirt that would eliminate his light forever.

Echo had been the only family he'd had in years. They'd met in the county jail three years prior and had been hanging since. If it wasn't him, it wasn't anyone. Echo was truly a stand-up guy and the only person that Don halfway trusted. He trusted him with business, but nothing personal.

Which was why they'd been friends for years and Echo still knew nothing about his living situation. Anytime they made plays, he'd either meet up at the spot or they hung out at Echo's crib. Nothing more, and Don planned to keep it that way until he could do better. He'd learned long ago to never let another man see him down bad. Hopefully, their current plan would open the door to all that.

With his heart beating a mile a minute, Don looked in his rearview mirrors to assure he wasn't being followed before taking the highway en route to the meeting place that no one except he and Echo knew about. Well, almost no one. Thanks to one lonely night in the run-down basement he'd been sleeping in, where he'd stumbled upon a life changing opportunity.

It had been freezing outside and way too cold to sleep under his normal bridge, so Don had gone on a hunt to find somewhere warm to sleep. When the raggedy old building with the boards and plastic up to the window caught his eye, he'd wasted no time kicking the backdoor in. It had been empty, minus the rats and stray cats that were seemingly unbothered by the other's presence.

Using plastic and the blanket he carried around in his tattered old backpack, Don made his bed on the bottom floor of the building. It was in the wee hours of the morning when he'd heard voices. Unsure who the men were, and afraid to move, Don lay deadly still beneath the dirty old blanket.

"It's the one they call Bishop."

"The pussy pusher?" The second voice questioned with a tainted accent.

"The one and only."

One of the men cleared his throat before the conversation continued.

"So, he sells dope and pussy? You Americans are a fucking joke."

Don strained to hear the conversation better. It was pretty easy, up until the one with the deep accent spoke. He was clearly a DeKalb county outsider. Nobody in Ellenwood sounded like that. Which only sparked Don's interest even more.

"Who gave you the information?"

"One of his hoes. I think her name is Mocha or some shit like that."

"Do you see why I say it's stupid? His own women are selling him out. Disloyalty is something my family doesn't tolerate."

The man that owned the first voice made some sort of noise with his mouth before talking again. "What do you think should be done?"

"You tell me. This is your area, right?"

Although he didn't know him, Don liked the second guy. His tone and wording sounded like a man that could be respected. In his opinion, the first one seemed to be a tad bit shifty. It was just something about him that didn't sit right with Don. Little did he know, his gut feelings would soon prove to be accurate.

"The only way to get rid of him is to kill him, is that something you want done?"

"You tell me."

"I mean, I could, but everybody would know. He's the man in this city."

"So, you mean to tell me I flew out here for this bull-shit? Not one muthafucka that I've met since being here has shown me anything to respect." Second voice cleared his throat. "Stop wasting my gotdamn time. Off that man, get me his shit, and call me when it's done. Got it?"

By this time, Don's heart was booming while his mind did numbers. If that nigga was scared to put in work, he had no problem picking up his slack. He just needed a way to get himself involved without seeming too eager. He lay beneath the blanket thinking over everything he was hearing and the best way in without getting killed for eavesdropping. The foreign man didn't sound like somebody he wanted to rub the wrong way.

"Yes sir. I got it."

"Good. Call me when you've figured this shit out."

The sound of footsteps could be heard clicking across the floor which let Don know the man was probably well dressed. Only nice shoes made that type of noise when being used. With his mind in overdrive, Don lay still for a few moments longer after hearing the door of the building slam closed, and got the break of his life.

"Hey, who the fuck is this nigga, man? Trying to call shots when he can barely speak fucking English."

Don slid the covers from his head slowly trying to grab a glance at the man as he spoke loudly on the phone.

"The only way he's willing to give me a spot in his ring is if I take Bishop out, and I ain't with that shit. I don't give a fuck how much money that nigga talking, Bishop is fucking royalty in the streets, killing him would be a sack move and I ain't going out like that. Fuck nah, nigga. I'm Ellenwood to the death of me."

Don was on pins and needles to sit up as he listened to the man he recognized as Jeff talk on the phone. Jeff was one of Bishop's right hand men; no wonder he wasn't feeling the proposition. Don had been hanging around the block doing odds and ends for Bishop and anybody else that paid him the right amount of money since he'd gotten out of his last group home, so he knew a few people. Jeff was one of them.

Even though he had no real idea what this job entailed, something inside of him wanted a part of it.

"I say we set that nigga up and give his shit to Bishop. We don't know his ass, at least we know if Bishop comes up, we all gone eat. This stupid-talking muthafucka might let us do all the work, then feed our asses to the fucking fishes."

What? Don was completely baffled as he listened to Jeff. Bishop was one of the greediest niggas in the hood, and that was a fact. Everybody knew Bishop was out for self, which was why Don had only done business with him once in the past. He promised one thing and had given another, something Don didn't forget. He was a man that took people at their word, so when Bishop burned him that once, their business relationship was over.

Don might not have had much, but he had his respect and he'd die about it. After pulling his heat on Bishop, and killing the two men he'd sent to kill him, Bishop accepted defeat and laid off. Don let him live off street credibility alone, and because of that, Bishop kept his distance and allowed Don to do him with no interruption.

"I'm supposed to meet up with him again at the end of the month. He said I can either have it done, or we can find us somebody else to do business with." Jeff paced the floor with the phone to his ear. "We met at the old barbershop on Thirteenth. You know ain't shit in here no more but animals and bums." Jeff laughed. "I just ain't with the shit. I say we dust his old ass and take it for ourselves." There was a pause. "Bet. Go ahead and tell Bishop what's up. I'm on the way."

Don's body stilled when Jeff walked past. He held his breath, unsure if Jeff would spot him or not, but when he heard the door slam again he figured the coast was clear. Don waited to move until he'd heard the sound of a car cranking up and peeling out of the parking lot.

He wasted no time getting out of the building. With his blanket stuffed into his backpack and a better life on his mind, Don set off into the darkness to find Echo and get them a plan going.

From that day to this current one, they'd been doing everything they could to get ready for the night at hand. It was the thirtieth, and the man would be arriving at the abandoned barbershop within the next ten minutes. Don had just parked Bishop's truck when he saw a pair of headlights shining behind him. He hurried to check his face in the mirror before getting out. He already knew they could only belong to one person. Echo wasn't set to arrive until Don called. Being in the streets, they both knew how first impressions could determine the outcome of life and death. The last thing they wanted to do was bombard the man and end up dying because of it.

With his hood still on his head, Don stood next to the truck with his hands still in his pocket. His heartbeat thumped rapidly as his hands opened and closed steadily in his pocket. He nodded his head to the beat in his mind as the headlights shined on him. He waited patiently on them to analyze the situation and make their move.

Nearly ten minutes passed with nothing happening, so Don made his first. With his head down and hands still hidden, he walked to the back of the truck and opened the back door. He pulled out the six large bags weighed down with Bishop's re-up money and new product. As a gesture of good faith, he unzipped two of the bags, pulling money out of one, and neatly wrapped drugs from the other.

He held them up, and for another few minutes the air around him was filled with uncertainty and regret, but he'd come too far to turn back now, so he maintained his cool and waited. It felt like forever for the front door to the dark-colored SUV to open. Out stepped a big burly man with a long ponytail and a neat black suit. His eyes were shielded by a pair of sunglasses, but Don could tell he was watching him.

The man's large stature seemed to grow another few sizes when he was in front of Don snatching him from the ground. The money and drugs fell to the ground as the man patted him down roughly, pulling at his clothes before snatching his gun from his waistband. He tossed it to the side before continuing his search. When he was satisfied, he stood massively in front of Don.

"Who are you? Where's Jeff?"

Don fixed his clothes while making the best eye contact he could make through the man's shades in the dark night.

"There is no more Jeff, and I'm . . ." Don pondered over his words. "Somebody your boss wants to know." Even with his body shaking in anticipation, Don was confident in his ability and decision making.

The man sized him up as the seconds passed before slapping him hard on the shoulder. "I will kill you."

"There will be no need for that," Don assured him.

With weighted footsteps, the man walked to the opposite side of the truck and opened the back door. A fancy white shoe that lit up the night emerged from the car. A pants leg the same color topped the ankle of the shoe as the other leg followed. When the man was upright, the two men spoke in hushed tones before the person Don was hoping would change his life rounded the door.

He was decked out in all white, from his head down to his feet. Even his hair and facial hair was white. Nothing like what Don had been expecting, but either way, he was there to do business and nothing more. Everything about the man looked expensive. Not that Don was privy to high-end brands or anything like that, but anybody with eyes could see this man was draped in nothing but the best. The iced-out watch and pinky ring further proved Don right.

The closer he got, the more profound his skin color became. The brownish-red hue to it made Don think of the beach. He looked like someone who lived and breathed under the sun and next to the ocean, but the dark lines in his forehead and heavy bags beneath his eyes told a different story.

"So, I've been told you're someone I would want to know? Is that correct?"

Don strained his ears to understand the man's heavy accent and nodded.

"What would make you think I would want to know someone like you?" The older man's eyes trekked up and down Don's clothing. He did nothing to hide his disapproval of Don's appearance. "You look like trash."

Don could feel himself getting hotter, but he took a deep breath and suppressed it. He needed this. On top of that, he couldn't argue with the truth.

"Whenever entertaining money, look the part. You got that?"

Don nodded.

"Appearance is everything. People see you before they hear you, and judging by what I see, nothing you have to say may be worth my time." He gave Don the once over again. "Speak, and hurry up."

Don glared at the man with fury burning behind his eyes. The confidence he'd had before had been washed away by the man's insults. In a world where Don had nothing but his respect, he'd fold before he let another man strip it away from him.

"Humility is also everything. If you present yourself like a self-absorbed jackass, people will treat you as such. Your personality can take you places that your money can't, and judging by what I just heard, I'd rather not do business with you." Don kicked the two bags in front of him toward the man before snatching the other four from the truck.

Once they were all on the ground in front of the man, he stood back to his full height. "In these bags is Bishop's most recent re-up and the money he was paid to cap your ass. He got the work from your competition as well as the cash. Him, Jeff, and that nigga Ditto from up north was planning on taking your old ass out tonight and pushing on without you, but I heard them and stopped the shit. But, I'm sure your head was too high in the clouds to know that shit." Don scoffed.

"How do you know this?"

"Because I heard them say it right after you left here the last time. They weren't feeling your approach, so they were going to push you out altogether."

The man's eyebrows rose. "What were you doing here that night? You work for them?"

Don shook his head once. "Nah, I'm more of an independent contractor."

"Don't fuck with me."

"I'm not. I work for myself and that's it. I do little shit here and there that nobody else wants to do for the cash that nobody else wants to make. I'm homeless and I do what needs to be done to stay fed. That's it."

"Do you know who I am?"

"Nope."

"So, why do something of this magnitude?" He motioned towards the bags sitting between them.

"The night you met with them, I was here on the floor sleeping. I overheard the way you spoke about loyalty and actually kind of respected it, so when I heard that nigga Jeff talking on the phone about all of this, I took matters into my own hands. I used that hoe Mocha to help me set it all up, and here I am." Don wrapped up his entire month of hard work in a couple of need-to-know sentences.

"And you did all of this with just the help of some prostitute?"

Don shook his head. "I had a friend, but he can come around later. Right now, it's just you and I."

With his hand to his chin, the older gentleman pulled at the white beard as he stared at Don in deep thought. Don waited on his next words, because they would decide his next move. It would take him absolutely nothing to grab his gun from the ground and kill them both before they had time to react. He was just that good, however he hoped it would go a different way. His lifestyle needed a change.

"Where are the traitors now?"

"No longer a problem."

His eyes widened in alarm, but he masked it just as quick as it had come. "I assume that was your doing?"

"You would assume right. Bishop, Mocha, and Jeff. Ditto wasn't here or he would be out of the picture as well." Don shrugged. "I figured you had ways to handle that though."

The air between the men was filled with unasked questions, but neither of them said anything to address them. Don had shot his ball directly into the stranger's court, it was up to him what he was going to do with it.

"Tell me your name."

"Don't have one. Yours?"

A steady hand went back to the long white beard. "Sergio Ortega."

"Never heard of you."

"And you never will." He looked over his shoulder to his bodyguard and nodded his head toward Don.

Before the man or Sergio could move another muscle, Don had fallen onto the ground next to his gun and aimed it at them. The guard had his hand on his waist in what appeared to be his attempt to retrieve his gun, but Don was faster.

"It ain't going down like this. Y'all can take that shit and count it as a favor, but I'm leaving with my life and that's on me." He stood to his feet slowly. "It's up to y'all if y'all do the same." Now in full combat mode, Don's eyes bounced between the two men, but stayed on the bodyguard.

Sergio hadn't moved to do anything, and didn't look like he was about to either.

"What's it going to be?"

"Quick reflexes, I like that."

Don said nothing.

"What is it that you said you do again?"

"I didn't say."

"Who taught you to move like that?"

"The hood."

Sergio chuckled a little before pointing a finger at Don. "You're something special, I can tell. You need a little help in the grooming department, but I can handle that." For the first time that night, he rendered a smile. "How much are your services? Since you're an independent contractor and all." His accent was heavier due to his laughter.

Don found nothing funny, so he didn't laugh. Instead he looked from the bodyguard to Sergio and back again before squeezing his hand around the handle of his gun. He wouldn't move until he was sure they weren't about to kill him first.

The silence grew as they all stood facing one another. Nothing in the air changed until Sergio stepped forward and pushed the top of Don's gun down. Don allowed him to do it, only because he stepped closer and began saying things he wanted to hear.

"I want you to come work for me. Tell me what you're good at." Sergio stood face to face with Don, invaded every ounce of his personal space. "I can use you."

"Use me to do what?"

Sergio laughed heartily. "Grow my empire, son . . . to grow my empire." More laughter flowed from Sergio as he grabbed Don around the neck and pulled him into a small hug. "You ready for this shit?"

Don looked into Sergio's smiling face and said nothing. He was still too busy trying to thank God that his plan had worked out. The only thing he hoped now, was that it was all that he'd been praying for.

"You have any family here, son?"

Don wasn't big on the "son" verbiage, but he'd let it slide for now. Maybe that was just the way he spoke.

"Just the friend I spoke of earlier."

Sergio stopped walking and turned Don to face him. With both of his hands resting on Don's shoulders he stared him in the face. Don's body shook lightly when Sergio gave his shoulders a firm shake. No more movement came from Don's body until Sergio slapped his face lightly. Don pulled his head away to free it from Sergio's range of motion.

Sergio dropped his hand from Don's face before a grin crossed his face. "Don't worry, son, we'll get to know each other soon enough. For now, on to more important things."

"Such as?"

"Take me to the bodies. I need to make sure all of this is true."

Don nodded his head backward toward Bishop's truck. "Your car or Bishop's?"

Sergio raised his eyebrows. "Bishop's?"

"Yeah, I drove it from the spot."

Sergio looked back at his bodyguard as he walked toward the truck. "Anybody saw you do this?"

"No."

"Are you sure about that?" Sergio rubbed his beard. Don noted that was clearly something he did when thinking.

"Yeah. No one snitches on me."

"Good." Sergio turned and walked back to his truck. "Since you've helped me, I'm going to help you."

Before getting into the car, he faced Don and observed him quietly. "Where are you living right now, kid?"

"Anywhere and nowhere at the same time."

Another smile. "I fucking love you. Get in."

"In your car?"

"Yes, son, with me. We have somewhere to be."

Don looked around at nothing in particular, just trying to process what was happening and how fast it was happening. He'd been hoping the meeting went well, but he hadn't known it would be of this magnitude. The feeling of it being too good to be true was heavy on him, but he pushed it away. He'd been on his knees before the creator for years begging for a break, maybe it had finally come. Sergio seemed like a cool dude, and was embracing him rather quickly, but that alone made Don a little eerie.

"How do you know you can trust me?" Don asked him.

Sergio clasped his hands together loudly and held them there before raising them to his mouth. He held them still for a few seconds before shaking them toward Don while walking toward him.

"Because I live off loyalty, and you were loyal to me before you even knew who I was." Sergio motioned for Don to come to him. "Come, we have work to do."

This time, Don went with no problem. Sergio was definitely a man he could work with. Not too many people shared his values in life, and anyone who did had to be trustworthy. It took a few minutes for everybody to settle down in the car, but once they did, Sergio turned to Don.

"To establish trust, we must be honest with one another no matter what, you hear me?"

Don nodded. "Understood."

"Once we're family, there's no going back. You good with that?"

Don was quiet for a while, contemplating how much that statement weighed before nodding.

"Give me your name."

"Don Free."

Sergio nodded before sitting back in his seat. "Free-Ortega."

Don fought the feeling in his chest.

"Would you prefer Don or Free?"

Don pondered his question for a minute because he'd never thought much about his name. It was what it was, and he was who he was, there was no need for specifics, but now it felt like more. His new identity, his new world, his new life.

"Free." Don glanced at Sergio before sitting back in the seat and looking out of the window. He didn't know what lay ahead, but he did know he was ready for whatever it was.

"Here's to a new beginning, kid." Sergio's outstretched fist hung between them.

Don pressed his against it. "A new beginning."

Don ran his open palms over the front of his jeans while trying to calm his nerves. It was really happening. The moment he'd been waiting for, or so he thought.

"You know, son, it's funny you picked the name Free."

Don looked his way. "What's funny about it?"

Sergio looked his way while digging in his pocket. "Because that's the opposite of what you'll be for the next few years of your life."

Don's eyebrows scrunched up at the sight of the shiny badge hanging from the wallet in Sergio's hand. Though he couldn't read the small words, the big FBI abbreviation hadn't lost his attention yet.

"Man, what the fuck!" Don slid down in the seat at the same time as two more large trucks pulled in behind him with flashing blue lights in their window.

Everything after that happened at the speed of lightning. All he knew was that Sergio's words definitely held some truth. Free was indeed the last thing he would be for years to come. But . . . who the fuck told? Don closed his eyes trying to think of any loose ends and they popped back open immediately. *Where the fuck was that nigga Echo?*

1

Who would have known?

2Pac's "Thug Passion" blared though the massive living room as people crowded in and out of her best friend Katara's house. The bass from the speakers was so loud that it vibrated the walls, the ceilings, and the floors. Guests packed the room from left to right as they danced, smoked, drank, and interacted with each other.

The potent smell of weed floated throughout the room as Danna passed through it trying to make her way to Katara's room. It was both Danna and Katara's mothers' birthdays and they'd brought the hood out to celebrate. Not only were Eva and Vonetta mothers and wives, but they were the queens of their hoods and their households as well. Eva, Katara's mother, was the bootleg lady, and Danna's mother Vonetta was the heart of it all. Everybody and their mama knew Vonetta, which was probably why Katara's house looked like an overcrowded bootleg house. Food, partiers, and liquor were everywhere.

Twenty-three-year-old Danna Mendoza, the daughter of old school drug dealer, Echo Mendoza, was a young hood princess with more attitude than people knew how to deal with. Hood but not ghetto, Danna knew all the ins and outs of the streets. Her father's only daughter, and her mother's youngest one, Danna was spoiled to the max. Vonetta spoiled all her children to be for real, but she really doted on Danna and Ezra. They were the youngest of her four children, and the only two that didn't drive her crazy with foolishness every day. Well, at least Ezra didn't. Danna had her days where she cut the fool and got cussed out like her older siblings, but those days were few and far apart.

Danna would rather spend most of her time spending money and playing with the hood niggas. At average height with long thick legs and wide hips, Danna kept the street niggas going crazy. A flat stomach, with glowing slanted eyes and a smile to kill, pushed Danna to a totally different level than most of her friends. She was a different type of pretty.

She didn't have the long hair or light skin that most men cherished. She was on the totally opposite end of the spectrum. A sexy li'l chocolate drop with killer style and a crazy yet funny personality. Danna was the bourgeois ghetto girl with the long locs and loud mouth. The one that was too good for the corner boys in the hood, but gave her heart to the kingpin that supplied them all. She was different; she was rare.

Though she was envied by a lot of girls her age for being one of the hottest in the city, she remained humble and nothing like people assumed she was. In everybody's mind she was street smart, and probably just as heavy as her father and mother, but she wasn't. Echo was halfway a daddy, and Vonetta didn't even deal in drugs, so that was most definitely a theory that needed to be proved wrong.

Much like her mother, Danna had no interest in involving herself in the street life. Too much came with it, and all she wanted to do was live life free, and happy. Her father would take care of everything else, when he felt like it, and Vonetta had it handled when he didn't, so for now, she was fine with hanging with people her age, getting her money, and admiring all the sexy men she encountered daily. Even though the majority of them were off limits, thanks to Echo's hating ass, she still admired from a distance.

Her mother's party had been on her mind all week because she knew it would be flooded with the men she watched day in and day out, but what she didn't expect were all the other people that would come along with them. The house was packed to the max, and it was becoming harder and harder to maneuver around. Katara's mother was always entertaining, but never had it been as packed as it was then.

"Excuse me," She pushed through the throng of men crowding the door. "Damn, I said move." She yelled in frustration when they didn't bother to acknowledge her request.

The tall man closest to her turned around so that he was facing her. His face had been frowning at first, but once he realized it was her, the glare was replaced with a small smile. Danna felt warm on the inside as she smiled back. It was Quay. He was one of her favorite corner boys, and the current crush of her life.

"Who you cussing at like that?" His gold grill shined through his plump lips.

Danna stood back on one of her legs and batted her long lashes at him. "I said it nicely the first time, but y'all were acting deaf, so I took a stronger approach."

Quay nodded his head slowly while smiling at her. "Where you trying to get to anyway? I know you ain't leaving your own party?"

"It's my mama's party, not mine, but yeah I'm kind of leaving. I was about to go upstairs." She looked around the room with her nose turned up. "This ain't my crowd. Too many of y'all dope boys in here."

Danna's eye circled the room for emphasis.

"I feel you, it ain't really mine either, but I had to show your mom some love. You know that's my baby."

Danna nodded at him. "Word? Vonetta your baby? Cool." She smiled and proceeded to squeeze her way through the men, but was stopped when Quay grabbed her arm.

She looked over her shoulder, and he was smiling. Danna raised her eyebrows at him just as he leaned down so that his mouth was near her ear.

"Stop acting like that and dance with me. You know you my baby too."

Danna wasn't completely sure how her father would feel about her interacting with his help, but since he was never around anyway, there was no way she was about to turn Quay down. She had been crushing on him for almost two years, and he hadn't begun paying her any attention until recently.

Without saying anything else, Danna slid in front of Quay, pressing her body against his. She made sure her butt was right on the hardness resting in his jeans before bending over in front of him. The way her body moved against his was like magic. Danna was tall, but Quay was taller, so that worked in her favor as she pulled him deeper into her space when she stood up and wrapped one of her arms around the back of his neck. With her hand above and behind her head, resting on his neck, Quay's hands slid possessively around her waist.

Danna could live and die in the way his arms felt on her. So strong, so protective, and so greedy. Quay was such a fucking vibe that she could literally get high off him, all day every day. He too had locs, but they were a lot shorter than hers, resting on his shoulders, but falling into her face right then. He'd leaned his head down and was whispering in her ear how much he'd been wanting her.

"I'm for real, I've been watching your sexy ass for a minute now."

Danna was blushing so hard she could hardly focus on dancing as his fingertips stroked her stomach.

"I know you be coming on my block so I can see you."

Danna giggled, and a light chuckle came from him as well.

"You ain't got to tell me I'm right. I already know. Why you don't stop and talk to me for a minute?"

Danna shrugged, because she honestly didn't know why she didn't stop and talk to him. She was far from shy when it came to men, but it was just something about Quay that kept her at a distance. Maybe it was his reputation, maybe it was the way he watched her; she didn't know. What she did know was the cat and mouse game they'd been playing gave her butterflies, and she wasn't quite ready for them to disappear just yet.

"Next time, stop."

Danna looked at him over her shoulder. "And do what?"

Quay's gold teeth could be seen through the small gap between his juicy lips. "Give me some sugar."

Oh Lord, get this country thug away from me.

Danna's stomach squeezed as her eyes focused on the shape of his mouth. His lips were so juicy she wanted to grab them with her mouth right then and suck on 'em until he made her stop.

"I can give you some now."

Quay smiled before raising his head to look around the room before looking back down at her. "Give me some then."

Quay's hands squeezed her waist tighter, pulling her further into his chest. The smell of his cologne wafted up her nose as she moved smoothly against him.

"I need to turn around."

Quay shook his head once while grabbing her chin, making the gold bracelet on his wrist shake. Though it looked a lot like a charm bracelet, it was still cute in a manly way and it caught Danna's eye every time she was in his presence.

"No, you don't. Lean your head back."

Danna moved her eyes from his wrist to his face as she stopped dancing and leaned her head back so that she was leaning to the side so that she could kiss his mouth comfortably. Quay wasted no time covering her lips with his. Though Danna had never died, she was sure it felt something like this. The way her soul had just left her body had to be a minor prerequisite of what it would feel like when it was time to go to Heaven.

Three soft pecks, followed by him sliding his tongue into her mouth, had Danna's body feeling foreign to her. She didn't recognize the tingles and shivers that took over her every time his tongue touched hers. The way her stomach mimicked the feeling of being on a rollercoaster was the only thing she could use to compare to the feeling she felt while kissing Quay. Danna wanted so badly to turn around and wrap her arms around him, but the grip he had on her waist wouldn't allow it.

"Nah, not here. Not like this." He whispered to her mouth. "Save it for me. I'll get it when it's time." Quay's words were so confident that it gave Danna hope. Hope that it would be more. More time, more kissing, more them, so she pulled away and smiled up at him.

"Vonetta gon' kill you. I know she's somewhere watching us."

Quay's handsome face got even cuter when he smiled as if he was nervous.

Danna waved him off. "Ain't nobody thinking about my mama. She gon' be alright. I'm grown."

Quay's eyes were back on hers. "What make you so grown?"

"Get to know me and see."

"I plan to." Quay held her closer to him again, and she went back to dancing.

Danna was busy twirling the bottom half of her body in a circular motion when she looked up and looked right into Don's face. He was standing across the room near her father's other friends watching her. For a minute, Danna stopped dancing because she didn't want to get into any arguments with her father if one of his people saw her, but she really liked Quay and didn't want to pass up on this opportunity to connect with him.

Don was one of her father's friends that came around sporadically, and had been in charge of "looking out" for her and family whenever her father was away. He'd been brought in by one of her father's other trusted friends, so they accepted him. Echo normally introduced them to all his people, but since he was becoming a pro at hide-and-seek and they rarely saw him anymore, they just went with the flow.

Being that he was around the same age as her father, Danna had never really liked him popping up where she was, and still didn't, depending on the day. Her parents had done their best to keep her and her siblings out of the streets as much as they could, but it was what it was. Some things in life just couldn't be avoided, and meeting her father's people was one. Whether she wanted one or not, she had her own personal bodyguards. Since they were always around, she knew them, but not on a personal level. Don excluded. Initially, they'd spoken and conversed only when necessary, but one day, that all changed and things hadn't been the same since. Don was no longer "off limits" or daddy's worker, he was now boo, bae, and whatever else Danna felt like calling him. All the pretend uncle and second daddy type shit had disappeared immediately.

So, for him to see her all cozied up with Quay in the corner was just the same as her father seeing it, maybe even worse. Don was something like her man and his possessiveness tended to float to a fatal attraction level occasionally, but that was only in private. He normally controlled himself in public, and when she involved herself with men her own age. Her entertaining other men wasn't something he was fond of, but since they weren't able to have a real relationship, he tolerated little stuff here and there.

After watching him glare at her for a few seconds, her heartbeat had sped up but slowed seconds later. Instead of continuing to frown as she'd thought he would, he smiled. Nothing too friendly, because Don wasn't friendly, but he did the best he could do around other people.

Danna smiled back before looking away. She and Quay danced a few more songs, and every time she looked up, Don was still looking at her. At first Danna did her best to look away, but after catching his eye for the fifth time she decided to play the little staring game he was obviously interested in playing.

The H-Town song that was playing in the background had her winding her hips slower and deeper into Quay, while staring at Don across the room. Danna wasn't sure if it was the lyrics or the aura in the room that had her feeling like a temptress, but she did.

With Quay's arms around her, and Don's eyes on her, she danced sexily doing her best to entertain them both. The longer Don stared at her and the tighter Quay held her, the sexier she felt. Danna didn't know what had gotten into her but by the time the song changed to a faster one, she was worn out and needed to get to her room ASAP. The feeling the men had given her was too much for her inexperience.

"Save your number," Quay handed her his phone. "I need to holla at you about something." His smile had Danna's own personal butterflies flying around tickling her insides.

She was on cloud nine as she programmed her number into his phone before pushing her way through the crowd once again. The further away she got, the better she felt. The air on the stairs felt a lot cooler than it had in the living room, probably from the lack of people occupying that area.

That was one thing Danna was thankful for. Katara's mother might have entertained regularly, but they didn't allow anyone past the bottom floor. There were only a select few that were allowed on the second floor of their home, and she could count all of them on one hand without using all five fingers.

Danna was quite familiar with that protocol because it was the exact same way at her house. Echo took his family's safety seriously when he felt like playing daddy, and did everything he could to maintain it. The only problem with that was he didn't always feel like it, so his workers also spent a lot of time looking out for the women of their family. Her father was a business man and a heavy hitter in the streets, but he liked to party. Along with partying, came other women, disappearing acts, and a lack of self-discipline to be the man for the family he'd created.

When she finally reached Katara's room, she grabbed a change of clothes from her bag and headed to take a shower. She showered quickly before wrapping her hair up and going back into Katara's room. Danna grabbed the remote to her TV, flipped the light off, and slid beneath the covers. She'd just flipped her movie on when she heard a soft knock at the door. Her face frowned momentarily before she fixed it and yelled for whoever it was to come in. Danna was inwardly hoping it was Quay even though it was probably Ezra's overprotective ass.

She wanted to pretend that Don was the last person she expected to see, but that would be a lie. After she kissed Quay, she kind of already knew he would be finding her sooner rather than later. Don dapped in coolly before closing the door behind himself and leaning on the edge of the dresser.

His tall muscular frame was maxed out with muscles. Bulges were everywhere, straining the fabric of his clothing. His brown skin was pretty, but edgy and scruffy from years of life. His thick black beard covered the bottom half of his face as his fresh haircut lined his forehead and jawline. He stood confidently, unaffected by his presence in the room. Like he belonged there.

Don was quiet, never really saying anything to anybody, but you would never miss his presence. He was so overpowering but in a relaxed way. It didn't ask for attention, but his appearance didn't make room for him to be ignored. An OG in the streets, with rough hands, and an even rougher demeanor, Don was the embodiment of intimidation. He never seemed angry, upset, or anything other than relaxed which made him easy to be around.

He was mad cool, and didn't bother Danna for the most part. He knew what they were and kept it at that. However, right then didn't appear like one of those times, and she was hoping he wouldn't do too much. She was sleepy and ready to get some rest, so she sat quietly, not sure what he was going to say, but more than positive it had a lot to do with the little staring contest they'd indulged in. Now that she was in a different atmosphere and not feeling as confident as she'd been feeling downstairs, she couldn't maintain eye contact. Hell, she could barely look at him straight, let alone stare at him.

"You feeling okay?" He broke the silence.

"Yeah, I'm cool. Just kind of tired. You?"

He took a sip from the beer he was drinking. "I'm always good, you know that."

Danna looked away with nothing to say.

"Danna, you do know I'm a grown ass man, right?"

Damn!

She cursed inwardly as she felt her stomach flip. She wasn't ready for where she could feel this conversation going.

"Yeah I know. I'm grown too." She spoke defiantly.

He looked at her with a smirk on her face. "I know you are, but you aren't grown as me."

"Grown is grown. You know Vonetta ain't raising no babies, we've all been grown for a long time." Danna laughed at her own shot at her mom's parenting.

Danna had been grown for as long as she could remember. Due to the lifestyle her parents led, she and her siblings had no other choice but to be. They'd been learning the streets and all the ins and outs of life since they'd been old enough to know better, so she may have been joking, but it was the truth. Danna cooked, cleaned, and made sure all the bills were paid. Vonetta made sure she was ready for the world when it was time. Her younger brother Ezra had just as many responsibilities as her, while her older brother and sister did their own thing. Their time with Vonetta and Echo had come and gone, now it was Ezra and Danna's turn.

"You right," Don drank from his beer again. "Downstairs . . . what was that about?"

Danna's stomach flipped again. She and Don had talked plenty of times in the past about her hanging out with other men, but right then it wasn't the same. She couldn't put her finger on what it was that made all their other interactions differ from this one, but they did.

"What you mean?" She asked him as she sat up in her bed.

The covers fell from her body showing her sprightly young breasts through her top. She wasn't wearing a bra, never did when it was time for bed, so when his eyes drifted from her face she was pretty sure she knew where they'd gone.

"Your daddy know you fucking with Quay?" His eyes left her breasts and went back to her face.

She shrugged. *Who was he really asking for? Him or her father?*

"You plan on telling him?" Another swallow of beer.

"It's not that deep, you know that. This is the first time I've ever really talked to him."

She could tell by the look on Don's face that he didn't believe her. "Word? That dancing looked pretty familiar to me." More beer followed.

Danna blushed as she watched him sip his beer continuously. It would be an empty bottle of fizz if he kept up that pace.

"You dance like you know what to do with that body."

There it was. He wanted sex. Danna held her head down for a moment before allowing her eyes to drift from the fresh sneakers on his feet up to the designer clothing he was wearing. Don was her father's age which made him a little over twenty years older than her, but his style was still hard to ignore. He was always dressed to death and smelling heavenly. He hadn't even been in her room long, and he had already smelled it up with his scent. He knew what he was doing. Danna smirked.

"I was just having fun. Nothing major."

"The way you were looking at me," More beer . . . almost gone . . . it was empty. "Was that just fun too? Or was it your idea of foreplay?"

Danna looked from the empty beer bottle and found his eyes and held them with hers. Her words were caught in her throat, but she felt them in her chest. She wanted to tell him something that would make sense of the way she was feeling right then, but she couldn't. Her words were failing her right then, and she couldn't think of anything witty to save herself.

"I didn't think so. Don't do it again." Don sat his beer bottle on her dresser and ran his hands over his face before sticking one of them in his pocket. "Come here."

Danna was out of the bed and going to him before she had time to think about it. When she was in front of him, he touched the side of her exposed leg, using it to pull her closer to his body. His nose went to her neck as his hand went further up, and palmed her butt.

"Go lock the door."

Danna took off with no hesitation. This was new to her, and she didn't have any idea what she was about to do, but she wanted it. Never had he ever initiated something like this in public, but right then it was exciting and welcomed. When she stopped back in front of him, both of his hands went to her body. He snatched her to him roughly before placing his mouth on hers.

Danna kissed him back eagerly, almost too eager for her liking, so she pulled back some. Obviously, Don felt her hesitation because he broke their kiss.

"You don't have to be worried. The door is locked, and nobody saw me come up here."

Danna nodded her head as her breathing increased.

His lips were back on hers immediately exploring the depths of her mouth. His thick tongue sliding in and over hers methodically. Danna had kissed a lot of men in her past, but the way Don kissed her topped them all. Well, almost. There was nothing in the world like Quay. His style, his touch, his kiss, everything was in a league of its own. Don was a close second though. He tongued her down like only a grown man could.

Her body was going crazy with need in ways she could barely explain. When she felt like she couldn't take it anymore, she broke their kiss and looked at him.

"Are we going to have sex here?" Her voice sounded immature and her question showed her inexperience, but it was too late, it had already come out.

Don's small eyes squinted as his tongue slid out over his bottom lip. "Is that what you want?"

Her eyes darted to the side as she nodded her head slowly.

"You know I don't like all that silent shit. Look at me, open your mouth, and say what's on your mind."

"I want you to give it to me here." She made herself look at him as she toyed with the idea of him teaching her things to show Quay.

As she listened to herself talking, she liked the way it sounded, and found a little more confidence than she'd possessed before. She grabbed the front of his shirt and kissed his waiting mouth again.

"Right now."

"You don't care about anybody finding you with me?"

Danna shook her head.

He smiled at her lazily before palming her butt with both hands and grabbing her bottom lip with his teeth. She pulled away gently and he let her go before sticking his tongue back into her mouth. Danna's hands went to his body. She touched and rubbed everywhere comfortably until he separated them long enough for him to pull his shirt over his head.

After he dropped it to the floor he picked her up and walked to the side of Katara's bed and lay her down. Danna looked up at him, watching him kick his shoes off before removing his jeans and boxers. For Don to be as old as he was, he was fine as hell.

He definitely had the body of a young man, minus all the scars and the indentations she knew to be healed gunshot wounds.

When his dick finally came into view her eyes bulged. Never in her life had she seen something that big. It was so big, she second-guessed her choice to have sex right then. He would surely have her screaming, as always. Don had shown her time and time again, that grown man dick came with grown man sex. Unfortunately, Don didn't look to be considering her fate. His hands were on her waist pulling her pajama shorts down. When her bottom was free, he removed her shirt as well. Her naked body was on display, and he marveled at every inch of it.

"You're so young and perfect." He leaned over and pecked her lips. "Nothing like these old raggedy-body bitches with cellulite and stretchmarks everywhere."

Danna giggled as she basked in his appreciation for her body.

"You mind letting me get a little taste before I put it in?"

She shook her head quickly.

"Try to control your fucking self." He smiled. "I know you love to get loud, but right now ain't the time for all of that."

Danna smiled wildly. "I'll do my best, but I can't promise you anything."

"I feel you, but try for me." Don placed an open palm over her stomach. "Relax and enjoy it."

Danna's mind went to the way she felt right then. She'd just gotten out of Quay's face and now she was in the same house as him about to do the unthinkable with another man. That was kind of flawed in her opinion, but she loved Don and only liked Quay. Danna closed her eyes and pictured Quay's face in her mind. When his sexy smile appeared, her stomach flipped. It fluttered a few more times making her feel bad. That wasn't fair to Don, so she did her best to clear her mind and enjoy the moment. Which wasn't hard to do since Don had some of the best tongue action she'd ever felt in her life.

"Um," She sat up, about to make a few requests, but couldn't. His mouth was already on her body.

Danna's eyes shut tightly as she lay back and covered her face. Never in her life had she wanted something so bad. It felt so good that she could hardly catch her breath. The way his tongue slithered all over her softness even slipping down between the cheeks of her butt had her losing her mind.

Danna didn't know whether to moan, scream, or continue muffling her sounds with her hands. Getting oral sex was one of her favorite things, and Don kept it coming. She honestly couldn't complain about sex with Don, everything was grade A, and she enjoyed every minute of it.

"You thinking about letting that young nigga Quay get some of this?" Don asked her from between her legs, lips still dangerously close to her love-box.

"No," She barely got out.

"How do I know you're telling the truth?"

She smiled down at him. "Because I only want it from you, now be quiet. You're messing up my focus."

Don laughed and she joined in.

"Bet. Focus then."

She nodded as he went back to what he'd been doing. The warm feeling in her stomach took over her body again and got even more intense the longer he stayed down there. Before long, she could feel goosebumps popping up all over her body and the shiver she'd thought she was going to feel was magnified by an eruption that took over every nerve ending in her body.

Danna's legs began to move uncontrollably as a feeling she would never be able to explain shot from the center of her body to her toes, and back up again. She didn't even have time to recover before Don rose from the floor and stood between her legs.

Don grabbed his dick and pushed it to the opening of her body. "You ready?"

She shook her head. "You don't have a condom?"

Danna may have been caught up in the moment, but she didn't trust Don as far as she could throw him. He might have played it cool as if she was the only woman he was really kicking it with, but she knew better. They barely got to hang out, and with the sexual appetite that he had, she was more than positive that he was getting fed somewhere else.

"Nah, I fuck these old bitches with condoms. I don't need one with you." Don leaned over and kissed her mouth. "I'm clean, and so are you. Let me just get it like this."

His whisper made her hot all over again. "No, Don."

"Please? I promise I'm good."

Danna shook her head adamantly, and instead of arguing with her, he released her legs and grabbed his jeans from the floor. He fumbled around in the pockets for a second before producing the condom. He got himself together rather quickly, before going back to his spot between her chocolate legs.

Don positioned himself at her entrance and used her thighs to pull her closer to him. "I'ma try to go slow as I can, but you already know how I get with you."

Danna smiled and braced herself for what was to come. Just like every other time, no matter how many muscles she clenched together, how tight she held the sheets, or how hard she bit the inside of her cheek, she was never prepared for the pain that Don inflicted.

"Ow, Don."

He leaned over her and kissed her face and mouth again. "I know, Danna. I'm going slow." He licked up the center of her neck. "It'll feel better in a minute. Just take it for me . . . you already know how this goes."

Don pushed himself deeper inside of her and her mouth fell open. Sure, she could take it, but she was going to die trying. There was no way she would be able to continue having sex with

Don. His dick was too big. It was killing her. Every time they were intimate, it felt like he was ripping her insides apart.

"You're doing good." He coaxed, as he moved above her going deeper. "Shit," he grunted. "I can barely get up in this shit, it's so tight."

Danna didn't feel like she was doing good, but if he said she was, then she had to be. The feeling of hot sticky fluids slid between her thighs when he finally put himself inside. Danna's body was burning and she was probably squeezing the life out of his big strong arms trying to manage the pain, but she had to do something. The heavy breathing and small sounds of discomfort she released in his ear over and over made her feel a tad bit better, but nothing rid her lower extremities of the agonizing hurt Don was delivering.

It took a little while for the pain to become manageable enough to enjoy the sex, but she wasn't new to that. It was always like that. Once she finally got it, it wasn't that bad. She held onto his back as he slid in and out of her at a slow pace.

The muscles in his arms flexed as did the ones in his chest every time he moved giving Danna something beautiful to enjoy while he worked her body over. The expertise in his movements along with the smell of his cologne took her to another place, eventually bringing about the same type of pleasure she'd gotten from his mouth being on her.

"You know we can never tell your daddy about this right?"

"I know." Danna's young eyes flashed up at him in uncertainty.

"Not anybody for real. They won't understand."

Danna rubbed her hands all over his back as she reassured him. "I know, this will be between us."

Don lifted one of her legs and wrapped it around his waist. "For how long because I don't really like you talking to other niggas." He licked and sucked her neck as he waited for her to answer him. "I might need to stake my claim a little sooner."

"It's all games. I never take any of them serious. You have nothing to worry about."

"That ain't what it looks like." He winked, she smiled. "You looked like you were enjoying Quay."

She shook her head and smiled at the same time.

"All games."

"So this mine?"

Danna gave him a reassuring nod.

"Good, I'll keep giving it to you as much as I can, or as much as you let me."

Danna's heart smiled at the simple assurance that he planned to keep having sex with her. His words always made her feel like a woman his age, not a newly legal woman with no real sexual experience. Filled with happiness and dick, Danna wrapped her legs around him and held on to him for the rest of their moments of love making.

Just as her goosebumps were about to return, he quickened his pace and stroked her deeper and harder than he'd been doing. Danna was sure she knew what was about to happen, but confirmed her thoughts when he pulled out and shot the creamy-colored fluid onto her stomach.

She waited for a minute as she watched Don breathe hard until he could move again. He used the towel that she'd had after her shower to clean himself up before handing it to her to do the same. Danna did the best she could before they both got dressed.

When he was back in his clothes he walked to her and grabbed her neck. He kissed her long and hard, making sure to hug her tightly the entire time. When Don finally pulled away, he looked mean again. Gone was the softness she'd just experienced with him.

He pecked her lips once more. "I'll see you again soon."

"Okay."

"Keep my pussy away from Quay."

"I am."

"Cool. You staying here tonight or you meeting me at my spot?"

"I think I'ma chill here tonight."

"Well, call me whenever you want. I'll be up for a while. I got some stuff I need to handle."

"Okay, see you later. Be safe."

"Later, Danna. Go take a hot bath." Don dapped to the dresser, grabbed his beer, and walked out of her room as coolly as he'd come in.

Danna stood there lost in the moment for a minute before grabbing more pajamas from Katara's dresser and running to the bathroom to shower. She washed her body again before running water for a bath. The music from downstairs was still booming as she relaxed backward in her large tiled tub and enjoyed the replays of her and Don's sexual encounter.

2

Words are "our" thing . . .

Second semester of senior year . . .

"I'm a rapper so you know I'm fly. I write liquor induced verses and get high. You don't like it, but I do. If you come to one of my shows and listen to my music you will too."

An array of suppressed chuckles sounded around the classroom as Jerald stood at the front near the chalkboard with a wide smile on his face. The large silver grills covering his top and bottom rows of teeth gleamed in the single ray of sunlight shining through the window.

"And you said you write raps for a living?" Mrs. Keating, the creative writing teacher, asked, as she walked toward the front of the room.

The same smile he'd been wearing since completing his poem got wider. "Yep. One of the best in the city."

"Well the city must not have much to offer then. Sit down boy, and think of you a new profession because writing isn't it."

Every student in the classroom laughed again, including Cannon, as Jerald made jokes and slick comebacks all the way to his seat.

It was the last semester of twenty-year-old Cannon Collier's senior year in college, and thanks to the promotion the insurance company had given her mother, Cannon was at her new school and missing her old one like crazy. Though it hadn't been her ideal year, she was okay with it. Moving wasn't new to her. From her stepfather having been in the military her entire life, to her mother's new job, she was accustomed to being snatched out of her comfort zone at any given moment. Though she would have preferred it not been in the middle of her senior year, she was adjusting just fine.

She'd hated it at first, but it no longer bothered her as much anymore. She'd grown into a loner so a new school didn't really faze her one way or the other. Besides, she was readier to graduate than anything, so as long as all her credits had transferred, that's all she cared about. If she could have, would she have picked another college? Of course! Her current one was outdated, overpopulated, and in desperate need of a makeover. It reminded Cannon of the rundown high school from the movie *Lean on Me*, all they needed was to shrink a little and a modern-day Mr. Clark, and they'd be identical.

The students were country as ever, the professors weren't too much better, and it looked to have a pregnant girl with long colorful nails and her ghetto homegirl at every corner. As if the girls and their babies weren't bad enough, Cannon didn't even want to start on the boys. Their jeans sagged so low they were darn near falling off, loud-colored clothing matched whatever shoes they were wearing, and there were more gold and silver teeth than she'd ever seen in her life.

It was as if there was one mandatory dress code and everybody stuck to it. Expensive sneakers and odd or solid-colored t-shirts to match. If one of them wanted to be a tad bit fancier than the others, they'd throw on a herringbone necklace to match their grill and probably win best dressed for the year. Cannon rolled her eyes and sighed. Country people shit.

Having experienced so many diverse areas of learning, Cannon was used to a more upscale environment, but Makenna State University was anything but. The presentations of their current assignment was the perfect evidence to support her feelings.

"I can't believe you even got your behind up here with that mess. I wouldn't listen to your CD if you paid me to." Professor Keating's smile was pretty as she and a couple of other students laughed at her joke.

"Now you know you're lying. I just gave you and all your li'l church members one the other day when I saw y'all coming out that li'l hot church y'all go to."

More laughter aroused as Jerald finally made it to his seat.

"A lie don't care who tell it." Professor Keating said nonchalantly as she looked down at her class roster.

Her short natural hair was gray and in a curly little box style, while her thick rimmed glasses sat across her nose. The gold bracelets on her wrists made an array of jingles as she wrote, then erased something before looking back up again. The long burgundy nails on her fingers had Cannon shaking her head. The pregnant ghetto girls had rubbed off on the old lady, had her wearing nails that she knew she was too old for. Cannon couldn't figure out for the life of her how women even functioned with nails that long.

"Well, that looks like everybody except for," her head went down again before coming up, this time with her pointer finger accompanying it. "You, Mr. Ezra Mendoza."

Cannon turned her head and eyed the dark-skinned boy next to her. His skin was smooth and so dark brown that it almost looked black. It reminded her of the soothing black sand on her favorite beach in California. Her stepfather had taken her there for her eighth birthday and she'd been dying to go back ever since.

It was so pretty and exotic looking, much like the boy Ezra. On top of him having some of the darkest skin she'd ever seen, he had the prettiest eyes she'd ever observed on a man. They were big and round with such a unique light behind them, they gave a sparkling illusion. It was weird because they lit up his whole face. Like miniature lamps shining down on him.

Thick black eyebrows scrunched together, while the curve of his smile ended in deep dimples on each cheek. His thick lips blended with his face, but gave way to a Colgate white smile. Cannon's eyes trailed over the long locs swaying around his shoulders as he moved subtly in his seat. She couldn't really tell if he dressed the same as the rest of the country people or not, because he'd been in gym shorts and white t-shirts, or school basketball paraphernalia, since she'd gotten there.

"What you mean I'm the last one? The new girl ain't went either." Ezra pointed at Cannon with his thumb.

A few eyes went to her as she sat in her seat scribbling on her paper. She stopped and looked up when she noticed the classroom had gotten quieter. She met a few stares head on, others she dismissed and looked back down at her paper.

"Boy, hush. Leave her alone and worry about yourself. Nothing she has going on is any of your concern. Get your behind up here."

Ezra sucked his teeth and began preparing to get out of his seat. Cannon's eyes darted to the paper on his desk, then to the paper in his hand, before traveling up to his face. He was looking at her with a sly smirk.

"You next, New Girl."

Cannon's small smile curved as her head shook from side to side.

"Watch and see," he whispered as he headed to the front of the class.

Cannon observed the slight lean at the top of his body derived from his height. The gym shorts hung just above the black athletic leggings he wore beneath them. The black Makenna State Basketball shirt stretched across his already widening chest, and cuffed a little beneath his arms. Cannon's eyes traveled over his body as he stretched lazily, before looking down at the notebook paper in his hand.

His face shined as he looked around the room with a comical smirk on his face. "Alright now, Professor Keating, don't be on no funny junk about my poem."

"I'll be on whatever I want to be on, now go ahead."

He chuckled a little before holding his paper up in a good enough distance for him to read. After a few deep breaths, he began.

"I dream big, I fight hard, I push myself to unimaginable limits of perseverance. A black man, a husband, a father, a protector and provider. They need me, as I need them. They serve me as I serve them. A lover who protects what belongs to him, one who eliminates sadness and replaces it with the stars and moon of the night's sky. For them, for her, for me, I can't get tired, I can't give up, and I can't let go. We fuss, we fight, we make life harder for each other, but that's our test. That's our strength. Hold my hand and lead with me, hold my heart and comfort me, hold my last name and be with me. You and I, untold, unnoticed, and unlike anybody else . . . A letter to my future wife." Ezra scratched his ear nervously before looking up at the quiet classroom. "The end!" He said loud and dramatically to detour the seriousness of his beautiful poem.

Everyone else laughed, but not Professor Keating, and most definitely not Cannon. She was exhilarated by his writing. Words were her thing, and his had stirred up a new infatuation inside of her. She inhaled deeply and even had to fan herself quickly before looking away from him.

"Now that's what I'm talking about." Professor Keating took her place back at the front of the room as she clapped her hands in praise. "Ezra, my Ezra. That was beautiful and well deserving of the A that you're about to get. Jerald, you need to get with him and see if he has time to sit in on some of those rap sessions. Maybe he can offer you some assistance." She continued to sing his praises as he walked to his seat with his classmates' laughter as his background noise.

"Your turn, New Girl." Ezra looked at Cannon before taking his seat.

His presence brought about another smile to her face. "No, it ain't." Her voice was low and somewhat softer than normal.

"Bet." Ezra raised his hand. "Professor Keating, the new girl said she want a turn."

Once again, all eyes were on her.

"Cannon, you don't have to do this, dear." Mrs. Keating told her. "You just transferred in, and I gave this assignment the first day of classes. There's no way you've had time to do it correctly."

"Why she don't? She got her poem right here." Ezra snatched the pink piece of paper from Cannon's desk before she could stop him and held it up in the air.

Cannon tried to snatch it from him, but was unsuccessful. "Stop, Ezra." She whined his name.

He looked at her with a smile that made her want to dive into it. "Alright now, New Girl, don't be saying my name like that."

A few snickers could be heard around the room, while another male voice said something in agreement with Ezra, further embarrassing Cannon. She held her head down and shook it.

"Cannon, would you like to go? It's up to you. I know you haven't had enough time to prepare, but you're more than welcome to share what you have."

Ezra sat the paper back on her desk with a mischievous smile. "Go ahead, you know you want to."

Cannon eyed him through squinted lenses before looking down at her paper. Heavy in contemplation, Cannon bit at her bottom lip. She'd been writing for years, so she was sure what she'd written was good, but that didn't mean she wanted to share it. It was a personal poem written for her own personal therapy more than anything, but good nonetheless.

"Don't feel pressured, baby." The sound of Professor Keating's voice came from the back of the room.

Cannon sat in thought for a moment longer before standing to her feet. Thicker than your average twenty-one-year-old girl, the tiny aisle between the desks didn't allot her much room to get through, but she made it work. Cannon wasn't overweight or anything like that, but she was thick and shapely. More bottom heavy than top.

At the front of the class, Cannon pushed her glasses up on her nose and made eye contact with a few people before taking yet another deep breath and looking at her paper. Her eyes scanned over the words quickly selecting the part she wanted to read.

"I miss you. I miss everything you were to me and what we were together. I'm not sure if it's your laugh or your smile that I miss the most. Maybe it's your hugs or the way you kissed my forehead every morning and night. It's too many emotions and too much pain to face, so I don't. Instead I think of you and smile at the sky because I know you're up there singing and flying high. See you again one day, until then I'll just miss you from here."

Cannon stopped there and put her paper down by her side. She hurried back to her seat and slid in smoothly. It didn't take long for her to situate herself, and look at Professor Keating. Her head was tilted to the side as she smiled at Cannon sympathetically.

"That was beautiful and delivered with so much passion. Awesome job young lady."

Cannon nodded her head but didn't say anything. Instead she folded her paper and stuck it inside the pink, black, and gold notebook on her desk. She stuffed the notebook into her backpack and looked up. Her eyes met Ezra's the moment her head raised.

"Who was that about? Your boyfriend must have died or something?"

Cannon could tell he was doing his best to whisper, but the bass in his voice still carried. With a quick shake of her head, she dismissed him and looked away. She could feel his eyes on her as she looked straight ahead, but she remained forward facing until he looked away. It wasn't long before the time came for them to be released from class.

Cannon was on her feet and moving through the throng of students in the hallway in no time. Her backpack was tightened securely on her back as she headed for the parking lot. Creative writing had been her only class for the day, so it was time for her to get home. She checked her watch as she sped walked to her car. She had fifteen minutes to get there.

"Aye, New Girl," someone yelled behind her.

She felt like she knew who it was, which was the only reason she broke her stride and turned around. Her eyes squinted until she used the side of her hand to shield her eyes from the sun. Ezra was walking to her but began jogging to get there quicker.

"Where you going? Why you always rush out of class like that? Fast walking ass girl."

Cannon's cheeks warmed with a smile. "Because I have somewhere to be right after this."

He hoisted his backpack on one side of his shoulder. "Where?"

A perfectly arched brow raised above Cannon's right eye. "Why you in my business?"

Ezra chuckled, as did she. "My fault. I was just asking because you ain't gon' never make no friends like that. You have to talk to people. You're always walking around looking so mean."

"So."

"So, that means ain't nobody gon' talk to your mean-looking ass."

Cannon tried to keep a straight face, but she failed and laughed at him. He laughed when she did.

"I'm for real. People be wanting to talk to you, but you be acting all stuck up."

Cannon leaned her weight on one of her legs, and his eyes followed her movement. His dark irises drifted slowly from her exposed thigh back up to her face.

"Who be wanting to talk to me?"

When he finally made eye contact with her again, he shrugged. "I don't know they names."

"Is that so?"

"Yeah, but I can find out for you if you want me to."

Cannon's eyes scanned over his dark skin and the way it glistened under the sun. "Yeah, do that for me and let me know."

He was smiling when he nodded his head. "Bet." He turned to walk away but stopped and turned back around. "You must gon' talk to them or something when I find out who they are."

"I might, it depends."

"On what?"

"Who they are for one, and what they want to talk about for two. I don't talk to everybody."

"Why?" He asked while pushing some of his hair over his shoulder.

"I'm not a friendly person."

"But you be talking to me."

Cannon could hear the underlying curiosity in his words. She allowed her eyes to roam away from him without saying anything else. Not because she didn't have anything to say, but because she didn't know what she wanted to say. There was a lot in her head that she could relay about him, but she wasn't sure if it was time for that yet.

"I'll get back to you with them names though." Ezra told her before holding his hand up for a high five.

Cannon looked at his large open palm before lightly slapping hers against it. The contact of their skin brought smiles to both of their faces.

"See you later, New Girl."

"See you later, Ezra."

His head shook and his dimples deepened. "I like the way you say my name."

"Why?"

"Because you make it sound different. It doesn't sound ugly like when these other girls say it."

"That's because I ain't country."

His laughter was cute and drew her to join in with him.

"Maybe."

"Bye, Ezra." Cannon waved and turned to head to her car.

The moment she was in, she checked her watch.

"Shoot!"

She needed to hurry up and get home or she wouldn't be talking to anybody for the rest of her life because she'd be dead. Her mother was going to kill her.

3

Mama's baby, sister's maybe?

Loud crying met Cannon's ears the moment she walked through the door of the three-bedroom townhouse that she shared with her mother and baby sister. Apparently, God hadn't heard the last part of her prayer on her drive home. The house was still clean and her mother wasn't at the front door waiting on her, so maybe God just stopped listening at the end, because she'd asked about that part at the beginning.

Cannon released one strap of her backpack and allowed it to slide down her arm and onto the floor before taking a few more steps into the house. The crying was getting louder and more intense which caused Cannon to panic. In a full out run, she took off for her mother's room. Her heart began beating faster and faster as she rounded the corner.

"What took you so long to get here?" Her mother walked to Cannon and practically threw the screaming baby girl into her arms.

Cannon cradled her baby sister, Yara, in her arms making sure to support her three-week-old head. The slick black hair that was lying down around Yara's head was wet from sweat as she sniffed uncontrollably, trying to calm her little body down.

"It's okay, Mama, I'm here. Stop all that. You're alright." Cannon soothed the baby while rocking her closely against her chest. "Has she eaten yet, Mommy?"

Cannon watched her mother look over her shoulder with an evil look on her face. "No, all she's done was cry. That's all she ever does. It's starting to drive me crazy."

With a low growl, her mother, Karina, turned back around and began fastening the buckle on her shoes. The black pencil skirt and mint green top she was wearing looked amazing with the mint-colored pumps. Her hair was pulled back into a neat bun, and her face was bare, but she was radiant. As always. Karina was a beautiful woman, and where Cannon had gotten her bright skin and shapely body from.

Cannon was the exact replica of her mother, just a younger version. Yara on the other hand was a little darker than them already due to her father's color. Her skin was brown like a cookie and she wasn't even a month old yet, so more than likely she'd have a little more color on her soon.

"You okay, Mommy? I tried to get here as fast as I could."

Karina stood and made her way to the full body mirror resting in the corner of her room. She nodded her head but didn't say anything at first. Versus pushing her for an answer, Cannon took a seat on the bed and just watched her mother. There was a bottle on the corner of the nightstand, so Cannon shook it up before placing it to Yara's little mouth and waited for her to latch onto the nipple.

She took it immediately, practically sucking all the milk down in one swallow. Cannon snickered at her before placing a kiss to her little forehead.

"I don't know why she likes you more than me. You weren't like that." Karina's voice was low and sad.

Cannon gave her mother an empathetic smile. "She loves you too, Mommy. She can just sense the irritation from you. I told you, you have to relax and she will too."

Karina stared at Cannon and Yara for a minute with a distant look on her face. Cannon felt so bad for her because she knew her mother loved Yara, it was just tough battling postpartum on top of the grief she'd already been feeling beforehand.

Cannon stood from the bed and lay Yara down onto the pillow with her bottle tilted so that she could drink it, and went to her mother. She hugged Karina as soon as she was close to her.

"Don't cry. She's fine, I'm fine, and you're fine. It's just tough right now, but we'll all get through it."

Karina's head fell onto Cannon's shoulder as a torrent of tears rushed down her face. "She's not supposed to be here, Cannon."

"Shh, don't say that. Yes, she is. If God didn't want her here, she wouldn't be. There's a purpose for her in our lives. Stop crying."

Karina sniffed and nodded her head against Cannon's shoulder, but didn't offer any supportive agreements. Cannon wasn't surprised, because it had been that way since her mother had gotten pregnant with Yara. She cried morning, noon, and night, and if she wasn't crying she was lying in bed in the dark. The only thing she did was go to work, and Cannon was sure that was only to get away from the baby.

Light crying came from behind them. Cannon looked to see Yara's bottle had fallen out of her mouth. Karina pushed out of her grasp immediately.

"I have to go. I'll see you later, Cannon."

"Okay, you're working both jobs today?" Cannon asked already knowing the answer.

Once out of Cannon's grasp, Karina snatched her work bag from her bed, nodded her head, and hurried from her bedroom. Cannon watched the door she'd disappeared out of for a minute before going to Yara and grabbing her from the bed.

"It looks like it's just you and me, little mama." Cannon pecked the center of her forehead. "You want to help me with my homework? Huh, Yara boo?" Cannon kissed all over Yara's little face before laying her on her shoulder and going back into the living room to grab her backpack.

With her backpack and laptop in one hand and Yara in the other, Cannon went to the living room and got situated to do her homework. It took a minute to get Yara back to sleep, so that she could work in peace, and the moment she was prepared to start, her phone began ringing.

"Hey, Daddy!" Cannon squealed when his face popped up on Facetime.

"What's going on sweetheart? Is your mother gone to work?"

"Yes, she's gone."

Her stepfather, Aaron, nodded his head solemnly. "How's my girl?"

"I'm good, just trying to get accustomed to this new school. I miss being up there with you."

"Well, you know I would love nothing more than to have you back."

Cannon sighed. "I know, but I have to stay here and look after Mommy. She's still not doing well."

"That's her business."

Cannon could hear the underlying anger in her father's voice. It had been there for almost a year now and probably wouldn't be going away any time soon. Though she hated things between her mother and Aaron had to end the way that they did, she understood his feelings and respected them.

"I'll come visit for Christmas, how about that?"

His smile returned. "That's perfect. I can't wait."

Out of nowhere a soft grunt came from Yara. Cannon's head whipped around to her to make sure she was okay. She was stretching, but no cries followed so Cannon was in the clear to keep talking to her father. Too bad, he didn't feel the same way.

"Whelp, that's my cue. I'll talk with you later, sweetheart."

"Nooo, Daddy, we're not done talking yet."

"I'll call you back a little later before you go to bed."

As much as Cannon wanted to keep talking to him, she didn't. Yara was still such a sore spot for him, that anything about her put him in a bad mood. So, once he ended the call, Cannon had no other choice but to put her phone down.

With sad eyes, she looked over Yara's little body. Cannon felt so sorry for her. Her precious little life had come at such an unexpected time and now she had nobody to love her except Cannon.

"How could they not love a little baby?" Cannon asked herself.

She still remembered the day her mother and stepfather had found out about Yara. It was such a sad day in their household. Back then Cannon didn't understand why because she hadn't been told anything, but the moment she was, everything made sense.

"What do you mean you're pregnant, Karina?" Aaron's deep voice bellowed throughout the living room.

Continuous sobs escaped Karina's lips as she stared at the white stick in Aaron's hand. Cannon, oblivious to the problem at hand, walked toward her mother.

"You're pregnant, Mommy? That's so good!" She squealed with glee while clapping.

Karina's melancholy eyes traveled to Cannon as her head began to shake from side to side. "No, it's not, baby."

"Why not? You all have been talking about another baby for a while now."

"Yeah, we have. We've been talking about adopting a child for years now, but I guess your mother couldn't wait anymore." Aaron tossed the test onto the floor and marched from the room.

Cannon was so lost as to why this wasn't a good thing. She stood there watching her mother nearly cry herself into convulsions, before following her father from the room. She found him seated on the edge of their bed with his head cradled in his hands. Once she was comfortable next to him, she leaned into his shoulder.

"Why are you so angry, Daddy? Your own baby is better than adopting someone else's, right?"

Aaron's large frame came up until he was sitting straight up. His wet eyes took in Cannon's face before he pecked her forehead.

"I can't have kids, Cannon. I had a procedure done in my childhood that made me sterile."

Cannon gasped and covered her mouth. Though she hadn't known before, she was more than old enough to know what sterile meant. Now she knew why their house was in such disarray. Her mother had cheated and gotten pregnant. Oh no! Cannon's sad eyes went to the only man she'd ever known as her father and watered.

"You're not going to leave, are you?"

Aaron's arm went around her shoulders and he pulled her to him. "I don't think I can stay."

"But I don't want you to go."

Aaron's eyes watered all over again as he held her and cried. Cannon even shed a few tears at the thought of not having her father with her every day. He may not have been her biological father, but he was everything that she needed.

"I can't make any promises, Cannon, but Daddy will try for you."

Cannon squeezed him tighter and nodded her head into his chest. She was a daddy's girl through and through, so she felt the pain from every tear he was shedding. She was young and had only had one serious boyfriend so she wasn't as familiar with the pain of her mother's infidelity, but she knew it had to hurt. When her boyfriend

had broken up with her for the new girl at their school,
she'd felt horrible, so she could only imagine what her
father must have been feeling right then.

For a while Aaron did his best to be there, but the pain of the situation was just too much for him to handle. Especially when Yara came home from the hospital. He packed his things and left immediately after. Karina fell into a depression that was nearly impossible for her to get out of, which was another reason for their impromptu move. She'd needed a fresh start, so there they were. In country little Columbus, Georgia.

"This is all your fault, little girl." Cannon said as she kissed Yara's bare feet.

Cannon stared at her sister for a little while longer before sitting back on the sofa and staring out of the window. It was such a pretty day, too pretty to be sitting in the house, so she decided to get out. Yara needed more milk anyway. It took her a few minutes to get Yara's stroller and bag together before they were out of the house and making their way down the street.

The sun was shining bright, making Cannon happy she'd worn shorts. The heat in Georgia was unlike anything she'd ever felt before. She had been living up north in Denver, Colorado for so long, she'd nearly died getting stuck in Columbus. The heat was just disrespectful. Slap you in your face, mess up your hair, sweat off your makeup kind of disrespectful.

Even with her liking to walk as much as she did, she was beyond thankful when she finally made it to Walmart. The atmosphere in Denver had been so peaceful that she would walk all the time, but she could tell that would be something short lived now that she was in Georgia.

The cool air from the store misted over her damp skin as soon as she walked through the door. Patrons were everywhere getting what they needed, her included. She was on the baby aisle picking up the milk that matched Yara's WIC voucher when the smell of cologne drifted up her nose.

She didn't want to turn around and look right into the man's face, but he smelled too good to ignore. When she looked up he was looking at the can of milk in her hand.

"Can you help me? My baby mama gave me this shit and I don't know what to do with it."

Cannon looked from him to the WIC folder he was extending in her direction. She giggled and grabbed it from his hand. She opened the folder and read the type of milk he needed.

"Okay, they give your baby the Similac with the blue top, so you get her these cans." Cannon used her pointer finger to show him the size to get. "Then, the number right here tells you how many cans in that size you can get."

"So, get six?" he asked her, still dumbfounded.

Cannon snickered again. "Yes, get six for this one," she flipped through the rest of the vouchers to check their dates. "Fill all of these, because they expire tomorrow."

"Aww shit, I should have known her dumb ass would do something like this."

Cannon's laughter escaped her lips again. The dude was average height and brown skin with a nice build, but nothing that made Cannon want to drool. The clothes he wore were flashy along with the jewelry he was wearing. Everything about him screamed he was the plug. Cannon knew a drug dealer when she saw one, and he was most definitely that.

"Appreciate it, baby," he told her as he fumbled in his pockets. "Here, take this and get your nails done." He pushed the hundred-dollar bill toward her.

"You don't have to pay me for helping you." Cannon declined the money.

"Just take it. Let me do something nice for you." His eyes roamed over her body appreciatively. "Where your man at? You still with your baby daddy?"

Cannon could already tell where their conversation was headed, so she decided to ease her way right on out of the trap he was trying to set for her.

"Yeah, that's why I don't want to take your money."

The dude nodded his head. "Aight, bet. I can respect that, but take it anyway." He stuffed the money into Yara's stroller before winking at her and walking away.

"You're not going to get the milk?" Cannon slightly yelled from behind him.

"Nah, she can come do this shit herself."

Cannon was amused by his behavior, but didn't render any further conversation. It was clear he'd just wanted to talk to her. Her eyes went to the money, and she smiled.

"At least I got some free money out of the deal," she whispered to a sleeping Yara.

It took her a little longer to get finished in the store before she was back out of the door and on her way down the street. Hopefully, she wouldn't die from heat exhaustion on her way home. Luckily, she hadn't. When she finally made it home, she stripped her and Yara of their clothes and collapsed onto the sofa. The air was just what they'd needed.

4

Because you're all
I need

The suds from the soap and water floated through the air as Don leaned down and scrubbed the dirty tires of Danna's car. It had been weeks since the last time her car had been cleaned and it was in desperate need of some tender love and care. She'd considered taking it to the local car wash, but what was the point of doing that when she had a man that could clean it for free?

With her large purple shades covering over half of her face, Danna sat on the small stool in the corner of Don's driveway. Close enough to see what he was doing, but far enough not to get wet. Her legs were crossed while she wagged one of her ankles absentmindedly.

"I don't know why you're always lying to me. I know you be out here entertaining these li'l niggas." Don squeezed the water out of the light blue rag. "Like they can do some shit for you that I can't."

Danna rolled her eyes. Here we go. "Don, what the hell are you talking about? What even made you say that?"

"That shit you just said about the nigga at the carwash. I know you said something to the nigga to think it was okay for him to ask for your number."

"Don, shut up." Danna fanned the fly from her face. "You love to take my words and spin them around to make me look like the bad guy. All I said was I didn't like taking my car there because of all the attention I get. The boy asked for my number one time. You act like I said he got down on one knee and proposed. You really need to get ahold of yourself."

Don's insecurity was really starting to get on Danna's nerves. Any time she mentioned anything about another man that wasn't as old as him, he immediately went off the deep end. She could understand the minor intimidation that might come from her being a young girl, but damn. She loved him, and had made it more than clear.

"You better watch your mouth," he eyed her from his crouched position near her tire. "You know, just like I do, you be enticing these niggas. You're a flirt; that's what you do. I know your ass, even if you think I don't."

Danna smiled because he was right. She was, and she did indeed throw herself around for attention, but that was only when she felt like it. Don made it sound like she was out in the streets smiling at every man that walked past, when she wasn't. She was young, fine, and men noticed her. What was wrong with that?

"Flirting doesn't mean I want them. It's just something to do to pass time by."

"You need to cut it out. I'm about fed up with that shit."

"Well, if you would stop being afraid of my daddy and what he has to say about us, then I wouldn't have to do this." Danna stood from where she was sitting and walked toward the garage opening and leaned on it. "This is your fault." A daring smirk rested on her face. She already knew what was going to happen next. It never failed.

"My fault!" Don boomed incredulously.

And there it was.

Danna smiled at him trying to suppress her laughter. She loved to provoke him into anger on her behalf. It was cute and always reminded her how much he loved her, whether he wanted to hide it from the world or not.

"How is it my fault? You knew I was too old for your ass when we got into this shit. Just like you knew I was your daddy's people. That didn't stop your fast ass then, and it ain't about to stop you now." Don grimaced as he walked toward her with the soaking wet cloth dangling from his hand.

Danna eyed him sexily as he approached her with a vicious glare that didn't intimidate her in the least. He may have scared everybody in the streets, but not her. She had him under a love spell that he couldn't break even if he tried. One of the main reasons why she never thought twice about provoking the animal in him. She was a remedy for his anger and tamed him every time. They just connected like that.

"You keep on trying me, fucking around with these young niggas and watch what I do." His face was so close to hers, she could have given him an Eskimo kiss.

"I don't fuck around with nobody but you, so whatever you plan on doing, do it to yourself."

"Yeah, aight." Don nodded while still standing in her face.

Danna crossed her arms over her chest and smirked. "You love me don't you?"

Don's frown deepened.

"Just say it because you know you do. That's the only reason you're always trying to shine on me about other men."

"Nah, I just don't like being disrespected."

"Disrespected by the woman you love. I get that." Danna grabbed the front of his tank top and pulled him the rest of the way to her mouth. "I love you too."

Her mouth was on his seconds later. With a twist here and a tangle there, Danna used her tongue to initiate the brewing passion she felt rising in her stomach. Don wasted no time matching her efforts. He'd even dropped the towel he'd been holding and grabbed her bare back with his wet hand. The short crop top left just enough exposed skin above her shorts to allow him to feel her skin.

"You like starting shit with me, don't you?"

Danna nodded her head but continued her assault on his lips. She kissed him deeply and even raised one of her legs to wrap around his waist. Naturally, Don's hand gripped her thighs and picked her up from the ground. With no effort, he held her and walked into his garage. The small futon in the corner was used as support as he sat down so that she could kiss him comfortably. Danna took full advantage.

"You're the only person that makes me forget shit. Like literally, forget everything." His lips found her shoulder and placed a kiss there. "I forget all the good, the bad, and the logical shit. When you're around all I care about is us. Fuck everything else."

Danna sat comfortably in his lap with her arms still draped over his shoulder. "That's a good thing isn't it?"

Don shook his head. "Hell nah. I've got too much stuff going on inside of me to be losing my mind like this. I got too much shit to lose to be that careless."

"Loving me isn't being careless though. I wouldn't do anything to make you lose your mind."

His eyes found hers at the same time his hands grabbed her neck. "Purposely." He spoke quietly. "You wouldn't do anything purposely, but some shit you just can't help."

"Like what?"

"Like who you fall in love with. You can't help loving my psychotic ass no more than I can help loving your young one. I ain't never wanted to be in no shit like this . . . with you of all people."

Danna got somewhat offended at that, because what was wrong with her? Yeah, she was young, but so? She was just as grown and capable of love as a woman his age.

"What you mean me of all people? What's wrong with me?"

Don stared at her with a tortured look. "You're Echo's fucking daughter. I ain't supposed to feel shit for you."

"He's your boss, but that's it. Your personal life and business life have nothing to do with the other."

Don was quiet as if pondering her statement. "You think so?"

"Yeah, and if it does we can just run away together. I'm tired of Columbus anyway."

His deep chuckles brought a smile to his face. "You'd run away with me?"

"Is the sky blue?"

Danna basked in the smile on his face. She loved the way he loved her. It was like an ongoing battle with his heart and mind. In one instant, he was doting on her and professing his love for her, in the other he was biting his tongue and trying to hold it back. He was always unsuccessful because everything he did showed his love for her, whether he vocalized it or not.

"One day we will. I'm going to kidnap you and we're going to blow this city."

The sound of leaving and living a life free of judgement made her smile. She couldn't wait for the day. Damn. Danna hung her head. An image of Quay's smiling face invaded her mind. Her crush on him was something serious. They'd texted back and forth a few times, but it had been nothing major. Every time he tried to see her and hang out, she declined.

As much as she would have liked to, there were two things prohibiting it. The first one being the man in front of her, and the other being her father. Though, he was never really around anymore, he'd expressed too many times to count that his people were off limits. It was a fact that Don fell into the category as well, but as long as nobody knew about him she was good.

Quay on the other hand had already made it known the moment he made her his, the world would know. It sounded too good to be true and she would definitely want it just like that, but only if her situation was different.

"But, until that day," Don pinched the side of her butt. "Stay out these niggas faces before I kill your ass."

Danna rolled her eyes and smiled as he removed her from his lap and sat her on the futon. He was out of his seat and headed back to her car moments after. She contemplated responding to him, but chose not to. She knew she wasn't going anywhere and he did too. The argument was pointless.

"What are you doing for the rest of the day?"

"Got a run to make. I was hoping you would go with me." Don sprayed the soap from her car.

It took Danna no time to decide that wasn't happening. It was a pretty day outside and the last thing she wanted to do was ride around collecting money with Don. That was tedious and boring. Maybe had he mentioned the movies or shopping, she might have obliged, but that street shit, he could keep.

"No thanks. I think I'ma stop by the nail shop." The chipped pink paint that had been decorating her nails for the past two weeks looked a mess, and needed to be addressed immediately. "If you're not out too late just call me and I'll come back through tonight."

"Go look on my dresser and get that money out of my drawer." Don told her with no hesitation.

Without an ounce of hesitation in her, Danna stood to her feet and proceeded into the house. She spent so much time at Don's house, it might as well have been hers as well. She was so comfortable there and he allowed her to be, which was why she thought nothing of looking at the receipt that had been balled up in the wad of money.

Her eyes scanned it for nothing in particular, just trying to see what he'd spent money on. Things were fine and she had just been about to put it down with the last item caught her eye. The fuck? She looked at it again to make sure it was what she thought it was. When she was certain, she saw what she saw, she threw it down, snatched the money and stormed out of the house.

"Don!" She yelled as soon as she got outside.

He looked up at her, now shirtless. Her eyes observed the excellence that was him, before they rolled back to the matter at hand. With the receipt in hand, she walked right to him and held it up so he could see.

"Who you buying pregnancy tests for?"

Don's poker face remained. Not an ounce of guilt blinked through. "My baby mama's broke ass."

"What the fuck you buying her pregnancy tests for? She pregnant by you again?"

"Hell nah," He frowned in disgust. "She's just broke as fuck. I bought my son some pampers the other day and she asked me to grab a few other things for her, and that was one of them."

"You must think I'm a fool?" Danna countered back.

"Nah, I'm telling you the truth. I bought some washing powder, dish washing liquid, Aleve, and a bra too. All of which is at her house. She asked me to grab the shit, so I did. That's it."

"Even if that is the truth, why in the hell are you buying her shit like y'all together?"

Don finally finished with her car and moved away from it. "She's my baby mama. I just help her out with stuff from time to time. It ain't nothing to it."

Danna's temper was rising and she could feel her hands starting to shake. That was that mess she didn't like. She didn't care if the girl was his son's mother, grandmother, or auntie. He didn't need to be buying her shit that didn't involve the baby.

"So, if I let another nigga buy me stuff even though you're supposedly my man, that's cool?"

Don leaned his head to the side stretching his neck. When he didn't say anything, Danna knew her words had struck a nerve, but that was good for his ass.

"Don't even worry about answering me. I'm out."

After retrieving her keys from the table in his garage, she snatched her purse from the futon and headed for her car. She was in her front seat and about to close the door when he stopped her. His hand was holding her door open as he moved around it and squatted down next to her legs.

"You're right. I'm sorry." He placed a couple of kisses along her thighs and knee. "I didn't think about it like that."

Danna said nothing.

"I don't give a fuck about her, only you. Aight?"

Determined to hold on to her attitude, Danna said nothing.

"I won't do it again. Stop being so mean."

"Whatever, I'll check you later." Danna reached around his head and grabbed her door.

Don licked his lips before standing to his feet and leaning into her car. He kissed her lips once before stepping away and closing the door. Danna cranked up and pulled away without another word. Don had her all the way fucked up if he thought she was about to play the fool. Angry and annoyed all at once, Danna needed a release, and had just the way to get it.

5

Games well played

With a quick detour, Danna headed for the block. As soon as she spotted *him*, she parked and got out. Using a fake errand to the corner store as her distraction, Danna got out of her car and sashayed toward the barred glass door with the raggedy OPEN sign.

"Aye, you!" A male voice came from behind Danna.

Holding in her smile, she turned to face the man that owned the voice. With one of her hands shielding the sun from her eyes, and the other holding her purse and keys, Danna stood back on one leg allowing a better view of herself.

"You talking to me?" Danna's voice was small but vivacious as she took in the fresh white sneakers and gold jewelry shining beneath the sun.

"Hell yeah, I'm talking to your ass. Didn't I tell you the next time you were on my block you needed to come holla at me?"

Danna's smile finally made its way out as she eyed Quay's sexy ass. The shoulder length dreads and arms filled with tattoos had her feeling stuff girls her age shouldn't be feeling. The white tank top he was sporting hugged his chest, while the gym shorts hung loosely from his waist in all the right ways.

"Bring your hard-headed ass over here."

The defiant Danna wanted to make him come to her, but the young girl crushing on that fine ass man in front of her moved her feet and got going. She was standing directly in front of him in no time. The jean shorts she was wearing gathered between her thighs giving her something to do with her hands. Before she could even pull her hands from between her thighs, Quay's had found them and stopped her movement.

His eyes were low as he took a step closer and invaded her personal space. "Let me get that for you." The gold charm looking bracelet around his wrist rubbed against her skin when his hand pushed hers away and grabbed the rugged material of her shorts. "You ain't got no business with these little ass shorts on anyway. Out here showing all these niggas my legs and thighs and shit." Quay's fingertips brushed the inside of her legs as he took his time pulling her shorts back to their rightful place.

Danna's heart fluttered with every word he spoke. She loved when a nigga talked that thug shit to her, and hearing him claim her body as his was setting her off.

"They ain't even that short."

"Shid," Quay finally allowed her to breathe again when he removed his hands from her body. "Got your stomach and shit showing." Quay half frowned, half smiled. "Hell, you out here trying to be fine for? You dun' lost your mind today I see. Out here dressing like you ain't got no man."

Danna was smiling harder than she'd ever smiled in her life. Quay was real life making her feel like a giddy little child. Never in all her years had a nigga made her feel shy, but Quay had her barely able to make eye contact. His smooth and cool aura was a turn on all by itself, but to pair it with his voice had her feeling like kissing. Jesus . . . those lips. Danna raised her hand to fan herself but put it back down the moment she realized what she was about to do.

Quay's eyes went to her hand before going back to her face. "Aye, be cool with them hands, I don't do all that moving while I'm talking, it's intimidating. I might mess around and swing on your ass."

More smiles. "Boy, please. You swing on me I bet you won't swing on nobody else."

Quay grabbed her hands and leaned back on the wall, still holding them. "What you gon' do?"

"Swing and see."

His dark brown eyes observed her face calmly before he smiled lazily. "Nah." His locs brushed his shoulders.

"What you want to do then?" Danna baited him.

The blazing sun was shining down on her back as she stood with her back facing the street. Cars could be heard in the distance as they stood lost in one another. Danna could even see people passing them in her peripherals, but she was so focused on Quay and all his handsomeness, that she could care less about anything going on behind her.

The feeling of Quay's thumbs rubbing across the back of her hands felt so good that Danna was scared to make the slightest movement and he stop.

"I low-key want to be on some boyfriend shit with you, but I need to feel you out a li'l more first."

"Feel me out for what?" Danna asked as she looked down at her vibrating phone.

When she saw the letter D, she already knew it was Don. He'd called her twice already since she'd been standing there and she hadn't answered either time. She'd call him back, right then she was enjoying Quay. He didn't want nothing anyway, other than to beg and plead his sorry case.

That pregnancy test stunt had her hot and Danna wasn't letting up that fast. Danna had done her best to play it cool at his house, but after the thought of him playing her like a fool continued to circulate through her mind, she got angrier. She'd been ignoring and dodging his calls the entire drive to Quay, and didn't plan on stopping any time soon.

"See, shit like that." Quay smiled at her and the sun caught his gold teeth. They lit up the block. "You'll fuck around and break my heart. Be ignoring my calls and shit while you in the next nigga face."

"No, I wouldn't. I don't even be talking to nobody like that." Danna told him seriously.

She and Don did their thing, and could probably call what they had something like a relationship, but it wasn't something she could really count on because they couldn't be seen together like her and Quay could. She and Quay were at least in the same age bracket. She'd been on and off with Don for a little over a year, and had even fallen in love with him, but it was hard with him with so many caution signs prohibiting their relationship.

His boundary-crossing baby mama being the biggest one. She didn't even really know who Danna was, and she was constantly becoming an issue. There was no telling what would happen if she and Don ever made themselves public. Too much drama!

"Who keep calling you then? Your phone been vibrating since I grabbed your hand." Quay brought her thoughts back to the present.

"Somebody that don't want nothing."

Deep chuckles came from Quay as he released one of her hands and wrapped it around the back of her neck, pulling her close to him.

"You too savage for me."

"I'm not trying to be though." Danna's words were spoken innocently as she looked up at his face.

The prickly black hair on his chin was in her direct line of vision as she rested against his chest with her face near his neck. The smoke and dice inked around his throat, next to the cross and bible, were entertaining as she waited for him to say some-

thing that might put her thoughts at ease, because they were flying around her head right then.

"How you know they don't want nothing? They keep calling
back, so they must want something." Quay leaned down some
and rested his chin on the top of her head. "I know if I was calling
I would want something."

With the weight of his chin causing an awkward amount of tension on her neck, Danna had no other choice but to lay her head
on his chest.

"Come on now, don't be doing this."

Danna had a feeling she knew what he was talking about, but
she asked anyway. "Doing what?"

Quay gave the hand he was still holding a light squeeze and
tightened the arm around her shoulder so that she was held snug-
gly in his grasp. Danna closed her eyes in the middle of the hood
with cars flying past, babies crying, the sun burning up her back,
and plenty of people that knew Don, all because Quay's embrace
felt that good.

"Being all up under me making me feel special and shit. You
know you ain't even trying to do this with me."

"How you know?" Danna pulled her hand away from him and
circled them around his waist.

"Because whatever nigga you got calling you, is still blowing
that li'l phone up." Quay pulled away from her and pinched her
cheek.

"How you know it's a nigga? It could be my mama."

Quay smirked at her. "Prove me wrong then."

As bad as Danna wanted to pull her phone out of her purse
and show him the screen, she didn't. She knew just like he did
that it was a man.

"See," Quay winked at her. "I'm fucking with you though. Just
text me later."

For some reason, his dismissal made Danna feel like an egg had
just been cracked all over her face, but she kept it G, and smiled.

"I got you." Danna winked back and took a few steps backward toward her car.

"Have me then, baby." Quay joked with her.

The feeling of awkwardness was lifted with that one statement, and she was back smiling. No more words were spoken as she turned away and walked back toward her car. She was on the other side and about to get in when she finally looked back at him. His eyes were focused on her with a wanting gaze strong enough to hold her in place.

"When we get our chance, we gon' ball the fuck out, beautiful. I promise you."

"I'ma hold you to that."

"Please do. That's one promise I plan to make good on."

Danna blushed before waving once more and getting into her car. She gave him one last look before cranking up and pulling off. As soon as she was down the street she pulled her phone out. Don had called and texted her a number of times, but she still wasn't trying to talk right then. All he would do is ruin the high Quay had just put her on.

Don was her baby, and she enjoyed what they had brewing, but he didn't make her feel how Quay did. The difference was massive. With Don, she felt like a grown hood rat. Everything they did was either ratchet or above her age bracket. Between drinking, smoking, and having sex, she rarely had time to do things people her age did. Don was bent on "exposing" her to real life, but that wasn't necessarily what she wanted all the time.

Sometimes, going to the movies, going bowling or out to eat, would appease her just fine, but of course they couldn't do that. If she wasn't sneaking in and out of his house, dropping him off at traps, learning street shit, or her newest pastime, stalking his baby mama's social media pages, they were laid up having sex.

Which was starting to scare her as well. That nigga never wanted to use condoms and she'd had one too many concerns about that.

Her life was all she had, so getting an STD wasn't something she planned to experience. It was just so annoying to have to argue about condoms every time they were about to have sex. The only thing more annoying than that was the fact that he wouldn't stop calling her. Danna rolled her eyes and answered her ringing phone.

"What?"

"Why the fuck you ignoring me?"

"Why do you think?"

"I don't give a damn about that little attitude. You can lose that shit. Where you at?"

"Headed to my mama house, why?"

"That ain't what I heard, but aight. I'll catch up with you." Don hung up.

Danna looked at the phone utterly confused. How in the world had he found out where she was? Niggas and the way they ran their mouths got on her nerves. She hadn't been on the block five minutes and somebody had already put her business out. Echo and his overprotective staff irritated her. She literally had no privacy, and since Don was considered her little bodyguard, niggas probably blew his phone up when they saw her with Quay. Stupid niggas.

Not even in the mood to get her nails done anymore, Danna headed for her mother's house. Vonetta always made her feel better. It didn't take long before she was pulling into the driveway of her mother's house. Her mind was so clouded from thoughts of Don, and fantasies of Quay, that she totally missed his truck sitting in her parents' driveway. However, that carelessness was short-lived the moment she opened the front door to their home.

"Look at this li'l sneaky thing right here." Vonetta called her out as soon as she came into view. "Come on in here Ms. Fast Behind." Her mother's words were laced with love and a smile as always.

Danna was smiling back at her while shaking her head. "Ma, leave me alone. I ain't sneaky." Danna looked over at Don, and hurried to look away.

The look on his face was annoying and making her eyes want to roll. Though he was laid back on the sofa chilling, she could tell by the scowl on his face that he was angry. His mouth was balled up and his left eye kept jumping. Two signs she'd learned to be aware of.

"Um huh. Tell that to somebody else," Vonetta scratched the back of her head, making the million bangles on her wrist jingle. "Echo, I sure wish I could meet whatever nigga that's got your mean ass daughter running around here like a chicken with its head cut off."

Danna finally closed the door behind her and switched into the living room as her father's voice boomed through her mother's cellphone. She was seated on her favorite side of the sofa, while talking to Echo's tired ass on the phone. Clearly, it was a good day for him because that was one some-timing nigga right there.

Old as he was, he still didn't know if he wanted to be a family man or a hoe, and though Vonetta was the furthest thing from being his fool, she still loved him and let him come and go as he pleased. Even talking to him on the times he was away.

"Let me call you back, Echo. I need to check little Miss Fast Ass out." Vonetta laughed and said a few more things before ending her call with Echo.

"I don't know why you got off the phone, Ma. It ain't nobody serious." Danna's mischievous smile said something the total opposite of what her words did.

"Let me catch the nigga, I'm killing his ass." Don's voice stopped Danna mid-step.

"Don, don't you start too."

Don sat up and looked at her. "Try me."

If only Vonetta knew, Danna thought to herself as her mother sat there laughing loudly. Don had Vonetta so fooled with his over-protective act that she probably couldn't see the real anger dancing behind his eyes. She could feel his gaze on her, but kept her composure; she'd deal with his ignorance later.

"Ain't nobody gon' try you. I just be chilling. I don't love these niggas."

She snickered inwardly when she saw Don run his hand over his mouth smoothing out the hair on his chin. He was big mad, and she didn't care. So was she. Had she known he was there, she would have stayed on the block with Quay.

"That's my girl." Vonetta smiled.

Don looked at her with a frown on his face. "See, that's her problem right there. You be encouraging this shit. I see I'ma have to talk to Echo about both of y'all."

"Nigga, shut up. Danna is grown. That girl can do whatever she wants to do. You ought to be glad she ain't taking none of these little boys serious. She fucks around and fall in love, get pregnant, and start tripping on our ass, it'll be a real problem then. You and Echo get on my nerves with that shit. Let her live her young adult life."

Danna couldn't even hold her laughter in after that. Her mother was savage as hell. She might have loved Echo's workers, but she would cuss them out at the drop of a dime. Especially about her kids.

"Y'all showing out up in here. Let me go." Danna looked from her mother to Don as she headed for the back of the house. Don looked pissed.

Danna giggled to herself but kept her pace. He would soon learn that she wasn't the one to play with. She may have been young, but a nigga was a nigga was a nigga. She didn't give a damn how old he was. Vonetta hadn't raised no pussy, so she wasn't about to act like one. He'd think twice the next time he allowed his baby mama to make him check her. If anything, he should have been checking that hoe since he was in a relationship with Danna.

Danna felt her phone vibrate. She looked at the new message.

>4SionbcheC!g[o]echanis9

Don's text message brought about more laughs from Danna as she tossed herself down onto her bed. She was kicking her sandals off when the door to her bedroom opened. Ezra's head peeped in.

"Aye, what you doing later on?"

Danna shrugged. "I don't know. Why?"

"Nothing, I'm going to one of my li'l shawty's house but I wanted to make sure Don's old hating ass don't be getting in my way. You know Mama don't care but he always has something to say."

"Oh, don't worry about that. You already know I'll cuss his ass out about you."

Ezra's face lit up. "Bet. That's why you my nigga." He told her.

"Your young ass needs to stop fucking off so much. Too young to be hoeing around the way you do."

Ezra's chocolate face lit up from laughter as he shot her a bird and left. Danna couldn't do nothing but laugh at her brother. He was such a cutie and the ladies loved him. She did her best not to be one of those overprotective big sisters, but she didn't stand off as much as she could either. The last thing she wanted was for him to turn out like their big brother Nuke. Baby mamas and babies every damn where. Nuke and their older sister Vonnie, were the total opposites of her and Ezra.

Danna and Ezra did their things, but they were both respectful and living lives according to their ages. Vonnie and Nuke both had a slew of children and way too much going on. Nuke spent his time dealing drugs and making babies, while Vonnie had moved up north with her dad's family and worked three jobs trying to make ends meet because she'd let her heart make too many foolish decisions for her.

Occasionally, Danna blamed Echo for their lives because he was a horrible stepfather, but hell, he was a horrible biological father, so his lack of interest in them didn't surprise her very much.

"You must think I'm something to play with?" Don's voice startled Danna.

She looked up and he was standing at her door with a frown on his face.

"I'm about to dip, you need to come on."

Danna looked at him like the fool he was. "What makes you think I'm finna' do that?" she whispered.

Don cleared his throat trying to calm himself down. "You heard what I said. Go to my house." He glared at her before leaving the room.

Danna released an irritated breath before sliding her feet back into her shoes and grabbing her purse and keys. As bad as she didn't want to go with him, she knew she'd might as well get it over with. The longer she ignored him, the madder he would get and that would only lead to him getting on her nerves.

Quickly, Danna walked back through her house and out the front door. "I'll be right back y'all."

"Be careful, Danna." Vonetta yelled behind her.

"Yes ma'am." Danna told her before shooting Don a knowing look.

She was certain he'd be right behind her soon enough. In a huff, Danna got into her car and drove the couple of blocks down the road to where Don lived. She pulled her car into his garage and walked into the house.

She hadn't even sat down good before loud knocking was coming from the front door. Danna looked toward it, but didn't bother going to it because it wasn't for her, and she wasn't about to answer it for him.

"Don't stay in there scared now, bitch. Open this door."

Danna's head snapped back as she heard the slurs. "Now, I know this bitch ain't over here." Danna mumbled to herself before going to Don's room and peeping out the window.

There was a small blue Honda with a red dragon painted on the hood, diagonally parked in the driveway. She couldn't really see who was at the door because of the angle she was looking from, but she was sure it was Don's baby mama. Let Don tell it, she was the only other woman that knew where he stayed, but what Danna couldn't understand was how in the world had she known she was there.

In that moment, Danna wished like hell she knew the girl personally, and whether or not her secret relationship with Don would still be safe after she beat her ass. Probably not, so she chilled, but the moment she figured out who Don's baby mama from hell was, it was over.

Don had spoken about her randomly whenever his kids became a topic, but he never expounded too much, so Danna didn't know her personally, but she knew enough. What she did know was that raggedy ass voice. The bitch did so much hollering and fussing on Don's phone, Danna would recognize her squawking anywhere.

More knocking and yelling came, but Danna ignored it all. She didn't have time for that mess. That was Don's shit. Versus getting comfortable, she held all her stuff in her lap and scrolled on her phone. She'd thought about texting Quay, but she didn't need Don coming in trying to go through her phone or any of that other crazy mess he did when he was mad.

Nearly twenty minutes passed with the yelling and knocking before it stopped. Danna heard voices outside, so she checked to see who it was. Don and a li'l light-skinned thot named Totiana she knew from around the way was in the middle of the yard fussing. Danna rolled her eyes in disgust.

"You running hoes where my fucking son lays his head, Don? Really?"

The chick's loud mouth could be heard through the window.

"Now, I know this freak ain't that nigga's baby mama?" Danna questioned herself shocked.

She knew Don's baby mama very well just off some street cred shit. Never would she have ever put them two together. She'd known Don had a son, just like she'd known that girl had one too, she just didn't know he was theirs, together.

"Ain't this some mess." Danna watched them in disbelief for a little longer, before taking her seat back on the bed and bouncing her leg agitatedly.

Her inner beast was dying to come out, but she wouldn't let it. She'd let Don and his cuckoo bird have it for now, but only because she'd rather keep her identity hidden. A mad baby mama would spread more lies than Danna cared to deal with. Especially Thotiana's pillow talking ass. That bitch was known for running her mouth to any nigga that was coming off some cash. A few more minutes passed before she heard Don coming up the stairs. As soon as he rounded the corner, he was fussing.

"Why the fuck you been dodging me all day?"

"The same reason it just took you ten minutes to get in your own house." Danna stood up and got into his face. "That foolish ass baby mama you have."

"Fuck her."

"Nah don't be hollin' fuck her, now. You weren't on that when you were in Walmart cashing out on the hoe."

"Wasn't nobody cashing out on shit. I was just making sure my son was good."

Danna sucked her teeth. "Nigga, please. That little boy ain't washing dishes or fucking, so why would he need a pregnancy test or dish detergent?"

Don's body language displayed his heated temper, but Danna didn't care. She was just as mad as he was.

"That's child shit you're on. Stop it. You're better than this shit."

"You stop it! You're the one doing dumb stuff." Danna screamed back. "I'm not about to compete with your baby mama. I shouldn't have to, since you ain't with her." Danna looked him up and down. "Unless you are."

Don walked away from her and began undressing. "You know

damn well I ain't with that fucking girl. You're my girl and my world. Believe that. Nothing comes before you."

Danna didn't believe him at all. If he wasn't with her, then there would be no reason for him to be buying her stuff, or for her to be outside of his house with nonsense. Niggas, lies, and flies, they all went together, and Danna knew that. Which was why she wasn't even about to trip. She'd just chill with him, but do her own thing as well.

"Next time I call your ass you better answer your phone."

"Um huh," Danna dismissed him.

Don was on her in no time, grabbing on to her waist trying to settle the mood. "Don't be acting all nonchalant with me."

Danna said nothing. She stood still allowing him to hold her. He kissed all over her neck while unfastening her shorts.

"You mad at me?"

Again, Danna said nothing.

"It's cool, I got something for you."

"No, you don't. Not as long as you're still messing around with your baby mama."

Don spun her around and began kissing all over her neck and face. "Fuck her, I love you."

Danna's defenses were weakening as he touched and kissed all over her.

"I swear it ain't nothing between us. I only love you."

"Whatever you say." Danna responded weakly.

She lay there rolling her eyes at her own self. She hated the way she allowed him to manipulate her emotions. The way she loved him could be so annoying at times. The current time, being one. With doubts and regrets running through her mind, Danna remained in his arms allowing him to have his way with her. Had she known that would be the last time she'd see Don outside of the walls of the city's local prison, she would have given him more of herself. Unfortunately for her and him, for a man with a past, freedom was hard to maintain and even easier to lose.

6

I want to talk to you

"Nigga, it took you forever in there. What were you doing?" Ezra asked his teammate Jazz as he got settled in the passenger seat of Ezra's pickup truck. "I should make you give me some gas money for taking all day."

"Talking to women." Jazz smiled as Ezra cranked up and backed out of the Publix parking spot. "You should have been in there with me instead of sitting out here whining."

Ezra cut his eyes at his brother. "Nigga, I ain't whining. I've just got better stuff to be doing."

Jazz shrugged nonchalantly. "If you say so, but ain't nothing better than talking to women except fucking 'em."

They shared a laugh as Ezra focused on what was in front of him. The parking lot was filled with people, but for some reason, his eyes were able to find *her*. He turned his head and slowed the truck some to be sure he was seeing who he thought he was. When he was positive that the thick thighs and pretty caramel-colored face belonged to Cannon, he pulled up beside her and rolled his window down.

"Aye, New Girl."

Her head turned, and her eyes squinted. She smiled when noticing it was him. "Ezra? You following me?"

Ezra's smile slid across his face as he reveled in the sound of his name on her lips. "Nah, not yet."

The pretty smile she was trying to suppress was just as cute as the little shorts she was wearing. With one ankle crossed over the other, she stood leaning on the handle of the stroller, making him want to feel on her. Her legs were so thick and juicy, all he could think about was how soft they had to feel.

"What you doing out here walking? You want me to take you home?"

"No thanks. I want to walk. I like the fresh air."

Ezra's face frowned. "Fresh air? Girl it's hot as the devil's front porch out here. Ain't nothing fresh about this air."

Soft giggles that made him feel some type of way flowed from her to the window of the truck. "I'm good, Ezra, thank you."

"Cool. Well, what you about to do? I found out one of them names for you."

Cannon's head tilted to the side some as she looked at him through her gold rimmed glasses. "I'm just going home to do my homework, that's it." She answered totally ignoring the part about the name.

"You don't want to know who the person is?"

Her shoulders shrugged as she smiled again. "Yeah, come tell me."

Ezra was grinning extra hard as he put his truck in park and got ready to hop out.

"Boy, what you doing? That girl is pushing a baby stroller." Jazz said to Ezra's back as he hopped out of his truck and walked toward Cannon. "Probably still with her baby daddy or some shit."

He'd heard Jazz, but he'd see what that was about in a minute.

As far as he knew, Cannon didn't even have a baby. But then again, it wasn't like he knew very much about her.

"What you cheesing so hard for, Ezra?" Cannon asked him as soon as he stopped in front of her.

With the bashful smile of a middle schooler in the presence of his crush, Ezra rubbed his hand over his face trying to wipe away the smirk that came naturally whenever he looked at her.

"Because you real fly, and I like looking at you."

Like he'd known it would, his response had Cannon blushing. It was real cute too, because it made her cheeks turn red just a little.

"Your face makes me smile."

Cannon pushed his chest lightly while turning her head. "You swear you running game on somebody."

Ezra's hand grabbed the one she was pulling from his chest and held it. "Not somebody, you." A wink and a quick lick of his lips had Cannon blushing nonstop.

This time a lot harder, because her whole face turned red. Ezra was a serious player and ran game on girls all the time, but spitting his lines to Cannon made him feel like a boss. Maybe it was the way she kept giggling and covering her face, or the fact that his words noticeably moved her. Whatever it was, he was loving it.

"Get out of my face, Ezra. I ain't got time to be playing with you."

Ezra let her hand go and looked around the parking lot dramatically. "Why you don't? Where you got to go?"

"Home."

"Who you stay with?"

"My mama. Why?"

Ezra nodded his head at the stroller. "Because I might have heard that you still with your baby daddy."

The frown on Cannon's face responded before her mouth could. "My baby daddy? Say what now? Where in the world did you get that mess from?"

"A source."

Cannon shook her head from side to side and waved him off. "Well somebody lied to you, because I don't even have a baby daddy." She was still frowning when she looked back at him. "And who running around here telling you my business like they know me? I don't even talk to nobody in this li'l country town."

Ezra found her little rant amusing, so instead of saying anything about Jazz, he stood back, smiling at her. When she noticed he wasn't saying anything, she stopped and turned toward the stroller like she was about to walk away, but he grabbed one of her wrists and stopped her.

"Aye, where you think you're going?"

"Home." She began pushing the stroller again.

She was even able to get a few steps in, making Ezra have to jog to catch up to her. "Why you acting like that?"

"I don't know. Ask your source and see what they say."

"Man, you're wilding out." Ezra grabbed the same wrist he'd held before and stopped her stride. "My teammate told me that shit, but he was just joking. He doesn't even know you like that."

Cannon's face relaxed a little before it slid into a small smile. "He doesn't need to be worrying about me or my fictitious baby daddy. Tell him I said to mind his business."

Ezra watched her with his eyebrows raised until she made eye contact with him and bucked her eyes at him. They both laughed before getting back to their conversation.

"Well, if you don't have a baby daddy, let me come see you then."

"When?"

"Tonight, when I get off work."

"Where you work?"

"KFC."

Cannon snickered. "Only if you bring me some biscuits with you."

Ezra couldn't hold back his laughter after that. He didn't know if she was being serious or not, but it was funny either way since she was already a little chubby, but in a cute way.

"You for real?"

"Yes, I love bread."

His eyes flowed down her body stopping on her legs once again. He couldn't get enough of those. "I see."

Cannon's face frowned again, this time a punch to his arm came behind it. "Don't try to make fat jokes."

"I'm not, but you are juicy as hell."

"Okay, see I'm finna' go home. Bye." Cannon walked away faster this time.

Ezra wanted to stop her but he was enjoying the view. He allowed her to get halfway down the sidewalk before once again jogging to get to where she was. This time he wrapped his arm around her neck and pulled her to him.

"Listen fast walking ass girl, our relationship ain't finna' be like this. I'm not about to keep chasing you. You gon' either come willingly, or I ain't never letting you go nowhere. I bet I won't have to chase you then."

"I don't deal with people that talks about my weight."

"You think I'm talking about you?" Ezra looked at her with a confused expression. "Man, listen, this the south. We love thick women. I only said something about your size because I can't get enough of it. I like how big your legs are. I know you see me staring at them every five seconds."

Cannon did her best to maintain her little attitude, but failed miserably, and was smiling from ear to ear. Ezra pulled her to him tighter before releasing her.

"Now, tell me how many biscuits you want and what time you want me to bring them."

"Three, and come whenever you get off. I'll be up. I don't sleep much at night because of the baby."

Ezra's eyes went to the baby in the stroller. She was cute little baby, but she was dark as hell compared to Cannon.

"Her daddy must be dark?"

Cannon looked at the baby and nodded.

"That's what's up. He ain't the kind of dude that be tripping when you talk to other dudes is he? Because I know niggas love to trip about their baby mamas."

"Ezra, this is not my baby. She's my sister. I just told you that, so you either gon' believe me or you're not."

"Okay, bet. My bad." He told her, smiling just as hard as he'd been the whole time they'd been talking. "Well give me your number so I can text you for your address and stuff when I'm on my way."

Cannon took his outstretched phone and typed her number in it before giving it back to him. He looked down at her number and smiled.

"Even your name looks pretty in my phone."

Cannon was all smiles and giggles as he stood in front of her running some of his best game.

"I can't stand you right now. You do know that right?"

"Yeah, I bet, but you'll get over that in due timing."

"I'm sure I will. Bye Ezra." Cannon pushed the stroller and began walking away again.

"Peace out, boo."

Cannon smiled at him over her shoulder once more before continuing down the street. Ezra watched her for a minute, getting his rocks off on her thighs before hopping into the truck with Jazz. He was on the phone fussing with somebody about something Ezra didn't care enough to hear about.

Once he was able to pull out of the parking lot, he merged into traffic and headed to Jazz's spot. He couldn't wait to get to work and get those hours out of the way. Being able to see Cannon was about to make his shift worth working.

He'd been checking for her since the moment she walked into his creative writing class, and hadn't stopped since. He wasn't sure if she noticed it or not, but he was always stealing glances at her, trying to make jokes with her, or accidentally bumping into her when they got out of their seats to leave. Hopefully spending time with her later would be just as exciting as their little conversation had been.

7

I can be the help you need

The sizzling from the grease in the frying pan had Cannon so zoned out, she almost hadn't heard her phone ringing. When she finally grabbed it from the counter, she already had two missed calls. Being that it was from a number she didn't know, she figured it had to be Ezra. When she unlocked her phone, and checked the text message that was waiting for her, her thoughts were confirmed.

He'd texted her once letting her know that he was on the way, and another letting her know he was outside. Since she'd sent him her address earlier, she wasn't alarmed by his presence. After clearing her screen, she sat her phone back down and checked the chicken. When she was sure she could leave it for a minute, she ran to the front door.

Upon opening it, she spotted the same black truck Ezra had been in earlier, parked along the curb. The tint was so dark she couldn't really see inside, but she was sure he was there. Neither her nor her mother really knew anyone in Georgia, so they most definitely never had any company at their house. On top of that, her mother's depression was at an all-time high, and they weren't really trying to broadcast that.

Cannon stood at the door for a moment just watching the truck to see whether he would be getting out any time soon. When he didn't move, she walked back into the house. He'd find his way when he was ready. The glass screen door slammed behind her as she made her way to the kitchen.

With a fork occupying one of her hands, and the other resting on her hip, Cannon waited with a stomach full of butterflies. For some reason having Ezra over had been affecting her since she'd agreed to his company. Cannon had been trying to figure it out all day, and couldn't. Ezra was cute and all but she wasn't really into him enough to be as nervous as she was right then.

Cannon's head spun around when she heard the screen door slam closed again. Her eyes went to the entrance of the kitchen in expectancy. When it took him too long to show his face, she rounded the corner and there he was. *Lord!* Cannon's eyes darted away quickly trying to give herself a minute to gather her bearings.

He was there alright, really there, and really fine as hell while being there. The black tank top and black gym shorts he was wearing were so fitting for his body, then to add the simple gold necklace with the E charm hanging around his neck, and the long locs, he was perfect. It didn't matter if she was feeling him for real or not, she couldn't deny the fact that the man was fine.

"Why you ain't wait for me?" Ezra's unique light bulb eyes shined on her as she stood taking in the beauty of the gift God had bestowed upon her.

In the back of her mind she knew that might have sounded like something straight out of a romance book, but that's how she felt. There was no way any other ordinary woman was in her exact place right then. A boy as beautiful as Ezra wasn't real. He was fictitiously gorgeous. Everything about him had to be make-believe, because real niggas didn't come that pretty.

"You were taking forever to get out of the truck." Cannon told him as she padded back toward the kitchen.

She hurried to remove the chicken from the grease before it burned. Just as she put the last piece on the plate, she heard Ezra behind her.

"Man, your ass don't know how to cook. You in here about to burn your mama house down."

"Boy, please. I can cook better than her." Cannon smiled at him over her shoulder. "You just better have my biscuits to go with my chicken."

Ezra smiled back before holding up the plastic bag with the red and white box inside of it. Cannon was just about to say something else to him, but stopped when she felt his chest on her back. Ezra was leaning over her shoulder looking at the chicken, but he was way too close for comfort, so with a quick elbow to his stomach, Cannon got her space back.

"You all over me. Move please," she pushed him back a little more.

Ezra chuckled and pinched the back of her neck playfully before taking a few steps back and hopping on the counter behind her. Cannon wanted to beg him not to put his hand on her body like that again, but she didn't want him to ask her why. That topic was surely off limits on their first little date. How was she going to explain she was easy? Like, really easy. The slightest touch would have her doing things girls her age shouldn't even know about.

"You was at home getting ready for these biscuits, huh?" Ezra was laughing again, but this time it was by himself.

Cannon's mood soured immediately. "I told you earlier about the fat jokes. I'm not going to say it again. Next time I'ma just stop fucking with you before I even start."

The kitchen was quiet for a minute, neither of them saying anything. Cannon didn't know about him, but she was angry, and as serious as a heart attack. She didn't like that fat girl stuff, and Ezra was getting more and more comfortable with it.

"I like to eat, so what? I ain't no different than these skinny girls that love to eat, and the world thinks it's cute." She turned her head to the side so she could look at him out of the side of her eye. "So, don't try me."

"I really didn't mean it like that."

"I don't care how you meant it, it sounded rude."

Ezra was off the counter and walking toward her. Cannon tried to sidestep him so that he couldn't touch her, but she missed and both of his hands were on her elbows pulling her backwards. He stilled her movement with a forceful tug when she tried to wiggle out of his grasp.

"Stop that." He told her once before leaning down and resting his chin on her shoulder. His hair rubbed against her face subtly. "I'm sorry. I promise I didn't mean it the way it sounded . . . okay?"

Cannon stood silent.

"I talk a lot and some of the stuff I say may sound rude, but that's because you ain't from here."

Silence filled the room for only a second longer before Cannon snickered.

"Because I'm not from here? What does that have to do with anything?"

"You're not used to the way southerners talk." Ezra's cute little laugh made Cannon laugh as well. "Just like you ain't used to what we like, because if you were, you'd know we love thick women." Ezra's hands dropped from her elbows and wrapped around her stomach. "The thicker the better."

Cannon shrank inward when she felt his hands on her stomach. Surely, he felt the extra softness she was trying her best to hold in. Her stomach wasn't filled with a bunch of rolls of fat, but it surely wasn't flat. She'd had a little more than her share of fried foods and sweets throughout the years, and her current moment was making her wish she'd avoided them altogether.

"You can go ahead and stop trying to hold your stomach in too, I can feel your muscles tightening."

"Oh my god," Cannon said aloud as she tried to step out of his hold again.

Utter embarrassment and shame was all over her. She was so ashamed she even covered her face with both of her hands. Ezra was killing her. Before the night was over she'd probably be in the local morgue, waiting for her toe to be tagged.

"Cannon, you don't have to hide who you are for me. I ain't nobody."

The coolness from his breath made the tiny hairs on the back of her neck stand up while his cologne and voice made her stomach churn. Hopefully he couldn't feel that too. She'd just die if he did. To go ahead and drop her casket six feet under, he gave her belly a light squeeze.

"Ezra, please stop."

"You damn stop. You the one acting crazy." His tone was accusing and comical at the same time.

The subtle sizzling from the cooling grease was the only noise in the small kitchen as Cannon stood awkwardly in Ezra's arms. Her back was still to him, while he'd raised his chin from her shoulder and was in place behind her.

"Now, are you going to keep acting a fool while I'm over here, or are you going to chill? I ain't got time for you to be not liking me already and I ain't even been here that long yet."

"Who told you I liked you in the first place? You asked could you come see me and I said yeah. That don't mean I like you. Pump your brakes, Mr. Southside."

Ezra's laughter caused him to finally release her, and for that Cannon was grateful. She even turned around so that she could watch him. He was leaned back casually on the counter with one hand over his mouth and the other on the granite next to him, laughing. He was freaking adorable. Almost cuter than Yara. Almost.

"I can't stand you. You think everything is so funny." Cannon pushed his hand that was resting on the counter causing him to lose his hold and fall forward a little.

Ezra stood to his full height and poked her forehead with his pointer finger. "Alright now feisty ass girl, don't be putting your hands on me."

"Or what?" Cannon walked into his space with her arms folded over her chest. Her face was serious as she tried to hold back her smile. "What you gon' do Southside?"

"First of all, I ain't say no damn Southside, I said Southerner. Get your shit straight."

"It's whatever I say it is." Cannon took a step closer to him. "Now like I said, Southside, what you gon' do if I keep putting my hands on you?"

Ezra's long hair fell around his shoulders, shielding the sides of his face some as he stared at her. His eyes dimmed a little as they squinted in the corners when his lips balled into his mouth.

"I don't care about your little serious face. Do something." Cannon stepped closer so that her chest was pressed against his. "I dare you." She pushed one side of his hair over his shoulder and held it back so that she could see his face.

Ezra remained stoic with an underlying smirk on his face. The two of them stood there pressed against one another, breathing, staring, and flirting silently.

"Don't dare me sweetheart, because I really do the stuff I say I'ma do."

"Show me." Cannon challenged, her confidence coming through with a vengeance.

Ezra stared at her for a little bit longer, before grabbing both sides of her face and pecking her mouth quickly. Cannon's first thought was to pull away, but like he'd been doing since he'd gotten there, he held her to him. His lips pressed against hers again. This time, remaining a little longer than before. Cannon's chest sank as she grabbed both of his hands with hers and pulled away.

"Boy, what you think you doing? How you know my mama ain't here?"

His smile spread across his face slowly. "She can get a kiss too if she wants one."

"I hate you." Cannon shook her head with a broad smile on it.

"You'll love me sooner or later, so I'll take that for now." Ezra walked past her and grabbed a piece of fried chicken and took a bite out of it. "Messing around with you, the food gon' be cold and I can tell you right now, KFC biscuits be nasty as hell when they cold. You might even choke on them bitches if you ain't careful."

"You ain't lying. Let me hurry up." Cannon grabbed the plate of chicken wings she'd fried and the bag of bread and told him to follow her.

Ezra was right on her heels as they walked into the living room. Yara was lying peacefully in her bassinet sleeping. Cannon checked on her before sitting down and placing the food in front of them. She'd thought Ezra was about to sit next to her, but he gave her his chicken instead and went to the bassinet to grab Yara. She squirmed a little until he placed her against his chest and began rubbing her back.

"Ain't nobody tell you to pick her up." Cannon told him while opening the pack of honey with her teeth. "If she wakes up, you seeing about her."

"You ain't saying nothing. I know how to take care of a baby."

"You must got one?" Cannon watched him sit on the sofa opposite of her and stretch his legs out.

Yara was balled up in the center of his chest, while he rested one hand on her body, while the other was behind his head. He looked extremely relaxed for a person that had never been to her house a day in his life. Though they didn't know each other from a can of paint, the chemistry was there. Not to mention, how cute he looked holding Yara. It didn't make Cannon want a baby or nothing crazy like that, but it did make her daydream a little bit.

"Nope. I've got a lot of nieces and nephews though. They love me too." A boastful smile lit up the living room. "Uncle Southside love the kids."

A series of coughs left Cannon's mouth as she tried to laugh and ended up choking on her bread. Ezra sat across from her with a grin on his face.

"I told you that bread was gon' choke you. You thought I was playing, didn't you?"

Cannon's middle finger served as her response as she sat with her hand on her chest trying to relax again. She could feel Ezra's eyes on her the whole time. She only moved when Yara's soft grunts came out of nowhere. With his head leaned over so that he could see Yara's face, he rocked her body softly until she quieted down.

"She needs to shut her ass up don't she, li'l mama? Keeping up all that fucking noise while you trying to get your beauty sleep." Though he was insulting every action of Cannon's, his baby talk was the cutest thing Cannon had ever seen. "Don't worry about it li'l mama, I got you. I'll make her behave."

"Nigga, please. I ain't thinking about you or Yara's little behind."

Ezra gave her a stern look and placed his finger to his lips before mouthing, *hush*. His eyes were bucked and everything giving Cannon yet another laugh. Something that had been reoccurring since he'd arrived.

"Let me get out of here before I knock you out." Cannon gathered the empty fast food box and walked to the kitchen.

When she came back she sat the soda she'd gotten for him on the table in front of him and took Yara from him so that he could eat. With the baby in her arms, Cannon walked to the back to get her together. After a quick change of her Pampers, and clothes, Yara's little round eyes were wide open.

"Hey Yara boo," Cannon kissed all over her face.

"Don't be trying to kiss all over my li'l mama now. You were just being disrespectful and shit while she was sleep. Keep that same energy you had in the living room, fam."

Ezra stood at the door sipping from the green and blue can of soda.

"I'm sick of your fan club, Yara."

Yara's small legs and arms waved around in the air as she got excited by Cannon's voice.

"I'm sick of you too. Give me the baby back and I'll be on my way." Ezra walked further into her mother's room, looking around at the pictures hanging on the wall. "Why your room look so dark and gloomy? You ain't got no posters, perfume, clothes, or none of that other girly stuff girls our age be having everywhere."

"You know how girls our age rooms be looking, don't you?" Cannon side eyed him knowingly. "Probably live in these hoe's house when they mamas be at work."

Ezra kept a straight face and held his open palm up toward her. "Talk to the hand, New Girl."

"Yeah, you know not to incriminate yourself."

"Just tell me why you got this old lady room and I'll mind my business." His locs dipped lower across his back as he tilted his head to admire the picture of the black lady above her mother's closet.

"Because, Mr. Nosey, this ain't my room." Cannon picked Yara up and cradled her in her arms. "It's my mama's, now get out." She stood to her feet with him following close behind her.

Cannon hit the lights and walked across the hall into her room. She pushed the door open and flipped the lights on. The lavender-colored decorations against the Cherrywood furniture came into view. Her full-sized bed was on one side, while Yara's crib that matched her furniture was positioned on the other side. One dresser, a changing table, and a vanity were all strategically placed around the room.

There were pictures on her wall as well, and Yara's name spelled out over her crib. It was neat and decorated nicely. Cannon's things were on her side, while Yara's were on hers. Cannon had made sure to keep their things separate, so that it would be easier to find everything.

Her eyes surveyed Ezra's face as she took a seat at the top of her bed. He was still at the door looking around the room.

"Why you looking around like that?"

His eyes went to hers and paused before going to the three poster-sized pictures on her side of the room. The first one was of her and her mom, the second was her and her stepfather Aaron, and the last one was of her and a boy from her hometown. His eyes stayed there longer than they had on the other two. Cannon could feel a question coming, but surprisingly, it never did.

"You're already too old to still be living at home with your mama, but you're most definitely too old to be sharing rooms with your baby sister."

Cannon's cheeks rose as she smiled at him. "Don't come to my house trying to talk about me. This arrangement works best, so that's how I like it. Plus, I'm not that old. I'll move once I graduate."

Ezra pushed his hair out of his face, and stepped further into the room. He moved toward her bed slowly and lay backward across the bottom of it. His back was pressed against the wall as his legs stretched out in front of him.

"I'm just messing with you. It's cool. I stay at home with my mom too. It's cheaper, and she don't be on me like that anyway. You on the other hand I'm not so sure about. You staying here taking care of the baby makes me think you're really her mother and not her sister, but I digress." He held his hands up in mock surrender.

"She's really my sister. Her arrival was just a little unwelcomed so I've had to fill in all the empty spots until everything is back to normal."

Ezra's eyebrows scrunched with concern. "What you mean?"

"My mama was married to my daddy, cheated and got Yara, my daddy couldn't take it and left. Yara's real daddy isn't in the picture anymore, so now my mama is suffering from postpartum really bad." Cannon's voice cracked a little, but she got it together quickly as she looked down at Yara, who was looking right back at her. "So, now I have to be sister-mommy." She held Yara up and kissed her nose before cradling her close to her chest again.

"Damn, that's messed up."

"Tell me about it." Cannon stated, exasperated.

Silence filled the room as they both sat deep in thought.

"I know that junk has to be stressful. Being a teenage mom when you really ain't one."

Cannon looked at him and nodded in agreement. She was sure the stress was written all over her face, but it was her life right then, so she accepted it. It was better for Yara to have her, than for her to be stuck with Karina all day. They'd probably kill each other.

"So, you don't be doing nothing?"

Cannon's head shook. "Not for real. I don't really trust my mom with her for too long, so I go to school and come straight home."

"So that's why you be leaving class so fast?"

Cannon smiled and nodded.

"I was wondering where you used to be running off to. I used to be like dang, she running."

They laughed together before Cannon continued.

"Anything else I do, I have to make sure it's something I can take Yara with me to do." Cannon resituated herself on the bed and sat against her headboard so that she was facing Ezra. "It's cool though, I don't really know anybody around here anyway, so I'm not missing much. It was worse when I was in Denver. It was like my life just ended."

"I know it did. Babies ain't no hoe. They real life blockers."

Another sequence of feminine and bass-filled laughter serenaded the room as Cannon sat reflecting on her current situation.

"I have to be here for her though. She's innocent, and can't control the hand she's been dealt, no more than I can."

Ezra's eyes were back on, and shining at her as she spoke. He looked so interested in what she was saying that it made her want to keep talking. It had been so long since she'd been able to actually enjoy a conversation about herself. Every time she talked to her daddy she was trying to avoid topics surrounding her mother and sister, when talking to Karina she was more of a therapist than anything, and she hadn't really kept in contact with any of her other friends from Denver.

"So, you plan on letting her call you mama?"

Cannon laughed and shrugged her shoulders. "I don't know. I mean not for real, but depending on whether or not Karina ever gets herself together, she may not have a choice."

"Karina is your mama?"

Cannon nodded.

"It's that bad?"

Another nod from Cannon.

"Damn. My sister be having kids like it ain't nothing and she be straight. I ain't know that postpartum stuff was that serious."

"I don't think too many black women take it serious because we're so used to just doing what we have to do, that we don't pay ourselves any attention. We just take it, tuck it, and take care of our responsibilities. Then men, y'all be in and out so," Cannon shrugged. "We don't really have time to focus on ourselves. Then the first time you say something about not wanting your baby everybody looking at you like you're crazy. Not knowing how real depression is."

"That's crazy, but true." Ezra touched her foot and rubbed up and down the top of it. "I'll help you out if you need me to."

Cannon's eyes went from his hand on her foot to his face. It was sincere and assuring. "You don't have to do that. I got it. Thank you though."

"Now, you just said black men be in and out. I'm sitting here trying to be in and be the baby's brother-daddy, and you telling me no."

Cannon's laughter erupted, scaring Yara. She whined for a minute until Ezra grabbed her from Cannon. He kissed the top of her head and rocked her against his chest until she calmed down.

"So, you gon' be her brother-daddy?"

"I'll just be her daddy, since she ain't got one and I ain't her brother for real anyway." He kissed her again. "I always wanted a dark-skinned little girl that looked just like me, and look at God." Ezra's tone was loud and humorous. "He sent the good writing ass new girl to my class."

More laughs came as Cannon stared at Ezra with stars in her eyes. It was funny how she'd gone from not liking him to feeling like she loved him within minutes. She was more than positive it was the way he'd taken a liking to Yara, but it was there nonetheless, and she liked it. Only time would tell if her feelings would continue.

8

I just want to say you're mine

The later it got, the more nervous Ezra got. Every time Cannon looked at the time on her cellphone, he held his breath. He was enjoying her too much to leave. He was sure he was going to have to be gone by the time her mama got home anyway, but he still wasn't ready.

"You said your mama work at an insurance company?" Ezra asked Cannon as he pulled her hair out of her ponytail.

"Yeah." She told him without moving.

They were in her room lying on the bed watching TV. Yara had been asleep for a while, so they'd put her in her little crib and cuddled up next to one another. Cannon's hair had been tied back into a ponytail, but Ezra had been wanting to pull it free all day. Especially once she lay on his chest. He had a thing for massaging women's scalps. It was relaxing to him in a weird way, and depending on the woman, could be used as a form of foreplay, and he was all for that.

"Well, where she at? I know ain't no insurance company open this late." Ezra stopped rubbing her head for a minute and looked down into her face. "I hate to tell you this, but your mama is selling ass."

Cannon pinched his knee in between giggles. "No, she is not, fool. She has two jobs. She goes to the insurance company during the day, and works at the hotel overnight. I think she did it to keep herself away from the house. When she's here she's sad, so she spends as much time away from us as she can."

"You be here by yourself every night?"

Cannon nodded.

"Oh, I'm about to be spending the night over here all the time."

Cannon turned her head and looked at him with a smile on her face. "Who told you that?"

"Me. I need to be here with my baby and baby mama. Y'all don't need to be here by y'all selves like this. Anything could happen."

"And what you gon' do to stop it?"

Ezra looked down at her face and smiled. The light brown freckles on her face matched the color of her eyes, while her pink lips and the light brown mole on her left cheek added to the beauty of it all. She had a round face with round eyes to match, and judging from the picture of Karina on her wall, that was something they got from her, because the baby's eyes were round just like Cannon's.

The blonde-colored hair spread across his chest was a good choice in hair color for Cannon too, because it meshed well with her skin color and features.

Ezra fixed her crooked glasses before answering her. "Don't let my handsome face fool you. I know I'm fine and stuff, but I'm cold in the streets and my hands so certified I should have snapped your neck for even trying me like that."

When Cannon's face curved from her smile, Ezra's heart raced. She was too pretty to be as self-conscious as she was.

"I'm for real while you're laughing. I should have folded your ass up by now. You been talking slick since I got here. I'm showing you way more mercy than I should."

"Mercy?" Cannon sat up so that she was facing him. With her

legs folded beneath her, he was able to really enjoy her thickness. It spread out wider, making him lick his lips. "You ain't got to show me no mercy. I'll beat your ass, Ezra."

Ezra tore his eyes from her wide hips and juicy thighs to look at her. Her tone was too much not to be addressed.

"Stand up and say that again."

Cannon moved backwards off her bed and stood up with her hands resting on her hips. Ezra twisted his mouth to the side to keep from drooling like a dog in heat. When he told her he loved thick women, he wasn't lying and she was that in such a gorgeous way.

The spandex shorts she was wearing cut across her thighs high-lighting the sporadic dents that rested in her legs easily. He took in the way her thighs touched slightly even with her legs spread apart. Cannon was crack and didn't even know it. Ezra could feel himself getting addicted and he'd only been indulging in her for a few hours. He was going to be a full-out fiend by the time he got done with her.

Though he'd been halted by some bad ass skinny girls, thick girls had his heart. All the women in his family were thick, from his grandma to his mama and sisters, and he loved them like no other which was probably why his wife would be juicy too. For now, he'd start with his soon-to-be girlfriend, Cannon. She was thick all the way to her ankles, and pretty as fucking hell.

"Don't stare, get up."

Ezra looked at her bright smiling face and hopped from the bed before she had a chance to defend herself. He snatched her up in his grasp quicker than she could stop him, and squeezed her whole body to his. Her chest was against his with both of her hands being held behind her back with one of his. Exerting more force, Ezra grabbed the back of her neck and held her backwards.

A lot taller than her, Ezra stared down in her face with his face only inches from hers. He didn't say anything as she stared at him, instead he ran his nose along the nape of her neck up to her ear, and over to her mouth. He could feel her breathing changing as he hovered in her face. Without releasing her, Ezra ran his mouth over hers softly. Not kissing her, just allowing their mouths to touch.

"You quiet, ain't you?"

Cannon didn't say anything, just swallowed and shuffled her feet a little.

"Don't get shy now, mama, talk your shit."

Cannon blinked a few times but didn't say anything.

"You ain't talking?"

"What you want me to say?"

His mouth was still so close to hers that whenever either of them said anything, their lips touched.

"Tell me you want to be my girlfriend."

Her radiance grew as she smiled.

"Nah, you got a lot of them already." She wiggled her arms and he let her hands go, but kept his hand on her neck so that she wouldn't move.

"No, I don't."

Cannon sucked her teeth. "The girls at our school love you. I be seeing them."

Cannon rolled her eyes, and Ezra smiled. He liked that she didn't like his groupies. That let him know that no matter what her mouth said, she liked him too.

"Well, I don't. I only be seeing you."

When she blushed, Ezra went ahead and stole the kiss he'd been playing around with, before going back to his spot on her bed. He lay back and looked at her as she stood there obviously not knowing what to do. He extended one hand out to her, she took it and lay back down with him. Naturally, his hand went to her round backside. With a handful of her soft curves, he pulled her closer to him. She came with no objections.

"You don't have no man back home?"

"Nah," her voice was low which took his mind back to the picture that was on her wall.

Despite every restraint he'd been placing on himself all night, Ezra showed his vulnerability. "Who is the boy on your picture with you? I assumed the old man is your daddy and the lady is your mama because you look like her twin sister, but who's the boy? I can tell it ain't your brother because of the way y'all posed."

He could feel the discomfort in her hesitation and movement, but he held firm in his question. As much as he hadn't wanted to ask it, it was out now and he wanted an answer. So, what if she knew he was feeling her, she needed to know. He wasn't a dude that could hide his feelings for long anyway, so she'd find out one way or the other.

"That's Matt."

Ezra remained quiet because if she thought that was going to be enough for him, she was sadly mistaken. When she didn't offer anymore, he gave her butt a light squeeze.

"And?"

"He's my old boyfriend."

"If he's old why is his picture in your new house? You still with him?"

She bit her lip and picked pieces of lint from his shirt. It felt good to feel her nails grazing his stomach lightly, but he still wanted an answer. Ezra sat up and looked at her. The look on her face let him know she didn't appreciate the change in their positioning, but she didn't say anything about it. Ezra almost dared her to when she was sitting there acting like she couldn't talk.

"Cannon?"

"What?" She yelled a little too loud for his liking.

"If he got you yelling and shit, you ain't got to tell me nothing. I don't even want to know no more." Ezra stood from the bed and grabbed his phone and keys from the dresser.

"You're about to leave?"

"Yeah, it's getting late, and clearly you don't feel like talking no more so I'ma go home."

Cannon turned so that her legs were hanging over the side of the bed. "You're really going to sit here and get mad like that?"

Now it was Ezra's turn to be quiet. He stuffed his phone in his pocket and walked over to Yara's bed. He kissed her head and turned toward Cannon.

"Come lock the door."

"Ezra, really?"

"Yeah, really. If I wanted to have a one-sided conversation I'd talk to your baby sister."

Ezra knew he might have been going a little hard on her, but he was serious. He was too old for stupid stuff. He got too irritated too fast to be playing with Cannon. She might have been used to that from other boys their age, but he wasn't like them. Never had been. He'd been mature his whole life because of Nuke. He spent so much time with his big brother, he was always more advanced than his friends.

"I told you he's my old boyfriend."

"I heard you when you said it the first time."

Cannon looked at him with an annoyed look before shrugging her shoulders and rolling her eyes at him. Ezra didn't like that little stunt at all. One thing he didn't tolerate was women that didn't value his presence. Not in an arrogant way, he just didn't like it. It felt too disrespectful.

"I'm out." He turned and left her room.

He could hear her following him down the hallway. He wanted to turn around and ask her again to give her a chance to answer him, but he didn't. He wouldn't beg her. She was cool and all, but she was new. It wasn't like he knew her too good to cut her off. They were fresh, he could ignore her and keep it moving if that's how she wanted to play it.

"Lock the door."

He heard her teeth suck behind him. "What you think I'm standing here for?"

Ezra was glad his back was to her, because that smart remark had caught him completely off guard. "Oh yeah, it's time for me to get up out of here before I knock your ass out for real." Ezra wasted no more time snatching the door open and walking out.

He didn't look back, pass go, or collect two hundred dollars on his way to his truck. He hopped in and fumbled around with his phone and the car charger until he watched her go inside. Once he was sure she was in the house safely, he drove away.

With his rising anger getting the best of him. Ezra drove to the nearest gas station and bought a Black & Mild. He needed to do something to calm him down, because he was way too riled up over a girl he barely even knew and her business with her old nigga.

Once he had his Black and was back in the truck, he drove home. When he pulled into the parking lot of his house, he sat in the truck smoking until he was cool. When he was straight he got out and let himself in the house. It was late into the night so he was sure his whole house was asleep, so he tried to be as quiet as possible when he went in.

His room was cool and dark as it always was. Without even bothering to take another shower, he kicked his slides off and removed his shirt. In nothing but his ball shorts and necklace, he put his hair into a ponytail at the back of his neck and slid into his bed. He tossed and turned for a minute trying to get comfortable. It took longer than he'd liked, but he eventually found it.

With his phone in hand, he scrolled through his social media. When he was tired of seeing the same people and posts, he looked up his new love interest, or at least tried. He didn't even remember Cannon's last name. He was just about to give up when he remembered it. He typed her in, and up popped her face. Ezra was hopping her page wasn't private, and God must have heard him, because it wasn't.

He scrolled down her timeline first to see what kind of stuff she posted about. All he saw was inspirational girly stuff, which worked for him because he hated ratchet bitches almost as much as he hated disrespectful ones.

Her pictures were just as breathtaking as she was in person. Ezra marveled at a few of them before continuing to scroll, hoping to run up on some pictures of her and her li'l old boyfriend she was trying to keep a secret. It wasn't until he checked the photos other people had tagged her in that he found what he was looking for.

"Let me look at this nigga," Ezra said to himself as he clicked the boy's name. Ezra's face was frowning when the boy's smiling face popped up in a picture of him and Cannon. "Matt Bridges? That's that white boy shit." He mumbled with jealousy as he stared at Cannon and how hard she was smiling. She looked just how girls be looking when they be in love.

Ezra sucked his teeth before trying to click Matt's picture to see the rest of them, but couldn't. He was destined to find their story, so he scrolled down to look at Matt's posts. Just like he knew he would, he found what he was looking for. Only it wasn't really what he was looking for. The very first post was from Cannon.

Cgcmmsiomigo]b&C!g^schachmc^_(Qbs!^siof_[p_g_ fce_nb[n9Jf_[m_]ig_\[]e&C][h!nfcp_qcnbionsio(@il_p_l siol\[\s(

"Ahh shit." Ezra's head fell forward as he realized how big of a fool he was. "This nigga is fucking dead." He said to himself again ashamed of his actions. "Why wouldn't she just say that?"

He asked himself a million questions, trying to understand why he'd cut a fool with Cannon before leaving her house. To say he felt like the biggest idiot in the world right then would have been an understatement. When Ezra finally began scrolling down Matt's page he noticed a host of rest in peace posts from Cannon and other people. The shit was sad to say the least, and he felt horrible about it.

Without even thinking about it, Ezra closed the app and dialed

Cannon's number. She didn't answer the first two times, so he called again while getting out of bed and sliding his shoes back on. He didn't even bother to put a shirt on before grabbing his keys. It was hot outside, he didn't need one anyway.

He was as quiet as he could be going back out of the house. He wasn't worried about getting caught or anything, he just didn't want to wake anyone. His mother was a cool OG, she didn't sweat him about curfews or girls, she just chilled. She knew him, and gave him space to be who he was. At seventeen, he was more responsible than men twice his age, and she treated him as such.

The whole ride to Cannon's house, Ezra tried to think of what he was going to say when he got there, and couldn't think of one thing. He could barely park before hopping out the truck. He was on her front porch in no time. He called her phone a few more times before knocking softly.

When she didn't come to the door he began knocking harder. He already knew her mama wasn't there, so there was no point in trying to be polite. She was going to talk to him before he went to sleep that night. Ezra knocked harder, and it payed off. Cannon snatched the door open with evil eyes squinted at him.

"What!"

Ezra disregarded her whole attitude and pushed his way inside of the house. He kicked the door closed behind him and grabbed her. He tucked her securely in his arms before kissing the top of her head. She was doing her best to put up a fight, but he was easily stronger than her.

"Get off me. I didn't tell you to come over here."

"You wouldn't answer the phone for me."

"I didn't want to talk to you."

"That's why I came. Anytime you're mad, I'm coming. I'm telling you that now so get used to it. I won't let you ignore me."

"You obviously didn't want to be here before, so why come back?" Cannon pushed out of his grasp and he let her.

He looked at her face. It was red and her eyes were a little swollen and damp. "What you crying for?"

"Why you ain't got no shirt on?" She sassed, ignoring his question.

"I hopped out of bed when you didn't answer and came straight back." He told her earnestly.

Ezra stood, bare chested in her living room waiting on her to forgive him. She had to know why he was there, even though he hadn't told her yet. Observing her tear-stained face made him feel even worse than realizing he was jealous of a dead boy. The only thing that eased the tension he felt in his chest was the small smile on her face.

"You're crazy."

"Yeah, I am for real." He walked to her slowly with his hands outstretched. "Don't hold it against me though."

Cannon stared at him with her arms folded over her chest before padding toward him. As soon as she got close, he pulled her to him and hugged her to his chest.

"I'm sorry for acting out. I was jealous."

Cannon's arms snaked around his waist. "I know, it's okay." He could tell she was crying again by the way her voice sounded.

"What you crying for?" She sniffed hard and shook her head, but he squeezed her tighter. "Tell me what's good, mama. Why you upset like this?"

Cannon cried for a few minutes longer before sniffing a few times and stepping away from him again. "I didn't like the way you left." She stepped away from him and wiped her face with the back of her hand. "You can't ever leave me like that, okay? If you're mad just stay with me until you're not anymore." She looked at him with misty eyes. "Please?"

"I got you." Ezra said with no hesitation.

"Matt and I had an argument one night and he left mad just like you did, but he never came back." Cannon's sobs took over her body as she covered her face with both of her hands.

Ezra went back to her immediately holding her. Her crying broke his heart. He'd never lost anyone like that, but his oldest sister had, so he'd seen first-hand how that could take a large toll on a person's mental state. His older sister's baby daddy had been shot up in a drive by and it had taken her almost two years to get over it, and she still mourned him depending on the day.

"He got hit by a drunk driver and died." She whispered. "I feel so bad because if we hadn't been arguing he would have never left, and he would have never been killed." Cannon wailed uncontrollably after that.

Ezra did his best to console her, which he was pretty good at. He'd spent more nights than he could count consoling his sister. That had been horrible for her, and him. To see her in that much pain crushed him every time he had to help her get herself together.

"You can't think like that, Cannon. It's not your fault, it was his time to go. God was ready for him, beautiful. Be happy about that. Don't keep stressing yourself out like this." Ezra slid to the floor with her and held her between his legs, as she lay with her head on his chest, crying.

The two of them remained in that spot for a while. When she was finally able to get herself together, he pulled her up and turned her around so that she was straddling his lap. She looked tired as she stared down at him. Ezra used the pad of his thumb and dried her face.

"You feel better?"

She shrugged.

"Tell me how to make it better." Ezra knew he probably sounded like a sap, but he felt too attached to Cannon to let her hurt like that without helping her.

"I don't know." Her voice was low.

Ezra pulled her to him and held her. Her head was on his shoulder as she scooted closer to him. Of course, even though the moment wasn't an easy one, when the heat from between her legs rubbed across his dick, it reacted.

"Sorry, about that," he told her as he tried to think of something else in hopes of his man parts relaxing.

"It's fine," she said as she sat up and wrapped her arms around his neck.

Ezra raised his eyebrows at her. "For real?"

She nodded with a light smile.

"Why is it okay for my dick to be getting hard while you're crying? That makes me look like a pervert. You're trying to pour out your feelings and I'm thinking about sex."

Cannon was all smiles and giggles as she looked at him through her glasses. "Sexual healing, I guess."

Ezra was blown away at her choice of conversation in that moment. "Is that so?"

Versus saying anything, Cannon grabbed his face and kissed him, and not the little pecks they'd been exchanging all day, she really kissed him. Tongue all over his mouth, lips sucking his, she was even rolling her hips in his lap. Ezra didn't know how much she thought he was going to take before giving her the D, but she was on the verge of making him lose control.

"You want to have sex with me, Cannon?" Ezra whispered breathlessly against her mouth.

Cannon disregarded his question and began sucking on his neck.

"Please say yes."

"Yes," she told him when she released the side of his neck to suck on his Adam's apple.

"Say no more, pretty girl." Ezra held her by her butt and stood to the floor.

"Ezra, don't you drop me."

Ezra gazed at her with compassion and kissed her mouth. "I got you, mama. Stop stressing."

He already knew her protest came from her feelings about her weight, but one day soon she'd realize it wasn't a lie when he told her how he felt about her body. Just thinking about it right then had him even readier for what was about to happen. When he reached her room, he kicked the door closed and locked it while holding her up with his other hand.

Their mouths were interlocked as he walked to her bed and lay her down. Cannon stared up at him, when he grabbed the hem of her shorts. He used one finger to dip inside of the band and began rolling them down. Cannon's body shifted allowing him the access to pull them all the way down. When Ezra noticed she wasn't wearing panties, he got harder.

Cannon's eyes went to the center of his shorts where his little man was making his presence known. It was straining the fabric of his shorts and taking up majority of the space between them.

"You're too young for your dick to be that big, Ezra."

Her bluntness made him smile.

"You're too young to be juicy as you are, but I ain't call you out." He picked up one of her legs and kissed the inside of her thigh. "I just love on you."

"You want me to love on you too?"

Ezra's hooded eyes looked down at her, still holding her leg. With her calf up by his face, Ezra rested it on his shoulder and leaned his head against it. With a swift movement, his shorts were on the floor and he was naked. He enjoyed watching Cannon marvel at his body so much that he remained standing a few seconds longer.

Cannon shook her head. "That don't make no sense."

Ezra looked down between them at his dick, before looking back at her. "It's yours if you want it."

Cannon's eyes rolled to the back of her head dramatically while she simultaneously released a deep sigh. She was turned on and he knew it. Women were the one thing Ezra knew. He'd been fucking since middle school, and getting schooled on game just as long. Nuke hadn't allowed him to lack in any area. Sex being one of the main ones. He'd been getting women to sex Ezra for years, and, thanks to them, he was a beast at a young age. He could finesse the panties off some of the baddest, especially the ones his age. Young girls were easy.

"Aye, New Girl, look at me." Ezra told her at the same time he looked down between them again.

Her body was so warm, he could feel the heat without even being up in it yet. He licked his lips as he opened her legs further and admired the juicy love that was waiting for him. It was glistening already and he hadn't even touched it yet. He couldn't wait to get up in it, he could already tell he was about to kill her. There wasn't no way he was going to be able to control himself once he felt her.

"I said look at me, Cannon."

Her eyes submitted to the bass in his voice instantly. She looked the most vulnerable he'd seen since meeting her, which was a good thing. With him, that was safe. She could be as weak to him as she wanted to be because he wouldn't take advantage. If anything, he'd make her better.

"Take your shirt off."

Cannon shook her head without even thinking about it. Ezra frowned his eyebrows at her.

"I wasn't asking you. Take it off." He turned and bit the side of her ankle before placing a kiss there.

Cannon's chest was rising and he wanted so badly to see her breasts. She needed to hurry and get that shirt off. He wanted it all.

"Please don't make me take it off, Ezra."

"Why not?"

Cannon looked away from him avoiding eye contact.

"I don't care about your stomach, Cannon. I already know you like to eat bread." He smirked as did she.

"Ezraaaa," she whined.

"Unless you got stretchmarks from having our sister-daughter, you ain't got nothing to hide from me."

Cannon covered her face. "But I do have stretchmarks."

Ezra smirked at how dramatic she was being. She was really cutting up. To get them both back into the mood, he slipped a finger inside of her, then another, and moved them slowly in and out of her body. Her thighs jerked a little almost as if they were going to close, but stopped.

"Are they from my baby?"

Her head shook but she didn't move her hands.

"They're from me being fat."

Ezra released a low chuckle and pulled her hands from her face. "Don't say that no more. I like stretchmarks, now take your shirt off."

He slid his fingers out and rubbed them over her opening before using the pad of his thumb to tease the sensitive spot he wanted so desperately to put his mouth on. Nuke had told him a million times eating pussy made girls wetter. Though Cannon didn't need any help in that area, he still wanted to do it to her.

"Cannon, this my last time telling you."

With a pout on her face, and with closed eyes, Cannon pulled her shirt over her head slowly. Ezra's eyes went to her stomach. The small stretchmarks on the sides of her waist was barely there, and her stomach was relatively flat. Sure, she was a little pudgy, but he didn't mind. More of her to love.

"You cutting up, now." He leaned over and tongue kissed her to ease her stress. "Open your eyes and look at me."

She shook her head and he smiled.

"You know how pretty your titties are?"

"Ezraaaa," she whined again and he laughed.

"Look, Cannon, having sex with me is intimate, baby. You're going to have to kill this shy stuff and let me connect with you."

It took a minute, but her hands slowly fell and her eyes opened. Ezra winked at her and licked his lips before removing his fingers.

"You got some condoms?" She asked.

"Nah."

"You need one. I'm not on birth control, and I don't know you."

Ezra nodded. "You will. You clean?"

Cannon nodded her head.

"Good, we'll use one next time." With both of her legs in the crooks in his arms, he yanked her to the edge of the bed.

He inhaled as he grabbed his dick and put it at her entrance.

"Ezra, we need to use protection."

He locked eyes with her and shook his head from side to side. "I said, no. Next time." He was forceful to make sure she knew he was about to get him some of her right then, and he wasn't about to let a condom stop him.

Yeah, it was dumb, but he didn't care right then. He wanted her too bad. It had been almost two months since he'd had sex and he was tired of jacking his dick. Cannon had enough wet pussy to appease him; he'd be a fool not to get it.

"Don't scream and wake my baby up."

Ezra didn't give her time to say anything else, before pushing inside. He'd be damned if she ain't do exactly what he'd just told her not to do.

"Hard-headed ass girl," Ezra managed to get out in between grunts.

His head fell forward as soon as he was submerged. Now he was the one with his eyes closed. He'd known her pussy was about to be a drug, but it was just as juicy as her body. The way it gripped him and held on, made him feel like he was being sucked in. He was holding on for dear life as she clenched her muscles around him.

"Ah man, Cannon." He moaned while grabbing her leg and raising it back up to his shoulder.

He needed something to hold on to. With his face lying against her leg and his hands on both sides of her hips, Ezra dove deep into the moment. The gushy noises and fountains of sticky waters immersing him right then had his heart beating fast. When he was finally able to open his eyes, he wanted to cry.

Cannon was so pretty. Her face was frowned in pleasure and pain, while her hair sprawled all over the bed. Her glasses were gone, allowing him the opportunity to see her entire face, and he was loving it. Her pink lips were parted and her tongue was resting along the bottom one.

"Look at me, baby."

Her eyes opened immediately. He could tell she was trying her best to mask the pain, so he eased out some. The leg that wasn't on his shoulder locked around his back, pulling him in deeper while she shook her head from side to side.

"Stay right there."

Ezra's mouth fell open before he grabbed his bottom lip with his teeth. With all the strength he had left, Ezra made love to Cannon the best he could. He wasn't able to show off all his tricks, but he was working her body out something serious. The constant moans she released let him know that. He, on the other hand, was barely able to say anything.

He was normally a talker during sex, but Cannon had him stunned silent with the dope she was drugging him with. When he was about to climax, he leaned over and kissed her deeply. She held him tightly rubbing up and down his back. Ezra could live and die in their closeness at that moment, but he needed to stay alive for a while. At least long enough for him to feel it again.

"I'm about to be out, mama. I can't hold it any longer."

"Okay," she moaned to him still rubbing his back.

Ezra loved how she coaxed his orgasm with her touch. With a low growl, Ezra snatched out rapidly. He grabbed the tip of his dick in his hand, while hoovering over Cannon's body. She was breathing roughly and staring at him passionately.

"You love me, don't you?"

Like he knew she would, she smiled.

"We'll get married one day, let's graduate first." Ezra was talking and trying to catch his breath at the same time. "That was crack, mama." He slapped her thigh and stood up to head to the bathroom.

He looked down the hallway to make sure her mama hadn't come back before darting to the bathroom quickly. He was about to wash off really quick, but when Cannon came in turning on the shower, he decided to hop in with her.

She looked nervous as she tried to keep her back to him. Ezra wasn't having that though. As close as they'd just been, there was no reason to be shy. He grabbed her and held her back to his chest as the water fell over them.

"What did you mean by that being crack?"

Ezra bit her shoulder lightly.

"I keep forgetting you're not from here and don't know our lingo."

Cannon turned to face him. Ezra took in all of her features, along with digesting the feeling she'd just given him with her body before giving her an answer.

"It means I'm addicted to you."

Though Ezra said it casually, his feelings were anything but. Only time would tell whether or not Cannon was worth what he had to give.

9

I'll never leave

Muscogee County Jail

"I just don't see how in the hell you ended up back in here after doing damn near ten years," the old man that Don shared rooms with said.

As always, he was in Don's business, minding shit that didn't concern him. Don was on the floor doing push-ups while his cellmate dangled loosely over the side of his bed looking down at him.

"I've only been in here for three months and I'm ready to get out and never come back."

There was some truth to what he was saying, but Don wouldn't dare tell him that. He probably would never shut up then. Don continued pushing his body from the floor, not paying the man any attention. It was bad enough that since he was older than Don by at least twenty years he felt compelled to offer advice. Don hated that with a passion. He was old as hell just like the man, and didn't need any advice. Being that he was in the same cell as Don, he clearly didn't make good choices either.

"I did some shit that sent me back."

"I know that, but what could possibly be worth this hellhole?"

Don pushed down and up once more before standing to his feet and making eye contact with the man. He retreated just a tad and scooted back on his bunk before continuing his line of questioning.

"I mean you don't have to tell me if you don't want to, just trying to get to know you a little."

Don offered an intimidating stare for a few seconds before looking away. "I ain't nobody you need to know, so let it go."

The old timer nodded his head and looked toward the door. "You headed out for visitation?"

Don shook his head. This nigga just didn't quit. "Yeah."

"Is it that pretty young thing I saw you with last week?"

Don tilted his head to both sides, stretching it as he tried to keep his temper in check. He didn't like the "pretty" remark that had been made about Danna. All that let him know was that he'd been watching her, and that was the quickest way to get on Don's bad side.

Although getting serious with Danna hadn't been on his agenda, he'd allowed himself to become too open to her, and now he couldn't take it back if he tried. He was in love with her young ass and hated the position he was in with her. But it was what it was.

"How old is that woman? She looks like she's about my great-granddaughter's age."

Don faced the man again with a grimace on his face. "You're treading a thin line right now."

The man's hands came up in mock surrender. "My apologies."

Don looked him up and down once more before grabbing his things and heading for the showers. Danna was indeed on her way, and he liked to look and smell fresh when she came. She was always so fresh and pretty whenever she came, he tried his best to be the same. It was bad enough he was in jail, he didn't want to give too many other niggas an advantage over him.

They could be out dressed in real clothes, while he was on the inside in the same thing he wore day in and day out. It may have sounded crazy, but Don figured if he at least looked nice, then he could keep her interested. Women loved a clean man. Danna especially. She made remarks about his clothing every time she came.

"Big D!" Someone yelled from the back when Don entered the showers.

Don nodded his head, but kept it moving. He didn't associate socially with people, but he'd done enough fighting and lowdown shit to earn his respect. The prison wasn't the biggest, so his name had gotten around fast. On top of that, his reputation had followed him from his previous prison. That had been hell on earth, but Don had managed to get through it.

After being set up by the only family he had, and slapped with eight years in prison on drug and weapon charges, Don had love for no one. It had taken everything in him to believe the undercover cops when they told him that Echo was behind it all. That was just so unfathomable, he'd literally sat in an interrogation room for damn near two days refusing to move until Echo showed up.

The nigga never did. Well, not that day anyway. The moment Don was in court being convicted of the crimes, guess who was front and center? Echo's snitching ass. Not only had he been there to tell on Don, but a bunch of other niggas Don knew from the hood as well. Turned out, Echo was an informant telling everything he knew, every chance he got. Real pussy boy shit that Don was going to get him back for.

He'd had eight long years to plot out his revenge, and once it was all said and done, Echo was going to realize he'd crossed the wrong nigga. He'd ruined Don's whole life, and Don was going to make sure he received the same justice. Which was why Don had become so cozy with Danna. Echo's family was his life. He'd spoken about them to Don many times when they'd run together, so of course, they were first on his list. It had taken a little digging to locate them, but he'd done it.

If he played his cards right with Danna, he'd know Echo's whereabouts soon enough. They all thought he was just a deadbeat that came around here and there, but Don knew the truth. That nigga was always so busy hiding out that he never had time to check on them himself. A small blessing to Don, because Echo's carelessness was exactly how he'd weaseled his way in.

"You headed up top?" The guard asked once Don finished his shower.

Don nodded. "You taking me."

The man nodded before grabbing the back of Don's arm and leading him back to his cell. Don complied with the guards easily. That was the best way to keep things running smoothly. He'd gotten knocked on a parole violation after being pulled over and having his gun on him landed right back in the pen.

At first, he'd been crushed thinking his plan was going to fold, but it hadn't. Danna was raw as shit. Made out of much better material than her weak ass daddy. She'd been there every step of the way, making things hard and easy for him.

Easy because his plan was still in play, but hard because he wanted her. She was so beautiful and vibrant it was hard not to love her. Her sincerity and genuine love for him turned him into somebody he wasn't. He'd been the one on the receiving end of love a few times, but nothing like what he had with Danna. She'd come in and changed that. Danna's love was irreplaceable. Maybe it was because she was so young and pure, or maybe it was just because he was an easy target.

Don had been loved incorrectly two times in his life, so when Danna gave it the right way, it was hard to fight off. He'd been thinking long and hard about taking her out of his plan and just keeping her for himself, but that would be too messy, so he was going to have to ponder that a little more. She'd laughed and joked all the time about running away with him, but if she knew how serious he really was, she probably wouldn't.

"Ready?" The guard asked Don just as he finished tucking his shirt into his pants.

Don looked himself over in the small mirror above his toilet to make sure he was good, and walked out. The guard's hand was on his elbow leading him toward the visitation room for the second time that week. The first one had come from his baby mama. She was cool, but couldn't hold a candle to Danna.

When it came to his baby mama, all he cared about was his kids. He'd been deep in love with Totiana at first too, but once he caught wind of her reputation it was hard to get over. He'd tried to make it work with her many times, but she always ended up doing something that pissed him off. If it wasn't for her loyalty to him when he'd first gotten out of the joint, he would have cut her all the way off by now, but he couldn't.

After dealing with so many disloyal people, finding one and doing her wrong wasn't in his blood. Totiana may have had her own motives when meeting him, but they'd clicked and gotten past it. She showed him love when he had no one else, so he'd always look out for her. If he could help it. There was only one person that could make him flip on Totiana, and he was headed to her. Hopefully, it would never come to that, but with the games Totiana played, there was no telling.

The loud buzz for the door to open sounded, bringing Don out of his thoughts. He waited patiently for the door to slide open so he could be seated at his table. He and the guard both maneuvered through the chairs until Don was at his regular one. Laid back and comfortable, Don looked toward the door where he was sure Danna would be coming through soon.

"What you over there smiling so hard for? You happy to see me?" Don licked his lips as he sat across the table from Danna.

Danna smiled even harder, not even realizing she'd been smiling before. It was mid-afternoon on one of her favorite days of the week. As soon as she'd gotten off work, she'd changed and driven straight to the barbwire-encased building with the tall brick walls that put too much distance between her and the love of her life.

With her chin resting in the palm of her hand Danna winked at Don. "I don't understand why you ask questions you already be knowing the answer to."

"Because I like to hear you say it."

The white-and-navy blue prison uniform that Don was wearing was freshly white and crisp as it lay across his big broad chest. It looked nothing like the rest of the uniforms around her. Though, it never did. Anytime she came to visit him, his uniform looked like he'd gotten it out of the cleaners before he got there. Clothes was so white, the nigga could have starred in a damn Clorox commercial. Nah, something wasn't right about that, and Danna wouldn't be Danna if she didn't find it out.

"What bitch came up here before me?" Danna squinted her eyes at him.

"Don't you start that shit, Danna, with your crazy ass."

Danna shook her head from side to side and pointed her finger at him. "That uniform look mighty crisp for me to be the only one seeing it. Unless you trying to show off for these niggas."

Don's face frowned like she knew it would. "You stay on that stupid shit."

Danna sucked her teeth and rolled her eyes. "Nah, I just stay watching your ass."

"Nah, you're just crazy as fuck."

"Call it what you want, but if you cheat on me nigga, I'ma kill you. Believe that."

Don's face remained balled up for a few seconds longer before he was back smiling at her. "You love to say that shit."

"Because it's true."

Don leaned forward on the table and grabbed the hand that she'd been holding near her face. "Ain't nobody fucking off on your ass."

Danna's smile matched his. "Better not be."

Don ran one of his hands over his black-and-gray beard before blowing her an air kiss. "You all in my business, I need to be wondering where the fuck you been in them tight ass jeans." Don looked around the room. "You already up in here and ain't got no bra on. Got your li'l titties all out and shit."

Danna looked down at herself and burst into a fit of laughter. "Well, blame that on that li'l yellow hoe that work in the check-in office. She wouldn't let me wear the bra that I had on because it had wire in it." Danna cheesed big at the hard grimace on his face. "So, it was either come in here with my titties out or don't come at all."

"Word? I'ma make sure I holla at her about that shit."

Danna's nose turned up as her stomach got tight. "Holla at her? Nigga, you ain't got to holla at her about nothing. Let her do her damn job. The fuck she need you in her face for?" Danna got hype immediately. When it came to Don, she had zero understanding. "That's probably the bitch that's been washing and ironing all your fucking uniforms." Danna snatched away from him and sat back in her seat with her arms folded across her chest. "I'ma hit her when I leave out of here."

Don's large shoulders shook lightly as he watched her make herself mad. The comical smirk covering his face only angered her more. Especially when he didn't say anything in objection.

"Oh, so you ain't gon' deny it? I knew it. Just wait until I leave up out of here." Danna nodded her head as she turned and began looking around the room for the guard. Don knew better than to play with her. "Guard!" She yelled alerting the guard near the door.

When the guard looked from her to Don and Don shook his head once, the man stayed in his spot near the door. Danna's temper really flared then.

"I see all y'all muthafuckas think I'm playing with y'all today."

Danna moved around in her seat. "He don't wanna do his job? He'd rather listen to your ass, I got something for him too."

Don's laughter finally made its appearance. "Shut your ass up."

"Fuck no. I'm about to go beat your li'l work hoe the fuck up as soon as one of these unprofessional workers let me out of here."

"Danna, calm your ass down and sit still. That girl doesn't wash and iron shit for me."

"Shut up. Yes, she does, but I bet she won't no more when I get done with her ass today." Danna sat in her seat bouncing her leg in agitation.

Her chest was heaving as she fumed in anger. Her already slanted eyes were smaller thanks to the frown in her forehead as she avoided eye contact with Don.

"Look at me."

"Fuck no."

"Who you talking to?"

Danna looked at him in defiance. "You."

They stared at one another for a long time before they both burst out into a fit of laughter. Danna enjoyed watching him laugh and play with her.

"Leave it to your ass to have me up in here being goofy and shit. You gon' have these niggas thinking I'm friendly."

Danna was still laughing when she looked around at the other prisoners and their visitors. There were a few eyes on them, but she didn't really care, and even with Don mentioning it, she was sure he didn't either.

"I don't never laugh, or even crack a smile until you come." He told her as he chilled out from his laughter.

"That's how it's supposed to be right?"

Don was quiet as he leaned his head to the side as if he was trying to figure her out. "I guess, li'l mama. Give me your hands." He sat both of his open palms on the table, so she rested hers in them. "Now, that you're done showing your crazy ass, talk to me."

Danna's rowdy demeanor diminished as she basked in the presence of her man. She'd been with Don on the low for the past three years, and they had been the best three years of her life. Even with him having been in prison for the last two months.

"I miss you. I went to the old Dairy Queen we used to meet at the other day, and I almost started crying." Danna's throat got tight as she thought about she and Don's favorite meet up spot. "I miss you so much, I'm ready for you to get out."

"I'll be home soon." Don released her hands and began massaging her arms instead. Something he did every time she came to visit.

"Why you always do that?" Danna asked looking at his hands on her arms.

"I like touching you. If I could massage your pussy I'd be doing that instead, but since I can't this week, I got to settle for making my dick hard just by rubbing your arms."

Danna was perplexed. "Rubbing my arms make you want to have sex?"

Don nodded casually.

Danna laughed in disbelief. "How?"

"Because you soft. Any part of your body makes me think about fucking you. Even when I just look at your face, I be wanting to put this dick on you."

With warm cheeks, Danna shook her head. "Why we can't do it this week?"

Don nodded his head toward the fat Hispanic lady near the door. "New guard. She been on my ass too. I don't know what the fuck her problem is, but she been riding my dick hard as hell. I don't even know her ass. Ain't never said two words to her, but she stays in my business."

"First of all, choose different wording. Saying stuff like she's been riding your dick makes me want to fight y'all."

Don looked from the guard back to Danna with a smirk on his face. "Girl, why you got to be so gotdamn crazy all the time?"

Danna stared at him with a straight face. He could make light of the situation if he wanted, but she wasn't playing. Danna's face didn't budge as she looked from him to the lady then around the visitation room. It was freezing cold and smelled like must and sanitizer. The tables were placed strategically around the room, while vending machines and a small picture area were stashed in the corner.

"Aye," Don shook one of her arms lightly. "Come back to me."

Danna gave him her attention, but held the scowl on her face. "I'm here."

"Well stop running off in your mind. I be waiting all week for you to come. Don't fuck it up getting mad for nothing."

"It's not nothing. I already don't have you. I don't like thinking about you and other women. It makes me mad."

"As it should, I'm your man. I be feeling like the Hulk when I think about you and other niggas. When you first walked in today, your nipples was hard and you could see them good as fuck through your shirt. I knew niggas was looking because you too fucking sexy to ignore, I swear on me I felt like my veins were about to explode with some green shit."

Danna's giggles were filled with embarrassment and excitement together. To know she still had that kind of effect on Don was an ego booster.

"You laughing now, but you wouldn't have been laughing had I started flipping tables and shit over."

"Don't do that. It ain't that serious."

Don looked at her with a crazed look. "Ain't that serious to who? I'll die bout you, Dan. Don't forget that shit. Everything that involves you, is serious to me."

Danna's heart moved rapidly in a burst of love. Words like that were the reason she'd held on for so long. Don was old enough to be her father, but he always made her feel so young and giddy, never treating her like a child.

"Well, I feel the same way about that girl washing and ironing your clothes for you."

Don tried to hold his smile in, but couldn't. "Will you let that shit go already? That girl doesn't do nothing for me, but what I ask her to do."

Heat began to rise in Danna's body. "And just what the fuck do you ask her to do?"

Don smiled mischievously. "Make you take your bra off, I knew I wasn't getting no pussy, but I had to get my dick tended to some kind of way." Don's eyes went from her face down to her breasts. "Slide your chair closer to me and grab my dick under the table."

"What?"

"You heard me. Do it."

"Ain't that lady gon' say something?"

Don looked at her with raised brows. "You scared of her?"

Danna shook her head.

"Well come hold my dick for me then." His lusty words sent chills down Danna's spine.

She was sliding her chair closer to him in no time. When she was close enough, she looked from the lady guard to the man one that hadn't come when she'd called him.

"Don't watch them, watch me. I got them."

Just like she always did, Danna ran her hands over her mouth quickly and did what he told her to do. His big heavy dick in her hands had her barely able to sit still. The pulsating veins thumping against the soft skin of her hands made her panties drip for him. Although it was him feeling all the pleasure, she probably felt better than he did.

After using her spit as lubricant, Danna massaged Don's penis the way he'd taught her on so many occasions. He had been grunting and keeping his composure as long as he could until his head fell backwards.

"Hold your head up and open your eyes before you get us caught," Danna urged.

Don sat up and looked toward the man and nodded his head. Danna watched the man nod toward the bathroom before walking toward the Hispanic lady.

"Aye, go to our spot, buddy finna' look out for me really quick."

Danna was out of her seat with no hesitation. She wiped her damp hands on the side of her pants and walked toward the bathroom. When she got to the door, she bypassed it and went to the small janitor's closet behind the vending machines. The door was unlocked like it always was, so she went in.

Much like she'd done every other week when she came to visit him, she removed her pants. Seconds later, the door opened and her eyes caught site of the white-and-navy uniform, but it wasn't Don. Her face frowned momentarily as she tried to cover her panties.

"Where's Don?"

The familiar eyes trekked up and down her body before quickly looking away. "He got held up really quick, so I came to let you know he was coming." The man sat the mop and yellow sign down next to her leg. "And, to put this shit back."

Danna nodded in embarrassment and looked away. "How long you been in here?"

"Two weeks, just got moved to this tier." He looked at her face and kept his eyes there. "So, you with Don?"

Danna nodded.

"Damn," He cursed. "Now I see why I never got my chance."

Danna finally mustered up the courage to look Quay in the eyes. "I wanted to give you one."

"Funny how life has a way of changing shit huh?"

Danna nodded solemnly.

"If life ever goes back in our direction, I want a do over, aight?"

Danna gave Quay a small smile and nodded. He left immediately afterwards leaving Danna to her thoughts. As much as she came to visit Don, she'd never seen him there before, but then again, he had just mentioned being on a different tier.

"Why you still got your panties on?" Don asked, disturbing her thoughts.

Danna's head shot up, and her hands went straight to Don. She needed a release and her man was the perfect one to give it to her. The strong grip he had on her body was divine as he picked her up and pushed her panties to the side. Danna slid right down onto him. Don's eyes closed as he released a deep breath.

"Wait, don't move. Just let me hold it in. I'm about to bust already from the hand job you gave me at the table."

"Don't nut in me, Don. I'm not playing with you."

A throaty chuckle released against her throat. "I won't."

Don moved and pressed her back against the wall and began thrusting inside of her. Danna had to close her eyes and ball her mouth up so that she wouldn't moan. Don had the best dick she'd ever had; even if it was the only one she'd ever had, it was still the best.

"I love you, Danna."

"Love you too, baby." Danna moaned in his ear as she rubbed the back of his head soothingly.

The sex between the two of them was always so magnetic. Don had broken her young body in. She knew so much stuff when it came to sex, she could easily put girls her age to shame. He'd been so patient and loving the whole time, but neither of those emotions had anything on how nasty he was. Danna had done so much stuff with Don that she would probably never do with another man, but she loved it.

"Thank you for this," Don told her just as he hurried to snatch out of her body.

Danna was still dangling in one of his arms as he snatched his white pants up with the other hand. Once he was dressed, he let her down and kissed her mouth hard.

"I got to slide out of here before they come back. Get dressed and then come out."

Danna told him she would and he left. A professional at sneaking, Danna hurried to get dressed, and was back out into the visitation room at their table in no time. The smile on Don's face would keep her coming back every time. She didn't care how long she had to keep him a secret, or how many guards she had to fuck up in the process, she would. As long as that meant he was hers.

"You wild," He smiled at her.

"I'm yours."

"Damn straight," Don told her with finality.

10

I never want to say how it used to be

The cinderblock walls of the University's gym were covered in an array of athletic accolades at the top and packed from wall to wall with people at the bottom. It was hot, loud, and way too crowded not to be over capacity. Surely, the fire marshal should have raided the building and thrown out at least a third of the crowd by the time the first quarter started. Men and women dressed to impress littered the walls and bleachers as two of the state's leading teams battled for the championship on the shiny wooden floor.

The damp air made Cannon feel sticky as she sat in the top corner of the bleachers trying to avoid too much commotion over Yara. She was nestled snugly in Cannon's arms looking around like it wasn't well past her bedtime. The smell of sweat and heat drifted casually around all the rowdy patrons as they cheered and fired off slurs in encouragement of their teams. When she'd heard everyone talking about how packed the game was expected to be, she had no idea it would be to that magnitude.

There was barely anywhere to sit, let alone any way to formulate one coherent thought amongst all the noise going on. Just from where she was sitting, she could tell this game was a fashion show mixed with a gambling opportunity. There were people everywhere doing a little bit of everything, including men arguing and yelling about money. The cheerleaders were scantily dressed, while the basketball players were either dripping with sweat from playing so hard, or seated on the bench in a freshly unused uniform.

"Girl, he's so fine. I wonder does he have a girlfriend at this school."

"I bet he does. Ain't no nigga that fine walking around here unclaimed."

The conversation going on next to Cannon had her full attention because she was more than sure the girls were talking about Ezra. What reason would they have not to be? He was indeed the finest person in the room. Anybody that said anything different, could take themselves and that lie right back to the pits of hell where it had come from.

"You ain't lying because if it was me, I'd be following that nigga around everywhere he went to make sure hoes know he's spoken for." She cackled loudly while high fiving her friend. "Look at them eyes! Jesus, he fine!"

Cannon listened while confirming her suspicions. Ezra's eyes were noticeable. Though they were nothing different from ordinary eyes that you'd see in passing any other day, they glowed. It was weird, but Cannon had noticed it too.

"Excuse me, do you go to this school?" The desperate girl with the long weave tapped Cannon's arm and asked.

Cannon gave the girl the once over, taking in the too big nose ring and overly curled bundles. "Yeah."

"Does that boy with the dreads have a girlfriend? Number fourteen."

"I don't think so."

The girl clapped and smiled as if she'd won the lottery. "Oh Yay! I'ma give him my number after the game."

Cannon gave a simple smile and went back to watching the

game. Her initial reaction was to be a hater, but she decided against it and just told the truth. He wasn't hers. Ever since the night at her house a while back, they had been keeping in close contact, but hadn't stamped labels on anything.

It was more her fault than anything, because he was there chilling with her and Yara every night, and sometimes during the day when he wasn't in class, working, or at basketball practice, but Cannon still kept her distance. Especially at school because Ezra had too many groupies, and groupies brought problems she didn't want.

"EZRAAAA MENDOZA WITH THE SLAMDUNK!" The announcer yelled over the raggedy intercom.

The crowd went wild as Ezra's long body hung from the rim. He'd just dunked the ball and was basking in his glory with a large smile on his face. Cannon's cheers erupted before she could stop them. She was yelling and screaming, darn near about to give poor Yara a heart attack as she hollered for him.

"Sorry, Yara boo." Cannon kissed her forehead as she took her seat again.

The crowd was still shouting and singing Ezra's praises as he let the rim go and began dancing in the middle of the floor. Cannon smiled at his silliness. He looked so handsome and smooth as he rubbed his hand over his hair dramatically before smiling largely in his opponent's face.

"This boy," Cannon said to herself with a smile.

When the referee blew the whistle and the game resumed, Ezra went off some more. He was really good, and Cannon was shocked. Now she saw why the girls loved him. He was cute and athletic. He was definitely worth the hype. The entire game was intense. None of their games were like that back in Denver; clearly Georgia was a totally different ball game.

"Where is your bottle?" Cannon asked a crying Yara.

She had been squirming and whining for pretty much the entire second quarter and Cannon had been doing all she could to console her, but the longer it took her to eat, the worse she cried. Cannon searched the diaper bag frantically with her one free hand.

"I know I ain't leave your bottle at home." A dejected sigh came from Cannon as she realized that was exactly what she'd done.

Either that, or she'd left it in Ezra's truck. She'd ridden back to the school with him for the game, and had been excited to hang out with him, but now she was wishing she'd driven her own car. It was too dark to walk even though she had Yara's stroller, but she couldn't possibly wait for the game to be over. Yara would probably be a lunatic by then.

"Fuck my life," Cannon palmed her forehead before closing Yara's bag and slinging it over her shoulder.

With Yara in her hands, Cannon stood to her feet and did her best to get through the bleachers and down to the floor so she could leave before halftime started and people got out of their seats. She had exactly one minute and thirty-three seconds before the buzzer sounded and the floors crowded.

As much as she didn't want to walk, she didn't have any other choice. Her house wasn't far from the school anyway. Plus, Yara's crying would be less embarrassing if she was alone. Her stroller was on the back of Ezra's truck so Cannon could just grab it and get on her way.

She'd just stepped off the last step and was headed for the door when she heard Ezra's voice, and she knew it was him because he was the only fool that still called her New Girl. Cannon turned quickly trying to remain as calm as she could. Yara's fit had her a little disheveled, but it was almost over.

Cannon pulled the jean material of her shorts down between her thighs as she turned around. Ezra was running toward her, which brought way more attention than she'd wanted upon her departure, but it was what it was now. She was just thankful she was extremely cute in her jean shorts, fitted top, and fresh blowout. Her hair was bouncy, and her nails were perfect as well.

Too bad they were attached to fingers that were rubbing up and down the back of a newborn, giving everybody the assumption that she was a young mother. Cannon hated that, but screw them. Life was life, she'd be fine.

"You leaving?" a sweaty Ezra towered over her with his hands on his hips.

Even though his hair was pulled back in a ponytail, it had slid over his shoulder and was resting against his damp skin. His face was etched in concern as he looked at her. As much as Cannon wanted to be embarrassed, standing there with all of Ezra's attention on her made it worth it. She was sure, if no one else, all the female eyes in the building were on them.

"Why you over here? It ain't halftime yet."

Ezra's hand pushed the piece of hair dangling in front of her glasses out of her face and smirked. "I was on the bench when I saw you walking down the bleachers. My coach told me I could come talk to you really quick."

"You saw me?"

"Yeah I found where you were sitting before the game even started. I wanted to watch you with my baby." His hand went to Yara's back, before he kissed the top of her head.

Cannon wanted to faint right there in the middle of the gym. Ezra was so much love, she could hardly wrap her mind around his existence.

"You gon' have these people thinking this your baby."

He looked at Cannon and smiled goofily with sweat dripping from his body. "She is." Without warning he leaned in and kissed Cannon's mouth roughly. "You are too."

If it were possible to see and hear fireworks in the middle of a college gym without catching it on fire, Cannon would have sworn that was what had just happened. Sparks were flying everywhere in her body at that moment. Even if she wanted to stop smiling, which she didn't, she wouldn't have been able to. Her face was so hot from the warm blushing that she could hardly keep from fanning herself.

"Ezraaaa," she whined as she always did when he said or did something that was too sweet for words.

"I knew that would make you calm down." He looked back toward his coach who had just called his name. He held up one finger before giving Cannon his attention again. "You out?"

"Yeah, I forgot her bottle at home and she's acting crazy, in here embarrassing me."

"She's a baby, Cannon. She's hungry. You think she ain't gon' cry?" he chuckled.

Cannon rolled her eyes at him. "You're always on her side."

"Because she's my baby. So you going straight home?"

Cannon nodded.

"Alright, come get my keys and drive home and I'll have my mama bring me to your crib after the game over."

Cannon's eyes bucked. "Your mama in here? She probably saw you kiss me."

Ezra's eyes lit up brighter. "I'm sure she did. Her and every other person that's up in here in my business." He kissed Cannon's mouth once more before grabbing her hand and pulling her behind him.

Cannon felt like she was on cloud nine as Ezra pulled her behind him to the bench where his stuff was resting on the floor. He dug in his bag and handed her his truck keys before standing back up.

"I'll be over there as soon as this over." He winked at her before slapping her butt and walking away.

Cannon nodded and hurried to walk away. She'd had enough attention for the night. Not to mention Yara's li'l hungry ass was still crying. It took her a little over ten minutes to get Yara settled in the back of Ezra's truck before she was in and driving out of the parking lot.

She was smiling like a crazy person as she drove home replaying her and Ezra's moment in the gym. How could he be so perfect? He was way too good to be true. She was still smiling when she pulled into her driveway and saw her mom's car. Her heart stopped because that was definitely going to put a pause in her and Ezra's nightly plans.

Karina was cool and all, but not letting-Ezra-spend-the-night cool. Just like that, Cannon's mood was ruined. With her face frowned, Cannon pouted all the way up the driveway and up to the front door. As soon as she walked in, she heard her mother on the phone laughing. That was alarming, so after closing and locking the door, she went to the kitchen.

Her mother was standing at the stove stirring a pot, with her cellphone resting between her ear and shoulder.

"Hey Mommy, who you talking to?" Cannon asked as she grabbed Yara's bottle from the counter and fed it to her.

Karina turned around with a large smile on her face. "Hey baby. I'm talking to your aunt Tessa. Where y'all coming from?"

"Basketball game at my school."

Karina's eyes went to Yara who was gobbling down the formula like a baby pig. "Did she give you a hard time?"

Karina's caring tone caught Cannon off guard, but she preferred that over her normal sadness.

"Yes! I accidentally forgot her bottle here, so the moment she got hungry she went off."

Karina touched the side of Cannon's face. "Aw, I'm sorry pooh. Give her to me and go get some rest. I'll keep her tonight."

Cannon gave Karina a skeptical look, while still maintaining her hold on Yara. She was happy to see her mother in good spirits but that didn't mean she trusted her with Yara for any longer than necessary, especially at night. Yara loved to wait until the wee hours of the morning to act like she didn't know what sleep was.

"Tessa, let me call you right back." Karina said a few more things before ending her call. "I'm okay today, Cannon. Let me help you."

"I can keep her. She's calm now since she has her milk."

Karina sighed and looked at Cannon with a sympathetic look. "Lord, I've ruined you. I'm sorry, Cannon. I really can take care of her. Go do something with your friends or something."

Cannon's mind wandered off to Ezra. Since he was probably not spending the night, they could possibly go somewhere else and do something fun. Cannon contemplated it a little because hanging out with Ezra outside of the house would be fun, but not at the expense of Yara's well-being.

"I know you want to, it's all over your face. Go ahead. I promise she'll be safe and sound when you return." Karina reached for Yara. "You see she was fine when you got home from school today."

Cannon nodded, because she was. Yara was dry and asleep while Karina sat at her vanity doing her makeup. Nothing like they normally were, where Karina looked on the verge of insanity while Yara screamed to the top of her lungs.

"Okay, but call me if you need me. I'll come right back and get her."

"I'll be fine. Go ahead."

Cannon smiled at her mom and handed Yara to her. Yara relaxed and continued drinking her bottle. "I'm going to go back to the game."

"Have fun, baby." Karina yelled to Cannon's back as she switched down the hallway.

In a rush, she freshened up her hair, sprayed on some perfume and left. She was in Ezra's truck in no time, headed back to him. Hopefully the game wouldn't be over before she got back. With her music blasting high, and baby free, Cannon rode peacefully back to the game. When she pulled up, the parking lot was still packed so she was sure it wasn't over.

With urgency accompanying her every step, Cannon strolled to the back door of the gym and stopped at the door. After smoothing her hands over her clothes and hair, she pulled the door open and walked back inside. The gym was still rocking with noise when she eased in cautiously. She allowed her eyes to survey the gym for somewhere to stand before walking all the way in.

When she found a small spot on the bottom bleacher next to Professor Keating, she walked in. She could feel eyes on her, but she kept her gaze straight and walked to the open seat.

"Hey, Mrs. Fast Behind," Professor Keating greeted her with tooted lips and a smile that she could tell held more than the small greeting she'd just offered.

"Fast behind? What I do, Professor Keating?"

Professor Keating's eyes rolled to the side as she smiled at Cannon. "I saw you and Ezra over there kissing like y'all grown."

"He kissed me."

"Well since there's no random man running around here kissing me without my permission, I'm assuming Ezra felt comfortable for some reason."

Cannon couldn't even deny what Professor Keating was saying because it was all true, so versus saying anything, she hugged her with one arm and gave Ezra her attention. He was on the floor balling. He'd just crossed up the point guard from the other team and was headed for a layup.

"Whooo!" Cannon yelled when the basketball slid into the net easily.

Once again, the crowd went wild, including Cannon and Professor Keating. They were both on their feet yelling and screaming for Ezra.

"Ezzzyyyy! Go baby!" Cannon screamed as he ran up the side of the court that was the closest to her.

His eyes went to her instantly. The breathtaking smile he shot at her had her stomach doing flips as she stood with a smile just as big plastered across hers. After blowing her a kiss and telling her his next shot was for her, Ezra made the rest of Cannon's night.

"Baby? Ezra's your baby now?" Professor Keating questioned mockingly.

Cannon hid her face and smiled as she tried to ignore the truth that she was hearing. Ezra was in fact, her baby. *Hers.* Cannon could get used to that. From the moment Matt died, she'd allowed her emotions to travel away with him. Never giving any other men the time of day . . . until Ezra. Although he seemed worthy of it, Cannon was still a little nervous when it came to him, but she wouldn't push him away just yet.

When the buzzer sounded for the game to be over, people were everywhere. Ezra was in the air on the shoulder of two of his teammates with the net hanging around his neck in celebratory glory. Both of his arms were stretched into the air as he nodded his head and yelled a host of boastful comments. The whole team was jumping up and down, making Cannon nervous. It would make her heart stop if they dropped him.

"Aye, girl, come with me." A thick, dark-skinned girl grabbed Cannon's arm and attempted to pull her behind her, but Cannon resisted with a frown on her face.

"Why you grabbing on me like that?" Cannon's face was still frowned in confusion as she stared at the girl she'd never seen a day in her life.

The girl's presence felt familiar for some reason, but Cannon knew for sure she'd never met her before. Even her face was recognizable, but Cannon couldn't place it for the life of her.

"Cannon, just come on girl. I'm Ezra's sister."

"Oh, dang." Cannon relaxed and followed her, still unsure of their current encounter.

The girl was about Cannon's size just a little bit taller and heavier on the bottom. Whereas Cannon had wide hips and a handful of butt, Ezra's sister had no hips and enough ass for her and Cannon to split and still have more to give away. She was a bad one. Her hair was also dreaded up and hanging past the middle of her back. Hers were dyed a dark blue that looked amazing against her skin. With her hand holding tightly to Cannon's, she pushed her way through the throngs of men trying to stop them.

When they were finally out of the mix of attendees, Cannon assumed she would release her hand, but she didn't. Well, not at first. They did once they stopped at the bleachers in the corner where a heavyset lady in an all-black dress and sandals was seated. Her hair was a short natural cut that curled up. It was freshly lined with two parts on the side. Although it wasn't something a lady her age should have been wearing, she was killing it.

The lady had two wrists full of gold bangles that went almost halfway up her forearm, with a handful of rings and a bright gold watch. She was so pretty, and looked like she was probably a thug in her younger days, but played it safer in her later years and just collected dope money or something. She had been waving her arms in the air cheering until she laid eyes on Cannon and Ezra's sister.

Her high cheekbones rose higher as she held her hands out to Cannon. "Hey, baby girl. Come here."

Cannon went with no problem. Judging from the way her eyes glowed with invisible lamps just like Ezra's, Cannon knew she had to be his mother. She grabbed one of Cannon's hands, and patted the bench next to her with the other one. Cannon sat down and scooted into the grasp of her outstretched arm. His mother squeezed Cannon to her firmly. She was so soft. Cannon was in love.

"Ezra wanted you to stay over here with us until he comes out of the locker room." She patted Cannon's shoulder lovingly before releasing her from their hug. "This is Danna, Ezra's older sister."

"Oh okay, you go here too?"

Danna shook her head. "Nope, I graduated from Columbus State in May. I didn't want to go here."

Vonetta cut her eyes at Danna. "Nah, she's just a sneaky little thing. She doesn't want Ezra all in her business."

"Vonetta, stop your mess," Danna smiled mischievously.

Danna's pretty dark skin glowed just like Ezra's as she winked at Cannon and looked back toward the floor where they were clearing people. She stood snapping her fingers while dancing casually to the music that was still playing. Bad dot com. Cannon could hardly take her eyes off Danna. She was breathtaking in a ghetto girl kind of way.

"Where's the baby?" Ezra's mother asked her.

Cannon turned to make eye contact with her and smiled. "It's so weird looking at you because it's like looking at Ezra. He looks exactly like you."

She smiled like a proud mother. "Girl, you should see his ugly ass, black ass, crazy ass daddy."

Cannon was cracking up as she sat listening to her.

"I wish my baby did look more like me, but he doesn't. He looks like Echo's old Jumanji-looking ass." She rolled her eyes and waved her hand dismissively. "But fuck him, Cannon, where's the baby. I've been waiting to see her."

"I just took her home to my mom for a little while."

Ezra's mom paused and looked at Cannon with her eyebrows raised. "She's with your mom?"

"Yes ma'am." Cannon could feel the question hanging in the air. "She's having a good day."

His mother nodded and her smile returned. "Well, that's good to hear. You have to make sure you bring her around so that I can see her. Ezra's lying ass can't stop talking about how much she looks like him."

Cannon squealed in laughter as she shook her head. "He kills me with that."

"You?" She bulged her eyes dramatically. "How in the hell that baby look like him?" she shook her head as if she really didn't understand.

"I hope I don't sound rude, but what's your name? Ezra hasn't told me." Cannon hadn't wanted to ask it, but she hated to continue talking to her without knowing what to call her.

"Vonetta Mendoza, but they call me Mendy for short."

"You look like a Vonetta." Cannon smiled at her happily.

Vonetta looked at Cannon and laughed in her face. "Girl, hush your mouth. You couldn't think of nothing better to say, could you?"

Cannon shook her head with a smile before looking away and looking toward the locker room entrance. Some of the players were walking out, preparing to go home. Danna was already headed across the floor by the time Ezra came out in his basketball sweat suit. His hair was out of his ponytail and hanging down around his shoulders. His face and eyes lit up when he saw his family. Mainly at Vonetta. She was waving her arms again the same way she had been when Cannon had first laid eyes on her, this time she even danced in place. She did a smooth little rock from side to side that let Cannon know she'd been a force to reckon with in her younger days. Cannon's eyes trailed to Danna, who was still dancing. They both had undeniable rhythm that Cannon enjoyed admiring.

"Look at my baby. You look so handsome Ezzy. You did good tonight, man." The way Vonetta spoke to him, somebody would have thought he was a five-year-old and not well on his way to twenty-one.

It was hilarious to Cannon. Especially since Vonetta called him Ezzy. He'd told her the night before that she called him that, but Cannon hadn't believed him until she yelled it during the game and he looked immediately.

"Ma, stop talking to this nigga like he a baby."

"Danna, stop hating. He my baby."

Ezra walked to his mother and hugged her tightly before pulling her from the bench. She screamed and slapped his back playfully until she was on her feet.

"This boy ain't got no sense." She laughed before slapping his arm again. "When I punch his ass, he'll stop fucking with me then."

Ezra kissed his mother's cheek before looking at Cannon with a wide grin. She was just about to smile back, but he grabbed her too fast and pecked her lips.

"Stop kissing on me like that in front of your mama."

"Honey, don't worry about me. After the shit I've seen Nuke do in front of me, it ain't nothing Ezzy can do that will surprise me."

Danna and Ezra both laughed at the disgusted look on Vonetta's face.

"When you called me Ezzy, I thought you was Danna." He released his hold on Cannon's body, but grabbed her hand. "Where's Yara?"

"At home with her mama, she said it's a good day, so mind your business and take this girl out on a date or something."

Ezra smirked at Cannon as he listened to his mother rant. "You want to go on a date with me tonight?"

"Yep."

"Aww Ma, ain't they cute?" Danna said sarcastically from behind them.

"Yeah child. I remember when I was young and in love like that."

"Not me. I don't love these niggas, Ma." Danna walked over to where everybody else was standing and leaned her arm on Ezra's shoulder. "I'm a playa."

"As you should be. These niggas ain't shit. Ezzy the only good one left and I still don't understand that shit. Living in the house with me and Echo should have ruined y'all."

Ezra nodded his head at Danna. "It did ruin her."

Danna shrugged her shoulders with a broad smile on her face. "Nah it put me on game, that's what it did."

With a quick high five, Vonetta encouraged Danna's banter. "That's my girl. Keep it that way," Vonetta winked at Danna before reaching for Ezra. "Ezzy, come on and help me to the car, baby. You know these bleachers be killing my back."

Ezra released Cannon's hand immediately. "Yes ma'am." He

grabbed his mother's arm and stepped as close as he could to her so that she could lean on him if necessary.

Cannon watched them begin walking before stepping back near the bleachers and grabbing the big black purse that she assumed to be Vonetta's. She was tossing it over her shoulder when the phone inside of it began to ring.

"Mrs. Vonetta, you want me to get your phone?"

Danna and Ezra both began shaking their heads in objection, while Danna actually reached for the purse and took it from Cannon. Cannon looked at them both in confusion until Vonetta started laughing.

"Baby, you have to enter that purse at your own risk. You might mess around and get bit."

Confusion was written all over Cannon's face as she stared at the three of them.

"Vonetta is packing honey, and she don't ever have that gun on safety so you have to be careful when digging through her purse."

More laughter came as they all continued out of the gym. The parking lot was almost empty minus a few of the players and their families. Ezra helped his mother to the car and made sure she was in before walking back to Cannon with a large smile on his face.

Cannon's cheeks warmed as she matched his smile with one of her own. The black sweat suit looked so cute on him as his hair swayed around his shoulders. With eyes that lit up the night, Ezra stopped in front of her and allowed his face to shine down on her.

"What you want to do tonight?"

"I don't know, whatever you want to do."

Ezra twisted his mouth to the side as his eyes rolled to the top of his head. "It's a party tonight at one of my teammate's house. You want to hit that?"

"I'll go wherever you want to go," Cannon told him honestly.

With Ezra she felt safe and free. It didn't matter where they went, as long as he was with her, she was ready.

"Bet." Ezra grabbed Cannon's hand pulling her to where his truck was parked so they could leave.

"Don't You Say No" by R. Kelly was blasting throughout the house as Cannon and Ezra made their way down the stairs. The dimly lit basement was cool and calming in a seductive way. There were a few people crowding the floor and sofas as others walked casually through the home's lower level.

The black leather furniture and large entertainment system decorated the middle of the floor, while a pool table and a weight set occupied opposite corners of the room. Red party cups, different finger foods, and sodas were here and there, while open pizza boxes crowded the coffee table.

The music was loud and drowning any conversation that was taking place at the moment, which was probably a good thing since everybody in the room looked to be boo'd up. Couples littered the room in the midst of various interactions. Some were kissing, some were dancing, and some were laid out on the sofas smiling and talking. There was even one couple seated on the floor in the corner darn near sexing with their clothes on.

Li'l fast behinds. Cannon turned her head and gave the fake grown people their privacy.

The further into the basement they got, the more Cannon recognized the boys as Ezra's teammates, and a few of the girls from various events at school. She could see some of the people's attention turning to her and Ezra as they came into view. A couple of the guys gave her the once over before smiling or winking at Ezra, while sly smiles came from the girls.

Well, all except one. She was seated on the sofa with a boy Cannon knew as Taki—he was the center and was like a miniature Lebron James. He was huge and fascinating on the court. He'd nodded his head in Cannon's direction as soon as their eyes met. They had one of their science labs together and spent a lot of days tripping out in class because they were at the same table. He was mad cool and could definitely do better than the little troll he had eyeing Cannon as if she wanted to kill her.

"It's about time your ass got here." Taki held his hand out for a dap. "I ain't think you were coming."

Ezra smiled and dapped Taki up.

"None of us did. You know this nigga don't ever do shit." Jazz, another player from the starting five chimed in as he rubbed his hand up and down the girl's thigh that was seated in his lap.

"Man cut it out." Ezra chuckled as the rest of his teammates chimed in with one thing or another that expressed their happiness to see him out with them.

"Then you got my homie with you." Taki's large smile got wider as he stood to hug Cannon. "I saw that li'l shit y'all pulled at the game today. I ain't even know y'all was fucking with each other like that."

Cannon's smile got wider as her stomach flipped. All attention was on them, and it was making her nervous. With one hand she covered her face, while grabbing Ezra's arm with the other one.

"That was him."

"Oh, we saw who it was," Jazz and the girl he was groping laughed.

Ezra's arm that she had been holding pulled out of her grasp and circled her neck instead. He pulled her to him and kissed the side of her head while releasing confident laughter.

"Damn right it was me." He pecked her head again. "Ain't that right, New Girl?"

All eyes were on Cannon as she stood tucked beneath his arm smiling like a star struck child. With a quick nod of her head, Cannon's arm went around Ezra's waist.

"I'm just glad this nigga finally gave a girl some real play. All he does is curve bitches." Another player from their team stated before Ezra grabbed Cannon's hand and pulled her behind him.

"I had to find one I liked first." Ezra winked at a blushing Cannon.

The girl Taki was chilling with was still eyeing Cannon, but Cannon decided to just ignore her. She wasn't there to make friends and didn't want Taki, so she didn't bother concerning herself with make believe drama.

As conversation died down, Ezra grabbed Cannon's hand and pulled her along. She followed closely behind him as they stepped over another boy that Cannon hadn't even seen lying on the floor. He was on his stomach talking to some girl on Facetime. Cannon almost felt bad for him that he didn't have anyone there with him, but he looked content enough just being on the phone, so she smiled at him and kept moving.

Ezra stopped at a small door in the corner of the room. When he opened it she realized it was a bathroom. It too was decorated in black and was extremely clean. Once they were both in, Ezra pulled the door closed behind them. The space between them was minimum which halted Cannon from doing too much moving. Though she loved being close to Ezra, she wasn't sure what he had in mind at that moment. It was a good thing he was a giving person and didn't make her wait long to find out.

As soon as Ezra was facing her again, his hands went to her waist and gripped it tightly. Cannon inhaled deeply when he stepped closer to her closing the distance between them. Naturally her hands went to his forearms and held onto them softly. With his hair falling down around them, grazing her exposed shoulders, Ezra licked his lips and allowed his eyes to travel from her eyes down to her breasts, before coming back to her mouth.

"You like the party?"

His voice was low and sexy, and Cannon's favorite thing to hear. Instead of saying anything right away, Cannon nodded her head while staring at his parted lips.

"Y'all always have team kissing parties like this?"

Ezra's personal lightbulbs glowed as a smile crept across his face. "Kissing party?" He chuckled. "You wild, but yeah kind of. Our coach be on us about getting into trouble after games, so we just hang out together at Taki's crib so we don't get into shit."

Cannon leaned her head to the side and made eye contact with him. "And, the girls?"

Ezra shrugged. "They be here too. We ain't trying to sit around looking at each other all night."

"How many girls have you brought here?"

"One."

Cannon twisted her mouth up on one side to show her disbelief.

"For real. I only came tonight because you came with me." Ezra leaned forward and rested all his body weight on her while sliding his hands to the back of her thighs and gripping them in both hands. "I don't do this shit regularly. I be at home chilling with my OG."

"So, you really expect me to believe you don't be having women?"

"Nah, I ain't say all that. I just said I don't be over here with none."

Cannon snickered and slapped his shoulder as he shared in her laugh.

"You make me sick."

"Man, listen, I ain't gon' lie. I do my thing here and there but not like this." He nodded his head downward, in reference to her and him. "I ain't really liked nobody in a long time."

"Well, what makes me so different?"

Ezra looked away for a minute in efforts to think of a good response. "Honestly, I'm ready to have a girlfriend. I've been chilling for a while now and I'm just ready to do the boyfriend thing for a minute. Plus, you seem grown like me."

Cannon giggled for a second, rubbing her hand over her mouth. "We are kind of grown ain't we?"

"Hell yeah. We too young to be this old too."

Their immature laughter showed their truest age while they stood face to face holding one another. Cannon's mood relaxed faster than his. After removing the eyelash that was on his cheek, she regained eye contact.

"So, the girlfriend thing, you want to do it with me?" Ezra's face was serious and sexy as he nodded. "I mean if you let me."

Cannon watched as his face went from calm and confident to a tad bit nervous. She could tell he was trying to mask it, but it was there. It was so cute how she made him nervous. She hadn't really enjoyed the company of another boy since Matt, but Ezra had been making it more and more enticing every time they hung out together.

"Yeah," Cannon smiled. "We can do it."

His smile matched hers as he squeezed the back of her thighs tighter before kissing her. Their tongues intertwined instantly, exploring the moist warmth of each other's mouths.

"Come on, let's go back out here with these niggas. I just wanted to ask you to be mine while we were by ourselves."

Cannon's heart melted hearing him call her his. Her eyes closed as she sighed deeply. Before she had the opportunity to open them back up, his lips were on her forehead.

"You gon' be straight with me."

"I know." Cannon finally opened her eyes. "You gon' be straight with me too."

Ezra's smile was the remedy to all her problems, and he probably didn't even know it.

11

Ain't no lovin' like the one I've got

The mood of the basement was just what Ezra needed when he and Cannon walked back out of the small bathroom. All of his teammates and their girls were still chilling doing their own thing, which set the mood for him and Cannon.

He could tell she was still a little apprehensive as they walked back into the darkness. It was enough light to see most of everything, but still dark enough to give everyone their own privacy. Ezra's eyes focused on the large La-Z-Boy in the corner behind the pool table. It had been occupied earlier, but was empty right then.

Although there were two people on the floor leaning against the wall next to it, they were so lost in one another they surely wouldn't be paying attention to him and Cannon. He tightened his grip on Cannon's hand as they moved through the sofas and went to the large chair in the corner. Once in front of it, he removed his backpack and sat it on the floor before sitting down.

His eyes traveled up the thickness of Cannon's thighs before stopping at the way her jean shorts hugged her body. With his bottom lip tucked between his teeth, Ezra's mind went to their sex and how good she'd felt wrapped around him. His dick jumped subtly. With one hand he covered it, and with the other he reached for her.

She was clearly still nervous because she had yet to make eye contact. She'd been standing in front of him looking around at everyone else. When she felt him grab her, she looked at him and blinked slowly.

"Sit on my lap, baby." Ezra could tell by the way he'd sounded when he said it that it would do something to her, and judging by the way her face flustered, he'd been right.

One thing Ezra had always been was smooth with the ladies. He wanted to believe that Cannon was no different, but after the way she'd let him fuck on her *that* night, he knew that was a lie. She might have been acting shy right then, but he'd never had sex with a girl their age like that.

Cannon had given it to him like a real grown woman, and he knew the difference because he'd had his share of old women too. Majority of his sexual partners had been Nuke's age which was why he was so good at sex with the college girls, but Cannon had been different.

"You gon' make me wait all night?" He rubbed the back of her hand with the pad of his thumb.

Ezra smiled when Cannon's head shook from side to side. He opened his arms for her as she moved toward his lap and climbed on top of him. He'd been thinking she was going to sit sideways, but when she straddled his lap, his earlier thoughts had been confirmed. She was different. Cannon was a grown ass woman.

She scooted around, slowly making herself comfortable before resting her hands on both sides of his body. Ezra's hands snaked around her body quickly as he scooted lower in the chair. Their eyes were trained on each other as he massaged up and down her back. The song had switched, and the Ying Yang twins were singing about making their bedroom boom as Ezra held onto his girl.

"You good?"

Cannon winked at him before smiling. "As long as I'm with you."

Ezra was blushing uncontrollably as he pulled her down to him so that she was lying with her head on his shoulder.

"That's how you feel?"

"Yep."

"Show me." Ezra's words were taunting as he urged Cannon to make a move.

It took her a minute, but shortly after his request she was sitting up just enough for their faces to meet. With no reservations, she grabbed his neck and kissed him, and not just any kiss, she kissed him like the grown woman he knew she was. With passion and lust radiating between them, Ezra's body movement took the green light and matched her advances.

He grinded slowly beneath her allowing her to feel how hard he was getting. Like she'd done that night at her house, she matched his grinds and sent them both into a frenzy. Hips ... thighs ... breasts, Ezra's hands journeyed over Cannon's body, massaging her firmly enough to encourage her actions, but still subtly enough not to fuck her in the basement of his friend's house.

"You feel me?" Ezra asked with his lips slightly touching hers as he spoke.

"Yeah, you want to feel me?"

"Your ass is a grown fucking woman, you know that?" Ezra looked in her eyes as he spoke.

A soft snicker came from Cannon as she nodded. "I'm really not. I've just had a grown-up life."

Ezra didn't make light of her comment, and planned to go more in depth about it at a later date, but right then all he wanted to do was feel his girl.

"How I'ma feel you?" Ezra pushed upward, poking her with his erection.

Cannon's hands came to her face to cover it as she smiled bashfully. Ezra pulled them away just as quick as they went up.

"I don't know. You tell me."

For a moment, Ezra sat in thought as to how he was going to get him a quick feel in the basement filled with his friends. His eyes surveyed their surroundings for a moment to see who was doing what, and ended up getting an eyeful himself. Taki had his shorty's skirt up, clearly getting a quickie in front of everybody, while Jazz and his girl was headed up the stairs.

His boy next to him looked to be on the verge of getting topped off which caught Ezra totally off guard. The girl was literally leaning over his lap unbuckling his pants. Although Ezra wasn't surprised, because most of the girls there were labeled promiscuously around school, he still hadn't expected to see it out in the open like that.

"Let's go to my truck. I ain't keeping you down here like this." With one arm wrapped around Cannon's back, Ezra scooted to the edge of the sofa.

Cannon was still seated comfortably in his lap with her arms and legs wrapped around him. She'd even gathered all of his hair in her hands so that he could see better.

"Why you want to go so far?" a soft whisper in his ear accompanied by a kiss to his neck had Ezra pausing his movements.

"I don't want you in here with these freaks, and I sure as hell don't want these niggas seeing what I'm about to get."

Cannon's thighs clamped tighter around Ezra's body as she squeezed his head closer to her soft breasts. "Ezra," She moaned quietly. "Hurry up."

"I'm hurrying, baby." Ezra grabbed Cannon's bottom with both hands and stood to his feet.

Her hesitant squeal grabbed the attention of the others in the room as Ezra began to walk toward the stairs.

"Don't drop me, Ezra."

"Hush, girl. I ain't gon' drop you." Ezra held her tighter to him.

"Y'all out, Ezra?" Taki asked.

"For a minute." He yelled over his shoulder without looking back.

Not that he could have anyway. With his hair still gathered in her hands, Cannon was going ham on his neck. Her hot tongue and wet mouth were sending all types of electric currents through his body. The way the blood was pulsating in his dick, he was almost certain that he wasn't going to last long once he finally got in. She had him teetering too close to the edge already.

"You need to stop that shit you doing, Cannon." Ezra warned.

Cannon completely ignored him as she continued her assault on his neck. Her arms were around his neck when she moved from his neck to his mouth. She kissed him so hard, that he had to pause on the upper level of the house and lean her against the wall.

With her back pressed into the dining room wall, Ezra kissed Cannon the way she was begging to be kissed. She'd been teasing him relentlessly and he was about to give her what she was asking for.

"Fuck that truck," he whispered as he walked up the second set of stairs they were next to. He walked until he pushed open the first door he came to. When he was inside, he noticed Jazz and his girl were already getting to it on the bed in the corner.

Since the cover was over them, all Cannon and Ezra could see was Jazz's upper body and one of the girl's legs. She was moaning and making all types of noises that probably made Jazz feel like he was fucking shit up. Ezra chuckled as he and Cannon watched the two of them for a minute.

"Stop, somebody else is in here." The girl said once she realized they were no longer alone.

Jazz looked over his shoulder momentarily before shooting Ezra a mischievous grin and turning back around.

"So, they finna' do they own shit." Jazz continued his movement. "Worry about me and you."

Ezra smirked at the girl. She looked unsure but turned away from him and Cannon and went back to what she and Jazz were doing. The room was Taki's other two roommates' room, so there were two twin beds opposite of one another.

"We staying in here?" Cannon asked, slightly alarmed.

Ezra looked at her. "You don't want to?"

He watched her look from Jazz to his girl, then around the room, then finally back to him before shrugging her shoulders.

"I guess it's cool."

"Let me know. If you ain't comfortable, we can dip."

Cannon sat in his arms quietly for a little while longer before biting her lip. Ezra watched her for as long as he could before he grabbed the same bottom lip she was biting and sucked it into his mouth. Soft and firm at the same time, he sucked her mouth until she was back into the groove of things.

"Don't worry about it, I'm not about to let nobody see none of this." He winked at her as he walked to the other bed.

With the room being completely dark, minus the outside lights shining from the window, Ezra pulled the covers back before lying Cannon down on it. She began fumbling with the buttons on her shorts as he climbed in on top of her.

"Here, hold the cover up real quick. I'll do it for you." Ezra instructed Cannon to cover them with the dark-colored comforter as he removed her shorts for her.

Once she was bottomless, Ezra marveled at her secret place. He kneeled in front of her going back and forth in his mind about what he was about to do, but ended up saying fuck it. He didn't care if Jazz told. All he cared about right then was getting his dick wet, and Cannon being the one to wet it. Throwing caution to the wind, Ezra slid beneath the covers until Cannon's love was inches away from his face.

"Open your legs," he told her without bothering to lower his voice.

Cannon's thighs fell open willingly. Before beginning, Ezra pushed one finger inside of her and moved it around. Cannon's body shifted some until he finally licked and sucked at the softness that she was pushing into his face. She was so warm and smelled so good that Ezra couldn't get enough. His lips and tongue said everything to her that his words hadn't been able to.

"See, he's doing her. You could have done me too," Ezra heard the girl with Jazz say.

"That's that nigga if he wants to put her pussy in his mouth, I ain't doing that shit."

A soft giggle from Cannon removed the seriousness of the moment, so Ezra raised back up her body and used one hand to push his shorts down. Once he was hovering over her, Cannon's legs wrapped around his waist.

"Ezra, you was giving that girl head?" Jazz asked.

"Bruh, do it look like I'm trying to talk to you right now?"

Goofy laughter came from Jazz.

Ezra ignored him and grabbed his dick in his hand, but it was removed by Cannon. She'd grabbed it with both of her hands and led it to her opening. Ezra licked his lips as he looked down at her with desire in his eyes. Cannon was staring at him passionately while guiding him to connect them. Ezra's eyes closed as soon as he was inside of her.

Cannon gasped as if she couldn't catch her breath. Ezra loved that shit. It was like his dick took her breath away, and that boosted his ego like a muthafucka. The continuous moans of pleasure mixed with pain that sounded from her lips afterward finished the job.

She was so pretty, as she did her best to take the pain he was pushing into her. Ezra could tell she was doing her best not to make too much noise since they weren't alone, but little did she know, that was the opposite of what he wanted. He needed to hear her.

With her arms around his neck, Cannon pulled Ezra down on top of her. His mouth was to her ear when she licked up the side of his neck.

"What you holding back for?"

"Because there's people in here," she whispered.

Ezra pushed as hard as he could and she yelped in discomfort. "So." He pushed harder again bringing about another loud moan. "I want them to hear me make love to you."

Ezra leaned up and looked down at Cannon. Her face was etched in discomfort as she stared at him lovingly while nodding her head. Ezra nodded his as well, making sure not to break their eye contact. Only moving the lower part of his body, Ezra gave one stroke of passion after the other. Cannon's moans were like music to his and probably Jazz's ears as well.

Her sounds were so melodic and peaceful that they had Ezra closing his eyes. "Damn, Cannon," he moaned before grabbing one of her legs in the crook of his arm. "What the fuck, man." He questioned, to no one in particular, just before placing a kiss on the inside of her knee.

"What's wrong?" she asked low enough for him to hear her.

"Ain't shit wrong, mama. Everything is fucking right." Ezra kissed her lips sloppily before diving deeper into her body.

He made love to Cannon as if they were at home alone, totally disregarding Jazz and the girl he had. Who had, all of sudden, begun to make more noise than she'd been making. Clearly in a losing competition with Cannon. Nobody could match her and the love she made with Ezra.

"She's so loud," Cannon mumbled into Ezra's ear.

"Fuck her. This real." He kissed the side of Cannon's mouth. "Hold on to me."

Cannon's arms went around his neck as he laid on top of her and made slow love. Ezra's sexual expertise was clearly driving Cannon crazy because she was mumbling all types of nasty stuff in his ear. Her words ranged from the way he was making her pussy feel to how she felt like she was in love with him. He smiled at that admission because it was probably the truth and she'd just been trying to hold it in, but good sex had brought it right on out.

"Y'all fucking shit up in here." Jazz chuckled.

Ezra peeped over his shoulder to see Jazz and the girl getting dressed. Jazz was smiling happily as he always was, while the girl looked annoyed and intrigued at the same time. She was on the edge of the bed pulling her skirt up while watching Ezra and Cannon in fascination.

"Shorty is watching us, give her something to see," Ezra whispered to Cannon.

Cannon's closed eyes opened as she smiled up at him and nodded her head. Ezra didn't know what the fuck Cannon had just done but the way she moved the bottom half of her body while squeezing the muscles in her love had him dropping his head in defeat.

"Cannonnnnn, damn, baby. What you doing?" He questioned in pure ecstasy.

"I love you, Ezzy," she moaned passionately while pushing his locs out of his face.

Ezra's face was distorted in pleasure as he felt the head of his dick tingling. The look in Cannon's eyes assured him that she would definitely be his baby forever whether she knew it or not.

"Ugh," the girl Jazz had been with said as she stood from the bed. "What you watching them like that for? You act like you ain't just get the same thing this nigga is getting." Her words were laced with envy as she ranted to Jazz.

"I ain't watching them like nothing, I just ain't never seen no shit like this. They fucking like real live grown people." Jazz chuckled again. "Your ass is just hating."

"Hating on what?"

"Her," Jazz chuckled again before letting himself out of the room with the girl in tow.

Ezra watched them over his shoulder as they left before giving Cannon his attention. "I love you too, mama."

Cannon's eyes watered as she smiled at him. Ezra pecked her lips softly until he reached his climax. Once they were done it took them a minute to clean themselves up and get dressed. When they were ready to leave, Ezra walked out first. As soon as the door opened, a plethora of noise and boys tumbled over each other in the hallway.

They were all running and scattering back down the stairs. Ezra laughed along with them while Cannon on the other hand looked embarrassed as hell.

"Y'all niggas lame as fuck for listening." He was still laughing when he pulled Cannon in front of him. He held on to her as they walked down the stairs. "Come on, I need to go grab my book bag."

Cannon nodded and led them down the stairs. Ezra could tell by the way she kept trying to hold her head down that she was embarrassed, but he wasn't having that. With his arms tightly around her shoulders, he kissed the side of her neck.

"Relax, you mine. Ain't no shame in that."

Cannon covered her face as she tried to hide her smile.

"Boy, we heard y'all all the way down here." Taki laughed.

"Shid, you should have heard they ass up close and personal like I did." Jazz joined in on the laughing.

"Fuck y'all." Ezra's laughter was just as hype as his friends.

"Aye, y'all she was moaning like that because this nigga be eating her out."

When Cannon spun around quickly and tucked her face into Ezra's chest, he kissed the top of her head repeatedly before looking back at his friends.

"Y'all niggas need not worry about what the fuck I be doing."

An array of laughter and comments sounded around the room. Some of his teammates agreeing with him, while others sided with Jazz about not doing it.

"It's your mouth, you can do what you want with it, but I'm making my girl feel good with mine. That's on y'all niggas what y'all do with y'all shit."

"Oh my god, let's go." Cannon shook her head into his chest.

"Don't be embarrassed, girl. These other niggas just childish." The girl that had been with Jazz told her.

Upon hearing her voice, Cannon turned around to face everyone. She smiled at the girl, and Ezra was grateful for that. He hated for her to have been the center of attention like that.

"Damn, New Girl, I ain't know y'all was in love and shit," Taki told her.

"Well, now you know." Cannon winked playfully.

"All that winking is unnecessary," the girl that Taki was with vented.

Ezra could feel Cannon's body tense in his grasp so he rubbed her shoulders. "Ignore her."

"Bitch, die." Cannon told her, totally disregarding what he'd told her.

"You die, hoe. You're the one over here fucking off when you barely even know this nigga." The girl taunted as she stood to her feet.

Ezra sucked his teeth. Monet was a groupie that had been checking for him since their ninth-grade year and had refused to give up until Taki tried his hand at her. Ezra had been happy as hell when she'd found her way out of his face, but clearly, she was still with the shit.

"Nah li'l baby, I ain't fucking off, I'm giving my nigga what he needs and your miserable ass is just hating." Cannon stepped out of Ezra's grasp. "Now if you want to square up we can do that shit, but I ain't about to argue with no jealous ass hoe about what I do with my body."

Vulgar commentary sounded from both the men and women in the room. Ezra waited patiently behind Cannon, giving her room to do what she needed to do.

"Let's get it then, hoe. I ain't scared of your fat ass."

Cannon moved to step toward the girl, but Ezra stopped her. "Nah, mama, relax. We're about to dip. Let her get hers another day."

Cannon stood in the same spot for a minute like she wasn't going to move. "Well, Ezra loves my fat ass, so fuck you."

Ezra could tell the situation was on the way to getting much worse, so he grabbed Cannon's hand and pulled her toward the chair where his book bag was. Once he had it on his shoulder he pulled her toward the stair. He could hear Monet still saying little lame shit about Cannon, but since Cannon wasn't acknowledging her, he was good.

"I'll holla at y'all boys later."

They all bid their goodbyes as he and Cannon made their way up the stairs and out of the house. Once they were back in Ezra's truck he looked at her. Cannon was relaxed in her seat looking unbothered as ever.

"You straight?"

"Yeah, I ain't thinking about her. She ain't really want this whooping she was asking for."

Ezra was smiling. "You think you so bad."

"No, I don't. I just know I would have mopped the floor with that little ass girl."

"You wild." Ezra grabbed her hand and kissed it. "You going home or coming to my spot?"

"I'm going where you go."

Ezra nodded and backed out of the driveway headed into the night with his girl. He didn't know where they were going right then, or in the future, all he knew was he wanted to go with her.

12

Never question my loyalty

"It's good to see you again, Miss Mendoza." Officer Terry rendered her a genuine smile.

Danna smiled back as she took the pen the officer was extending to her. "It's good to see you too, girl. I like your hair like that."

Officer Terry ran her hand over the long-braided ponytail and pushed it over her shoulder. "I needed something for this heat. It's too hot out there for all that weave."

"Honey, who are you telling? I almost melted walking from my car." Danna finally looked down at the paper, preparing to sign in, when she felt a funny feeling rising in her chest.

Her eyes scanned the paper a couple of times, reading the same name over and over again to be sure she was seeing what she knew she was.

"That fucking liar, I knew it," Danna mumbled to herself.

She studied the paper a few more seconds, making sure that it was Don's baby mama's name, before looking up at Officer Terry. She was leaning over scrolling on the computer. Danna watched how Officer Terry's hand shook slightly as she did her best to avoid eye contact. A clear sign of nervousness.

"Hey, Officer Terry, let me ask you something really quick."

As soon as Officer Terry turned her head, Danna could see the guilty expression plastered across her face. Although, she knew Terry was cool with her, she was sure her loyalty lay with Don, so asking her about his Totiana's name being on his list was probably pointless, but it was a good thing Danna was the queen of doing pointless shit.

"Don's got somebody back there now?"

"Umm. I'm not sure. Let me check for you."

Danna watched as Officer Terry observed the sign-in chart before walking over to her computer. In Danna's opinion, it took her a little too long to do something she did all day every day, but she was going to give her the benefit of the doubt. It was obvious she knew Don's ass was caught up and wasn't exactly sure what she was to be doing at that moment.

"You can sit down, Danna. I'll let you know as soon as I find something out." The fake smile plastered on Officer Terry's face was nothing like the one she'd had when Danna first arrived.

"Make it quick if you can, please," Danna told her before taking a seat in the corner.

All types of thoughts and scenarios were racing through Danna's mind as she sat still trying to keep herself calm. It was literally taking everything in her not to go off at that moment. She knew Don was on some shady shit. Most niggas in prison were, but she had honestly put it past that fool. Or maybe she was the fool. She was the one being played by a nigga sitting in a damn jail cell.

Danna sighed and grabbed her head in both of her hands. Her mind was on a million and she wished for just one moment it would calm down.

"Okay girl, thank you. I'll see you next time."

Danna's head shot up at the sound of the voice. When she noticed Totiana, she just knew it was her lucky day. She was so busy waving and talking to Officer Terry that she was about to bump right into her. Danna had gotten out of her chair the moment she saw her coming.

"Oh, damn. Excuse me," she said as she turned around and saw Danna in her personal space.

Danna looked her up and down trying to contemplate her next decision. She wasn't big on letting people know about her and Don, but she most definitely wasn't about to let this moment pass her by.

"Why you here seeing Don?" Danna cut straight to the chase. Fuck it. If it got out to anybody, she'd just deny it. She was sure Don would too.

"I'm sorry, why is that any of your business?" Totiana asked with attitude.

"Because I asked, now tell me." Danna stepped closer to her.

Totiana's hand went to her belly protectively, immediately drawing Danna's eyes to it. It wasn't the biggest but it was definitely round with an enormously ugly belly button poking out. *How in the fuck did I miss this?* Danna's mouth began watering as she felt herself getting physically sick.

She knew they already had a child together, but she was most definitely unaware of the growing one that was clearly being housed by Totiana's ugly ass. *That fucking pregnancy test!* Danna's mind went straight back to their fight that day and how Don continued to reassure her that the test hadn't been on his account. He was such a liar.

"Listen, I don't know who you are, but you better get out of my face. You're asking about my baby daddy, but you clearly don't know him very well because if you did, you wouldn't be all up on me like you are."

Danna was definitely going to throw up, but not in front of Totiana. "Girl, of course I know that nigga. Why you think I'm here?" Danna waited for her to say something. "And trust me, he knows me too."

"So. What you want? A cookie?" Totiana looked her up and down smugly. "Your li'l bitty young ass. Probably ain't even old enough to be up in this damn jailhouse."

"Well, tell that to your baby daddy."

Totiana's eyes squinted as she pushed some of the long weave over her shoulder and laughed. "Oh, I see. You're one of Don's little hoes huh?" More chuckles came. "You'd might as well go ahead and go home, baby girl. Whatever you and him had is over now."

Defiantly, Danna stood her ground. "I'll let him tell me that."

"Well, you do that then, you fucking toddler."

Every nerve in Danna's body began to tremble as she tried to keep her fists from coming up and knocking Totiana's head off her shoulders. She'd owed her an ass whooping for cutting up in Don's yard that day anyway.

"You big and bad today, huh? Is it because you think I won't beat on a pregnant woman, or because Don dun' sat his lying ass up in there feeding you some bullshit about y'all being a family?" Danna smirked at her.

"Bitc—"

"Danna, it's your turn." Officer whispered just as she stopped next to the women.

Danna looked at her, but Totiana's gaze stayed on her. "Danna? As in Danna Mendoza?"

Danna wasn't surprised that she knew her, most people did. Echo didn't do a very good job at being a father, but the streets would never know that. He could win a "father of the year" award, if it was up to people in the hood. Not to mention he was Don's boss. No wonder Totiana knew him. Danna knew all of Don's friends too.

When Danna didn't bother responding, the urgency in Totiana's voice picked up. "You're Danna Mendoza?"

Danna looked from Totiana's shoes to her face before walking off. Totiana's hand was on her elbow immediately, and just as fast as she'd put it there, it was smacked off.

"Don't touch me, girl."

"Ladies," Officer Terry intervened.

"This is some bullshit. You've been fucking with Don?"

"Ask him."

After that, Danna and Officer Terry left the waiting room. Danna's tongue was practically jumping in her mouth as she walked to the visitation area. As soon as she walked in, she spotted Don. He was at his usual table, leaning over the top of it casually. He smiled upon noticing Danna. The nigga even had the nerve to wink.

On a mission, Danna continued to the table, completely ignoring his attempt at cordiality. She took her seat before looking around the room. She recognized a few of the faces from her other visits, but the only one that stood out was Quay's. He was near the vending machines with that same dirty ass mop and bucket he'd had the last time she saw him there.

Her eyes lingered a little longer than they probably should have, but his didn't. He'd watched her for not even a whole second before he was back pushing the bucket and carrying the yellow sign over his shoulder. He was so muthafucking fine—too fine to be in jail, that was for damn sure.

"You must want me to fuck you up?" Don's voice brought her attention to him.

Danna's eyes rolled as she turned to face him. "What?" she asked, disgusted.

Don looked a tad bit surprised at her tone, but she held her ground. The two of them stared at one another until Don nodded his head and sat back in his chair. His interlocked fingers rested across his stomach as his eyes remained focused on her.

"If you want that nigga, maybe you should be over there with him."

Danna ran straight through the door he opened for her. "Maybe I should, that way you'll have all the time you need to be with your Totiana and y'all kids."

The anger in Don's eyes retreated some upon hearing her statement. When she'd first mentioned being with Quay, that nigga looked like he was seconds away from jumping across the table, but he looked pretty rooted in that chair then. Danna sucked her teeth and leaned her elbow on the table.

"Cat got your tongue?" Danna rested her chin on her fist. "Oh, wait. Maybe Totiana took that shit back out of here with her, because she sure as hell had a lot to say to me."

Don's agitated demeanor was a clear sign of guilt, but he was holding it together. "What she say?"

See, that was the one thing Danna could appreciate. The nigga knew better than to lie to her. That was one of the main reasons anything the streets had to say about him didn't mean much to her. If it didn't come out of his mouth, it didn't matter.

"She told me that y'all about to be family." Lies slid through Danna's teeth as she sat stone-faced in front of him.

A quick pop of his neck ruined the silence between them, but as soon as he was still again, it returned. "That's it?"

"That's the most important part."

Don nodded once. "You believe her?"

"Should I?"

"Not really."

Danna blew out a frustrated breath. "Look, I ain't got time to play with you, Don. You're just sitting here trying to buy yourself some time and I ain't about to do that shit with you. Is that your damn baby that girl is carrying?"

The cool rigid air between the two of them set off so many alarms in the back of Danna's mind that she could barely hear herself think. All she saw was his lying face and how big of a fool she was.

"Yeah."

Fuck!

Danna's insides trembled at the thought. Her stomach weakened at the same time as her mouth began to water again. Surely, she was going to throw up. With one hand, she covered her stomach and held it. With the other hand that had just been holding her chin up, she grabbed her forehead and allowed it to drop into her open palm.

"Danna—"

"Shut up, that's what the damn test was for. You knew this shit and still tried to play me like a fool."

"Just let me explain."

Danna's head finally raised. "Save it. I'm done."

Don finally lost his composure. "Danna, come on. It ain't like that. I'm not about to be with that girl."

"You might as well, because you sure as hell ain't about to be with me. I've been up here fucking you the entire time you've been here. There's no excuse for this shit." Danna sat back roughly in her chair before crossing her arms over her chest. "I can't believe you. Got me up here flouncing around like I'm the only bitch you be seeing. I knew you ain't keep them damn uniforms that white for no reason." Danna's heart was overflowing with hurt. "You know what, I'm out. Fuck you."

Danna was out of her seat preparing to leave, but Don stood to his feet and caught her arm. "Danna, sit down. Just let me tell you what happened."

"Fuck you," she spat.

"Tot don't mean shit to me. I just messed up."

"You sure did." Danna snatched her arm from him just as the guard came to their table.

"You two need to take your seats."

"Nah," Danna looked at him with water in her eyes. "I'm good. I'm leaving."

Danna walked away without looking back. She was out of the main visitation room and marching down the hallway when she caught sight of Quay, pushing the mopping bucket up the hallway. He stopped when he saw how upset she was. Danna held her head down, attempting to shield the tears that were about to run down her face.

"Yooo, Danna, chill." Embarrassed, past words, Danna tried to keep walking but he wouldn't let her. "Tell me why you're crying."

She shook her head. "I'm good."

"Nah," Quay shook his head and grabbed her chin.

The plastic glove on his hand made her think of how many toilets he'd cleaned that day, but she didn't say anything. Instead she pulled away and just kept her gaze on him. She was sure she looked a mess crying behind a nigga, but she couldn't even think enough to feel at that moment. The hurt stung too bad.

"You ain't good right now, but you will be," he told her with a straight face.

The gold that she'd grown so infatuated with shone between his lips. His hair had gotten longer, and he was still just as self-assured as he'd always been. Even in the dingy white prison uniform, his confidence was on one thousand.

"How you know?"

"Because you made for this shit. Don't let that nigga get you down."

Danna's bottom lip began to tremble at his thugged out sympathy. She cleared her throat and even began to bounce her leg trying to gain control of herself.

"Quayyy," she whimpered and held her head down when she couldn't make herself say anything else.

The wooden mop stick was out of his hand instantly, and she was once again wrapped in his warm embrace.

"Quit this shit, Danna. You're grade fucking A, and if that nigga can't see that, then fuck him." Quay gave her another light squeeze just as jingling keys could be heard at the other end of the hallway.

Danna pulled away and looked toward the sound. Don and the male guard from visitation were coming through the double doors she'd come through. His face showed his disapproval for her and Quay. Danna, already knowing his anger would be focused on

Quay, snatched out of Quay's embrace and tried to lean against the wall instead. Quay, on the other hand, didn't look like he gave two fucks. He even went as far as grabbing Danna's hand back in his.

"Write me."

Danna finally looked away from Don and nodded at Quay before practically running out of the prison. She wasn't sure what was going to happen between the two of them, but for Quay's sake, she hoped it wasn't much. She'd feel horrible if he got caught up in some mess on her part.

The rest of her day went by in a blur. By the time she was able to get her thoughts together and focus on her next move, it was a little after one o'clock in the afternoon. She'd been riding around thinking all day and was ready to go home, but had one last stop to make.

The strip mall was crazy packed with people, and it seemed as if the sun was at its hottest hour. The rays were beaming and sizzling everything resting beneath them. Heat radiated from the ground and disappearing into the still air. It was the middle of the summer and if Danna had forgotten, she was quickly reminded the moment she stepped out of her ride.

Nothing caught her eye at the mall, so after soaking up the air conditioning and a lemonade, she headed toward the exit. In a hurry and not paying attention, Danna raised her hand to put her sunglasses on while she walked to her car, but inadvertently bumped into a mom and her baby. The things that had been in the lady's hand hit the ground and rolled along the cement in a mess.

"I'm sorry, excuse me." Danna bent down to pick up the baby bottle, cell phone, and diaper cloth that she'd just knocked to the ground.

The mother of the pretty baby girl smiled with her hand outstretched to retrieve her things.

"You're fine. I shouldn't have been trying to carry all of this stuff anyway." The clearly flustered mother admitted, as she switched the baby from one hip to the other.

"No, it was really my fault. I don't even know where my mind is right now," Danna expressed truthfully.

The water in Danna's eyes that she'd just been doing a perfectly good job holding back swooped in and ruined her eye liner. A puddle of tears pooled in her eyes as she stood in front of a complete stranger on the verge of losing total control.

Instinctively her hand went to her face to stop the tears before they could fall, but unfortunately she was unable to stop the disaster that had been waiting to happen. Tears were on her cheeks and clouding her face before she could stop them. As if it were second nature, the lady grabbed Danna's arm and pulled her away from the bank's entrance.

"Oh, you poor baby, what's the matter?" Motherly concern laced the lady's words as she stood with one arm filled with a baby and host of other things, while her free one stroked Danna's shoulder. "Are you okay?"

Danna's head began to nod immediately, even though that was the furthest thing from the truth. "I . . . I'm fine," she stammered. "Just having a bad day." Danna wiped at her eyes with the back of her arm. "I'll be fine."

The woman's blue eyes were a mirror of Danna's sadness as she stared at her in sympathy. "Would you like to talk about it? I know you don't know me, but I wouldn't feel right leaving you out here like this."

"No, ma'am, really, I'm fine."

"No, you're not, but I understand you don't know me." She continued to rub Danna's shoulder as the baby girl kicked and squealed with glee. "I'll just stand here with you until you feel better."

The infant's joyful carrying on brought a smile to Danna's face, but wiped it away just the same. With the feeling of fresh tears surfacing, Danna hurried to look away.

Dammit, Don!

"I'm fine, thank you so much, but I'll be okay." Danna gave the lady her best smile. "I just had a moment, but I need to get going."

The thin, untamed eyebrows of the woman raised as she allowed her facial expression to let Danna know she didn't believe her.

"Can I please pray for you before you leave?"

Pray? What?

Danna twisted her face to the side, not really feeling the whole praying for her thing, but if she was truly honest with herself, she was open to any form of comfort she could get at that moment. Even if it was from an overworked house wife, and a God she couldn't see. She'd take what she could get.

"Sure."

The lady shifted the squealing baby once again before stepping toward Danna and subtly pulling her closer. Once the distance between the two was minimal, the lady bowed her head and closed her eyes. Danna preferred to keep hers open because she didn't know that lady from Adam, and didn't want to take any risks.

"Dear Lord, amazingly sweet Jesus, I ask you right now to wrap your loving arms around this young lady. Strengthen her and let her know that no matter what may be going on her life, you're always there to see her through it. Give her the strength and comfort that she needs right now, Father." A tighter squeeze came from the lady. "Just rush her with your love, grace, and mercy, O Lord. In Jesus' name, I pray. Amen."

With a smile on her face, the lady stepped back only a few steps before pulling Danna in for another hug. "I love you sweetie, and I'll be praying for you. You behave, okay?"

"Yes ma'am." Danna nodded obediently before they parted ways.

She could see the lady still watching her as she walked to her car, but she eventually turned and walked inside. Danna was grateful for that, because for as long as she was near her, she kept getting choked up. The fit that had been lying dormant all day was on the rise and Danna wanted to be alone whenever it happened.

With a quick turn of her wrist, Danna cranked her car up and pulled out of the parking lot. It had been a long day and she was positive it was only about to get longer. From the moment she'd walked out of the prison, her stomach had been a mess, and so had her nerves. All she wanted to do was go home and climb into her bed. The only reason she hadn't gotten there yet was because she'd needed to get what belonged to her.

When Don found out he was going to be past angry, but Danna didn't give a damn. Maybe with all his money gone, he'd feel just as brokenhearted as she did right then. She'd helped him run that fucking dope, he owed her. Him and his baby mama wouldn't ride off into the fucking sunset with no worries.

Though she'd heard plenty of rumors while being out in the city, she hadn't believed them. All she believed was Don. He had never lied to her before, so why start now? Stupid ass nigga. Danna shook her head and allowed the reality of her situation to set it in, with the saddest part being that she was probably going to forgive him. She loved him like that.

The imaginary steam blowing from Don's head was sure to set off every fire alarm in the prison. He and the guard were both marching down the long corridor toward his cell and all he wanted to do was turn around and throw the man over the third-floor railing. Luckily for him, all that would do was prolong Don's time there, and that was the last thing he needed to be doing right then.

It was bad enough he still had another few weeks before he would be a free man again; he didn't need any unnecessary time added on. Plus, the man hadn't done anything to deserve that type of pain. If Don wanted to throw anyone over the balcony, it needed to be himself. He was the only person responsible for what he was going through.

From Danna finding out about Totiana's baby, to her being hugged up in the hallway with Quay, it had all been his fault. The first problem was that he'd fallen so hard for Danna. He really cared that she was angry enough to call it quits with him. Then, for her to find comfort in another man—that sent him flying over the edge. She may have started out as a job to him, but that shit was so far gone, he'd kill Quay and any other nigga that thought they were going to take her from him.

"Aye, I need to make a stop." Don turned his head to the side to be sure that the guard had heard him.

"Where?"

"The janitor's closet."

The guard nodded but said nothing else. They'd long ago learned that Don wasn't to be played with. Majority of what he wanted, he got it. His peaceful behavior in the prison played a big part in their daily operations, so, as long as he was happy, everyone else would be as well. Don was the type of inmate who had nothing to lose, so he'd do anything. Including starting a riot that could potentially put the guards in a life or death situation.

"Big D." An inmate hit his elbow against Don's as he passed by.

Don nodded, but kept it moving. He was in no mood for pleasantries at the moment. Danna and Totiana had him on ten. Totiana stayed on some hot shit, which was why he didn't necessarily deal with her the way he could. She was way too messy, and Danna . . . fucking Danna. Don hung his head again. This love shit was too much. Leave it to her to complicate everything he'd been plotting for eight years.

He'd planned the death of Echo's family out in so many different scenarios, and because of her, he hadn't carried it out. Vonetta had been first on his list, but after seeing how much Danna loved her mother, he couldn't bring himself to do it. His mind moved from Vonetta on to Ezra for a while, but that li'l nigga was so fucking cool he'd made Don like him as well. He was like a son and no matter how hard Don's heart was, he couldn't kill a kid. Especially when his future was as promising as Ezra's.

"Fuck!" Don gritted out as he thought about the mess he'd made.

He was too fucking hard to give a fuck about these damn people. Going from never having a family to finally having one had him in such a bad head space. Echo's people had been so receptive to him since the moment he'd shown up. Showing him love, and making sure he was good no matter what. So, to turn around and kill them was really fucking with him.

"Ten minutes." The guard spoke before removing the cuffs from Don's hands.

Don snatched the door open in search of one person. The closet was small and crowded with an array of cleaning materials, so Quay's tall frame stood out immediately. He was standing near the sink mixing up some shit in his bucket that had smoke coming from it. Don watched him without saying anything. Quay was a street nigga too; he knew Don was there.

"Clear your chest, my nigga," Quay told him without turning around.

"Don't fuck with what's mine."

"Cool."

Don didn't like his response so he didn't move. He continued watching his hands and what he was doing with them. The mixture was still smoking and since he didn't know Quay very well, he didn't know what he might have been plotting.

"So, Danna's yours?" Quay finally looked at him.

"Been that."

"A'ight. So, she's cool with Tot being yours too?"

Hearing another man abbreviate Totiana's name angered him again. He'd known she was an around the way girl when he'd met her, but once again, his decision making when it came to women was weak, and he'd fallen for her too. Even gotten her pregnant twice. Dumb nigga shit. She had been easy and persistent, before long she'd become his and it had been that way ever since.

"She ain't got to be cool with it. It is what it is."

Quay made eye contact with Don and shook his head. "Nah, it ain't. Not when it comes to Danna. That's my li'l people and she doesn't deserve no jailhouse love triangle shit with you and the hood hoe." Quay pushed the bucket towards Don and grabbed the mop that had been leaning against the wall. "Either fuck with her right, or I'm taking her from your ass. Straight like that."

The blood pulsating through Don's body was getting hotter by the second as he listened to Quay disrespect him.

"Is that a threat, young nigga?" Don's large chest swelled.

Quay smirked. "Nah, I don't make threats. You know that."

That was a fact. Don had saw Quay in action plenty of times in the past and the nigga did in fact have heart, but that didn't scare Don. Don was an old school hustler; there were only a few young cats that could hold a candle to the shit he used to do with his guns, and Quay was definitely one of them. He respected him, but that wouldn't keep him off Quay's ass. If anything, it would make him act sooner and faster.

A deep chuckle came from Don as he and Quay stood face to face eyeing each other. "So, you think you can take her?"

"Ain't no thinking in it. You knew she was mine before you snuck her." Quay grazed his teeth over his bottom lip before pushing his hair back over his shoulder. "I let you have that, but I ain't doing that shit no more. You old enough to be her fucking daddy any damn way."

"You got some big balls."

"Because I can carry them muthafuckas." Quay looked Don square in the eye. "You want her, do her right and I'll fall back. You slip up, she's mine. Period."

Don balled his fists up and held his head back a little. He and

Quay traded murderous glares, but neither of them said anything further. Don would let Quay have this round, but he wouldn't hesitate to end his life if the opportunity presented itself.

Don held his closed fist out toward Quay. "Respect."

Quay pressed his fist against Don's and moved past him and left the small room. Seconds later, the guard came in and shackled Don's wrists again. They walked together to Don's room. Once he was back in the comfort of his cell he hit the floor to do some push-ups. He needed to do something to get his mind together. He needed to pick what side of this he wanted to be on. He was either going to be all in or all out. Kill them all, kill them and keep Danna, or do neither and just take his vengeful heart and bruised ego elsewhere to live out the rest of his days.

13

How bad could it be?

Slow melodic tunes of R&B played throughout the speaker of Cannon's phone as she and Danna sat on the bleachers of the local basketball court. The sun was blazing as always, and the sweat pouring from Ezra and his teammates was mouthwatering. Cannon and Danna had been practically drooling over the men as they moved around the court shirtless.

It was Saturday evening and the perfect way to end a long day. Danna had been cooking and cleaning her house all day and she was dog tired. The moment Cannon mentioned meeting Ezra and some of his friends at the basketball court so they could work out, she'd tagged right along. She'd been an isolated mess for the past two weeks, so she figured what was better to break her out of her funk than sexy, single, sweaty men.

"I owe you for this shit here, Cannon," Danna mumbled as she salivated at the guy who'd just come off the ground to make a jump shot.

"I told you. Every time I feel bad, or something is on my mind all I have to do is look at your brother with no clothes on and bitch, everything is alright in my world."

Danna turned her nose up and began gagging dramatically.

Cannon's face was bright from her laughter as she pushed Danna's shoulder playfully.

"He may be your little brother and all, but don't act like you don't see how fine Ezra is. You know that nigga is the fucking greatest. Don't do him."

"Baby, I ain't doing nothing surrounding Ezra, and I wish you wouldn't either."

"Well I wish you wouldn't walk around moping every day, but you do it. So," Cannon nudged Danna's shoulder.

"Girl, I'm doing my best. I just can't seem to shake this shit."

"I empathize with you Danna, I really do because I know what heartbreak feels like, but I also know what happiness feels like too. From the moment you told me about the prison incident, I've been wanting to make you move on from Don and just find someone else, but I've never been the leave-your-man friend. I'd rather just be a listening ear or shoulder to cry on, but you do need to get yourself together. This crybaby stuff is getting old, sis."

Danna looked off into the distance. "You're right. It feels like it's taking me forever."

"It feels like forever because you ain't talking to nobody else. I've already told you a million times, if you'd just find somebody else then you would be okay, but no, you don't listen to me."

"I do listen. I just don't know who to talk to. I like grown niggas, not these little ass boys." Danna motioned toward Ezra's teammates. "They're cool to look at, but I need me a man."

"I feel you on that." Cannon agreed. "What's wrong with Quay?"

"Nothing," Danna's smile slid across her face. "Everything is right with that nigga. He's just locked up right now too and I honestly ain't trying to deal with that."

Quay had been in the back of Danna's mind since she left the jail that day, and though she'd written him once, that had been it. She hadn't executed any other forms of contact, and she was fine with that. Right then she just wanted to give her heart a break. Even if it did speed up at just the thought of Quay.

"You're in denial, Danna. You like Quay. I don't care what you say. Every time I bring his name up you be smiling."

"I do not."

"Lies," Cannon told her as Ezra winked at her.

Danna sucked her teeth. "You and him make me sick."

"If you would check Quay out, then you could get like us instead of hating all the time."

Danna snickered and shook her head. "Nope. Quay is going to break my heart just like the rest of the men."

"You won't know until you try." Cannon's light face shone beneath the sun.

Though she was saying it in a joking manner, Danna knew she was serious. Maybe Quay wouldn't be so bad, at least not while he was in jail. What harm could talking on the phone really do? Fortunately for her, it didn't take her long to find out.

"What took you so long to write me?" Quay's deep voice sounded throughout Danna's phone speaker.

It was a little after ten o'clock at night and she was lying across her bed smiling too hard for her to be in her room alone. It was a good thing Quay wasn't there to see the effect that he had on her. Even after so many years, anytime she was near him she felt like a teenager all over again. Whether in person, or over the phone, she was a puddle of water when he was involved. Cannon had been right.

"I don't know. I guess I was just trying to get my mind right first. What took you so long to call me? I sent you my number days ago."

"I had to wait until my home boy could get me his burner phone. Can't be moving too fast up in here. Mess around and get caught with this shit, these niggas will be adding all kinds of time to my books." Quay released a long breath before resuming their conversation. "But you know I could have helped you get your mind together, right?"

Danna snickered. "I feel you, but nah, you would have only made it worse on me."

"How? I'm just here to help you, beautiful. No pressure this way."

Danna flipped over on her stomach and picked up her phone. "That's what your mouth says, but your presence is something else. You make me feel so childlike." Danna fiddled with one of her long locs. "Talking to you makes me forget everything."

The sexy yet soulful chuckle filled her room as Quay's deep laughter mesmerized her. It had been so long since she'd heard him laugh, she wanted to savor it.

"That's a good thing. If I make you forget stuff, you should have been rushing to talk to me." He paused for a minute. "You good on that? How you feeling?"

Danna's mind went back to the heartbreak that she'd been enduring for too many days to count. Don had really done a number on her with that baby Totiana was pregnant with. It was like everywhere she looked, there was something that reminded her of his betrayal. If it wasn't Totiana posting pictures of her belly on social media, it was Don's constant calling.

If she could have it her way, she would just run away for a few weeks until she could find a heart that wasn't as raggedy as hers was right then. She'd gone against everything Vonetta had taught her and opened up to that nigga, and he had run her right over. She hated the vulnerability she'd shown with him, because it had amounted to nothing more than sad songs and tears.

"I'm straight. It's fucked up, but it's not like I didn't know he was still fucking around with her."

"You knew about that shit and you let it happen?" Quay's voice held a hint of shock mixed with disappointment. "Come on now, Danna. I gave you more credit than being one of these dumb block bitches. You too fly for that kind of behavior."

Danna's eyes watered because Quay was right. She was too fly for it, and she was lying. She hadn't known a thing. That betrayal had cut her so deep that it was hard to keep her tears at bay. Anytime she thought about it her emotions took control. The warm tears cascading down her cheeks right then were proof of her long-lasting pain.

"Danna? Are you crying?" Quay asked. His voice was a lot softer that time. "Ah man, I didn't mean to upset you. I just don't like you playing yourself like that."

Danna sniffed. "I know. Neither do I. I didn't know."

Quay sighed. "I figured you didn't. You're too savage for that shit. You would have been beat old girl's ass if you had."

Danna's mood heightened again as laughter replaced her tears. "You're right about that, but that ain't even what I'm trying to do no more. I don't want to be in a love that drives me to be somebody I'm not. I'll fight and whoop ass all day, but I don't want to do it because my man is fucking off. Then what's the point? What am I really fighting for?"

The line was quiet, both of them in their own thoughts. Danna could hear the background noise on Quay's end so she knew he was still there, but she wanted to know what he was thinking.

"Quay?"

"What up?"

"Why you let me stay away from you all this time? Why you ain't make me yours?"

"Because I shouldn't have to make you do anything; if you were mine, you would have come willingly. You never came." Quay said something to someone in his background before directing his attention back to her. "Plus, I knew you was fucking with that old dude. I ain't the type to get in another man's way."

That was news to Danna. She'd thought she'd been as discreet as possible during her little fling with Don. How in the world had Quay known? She and Don had never gone out in public together other than when her entire family was with them. Any other time they were ducked off in his car or at his house. Never at hers, and never in public places.

"You ain't know shit." Danna played her surprise off.

"I knew enough to know you were giving my pussy to that old ass man when you should have been giving it to me."

Danna's chest sank at the same time that her eyes closed. "Quay, you're the fucking remedy, baby."

He was laughing again and making her whole night. "I could be more than that if you'd ever let me."

"What about Don?"

Quay scoffed. "You're asking me about that man like I'm supposed to be scared of his ass. You need to be asking that nigga about me. Don manipulates y'all women, I don't give a fuck about him."

See, that was that thug shit that Danna loved. If it was one thing that made her panties wet, it was a dominant man. One that didn't allow nothing or no one to intimidate him, and Quay had been that. From the first time she'd ever seen him putting in work for her father, her girl had been juicing for him ever since. He was fearless and standup about it. He didn't throw a rock and hide his hand. He owned the things he did.

"He's not going to cause you any trouble in there?"

"He can try," Quay's voice took on a more serious tone. "Listen, baby, I'm not trying to talk about that nigga all night. I have ways to handle that. You just tell me what you want from me. You said I could have a do over, your mind still on that?"

Danna looked up at her ceiling and pondered his statement. She was still in so deep with Don. They hadn't talked since the day she'd left the prison but they hadn't officially ended things and the last thing she wanted to do was mess over Quay because she wasn't ready. He was too real for her to be on some phony shit.

"I don't know yet, Quay."

"Cool. Handle your business. I'll be here when you're ready, but I ain't waiting on you."

Danna's face frowned. "What you mean you're not waiting on me?"

"I mean, I'm not Don. I'm not going to lie to you about you being the only one. If you ain't writing and talking to me somebody else will. I have needs that have to be met, boo. I ain't about to stand by watching you give your pussy to another nigga while my balls turn blue."

Why did Danna's heart break like that? It literally broke into pieces as she listened to Quay talk about giving himself to another woman. Yeah, she really needed to get herself together because she was allowing these niggas to do her too dirty. The old Danna that didn't love niggas never would have let that shit happen. She needed to shake back, and shake back in a hurry.

"Dan, I ain't trying to hurt you or nothing like that, I just don't want to lie to you either. That ain't me."

Danna sniffed, but said nothing. She was tired of crying. These niggas had her fucked up. Fuck Don and fuck Quay.

"Danna?"

"What!" she yelled.

"Whoa, calm your ass down. All that yelling is unnecessary. If you're angry then say so, but don't be doing all the fucking hollering like I'm not a grown ass man."

Yes, Daddy check me. Danna's insides leaped with momentary joy. Quay was her dream come true. She sniffed again trying to get herself together.

"Danna!" He spoke her name so forcefully that she wanted to fall to her knees in front of him and he wasn't even there.

"Yes?"

"You got you shit together?"

"Yes," she mumbled.

"That's better. Now talk to me like you've got the sense that I know you have."

A giggle escaped her tight throat. "I hate you."

"No, you don't. You love this shit that's why you got your fucking act together. I ain't Don. You ain't about to come up here to this damn jail showing your ass on me."

He and Danna both laughed.

"I be seeing you yelling and clowning on that man, wishing it was me. I'd hem you up so fast, you wouldn't dare be that defiant if I was your man."

"Yeah, yeah, yeah. Niggas love to say what they would and wouldn't take. I'd clown with your ass too, and slap you if you tried to buck."

Quay's laughter was so sexy as he chuckled at her. He laughed so hard that Danna had to join in.

"Danna, I'd beat your ass."

"Good. It needs to be beat."

"Word? I got that for you."

Danna rolled back over onto her stomach and picked up one of her locs. She was smiling bashfully as she nodded as if Quay could see her.

"I hope you do because I need it."

"Come get it then. You know where I'm at."

Danna's mouth went against everything her body was telling her. "I can't do that right now."

Quay's cleared his throat. "I know you can't. It's cool though, I'll just let another one of my li'l freaks keep it warm until you're ready."

"I hate you. Bye." Danna picked her phone up about to hang it up.

"I wish you would hang up this phone in my face."

Stopped in her tracks, Danna just held her phone in her hand afraid to hang it up. Quay had already warned her that he wasn't the type of man that let his women run over him. She didn't want to test him just yet.

"If you don't want that to go on, then change it. But as long as you're up here giving this nigga your body, I'ma do the same."

"I ain't giving that nigga shit," she spoke defiantly.

"Well then I won't either. The ball is in your court, Danna. I've been wanting you for too long to keep playing these little kid games. You think I want to watch you walk in and out of here doing all the shit for another man that you should be doing for me? Fuck no. I wanted to drag your ass out of that damn closet the day I saw you in there." Quay sucked his teeth. "In there with all your ass and shit out waiting on that old ass nigga." He fumed and Danna could finally hear the feelings that he had for her. His anger made them loud and clear. "I'm telling you now, you do that shit again, I'ma be the one fucking you. Either that or I'm knocking that nigga the fuck out, so don't try me Danna, because I'll do it for real."

The smile on her face would remain for days as she replayed this conversation in her head. Quay was the man she'd been begging God for. Everything about him was what she liked. How had she allowed herself to look over him for Don? She shook her head and chopped it up to her inexperience, because the two were drastically different, and in ways that mattered.

"I'm sorry, Quay."

"You should be."

The line was quiet as they listened to one another breathe. Danna didn't know what he was doing but she was busy picking out their wedding colors in her head. Quay was going to be her husband whether he knew it or not.

"Dan?"

"What's up, baby?" Her eyes were closed as she listened to his voice.

"Hurry up and stop playing with me, aight?"

"I am."

"When?"

"When you tell me you love me," she joked.

"I love you," he told her in the most earnest voice he'd ever used with her.

Danna's eyes squeezed tighter. "Let's get married."

"The day I get out."

Her smile got bigger. "You play so much."

"I ain't playing. I'll probably need to take a shower and shit but I'll marry you whenever and wherever."

"Oh yeah, I forgot you love me." Her giggles brought about some of his own.

"Shid, I do. I'll be even more in love once you let me get some of that loving you got. I know it's hitting right."

"And you would be correct."

Quay cursed under his breath and Danna smiled even harder.

"Let me make you cum real quick, Danna. I need to hear you moan my name."

Danna sat up on the bed, unsure of what he expected her to do. She had an idea but she'd never done that before and didn't know if she wanted to start with him. Quay would probably laugh at her or say something silly that would make her feel crazy.

"You with it?"

"Who's in the room with you?"

"My cellmate, but don't worry about him. Worry about me and how my mouth gon' feel kissing your pussy."

Danna's legs clamped together as she closed her eyes and covered her face with one of her hands.

"Take your panties off for me. I want you to play with my girl . . . let her know I love her."

Danna wasted no time pushing her pajama shorts off. She didn't wear panties to bed, so the moment her shorts hit the floor she was ready. She waited to get beneath her covers before she allowed her legs to drop open. She found her already throbbing center and covered it with her fingers. Her eyes were closed as she waited to hear his voice again.

"You touching her for me? She needs to know Daddy can't wait to see her."

"Yeah, I am." Danna's voice was a little hoarse from her excitement. "She's dripping wet for you too, Quay."

"She knows what to do when I'm on my way." Danna could hear Quay's muffled voice telling his cellmate to give him a minute. Afterwards, there was a tad bit of shuffling, then he was back. "I had to send that nigga on his way so I can get me one. I can already tell you're about to have me rocked up with that sexy ass voice."

Danna's fingers moved to the rhythm of Quay's voice. Slowly, sliding over and across her love button that was beating terribly for him.

"Quay," she whimpered. "I want to ride your dick so bad."

"It's yours baby, you can do whatever you want to do with it after I get me a taste of you. I want to run my tongue over every inch of you. I'm talking about touching titties and sucking toes, baby."

"Ohmygahhh," Danna moaned as she felt her body tensing up. "Quayyy."

"Yeahh, say my name like that," he grunted. "My dick so fucking hard right now, Dan. I can see your pretty chocolate ass sliding up and down on me right now. Drowning me in that wet, putting it all over my dick and my face. Fuck," Quay's husky voice went low for a moment. "I'm jacking my dick right now with my eyes closed so I can see your face. You're so fucking beautiful. I bet you'd look like a fucking dream with my dick inside you."

"I would, Quay. Your voice alone makes me creamy, I would be sexing you like crazy." She sped her fingers up when she heard his breathing get heavy in the phone. "You close, baby?"

"Hell yeah," he grunted.

"I wish I was there now, on my knees in front of you. I want you to grab my hair and fuck my face. I love rough shit and I know you'd dog me."

"Fucking right I would. I'd fuck the shit out of that pretty ass face. I can see your thick lips wrapped around my shit right now. Goddamn, Danna." He was breathless, as was she.

"That's right, Daddy. Fuck me deep. I want to be your favorite. I'm doing whatever it takes to make you fall apart for me."

"Tell me you love me, Dan. I'm about to bust, baby."

In the exact same spot as him, Danna gave herself all she could with visuals of Quay in her head. Moments later she could hear him inhale deeply.

"Ohhhh, Quayyyyy, I love you, Daddy," she moaned as her orgasm took over her body.

Her breathing was ragged as she fought to control the subtle tingles shooting through her body. The light sheen of sweat covering her body trickled along her skin tickling her in certain spots.

"Fucking, Danna! That was the shit, girl. Who taught you that nasty shit?"

"You. I've been daydreaming about you for years. This pussy been cumming for you and you didn't even know it."

"I swear you're trying to drive me crazy."

"I'm just being truthful."

"Keep it like that. I'll be home soon and when I get there, we're making up for lost time."

Danna lay exhausted from her long day, topped by her Quay-induced orgasm. "I'm so tired."

Quay chuckled. "Good dick will do that to you. Get you some rest. I'll hit you up again soon."

"How soon?"

"As soon as I can. It won't be too long though. Niggas just be tripping about their li'l phone and shit."

Danna didn't like the sound of that. "Why not get your own?"

"It takes too much to get a cellphone up in here and I ain't really trying to pay no nigga hundreds of dollars for no damn flip phone."

"How much are they?" Danna's voice perked up.

"Too much, but I'm straight. I don't care if I have to walk across the moon, I'll find my way to you."

Danna was smiling too hard to respond with anything witty, so she didn't.

"Go to sleep, my love. I'll get to you."

"No matter what?"

"No matter what. Peace boo."

"Quay!" she called his name in a hurry.

"What up?"

"Tell me you love me."

She could hear his low laughter.

"I love you, Danna."

Once again, she was all smiles.

"Goodnight. Dream about me, pretty girl."

"I will, Daddy."

"Yo, that daddy shit is fucking insane. Keep doing that."

"I will, goodnight." Danna told him before hanging up the phone and pulling herself from her bed.

She needed to take a shower and move to the other side. She was sticky and had wet that other side up. Once she'd gotten herself back together, she was in her bed and asleep in no time. Unfortunately, it didn't last long. Her ringing phone startled her out of her sleep. She lay there for a minute trying to decide if she felt like moving to get it. When she figured she might as well, she snatched it from the charger and looked at the screen. Her eyes rolled before she answered.

"What, Don?"

"You still mad?"

Danna yawned. "Yep."

"How long you gon' stay mad with me? You know I can't take it."

Danna lay still, not saying anything. Don was a liar, but she loved him. She'd been purposely avoiding his calls because she hadn't been ready to forgive him, but clearly that was about to go out of the window. It never failed.

"Danna, I don't give a fuck about that girl. I only love you . . . you know that right?"

"Yeah."

"Wake up and talk to me. I miss you."

Danna rolled her eyes but rubbed her eyes and sat up anyway. *Here we go again.*

Don lay in the bed listening to Danna talk to him crazy. It was clear that she was still extremely angry with him, but she was going to have to get over that. He had things to do and couldn't do them with her acting a fool. She was his ticket in and he needed her to be in accordance with his plan for it to work out. He'd finally made his mind up about what he was going to do, and didn't have much time to do it.

After hearing from an outside source that Echo had been showing up around the house a little more frequently, Don figured it was now or never. He had no more time to waste because Echo was a disappearing act and it was no telling how much longer it would be if Don allowed him to slip through his fingers again this time. He'd already been waiting months just to catch him up this time.

Wherever that nigga had been hiding, he was good as fuck with it because no matter how hard Don tried, he never caught him out in the streets. His family could believe he was out making moves, but Don knew better. The feds had that nigga tucked away in hiding somewhere. There was no way possible that he was out in the streets snitching on people and hadn't got capped for it yet. Don wasn't going for that. With one more day until he was released on his parole violation, Don had to make this hit quick.

"I'm just saying Don, I'm too good for this. I could have any nigga I want. I don't have to play second to Totiana's nasty ass."

"You're not playing second to anybody, Danna. There is nobody else but you. She's just some shit to do. I don't love her."

Danna sucked her teeth. "Fuck you. If she's just something to do how does she keep ending up pregnant?"

Don sighed because he didn't want to lie to her, but he most definitely wasn't about to tell her the truth.

"It's alright. I know you ain't got nothing to say. I don't even care though. You can have her if that's what you want."

"She ain't what I want, you are!" He yelled, allowing his anger to get the best of him. Don pinched the bridge of his nose and took a few deep breaths. "Danna, listen, I love you and that's it. When I get out of here, we're getting married and leaving this fucked up city. You hear me?"

"Yeah I hear you talking."

"So, you don't believe me?"

"Nah, your word doesn't mean much to me anymore. I need to see some actions."

"Aight, I can deal with that. Well, I'ma show you how I feel. You have my word."

Although Don could tell Danna didn't believe anything he was saying, he'd show her. The moment he touched down, he was killing her pops and kidnapping her. She'd see just how serious he was soon enough.

14

Real love, I'm searching for a real love

The smell of grits and eggs permeated throughout the house as Ezra sat at the kitchen table waiting on his mother to finish cooking. It was Saturday morning and he and his family were headed out of town for a NBA combine. With it being his senior year in college, he'd been making appearances at a lot of combines trying to get his foot in the door. A few teams had already been beating down Vonetta's front door, but he was chilling.

He hadn't been given anything firm yet, but he had a lot of great offers to consider. Coaches from all over the world wanted him for their basketball team, and were offering him major incentives to come. Vonetta was on cloud nine, and so was Echo. Even though he didn't show much excitement, Ezra knew he cared. He too had been a basketball star in his younger years, which was why Ezra started in the first place.

Although his father, Echo, had been absent most of his older life, he still pretended to care every now and then. He wasn't Ezra's favorite person in the world, but his approval still carried weight.

"You got all of your stuff ready?" Vonetta asked, as she stood in front of the stove scrambling eggs.

Bare-chested in a pair of gym shorts, Ezra leaned back in his chair. "Yes, ma'am. I packed it last night when I got home."

"You mean to tell me you had time to do something other than go to sleep?" Danna asked comically. "You got back from Cannon's house so late, I just knew you would be too tired to do anything else." Her laughter came immediately after her corny ass joke.

Ezra shot her a bird before kicking the bottom of her chair. "You always in somebody business."

Danna stood from her chair and pushed the purple flower headscarf on her head, backwards. "Not somebody's business, just yours, because you think you're grown."

Ezra's face frowned as he watched Danna walk to the refrigerator. "You need to be worried about that old lady headscarf on your head while you worried about me. What you doing over here this early in the morning anyway? Why you ain't at your own house?"

"Because I'm grown and hungry. Plus, I can be in your business if I want to be."

"Be in your own sneaky business, you're the one always sneaking off somewhere and not telling nobody where you at," Ezra burst Danna out.

Danna slapped the back of his head and rolled her eyes. "Don't worry about me."

"Both of y'all need to be worried about me putting my foot in y'all ass if y'all keep up all this damn fussing. Now shut up." Vonetta scolded them with her back still turned.

Ezra and Danna traded ugly faces at one another, but neither of them opened their mouths again. Not to each other anyway.

"Now, Ezra, Danna does need to mind her own business because my eyes are on her fast ass, but they're on you too. You have been spending a lot of time over there with Cannon lately. Don't get your ass over there and make no damn baby before you leave up out of here. You're doing something with yourself after college and I mean that."

A deep sigh came from Ezra as he slouched down in his seat. He had already known his mother was going to take Danna's bait, which was why he got so annoyed when she'd brought it up.

"Maaa," Ezra dragged her name out.

"Don't Ma me, li'l nigga. I'm just telling you. Ain't nothing wrong with hanging out with her, I'm just telling you don't get her pregnant." Vonetta turned to look at him. "You hear me li'l boy?"

"Man, ain't nobody gon' get that girl pregnant."

"Better not." Danna smirked as she leaned against the counter with her glass of orange juice.

The spatula Vonetta had been using to cook came up and pointed in Danna's face. "Leave him alone, heffa."

Danna held her hands up, surrendering, with a guilty smile plastered on her face. "What? I ain't doing nothing to him. I just don't want him running around here like Nuke and Vonnie." Danna rolled her eyes dramatically. "Kids every darn where."

Ezra sucked his teeth and Vonetta looked at him. "She ain't lying, Ezzy. Your big sister and brother have set a horrible example that you don't need to follow." Vonetta's head shook as she went back to cooking. "I've got enough grandchildren to last me a lifetime. I don't want that for you."

"Why you always single me out?" Ezra whined. "Why you don't want it for Danna?"

"I ain't singling you out, because Danna doesn't want it for herself, so I ain't worried about her. Even if she is out here fucking off," Vonetta side-eyed Danna before placing a plate of food on the table in front of Ezra. "You on the other hand, I need to keep my eye on. You and Cannon have gotten mighty close these last couple months. I don't want no shit out of y'all."

Ezra huffed and puffed to himself as he pulled his chair closer to the table and said his grace. Once he raised his head from prayer he began eating. He didn't have time to sit there listening to his mother or his nosey behind sister. He and Cannon knew what they were doing. True enough they'd been on each other like rabbits since their first sexual encounter, but it was good, so they did it a lot.

A small smile curved his lips as he thought about the way Cannon had told him she loved him in front of Jazz. That still rocked his heart any time he thought of it, and that had been almost two months ago. She'd been his baby before, but after that they really began going hard. All the girls at their school had been hating in the beginning, but Ezra didn't care. Cannon was bad, and his. He'd made sure of that every time she let him enter her.

"Is she coming with us today?" Danna interrupted Ezra's eating.

Still a little annoyed with her, he shrugged but didn't say anything.

"Eww, you ain't got to be like that. I was just joking with your stupid self."

"I ain't being like nothing. I'm just trying to eat my food."

Danna rolled her eyes and grabbed her food from Vonetta before taking a seat at the table next to him.

"Is she coming, Ezra? I think you should invite her." Vonetta voiced her opinion.

Now, Ezra was confused. "Both of y'all was just tripping about how much time I spend with her, and now y'all worried about me inviting her somewhere?" Ezra's attitude was evident, but he did his best to calm it down for his mother's sake. He didn't give a damn about Danna.

"You can stop acting like a victim. We ain't say nothing about you being with her, we just said don't get no babies, so get out of your feelings, little girl." Danna sucked her teeth and rolled her eyes at him.

"Yeah, whatever." Ezra finished his food and stood from the table.

After putting his plate into the sink, he grabbed a bottle of water and went to his room. His cellphone was on the dresser and had just begun ringing. He snatched it up, already knowing who it was because of the ringtone.

"What's going on baby?"

"Nothing, just got out of the shower. Y'all left yet?" Cannon's soft voice came over the line.

Ezra lay flat across his bed with the phone to his ear. "Not yet, why? You changed your mind about coming with me?"

Ezra held his breath awaiting her answer. He'd been asking her to tag along for weeks and she'd been declining for one reason or another every time. Since she hadn't agreed to go, he chose to keep his invitation a secret from his mother and sister. The last thing they needed was to assume he was more in love with Cannon than she was with him. That would be nothing but more problems.

"I don't know. I thought about it, but my mama hasn't gotten back to get Yara yet."

"Just bring her."

Cannon's immediate rejection was loud and clear. "Nope, nah. You don't need none of those people up there thinking this is your baby for real. You already know how she get when you're around."

Ezra's smile was bright as he thought about how attached he and Yara had gotten to one another. "Yeah, that's my baby right there. I don't know who I love the most out of y'all, you or her."

"It better be me." Cannon said through a mouth full of whatever she was eating.

"What's in your mouth? You're smacking hard as hell."

"Some cereal."

The line went quiet for a minute as Ezra listened to Cannon eat and talk to Yara about having a dirty diaper. An unexpected smile came to his face as thought of how good of a mom she might be when the time came. The way she handled Yara was such a sight to see.

"Ezzy, baby, what you doing over there, handsome?"

Ezra sat up and ran his hand over his face. "Let me come see you real quick."

"Come on, I'm here."

"Bet. You need anything before I come?"

"Nope, just you."

Ezra was blushing too hard to be standing in his room alone. With the speed of lightning, he slid his feet into his Nike flip-flops, grabbed his shirt, and headed out of his room.

"I'll call you when I'm outside."

After Cannon ended the call, Ezra slid his phone into his pocket and went into the kitchen. His mother was now sitting on the sofa watching TV. Her hands were folded across her stomach, with Danna's head resting on her thigh. She was lying down on her back with her head turned toward the television. They were both deeply enthralled in the show on the screen until he walked in. Both sets of eyes came to him.

"Where you going?" that was obviously loudmouth Danna.

Vonetta looked at him as she bit the inside of her cheek.

"I'm about to run up on Cannon really quick. I'll be right back."

"Alright now, we're leaving in a little while. Don't be over there all day." Vonetta warned.

"I won't."

"If she's going with us, bring her back with you, so we don't have to go all the way back over there to pick her up when we leave."

Ezra told her he would before kissing her cheek and heading out of the door. He was halfway down the driveway when he noticed his father's gold Cadillac pulling in. A part of him wanted to ignore him, and the other half was hoping he was there to accompany him on his visit. But with Echo being who he was, it wouldn't take Ezra long to find out what his impromptu visit was for.

"Where you headed?" Echo yelled to Ezra as he stood halfway out of his car.

"To see my girl before I leave."

Ezra watched his father's eyes dart away at the mention of him leaving. Clearly, he knew about the visit, but had no intent to join.

"Cool, well make sure you strap up. You're going somewhere, you don't want to make the same mistakes I did."

His father's words felt like a blow to his chest as he stood there, assuming he and Danna were the mistakes that his father spoke of. Nuke and Vonnie had their own daddies, and didn't give a fuck about Echo's ass. Had Ezra not been so young and naïve, he probably wouldn't have felt the same way, but he was, so he did. He'd been trying to find the good in his father for so many years that he had yet to face the fact that he really wasn't shit.

"I'll make sure I do that." Ezra cleared his throat and hit the locks to his truck before hopping in.

He cranked up and backed out of his driveway before Echo could say anything else to ruin his mood. With tears in his eyes, Ezra sniffed hard and wiped at his eyes trying to rid himself of the liquid pain that was threatening to cloud his vision. With one foot on the gas and the other on the steering wheel, Ezra sped until he reached Cannon's house.

With God looking out for him, he made it there in twenty, going above the speed limit and no ticket. Once he parked, he checked his eyes in the rearview mirror and hopped out. His long legs got him to her doorstep and knocking in no time. When the door opened, Cannon stood there in nothing but a large t-shirt and panties.

Though Ezra couldn't see her panties, he knew they were there. With one hand, she held Yara over her shoulder, with the other, she pushed her screen door open for him to walk in. Ezra closed the door behind him as soon as he was all the way in, and just stood there. With his back pressed to the door, he crossed his legs at the ankle and gave her his attention.

"What's wrong, Ezra?" Cannon walked closer to him.

"How you know something wrong with me?"

Cannon's head tilted as she gave him a sympathetic smile. "Because the lights behind your eyes are out."

Why her words weighed so heavily on his emotional state at that moment, he had no idea, but the moment he heard her speak about his eyes, they watered again. He did his best to wipe the tears away, but they kept coming. Cannon turned away from him quickly and went into the living room. When she came back, she no longer had Yara.

Ezra's eyes searched for her until they landed on her little bassinet. She was in it, sound asleep, and not thinking about his crybaby ass. Cannon on the other hand was a totally different story. Her arms went around him the moment she was back in his space. As much as Ezra wanted to cry and just let out his feelings, he didn't want to do it in front of Cannon like that.

He sniffed his tears back as much as he could while hugging her. Her thick body was always so soft and welcoming. Her curves filled his arms with little to no effort.

"Tell me what's the matter." Cannon's hand rubbed up and down his back as she urged a confession.

"Nothing, just my deadbeat daddy."

"Aww, Ezzy, it's okay. He's going to regret not being here for you."

Ezra nodded against her shoulder because he'd heard that before from his mother and believed it just as much when she'd said it.

"What'd he do?" Cannon questioned.

Ezra pulled away from Cannon and grabbed her hand without saying anything. He pulled her into the living room where he picked Yara up and cradled her to his chest. He placed kisses all over her head and rocked her close to his chest. Her small body squirmed in his grasp for a few seconds until she released a loud yawn and relaxed.

Ezra closed his eyes as he lay his head against hers. Even though Yara wasn't his baby he'd grown so attached to her that she might as well be his. The way she made him feel was beyond words. He'd loved his nieces and nephews for years and the one thing that stood out amongst them all was how peaceful he felt when he was in their presence. Babies were a blessing.

"I don't know how my daddy is okay with being the way he is. Like, how do you have kids and not want to be there for them? That's crazy as hell to me. I ain't gon' ever do that when I have mine."

Cannon stood fidgeting with the hem of her t-shirt and nodding. "I know you're not."

Ezra's eyes found hers and held their gaze for a little while before they traveled down the front of her body. Braless, Cannon had his mind bouncing from one thing to another. Before he could stop himself, a small chuckle came.

"What you laughing at?"

Ezra ran one hand over his face. "Man, I need some help, baby."

Cannon's face showed how perplexed his change in attitude had her. "Uh, yeah, you do." She looked away before taking a seat on the sofa, making his thoughts go even deeper.

"I was sitting here on the verge of crying but then I looked at you and I can see your nipples through your shirt and it made me want to suck 'em."

Cannon palmed her forehead and shook her head simultaneously. "Oh my god, Ezra. You're terrible."

Ezra burst into laughter. "I know man, that's what I was saying." He took a seat on the sofa across from her still rocking Yara. "Then you sat down and your thighs spread out on the sofa and it made me think about how I be kissing on them when I be eating you out."

"Oh Lord, Ezra please stop." Cannon pulled her shirt down as much as she could, trying her best to cover her exposed legs.

"You'd might as well stop. You already know you can't hide from me."

"Clearly, pervert."

Ezra's laughter flicked the light in his eyes back on. He was laughing so hard, he almost missed Cannon staring at him.

"What? You thinking about sex now too?"

"No, nigga. I'm thinking about how your lights came back on. Sex shouldn't make you that happy. You need to be ashamed of yourself."

"It's not just sex, it's sex with you." Ezra leaned over and lay Yara down on the sofa cushion. "I be feeling like I'm married to you when we have sex. You make me feel like a grown man."

"What?"

Ezra smiled and nodded at Cannon. "For real. Anytime I'm with you I be feeling like I'm your husband."

Cannon's laughter took the place of Ezra's as she tried to cover her smile. "How I make you feel like that?"

Ezra shrugged. "I don't know. I don't know if it's your body or the way you be working it. Whatever it is makes me feel like a grown man in the pussy."

Cannon's face turned bright red as she hid her face with both of her hands. Ezra's smile was big as he watched her blush from his words. It was still so comical to him how he easily he made her blush.

"When we graduate and leave Columbus, you're not going to be with another man are you?"

Cannon removed her hands and looked at him with a straight face. "No, but I bet you're going to have other girls. You're too cute not to. Then you're going to be an athlete. You're going to have women everywhere."

"No, I'm not. I only want you."

"That's what you're saying now, but I know once we're not together anymore that's going to change."

"You don't know that, so don't say it."

"I'm not crazy, Ezra. I already know you're going to cheat then eventually break up with me. I'm just waiting on it."

Ezra could hear their conversation taking a turn for the worse, so he moved from the sofa and kneeled in front of her. He kissed both of her knees before replacing his lips with his open palms.

"We're going to be together forever. Watch and see. You're going to be my wife."

Cannon smiled but he could still see the doubt in her eyes. Ezra wanted to do whatever he could to reassure her that he would be there, but words would probably fail him, so instead he kissed her. They kissed and touched until she felt better, and it was time for him to go. He begged and pleaded for her to go on his visit with him, but she continuously refused so he stayed a little while longer before leaving. Whether she believed him or not, Cannon would indeed be his wife one day.

Two months later . . .

"So, you want me to bring her to you?" Cannon asked for the third time to be sure she'd heard her mother right.

"Yes, Cannon." Karina snickered. "I know how to take care of my own baby, girl."

Cannon laughed too. "I'm just checking because I can take her with me."

"No, you go shop with your friend. I'll keep her. Thank you though, Cannon ball. I don't know what I would do without you."

"You're welcome. We'll be there in a few."

Karina blew her air kisses before hanging up the phone. Cannon tossed the phone onto her bed and continued putting Yara's diapers and wipes into her baby bag. It was the last week of school and she, Ezra, and Danna were about to go to the mall to get their clothes for their graduation party. Cannon hadn't been too concerned with her graduation attire, but between Karina and Vonetta, she'd practically been forced into it.

Somehow, the two of them had conspired to have her and Ezra's graduation party together, and the pressure had been on ever since. From combines and training camps, to prom, to signing day, the two of them had done it together. Danna only came around when she wasn't off somewhere with whoever she spent all her time with.

Cannon and Ezra had concluded that she had to have a secret boyfriend somewhere that no one knew about. She spent so much time acting as if she didn't love niggas, but Cannon was sure she was lying. Only a man would keep you ducked off the way Danna always was. She could tell that single lie to Vonetta and Ezra all she wanted, Cannon knew better.

"Okay, I got all your stuff together for Karina, can you please just behave yourself today?" Cannon cooed to Yara.

She was lying on the bed biting on her fists and staring at Cannon as she moved around the room getting them both ready to leave. It took her a little over ten more minutes before they were out of the house and heading to the hair salon where Karina was. It took Cannon no time to drop her off and get to Ezra's house. She'd parked and was pulling the screen door open when Ezra grabbed her.

His face was bright with a smile as he hugged her to his tall body. Since in his arms was her favorite place to be, she went willingly.

"You must have saw me pull up?"

"Nah, I heard your music. I already told you to stop playing it so loud, hard-headed ass girl."

Cannon was all smiles as she stared at the handsome young king that had stolen her heart. "I'm always something when it comes to you."

"You're always my baby, how about that?" Ezra's mouth found hers as his hands pulled her to him tighter.

"Here we go," Danna's voice broke their kiss. "Y'all always up on each other. Can y'all not do that in front of me today? I honestly don't want to see it."

They both laughed, but remained entangled in their embrace.

"You ain't got to worry about it, I ain't going with y'all today."

Cannon looked up at Ezra quickly. "What? Why not?"

"Why you ain't?"

Both women got into his business immediately.

"I got some stuff to handle, y'all go head. I'll catch back up with you later, baby." Ezra looked at Cannon as he finished talking.

Cannon's mood changed as soon as she found out he was no longer going with her. As unhealthy as it sounded, she wanted to spend all her time with him, so for him to be trying to dip on her made her wonder. With her face frowned in confusion, Cannon watched Ezra for any sign of disloyalty. She found none. Instead, she was rewarded with a smile that brought about one of her own.

"What, Cannon?"

"Nothing, I'm just trying to figure out what you got going on."

Danna walked up and grabbed Cannon's arm. "Girl, come on. His dusty ass ain't finna' do nothing."

Cannon was reluctant to let Danna pull her away, but she went anyway. Her eyes stayed on Ezra until she was wrapped back in his arms. He was behind her walking her to the car. His lips kissed the side of her face repeatedly as she held on to her attitude.

"Stop pouting. I just need to go do something really quick. I'll be here when you get back."

Cannon still didn't say anything.

"I already told you I'ma come spend the night with you tonight. Why you acting so mad?"

Cannon was doing her best to relax, but it was hard. She wanted to be with him. She enjoyed hanging out with Danna, but being with Ezra was better.

"Chile, get away from this nigga for a minute." Danna encouraged. "He wasn't gon' do nothing but cock block all day anyway."

Ezra chuckled at his sister before turning Cannon around so that he could see her face. He pecked her forehead once before squeezing her in a tight hug.

"You gon' let me get some later?" He whispered in her ear before sticking his tongue in it.

Cannon's whole body jumped as she shied away. "Yeah," her smile was wide as she felt herself getting hot.

Ezra's eyes shined down on her as he bit his bottom lip while staring at her. His hair was pulled back in a long braid showing his whole face. He was so chocolatey and handsome.

"I can't wait. I been thinking about you all day."

"Well why you ain't coming with me then?"

Ezra pecked her mouth again. "Because I have something to do. Just go with my sister and have fun. I'll be here when you get back."

Cannon crossed her arms and continued to pout until Ezra pecked her lips.

"Just text me while you're gone. I'll talk to you all day."

Oddly, that made her feel better, so she agreed. They hugged and kissed once more before she joined Danna in her Altima and pulled off. Cannon didn't know what Ezra had going on, but she'd let him do his thing. They literally spent every minute together since they were about to leave for school, so maybe he just wanted to hang out with some of his friends for a change. Either way, she was missing him already.

"I'm gon' die when I move to Atlanta for grad school and I don't have your brother," Cannon vented dramatically.

Danna looked at her with her nose turned up. "Bitch, you need to get a grip. Ezra cute and all, but that nigga ain't all that."

Cannon burst out laughing. Danna was so raw.

"You need to let your secret man out of hiding and fall in love."

"Why, so I can be like you? No, thank you. I ain't got time for that sucker shit. I'm too playa for that."

"You can keep telling yourself that, but I know you're lying. You've got a man somewhere around here. You always sneaking off, or hanging out by yourself. Ain't that much alone time in the world, hoe. You can fool your mama and brother, but I ain't buying that shit. Somebody's got your behind out here running." Cannon looked at Danna with a smirk on her face. "I'll meet him soon enough."

Danna was smiling and laughing uncontrollably. "Girl, gone."

"Nah, you gone. You love to come for me and my boo like you ain't on the same mess. I know better. I be watching you. You think you're slick."

More laughs came from Danna. Further proving Cannon right.

"Guilty ass." Cannon laughed with her.

"Listen, don't watch me. Watch yourself. I'm good over here."

"I just bet you are, Mrs. Sneaky."

"Whatever nosey ass girl."

Cannon shook her head. "You and your brother kill me always talking like that."

Danna and Cannon shared more laughs all the way to the mall. The more Cannon relaxed, the more she realized hanging with Danna without Ezra was in fact a good time. They were free to laugh and talk about stuff that would never fly if Ezra was around. Maybe she would be alright when school started. Especially since she and Danna had gotten close like best friends. Now she had somebody to talk to and hang out with outside of Ezra. Hopefully she wouldn't have Cannon doing too much, but then again, maybe a change of pace wouldn't be too bad.

15

That's what friends are for

Cannon's eyes darted over to Danna again for the thousandth time within the last couple of minutes. She looked her up and down again before stopping on her face. She was holding her phone to her ear and looking crazy but hadn't said anything. The look on her face warned Cannon that there was clearly something wrong with her, but she didn't know what it could have been because Danna was quiet as a church mouse.

She'd considered asking her what was wrong, or taking the phone to see what she was listening to, but she didn't. Invading Danna's personal business wasn't the first thing on Cannon's to-do list, but it wasn't scratched off either. If she kept following behind her looking like a lost puppy, Cannon was about to do some digging. Especially, since sadness was the one thing that hadn't been in Danna's character since Cannon's first time meeting her.

"You ready to go?" Cannon mouthed to Danna as they neared the exit of the mall.

Danna nodded but didn't say anything. Cannon led them from the mall and to Danna's car. Danna hit the locks and they got in. It was on the tip of Cannon's tongue to ask what the hell was the problem, but she restrained herself. If Danna wanted to tell her, she would. The ride out of the parking lot was extremely quiet and awkward as hell as Cannon watched Danna drive with the phone still pressed against her ear.

When she could no longer take the silence, Cannon reached to turn the radio up, but Danna slapped her hand. Not hard enough to hurt, but enough to halt Cannon's movement. With a quick roll of her eyes, Cannon sat back and looked out of the window. When she noticed they weren't going in the direction of Ezra's house, she turned in her seat and whispered.

"Where we going?"

Danna held up one finger to silence her. Cannon was nearly annoyed when Danna stopped at the traffic light and slammed her open palm across her chest.

"What's wrong, Danna?" Cannon questioned, overly concerned.

Danna's head fell forward onto the steering wheel as she held her hand over her chest with one hand and the phone to her ear with the other. It was driving Cannon crazy, so instead of questioning her further, she snatched the phone from Danna's ear and put it to hers. Danna put up a weak fight that Cannon overpowered easily.

There was a conversation happening, but Cannon couldn't really hear it good enough to make anything of it. There was a man and a woman arguing, but that was it. Still nothing that made sense, so Cannon pressed the phone further into her ear to gain a better understanding of what had Danna so upset, but when she couldn't understand it, she just handed Danna the phone back. She'd driven away from the light and was now parked in the parking lot of Burger King with water in her eyes.

"Danna, what is all of this?"

Danna's sad eyes turned to Cannon as she shrugged. "I don't know."

"Yes, you do." Cannon's eyes went to the name on the caller ID. "Is D your nigga?"

Danna nodded slowly.

"Kind of. We stopped kicking it for a while because I got mad, but we ended up getting back right."

"Cool, is this him talking?"

Another nod from Danna made Cannon's stomach flip.

"Did he call you?"

"That's what I'm trying to figure out because from where he at, he shouldn't have been able to, but that's what got me tripping." Danna scratched her head in confusion. "That's his baby mama I heard him talking to. I just don't understand how or why they're together."

"What you mean? How you know this her?" Cannon was lost as hell and Danna wasn't making any type of sense.

"This some bullshit, Cannon," Danna ran her hand over her face quickly before throwing her car back into gear. "I know it is, but I'm about to find out today. I can promise you that."

"Danna, what's some bullshit?"

"This nigga, but I bet you I kill his ass today. Watch me." Danna's head nodded in reassurance of her words as she sped out of the parking lot like a madwoman.

Still as confused as she'd been the whole time, Cannon watched her without saying anything. She had too many questions at once that Danna had yet to answer, but judging by the angry look of determination on Danna's face, she was certain she would be finding out soon enough.

"Can you at least tell me what's going on so I can know what you're getting me into?"

Danna's face remained the same as she mumbled stuff to herself about him having her fucked up and how she was going to kill him. Cannon's mind was completely blown, but she was down for whatever Danna was down with, so she just sat back and rode.

"Danna?"

"What, bitch? Don't you see me over here thinking?"

Cannon looked at her for a minute before laughing. "Don't yell at me cuz your nigga fucking off. I'm just trying to see what you want to do when we get there."

Danna snickered to herself before making a quick left turn. "Fight her."

"Bet."

A small smile curved Danna's lips. "Bet? So, you're down to beat their ass?"

"I'm game."

Danna nodded again before smiling mischievously. "Bitch, you don't even know these people, talking about you with what I'm with. They could be stone cold killers and you talking about fighting."

Cannon looked at Danna like she was crazy. "Well, that makes you just as dumb as me. It was your idea, I'm just not about to let you cut the fool by yourself. If you hitting, I'm hitting." Cannon shrugged as if it was no big deal.

"Ezra gon' kill me for having you in the shit."

"Don't tell him."

Danna nodded but didn't say anything else as she drove. The car grew too peaceful for Cannon's liking, so she changed the slow song that was on Danna's phone to something more upbeat and fitting. When Yo Gotti's "Shawty Violating" blasted through the speakers, Danna looked at her with a wide smile on her face.

"Man, Cannon you so fucking stupid. What you turn this shit on for?"

Cannon grabbed her hair that had been resting on her shoulders into her palms and began smoothing it into a ponytail.

"Because that crybaby ass song you just had on made me want to cry, not fight, and I'll be damned if you make me get my ass beat because I'm sad and not mad." Cannon tied her hair back with the rubber band she'd taken off Ezra's wrist before they left his house. "I need to hear fighting music so I can get ready to take these hits."

The feminine laughter floating around the car was a joy to hear until Danna's car came to a slow stroll. She'd just turned into a neighborhood filled with brick houses, and had been driving slower ever since. She was looking out of the window, clearly looking for something in particular, when she pointed at the red car parked along the side of the street, she pulled over and parked.

"Why you park way back here if that's the house?"

Danna was busy snatching her earrings off as she answered. "So, they don't see me coming."

"Fuck that, let them see."

Danna shook her head. "Nah, this ain't that hoe house, this her mama house. Bitch ain't even got her own spot. Grown ass." Danna's rant continued.

"How old is she?"

"Thirty."

Cannon's mouth fell open. "What? What that nigga want with that old ass lady?"

Danna stopped moving and looked at Cannon with a smile on her face. "He older than her."

Cannon's eyes bucked as she sat back in her seat dramatically and covered her face. "Lord, we going to jail for fighting these old ass people. How old is he?"

"Old enough to be my daddy."

"You need your ass beat," Cannon shook her head at Danna. "I'm still with it though." Cannon checked her face in the mirror and began removing her necklace and earrings. "I knew your sneaky butt had a man. Now I see why you kept him a secret. He old as hell."

Danna was smiling again. "Nah, that ain't why I'm hiding him. I'm hiding that nigga because he one of my daddy workers. If Vonetta knew I was laid up with the OG, she'd beat my ass to death."

"Ah shit, you stay bucking. Is he somebody I know? Have I seen him before?"

Danna shook her head. "Nah, he's been away since you've been around. You don't know him."

The two of them laughed together again before the car suddenly got quiet. Danna sat back in her seat, just staring at the house. She'd turned the music down and bitten her bottom lip, obviously in deep thought. Cannon wasn't sure why, but she wasn't about to wait too long.

"Look, I'm hype now so let's go get it. If I calm down I might not be as strong."

Danna was laughing again. "Man, I swear I'm sick of your ass preparing for this fight."

"Shoot, we need to. We done pulled up on these people we need to be ready to scrap, bitch. I ain't getting beat up."

Danna looked at her with a frown on her face. "Neither am I."

"You sit there too long, yes you is, too."

Danna shook her head. "Nah, for real I'm trying to decide whether or not I'm finna' take my gun or my bat up in here."

"What the fuck? A gun?"

"Yeah, you think Vonetta my mama and I ain't got no heat?" Danna leaned forward and pulled her gun from under the seat. The black gun was shiny and looked heavy as hell. "I don't play, Cannon. My mama ain't taught me to be no hoe, that's why I'm chilling because I'm mad enough to go shoot his ass right now. Plus, that nigga big as hell, he can pick me up with one hand, so I might have to shoot his ass."

"Oh, see hell nah. I ain't got time for this." Cannon sat back and started to shake her head. "He ain't gon' do nothing to you because you his woman, but he might knock me the fuck out."

Danna shook her head while opening her door. "No, he ain't. I got you. Go get that bat out my trunk."

On cue with Danna's words, her trunk popped open. Cannon looked back before opening her door and hopping out behind Danna. She met her at the trunk and took the steel bat she was extending to her. Cannon's hands began to shake as she thought about how real this fight was about to get. She'd meant she was down with what Danna was down with, but that was before she knew Danna had weapons.

"Don't let that nigga hurt me, Danna." Cannon whispered as they walked down the street.

"I got you, sis," was all Danna said.

Her face was serious as she held her gun down by her side. The aura exuding from her was totally different from the one she'd had in the car. She looked to be on some other shit right then. Her face was straight, devoid of any type of emotion. No tears, no talking, no nothing. She wasn't even shaking, which was odd to Cannon, because anytime she got too nervous or too hyped, she could barely keep herself still. Much like right then. Danna was clearly a different breed of woman. The way she walked with so much relaxation and power made Cannon feel somewhat untouchable as well. Danna was so confident in her steps, that it almost wiped Cannon's fears away. Almost.

Her long locs were pulled back into a ponytail, swinging against the middle of her back, while the subtle frown on her face yelled to the neighborhood that she wasn't to be fucked with. Vonetta had raised a real-life girl gangster. Danna wasn't fucking around, and it low-key made Cannon want to be like her. Even with her still not knowing the full story, she was sure she wouldn't have been handling it as well as Danna was.

"You ready, Cannon?" Danna looked at her with bold eyes as they approached the front door to the house.

"Yep."

"Bet, don't be no hoe when we get up in here. Use that fucking bat."

"I got you." Cannon reassured Danna just as she snatched open the glass screen door to the house.

The butt of Danna's gun sounded against the front door as she banged on it with all her might. Cannon's heart jumped with each pound of the gun. On one hand, she was scared it would accidentally go off, and on the other she was scared what would happen when the door finally swung open. Her anticipation was cut short the moment the lock began to turn. Oh hell! What the fuck had Danna gotten her into?

16

I may be young but I'm ready

Danna's mind was on one hundred as she stood face to face with the one hoe that had been giving her problems from sun up to sun down any free moment she got. Totiana, or Tot, as the streets called her, was a tall red bitch that thought she was God's gift to niggas. Trashy, but hood classic at its finest. She was one of those hoes that fucked with you for what you could do for her, and nothing more. How in the hell had she gotten stuck with Don was Danna's biggest question? His stupid ass.

Tot's long burgundy bundles of weave in her head fell around her face as her light skin grew brighter from anger. The scanty clothes she had on showed how much class she lacked, as the round stomach full of stretch marks poked from her crop top displaying the one "up" she had on Danna when it came to her nigga.

Her eyes went from Danna's face to the gun in her hand. Though Danna could tell it took her nerve, she saved face and threw her weave over her shoulder, slapping the baby right across his dirty face. He was wrapped around one of her hips, with a nasty onesie on and face full of dried up snot. Danna frowned immediately.

"Bitch, go get Don and get this li'l dirty ass fucker out of my face."

Tot's face distorted in fury as she took a step toward Danna, totally forgetting about the gun she'd been holding until it was pointed in her face.

"Bitch, go get Don before I come in here and get him myself."

"He ain't here."

Danna chuckled in disbelief. "Yes, the fuck he is. Go get his ass right now and leave that crusty ass baby back there so I can beat your ass once I get done with Don's."

Danna's chest heaved up and down as she and Tot glared at each other. Tot could think she was playing if she wanted to, but she would real live walk up in that bitch's mama house and drag Don's ass out of there.

"Don't keep talking about my baby, Danna. I'm trying to stay off your ass because you're young and I'm pregnant, but you're pushing it."

Danna turned around and handed Cannon her gun before looking back at Tot. "Don't do me no favors, hoe. That's what I been waiting on. I don't give a fuck about that damn baby." With her fists balled up and swinging lightly at her sides, Danna taunted Tot with a smile on her face. "Come out and do something."

"Man, Danna, care your young ass home."

With a small chuckle and a shake of her head, Danna pushed past Tot, palming her whole face along the way. She made sure to push her head into the door as she moved. Cannon was hot on her heels bumping into Tot as well as they rushed into the house.

"Don!" Danna yelled while walking through the living room. The older lady seated on the sofa looked alarmed as she moved to protest. "Don! Bring your ass out here right muthaf—"

Danna's words were cut off by the large stature of a man rounding the corner. In nothing but a white tank top and some black sweatpants, Don, the muscled, drug-dealing, hardcore, life-taking criminal, stood face to face with the one thing that made him weak. His fresh haircut and long beard were lined to perfection, further angering Danna. This nigga had gone out and gotten cute for that bitch Tot, and hadn't told her shit. Rage rushed through Danna's veins as she thought about him disregarding her and going straight to Tot's hoe ass.

"I'm finna' kill your ass." Danna's hand moved, momentarily forgetting she'd given Cannon her gun. "Cannon, give me my heat." Danna's words showed her history in the streets.

She was used to being the main chick to a street nigga, even if it was on the low, and she was about to show him that even though he obviously had forgotten who she was, she hadn't.

Don's hazel eyes went to Cannon quickly before the vein in his jaw flexed. With cold eyes staring back into hers, Danna stood unmoved and angrier than she'd ever been in her life. Her heart was beating, and her body was shaking. She could literally feel the heat encompassing her, as thoughts of him fucking Tot as soon as he touched down crossed her mind. She'd wanted to be his welcome home, but clearly he and Tot had other plans.

"Give me my gun, Cannon!" Danna yelled again.

"Oh Lord!" The older lady that had been seated on the sofa screamed before running from the room.

"Don, get this baby ass rat out my mama house." Tot's annoying yell came from behind Danna. "If you don't, I will."

"Bitch, you ain't gon' do shit but shut the fuck up and let Danna talk to her nigga." Cannon's voice simmered the rapid beating of Danna's heart. For a second she'd felt overwhelmed with the decision of who she was going to handle first. "I ain't Danna, I'll beat your ass with the baby in your arms."

Again, Don's eyes went to Cannon. His massive presence in the living room said everything he wasn't saying. Even though he hadn't opened his mouth yet, Danna could tell by his posture and oddly enough, his silence, that he was just as mad as she was. Don had been a quiet dude for as long as she'd known him. Never saying more than necessary, and especially in moments of irrationality.

"The fuck you doing here, Danna? Bringing strangers to my

kid's crib and shit." Don's voice boomed, but it didn't scare Danna one bit. After all she'd been to that nigga, she'd punch his ass right in the mouth.

"What am I doing here? Nigga, the fuck you doing here? The last time I checked you was supposed to still be locked up somewhere, when the fuck you got out?"

"Oh shit," Cannon's words were just above a whisper, but Danna heard her.

She even smirked a little at the surprise in her voice.

"Danna, let's go outside and talk."

Danna's head began to shake instantly. "Nah, tell me when you got out. It was obviously recently because I just talked to your ass the other night. Got your li'l haircut and shit. Oh, you getting fine for this hoe huh?"

"Chill, Danna. Let's go outside."

"Fuck no, Don! Stop playing with me." Danna spun around quickly and snatched her gun from Cannon. She shot Tot an evil glare. "Hoe, you getting this ass whooping today, pregnant and all. Just wait on it."

Cannon's eyebrows raised as she looked at Danna. "You want me to go ahead and do it for you? I don't give a fuck about her being pregnant, shit, her head ain't."

Danna looked at Cannon for a minute, weighing her invitation. She wanted to get Tot for herself, but right then she really wanted to get in Don's ass.

"Let me know, because I'll skull drag her all around her mama's shit." Cannon looked Tot up and down. "Her skinny ass."

"Aye, Danna, get all this shit up out of here." Don's tone of voice showed his anger. "You know I ain't even the one for all this messy shit."

"Yeah, you go ahead and handle him because he clearly has a problem with you being at his baby mama's house with him." Cannon relayed with plenty of disgust and attitude to burn the house down.

"Bitch, you better shut up before I knock your ass out." Don pointed at Cannon and told her coldly.

"Sure, you are."

"Don, you need to handle this shit." Tot's unwanted opinion warranted her a slap from Cannon's left hand.

Scuffling came soon after that. Danna wanted to watch what was about to happen, but movement from Don grabbed her attention instead. He was trying to get to where Cannon and Tot had just begun exchanging licks.

"You ignoring me for this hoe, Don?" Danna yelled while raising her gun. "Ahhh, I hate you!" She yelled in pain and anger.

Don's attention came to her rapidly. With one swift motion, he took her gun and snatched her body to him. Danna fought with everything she had in her to get out of his grasp. Nothing worked until he'd just dragged her out of the house, and she bit him, trying to get back inside the screen door.

"Stay your muthafuckin ass still." He yelled.

"Fuck no!" Danna followed him right back into the house.

He was in the middle of snatching Cannon off Tot when he slapped Cannon so hard she fell to the floor. A feeling Danna couldn't even describe cursed through her body as she searched for her gun. When she didn't see where it was, she snatched the bat that was on the floor next to Don's nasty faced ass son. Without even thinking about it, she swung it at Don and hit him across his back.

"Fuck! Danna!" He pushed her backward with one hand while snatching Cannon up by her shirt and dragging them both from the house.

Both girls were kicking, screaming, and putting up the fight of their lives, as he handled them with no effort. Once they were both outside and in the middle of the yard he pointed at Cannon again.

"Bitch, you better get your ass on. Danna knows better than to pull this shit. She's about to end your life for no fucking reason," he bellowed.

Danna looked to Cannon who was standing her ground. She was breathing hard and looked on the verge of charging at that nigga at any minute, and because Danna didn't know what she was really capable of, she intervened. The last thing she wanted was for her to test Don and he snap her neck or some shit they couldn't come back from.

"Cannon, just go get my gun and get in the car. We're about to dip. Fuck this nigga."

Cannon stood still, not acknowledging nothing Danna had said. Instead she kept her gaze on Don, who was also unmoving.

"I'm good, Cannon. Just get my shit so we can go."

Cannon looked at Danna. "This what you want to do?"

"Yeah, go head."

Cannon walked past him slowly, headed for the house, keeping her eyes on Don the whole time.

"Bitch, keep watching me like you got some shit on your heart, and see don't I kill your dumb ass."

"Nigga, fuck you." Cannon spoke at the same time Danna rushed to get in Don's face.

Cannon was seriously trying that nigga. Danna chopped it up to her not really knowing who that nigga was. Either that or she had some real heart, and Danna could definitely fuck with that.

"Don, this really what you doing? Talking to this bitch at my house?" Tot's maggot ass was back at the door with her whining.

"Don't worry, bitch, I'm about to go. You can have this nigga." Danna said, in front of Don.

When he finally turned away from Cannon and looked at Danna, she acted as if she didn't see him. Instead she watched Cannon push Tot out the way and walk back into the house to find her gun.

"Bitch, get out my friend's business and come help me find this damn gun before I finish beating your ass."

Danna chuckled before looking back at Don. His eyes were dark, but not as cold as they had been. His body was tense and his mouth was balled up.

"Why you come over here like this?"

"Shit, you came. I thought this was the meetup spot."

"Stop talking to me like you don't know who the fuck I am."

Danna rolled her eyes. "I ain't. I'm talking to you like you don't know who the fuck I am. I been holding your ass down this whole time and the moment you get out, you run over here? You ain't even tell me you were home. That's fucked up, Don." Her voice broke as her emotions got the best of her. With watering eyes, she stared at him. "You just don't give a fuck about me, do you?"

"Quit that shit. You know I love you. All of this with Tot ain't shit. I had her come scoop me so I could surprise your ass."

"You're a fucking liar, Don." Danna shook her head and wiped her tears away. "I'm good though, if you want that hoe, you can have her ass." A few sniffles came again as she tried to keep her tears at bay. "It's funny that you chose her over me though, because she's probably the one that called me."

Confusion was written all over his face. "The fuck you talking about?"

"How you think I knew you was here? The damn prison surely didn't call and tell me." Danna shook her head at his ignorance. "Dumb ass." She mumbled before trying to walk away from him.

"Nah, you stay on some bullshit. Ain't no telling how you found out. You're just blaming it on that damn girl."

Danna was flabbergasted at how he was defending Tot. If him being there hadn't done it for her, that had surely sealed the deal. With a disbelieving sigh, Danna looked him up and down with pain filling her chest.

"Fuck you, Don."

"You ain't going nowhere. I don't even know why you're playing. What we got don't come this easy."

"It sure as hell don't. That's why you were a fool to let his hoe trick you up out of it."

Don grabbed Danna and pulled her back to him. "Danna, come on baby, stop it. I was really coming to surprise you. All of this was for you. You know don't nobody love me like you do."

Danna was motionless in his arms.

"Baby?" his voice softened. "Please don't do this." He ran his nose along the side of her face and neck. "Danna, I love you baby, please don't be mad at me. I promise this was for you."

Danna's heart was breaking as she listened to him plead with her. "You could have just called me to come, I would have come. It still could have been a surprise."

"I know you would have, but I really wanted to surprise you. I needed to make up for all of this shit I've put you through."

Danna's tears finally escaped the corners of her eyes. "So, you telling her you love her and you're going to do right by her and your boys so y'all can be a family was what? A lie? Because it sounded pretty truthful to me." Danna surprised him with the words she'd heard him speak to Tot earlier when she'd heard them over the phone. "I already took you back after the bitch mysteriously got pregnant, with your lying ass."

"I know, Danna, I'm sorry."

"You not even supposed to have that raggedy ass baby with her!" Danna screamed as his most recent betrayal resurfaced in her mind.

Don's silence let her know that he was caught. Danna shook her head as she watched him realize there was no way out of the hole he'd dug himself into.

"Just put me down."

Don held her closer to him, hugging her tight to his chest. "I don't want to hurt you, Danna."

"Too late."

The heavy sigh he released made Danna's soul shake. It was clear he was earnestly sorry, but so was she, and sorry wasn't about to do shit for either one of them.

"I know I fucked up, but I don't want you to leave me, Danna."

"Yeah, neither do I, but I didn't want you to choose your baby mama over me either, but it's life, right?"

"No! No, the fuck it ain't life. You're tripping right now."

Danna wiggled, trying to release herself from his grasp. "Please put me down." Her words stirred up some more.

Being in his embrace was beginning to be too much for her. She couldn't ignore her feelings for him, being that close to him. She needed to get away, right then. She had to go. With the little fight she had left, Danna pushed at his chest trying to break free from his stronghold on her. His arms felt like vice grips, slowly sucking all the fight out of her.

"Don, please," she sobbed weakly. It irritated her how her weakness for him was beginning to show. "Let me go." She allowed her head to fall forward onto his shoulder. "Please just get off me. You did this to me, let me down so I can heal."

"The fuck you need to leave me to do that for? I can heal you right here with me." Don's head began to shake adamantly. "Fuck nah. I ain't letting you leave me."

"You ain't got no fucking choice!" She yelled in rising anger. "You did this to me, so you have to deal with this shit." She grabbed his face and looked at him. "I'm too strong for this weak shit you got me in. Leave me the fuck alone and let me move on. Don't keep puppy dogging me to come back to you because you know I will, so just move out my way and let me see past you."

Danna wiggled and fought while Don held her with emotion pouring from his eyes. She knew what they had was past real. No matter what anybody said, no matter the age difference, none of that shit mattered. Love was love, and they'd shared some real moments of it. This nigga was truly her everything and he'd hurt her in one of the worst ways. Hell nah, she had to go.

"Danna."

"Stop calling my fucking name, Don. Go be with her."

"But I want you."

"No, you want both of us, and you can't have it like that. I'm out." Danna told him as he finally released her. "Fuck all y'all niggas. Y'all don't do shit but hurt people. You can't never be real with no nigga because y'all don't do shit but fuck over people feelings, but nah," Danna shook her head adamantly. "I'm too good for this shit. You take that hoe and live happily ever after with her and that dirty ass baby that looks just like your sneaky ass." Danna glowered at him. "You too old for this immature bullshit."

Don's chest sank as he stood in front of her stuffing his hands in her pockets trying to save face. The nigga was clearly hurting behind the situation, but was doing his best to hide it. Danna didn't care either way, his feelings was his business. Danna stared at him getting sadder by the second, but not really wanting to look away.

"You're the last person I wanted to hurt. You're my fucking baby, Danna." He reached to grab her as she began backing away.

Danna snatched her hand away and shook her head. "Leave me alone!" She screamed in agony.

"Danna, No! You ain't fucking leaving me. We ain't never gon' be over." Don's voice raised as he began walking towards her.

Danna's hands went to both of her ears as she did her best to not hear the words he was saying. Why wouldn't he just stop, and leave her alone.

"Me and you gon' always be together. You mine. I ain't never felt like this, I'm not letting you leave me." He was finally able to snatch her to him and hold her. "And I mean that."

Danna's mind went blank. She couldn't think, all she could do was feel and it was making her want to find her gun and shoot herself.

"Cannon!" She yelled in desperation. "Cannon, please come help me. Make him leave me alone." Danna cried hysterically.

Unbeknownst to Danna, Cannon had been silently crying behind them the whole time. She'd long ago gotten Danna's gun and had been stopped by Don's pleas for Danna not to leave him. It had already been heart-wrenching at first to see a man like Don turn that soft, but now it was just overwhelmingly sad. Danna was falling apart. Cannon rushed to her immediately.

"It's okay, Danna. Stop crying." Cannon tried to fight back her own tears. "Don, please let her go. Please." Cannon's voice was much softer that time around.

"No," He shook his head stubbornly. "If I let her go, she'll never come back," he told Cannon, as if his handprint wasn't still branded across her cheek.

"Yes, she will. She just needs time."

For an instant, Danna stopped crying and looked at Cannon. "No, I'm not, Cannon. It's over. He'll never hurt me like this again and if I come back that's what he's going to do." Danna was doing her best to break free.

"See," Don told Cannon as if she could do something to change Danna's mind.

The whole ordeal was too much. They would have probably still been standing there had Tot not come out of the house. All day they'd hated the day she'd been born, but right then, Danna was thankful for her.

"Don, I can't believe you're crying behind this young ass girl when you just got done telling me you were going to marry me."

Danna and Don's eyes met as Totiana stood behind them, pushing the knife into Danna's heart deeper and deeper. Turning it with each word she spoke.

"You promised me when you got out you was going to marry me so we could raise DJ and Donte together. You said you loved me, were you lying all of this time?"

A loud thud could be heard as Danna's heart fell out onto the ground and splattered into a million pieces.

Don looked helpless as his gaze went from one woman to the other. "No, I do love you, but I love Danna too."

It sounded like broken glass being scrubbed across a chalkboard as Don began stepping on the splattered pieces of Danna's heart.

"Jesus," Cannon palmed her face.

"I have to go." Danna freed herself from his grasp again. "Y'all can have each other. Let's go, Cannon,"

With the gun and the bat in hand, Cannon followed Danna from the yard. Don was hot on their heels following them to the car. Danna wished on everything she loved that he would just stop, but he wouldn't. It took her and Cannon another thirty minutes to finally pull away. The emptiness in Danna's chest showed her what a gaping hole might feel like. Her heart was gone.

"It's going to be okay one day, Danna. Not today, or even tomorrow, but one day the pain will ease and you'll be back to yourself." Cannon's words were low and soothing as she looked out the window while holding Danna's hand.

"I just feel so empty."

"I know . . . I've felt that pain before. It'll pass. I promise."

Danna didn't know when Cannon had ever felt the type of agony she was experiencing before, but she believed her. Her words sounded so sure, that she had no other choice but to feel her.

"Please, don't tell my brother about this."

"I won't. Don't nobody need to know about this shit."

Danna agreed wholeheartedly. "Thanks . . . for everything."

"No thanks needed, that's what sisters are for."

The future seemed so blurry without Don in it, but Danna had no other choice but to face it. She'd faced tougher situations, felt worse pain, dealt with harder trials . . . or so she thought. Little did she know, nothing had anything on the feeling of a broken heart. Danna had been through a lot and would go through even more before it was all over with, but one thing was for sure, it wouldn't be with Don. He'd buried himself and she had no plans of resurrecting him.

17

When it all falls down

The soulful sounds of Marvin Gaye crooned throughout the house as the Mendozas moved around the living room and kitchen getting everything set up for Ezra's going away dinner. He'd signed a nice deal with the Houston Rockets and would be leaving the next day. It had been a long summer and even longer process with his signing, but praises be to God, it had all worked out in his favor. Now that the day had come for him to part ways with his loved ones, his nerves were getting the best of him.

He'd been trying his best to get ahold of himself and prepare for what was coming, but every time he thought about leaving his family, Cannon and Yara, he got sad all over again. Becoming a part of the Rockets' organization should have had him on cloud nine, which it did, but family was everything to him. He was sure he would enjoy it once he got there, but until that moment came, he'd be drowning in his thoughts.

"What's wrong, baby?" Cannon's voice came from behind him as she wrapped her arms around his stomach. A kiss on his bare back came next.

Ezra was fresh out of the shower and standing in his bedroom mirror with his towel draped loosely around his waist. His eyes found Cannon's when she looked around his arm so that she could see him. Her bright skin was flushed a tad bit red from the orgasms he'd just finished giving her, while her hair dangled loosely in the mess of a ponytail he'd left it in.

She smiled and he grinned back. "That dick got you happy, don't it?"

"Always," she kissed his back once more before moving around so that she was standing in front of him.

The moment she stopped moving, Ezra picked her up and sat her on his dresser. Her juiciness weighed his arms down just the way he liked, before pulling him closer. Her open legs circled the sides of his body and dragged him further between her thighs. Ezra leaned the rest of the way lying his head in the center of her chest. Her breasts were just as soft as the rest of her body, and always put him in a much better mood. When her hands came up and massaged his back smoothly, his eyes closed and he exhaled.

"You always make me feel so much better."

"That's what I'm here for? What's wrong? I thought me sneaking into your shower with you had put you in a better mood. I didn't help?"

Ezra's arms circled her waist and squeezed her tightly. "Hell yeah, it did. It just also made it worse." He sighed. "I don't want to leave you and my baby."

He felt Cannon's breasts sink beneath his cheek when she exhaled. "I don't want you to either, but you deserve this, Ezzy. Go have fun, you'll always have us."

"I don't know that. People always say one thing, but turn around and do another. Take my daddy for instance, I remember him telling me that he'd never miss a game. Now I can count on one hand how many he's been to." Ezra scoffed. "But now he has his ass front and center at my mama's dinner table like he has something to do with my success."

"I'm not your daddy. I'd never lie to you or leave you." Cannon's head rested on the top of his as she lay her cheek against his locs. "I promise to be at every game. Me and li'l crying ass Yara."

Ezra smiled at the thought. "I can see you now, wearing one of my jerseys looking all extra pretty and shit."

Cannon laughed and continued rubbing his back. "I just love that you think I'm the prettiest girl in the world."

"Ain't no thinking in that. I know that for a fact. Don't nobody look better than you, and there's most definitely nobody that loves me like you."

"I'm glad you know." She raised her head and pulled his head backward so that she could see his face. "Stop stressing. You're going to do amazing and I'm going to be here cheering for you the whole way. Me, Danna, Vonetta, and probably even Echo. Just embrace your blessings boo." Cannon pecked his nose before going for his mouth.

Ezra stood back some so that he could hold her while they kissed. Upright, with two handfuls of her body, Ezra explored her mouth with every ounce of passion he could muster without going overboard. Cannon's body scooted subtly closer to the edge of the dresser and before either of them knew it, she was in his hands and being carried to his bed.

"Did you lock my door?" Ezra broke their kiss to ask her.

Cannon nodded and pulled him right back to her. "I can't get enough of you."

"Who the fuck you telling?" Ezra moaned as he pushed the towel he'd been holding onto the floor.

Cannon sat up in a hurry removing her clothing. Once she was nude again, Ezra dove face first into her loving. He'd live and die in Cannon if she'd let him. The love and warmth that he got from her made him feel like he could conquer the world.

"Make love to me good, baby. I'm tired." Ezra pulled away and lay on his back so that she could get on top.

Cannon moved with urgency to connect them. The moment she did, his eyes closed and her breath left her body. Pure fucking ecstasy. The slick softness of Cannon's body took him to another place. Somewhere where he had no problems, no cares, and no fears. Their lovemaking was intense and much needed, as always. By the time they'd finished and gotten put back together, his entire family had arrived.

Nuke, Vonnie, and Danna were all standing around the kitchen talking to Vonetta as she finished preparing food. Karina was seated at the table spreading whipped cream on some sort of dessert, while a host of loud children ranging in ages ran around the living room.

"Where's Yara?" Ezra asked, making his presence known.

All eyes went directly to him and Cannon. She was behind him, but he was sure they could see her. They all looked at him with knowing looks, but only loud mouth Danna said something.

"Somewhere trying to enjoy being the youngest as long as she can." Danna and Vonnie both snickered. "The way you and Cannon be going at it, she'll be somebody's auntie before she even turns one."

An array of laughter sounded throughout the kitchen, including his. Ezra was smiling guiltily as he pulled Cannon around in front of him. She was bright red and covering her face with both of her hands.

"Don't be embarrassed, baby. They're just jealous because we're in love." Ezra pulled her hands from her face.

"If that's what love is, I don't want it." Karina shook her head. "I'm too old for all that mess y'all be doing."

"You better tell them." Vonetta consigned. "I'm too big and I get too tired too fast."

"Maaaa," Nuke's face frowned as he looked at his mother in disgust. "Don't nobody want to hear that mess."

"Why not?" Vonetta asked incredulously. "I have to hear about how much all of y'all be fucking, but as soon as I say something, it's a problem? Nigga, please. How you think you got here?"

"I know that's right, Ma. Tell him. Ain't nothing wrong with getting your groove back." Vonnie chimed in.

"Yes, the hell it is too. Mama better not be doing shit she ain't got no business doing." Nuke continued ranting while grabbing a slice of cornbread from the platter in front of him.

"Boy, me and Karina are the only two old enough to be fucking. That's the rest of y'all that ain't got no business fucking."

"Who's fucking?" Echo came walking into the kitchen with Yara thrown over his shoulder.

The kitchen was awkwardly quiet for a second, until Danna walked to him and wrapped her arms around his waist.

"Your wife and your nasty sons. Not me and not Vonnie." She smiled at her siblings as she held onto their daddy's waist.

Ezra smirked but only at her. He wasn't thinking about Echo's ass. It was obvious that she knew the rest of them weren't going to speak to him, so she'd had to do it in a hurry. Danna was such a daddy's girl and it angered Ezra because as much as she loved him, Echo still wouldn't do right. That nigga came and went, not thinking twice about it. The rest of them had gotten accustomed to it, but not Danna. She still had hope for whatever reason.

"Good. Don't y'all be like them." He told her before kissing the top of her head.

"I'm good. Me and my girl getting married." Ezra spoke before taking his seat, pulling Cannon behind him.

Once in his seat, he pulled her down so that she was seated on his lap. The weight from Cannon's body made Ezra fall in love. Her thickness drove him wild. As naturally as he breathed, Ezra circled her body with one of his arms as he rested the other one on the table. Echo watched him and smiled.

"Married? When?"

"That's what I'm trying to see," Vonnie was looking at him as well.

"Whenever we feel like it." Ezra scooted down in his chair some, holding on to Cannon so she wouldn't lose her balance. "That way we can do it as much as we want, whenever we want."

"Jesus," Karina grabbed her forehead and shook it.

More laughter came as conversation continued. A few hours

had passed before everyone was seated around the table preparing to eat. The grace had been said and everyone had just begun digging in when the doorbell rang. All heads shot up, because everyone that had been invited was there already. Vonetta moved to get it, but Ezra stopped her.

"Sit down, Ma, I'll get it." Ezra was on his feet and headed to the door within seconds.

The conversation behind him had resumed and the house was lively with interaction as he passed the small table of kids eating their food. Ezra checked the peephole before opening the door. As soon as Don came into view, he held his hand out and dapped him up.

"What's good, bruh? What you doing over this way?"

"Just came to check in on my people. I heard you out of here tomorrow." Don's voice carried into the dining room, gaining a few of his family members' attention.

"Cool, well come on in. We're just about to eat anyway."

Don followed Ezra after he ushered him inside and closed the door. The moment they walked into the dining room, conversation ceased.

"Don, I didn't know you were coming." Vonetta smiled at him while ushering him into the chair beside her.

"I know. I'm sorry for dropping by unannounced. I was in the neighborhood and saw all of the cars, so I stopped to wish my li'l homie well." Don's words were nice, but his face was anything but.

He hadn't taken his eyes off Echo yet. Ezra was still standing near the door for a minute, and caught the glares that were being sent his way. He wasn't sure what that was about, and honestly didn't care. It was probably some shady street shit anyway, so he went back to his seat and continued eating.

"Echo, long time no see." He spoke across the table.

"Ye . . . yeah," Echo cleared his throat. "You know me, I'm always sticking and moving."

Don nodded. "Don't I know it. How long you around for this time? You know the streets missing you."

Danna's hand went to Echo's shoulder. "I keep telling him that. I miss you too, Daddy." Danna smiled up at him.

Echo looked a little unstable as he wiped his mouth with the napkin that had been in his hand. "Duty calls, sweetheart. I can't take care of y'all the way I do if I'm here every day."

"We're grown now. We can take care of ourselves. Whatever we can't handle, all of your workers take care of for us." Ezra stated, unknowingly adding fuel to an already blazing fire.

"Right! Even if we don't want their asses to." Danna rolled her eyes toward Don. "Him being the main one. He follows me everywhere. It's so annoying. I can't even talk to men because they always think I'm with him."

Echo coughed roughly as if he was choking on his food. Danna patted his back softly until he calmed down.

"He follows you?"

Danna nodded dramatically. "Everywhere. He's such a creep. I don't know why you hired him. I don't need a babysitter."

Vonnie and Cannon both giggled at Danna's dramatic revelations.

Echo and Don locked eyes for a minute before they shifted from Danna to Ezra. "I'm sorry it has to be this way. This isn't how I thought life would be for us. I really thought the choices I made in the streets were for our good." He looked around at everyone with water in his eyes.

Ezra was thrown completely off by the tears. He'd never known Echo to show any emotion when they were around. He was always smiling or straight faced with some sort of lecture accompanying his words. His current demeanor was anything but normal.

"Aye, Echo, you good?" Nuke asked.

Echo smiled and ran his hand over his face, wiping away his tears. "Yeah. Just getting a little emotional. I've spent so much time trying to give y'all a good life, that I've missed it all." His lips trembled as he fidgeted in his seat. "All of y'all are grown up, starting your own families and shit, and I've missed it all."

Being the woman that she was, Vonetta stepped in and saved him. Her bracelets jingled when she reached across the table to hold his hand.

"You did what you had to do. I understand, and have raised these kids damn good. Don't be sorry, just enjoy what you have left. We know how this street shit goes."

"We really do, Daddy. We're not mad." Danna scooted her chair over so that she was lying her head on his shoulder.

Don cleared his throat at the same time Ezra reached for Yara. Karina had just gotten up to answer her ringing phone and passed her off with a quickness.

"Let's just eat and enjoy each other. Tonight is a joyous occasion, our baby is going to the NBA!" Vonetta switched the mood of the room.

Everyone cheered and expressed their congratulatory praises as they began eating again.

"Danna, can you grab Don a plate from the cabinet?"

Danna's nose turned up and she rolled her eyes. "No. Don is grown. He can get it himself. He ain't no guest." Her tone was so nasty that Ezra had to turn and look at her.

"Damn," he said while trying to suppress his laughter.

Cannon, on the other hand, didn't find anything funny. She elbowed him and stood up instead. "I'll get it."

"Thank you, Cannon, because my rude ass daughter has lost her mind."

Don looked at Danna and winked at her. Ezra hadn't missed that, and would make it his business to check Don on that shit later.

"It's cool. Danna is always mean to me."

"Because I don't like you." She came back without missing a beat.

Ezra, along with all his siblings and Cannon, were laughing at

Danna when Karina came back in. She smiled politely at everyone before stopping on Vonetta.

"Thanks for the invite, Vonetta, but that was my second job. They need me tonight. Somebody called out." A sorrowful expression covered her face until she looked at Ezra. "I'm proud of you, sweetie. Go down there and live it big, my baby."

"Yes ma'am. Let me take your daughters with me." He responded with a large smile on his face.

"You can have Cannon, but I'm going to have to keep my Yara."

"Well just throw me to the wolves," Cannon laughed.

Ezra pecked her cheek quickly. "Not the wolves, baby. The Rockets. Throw you to the Rockets."

Everyone began laughing again before Karina excused herself once more. Echo stood behind her.

"Let me walk you out. It's too dark for you to be out there alone."

Karina nodded and the two of them exited. The room's energy picked back up immediately with everyone conversing and eating. Well, everyone except Danna. She wasn't as lively as she had been, but she was still talking. Ezra noticed the change in her and wasn't necessarily sure what was going on, but he'd find out one way or another. Although he knew she most definitely wasn't going to tell him, he also knew if he fucked Cannon good enough, she'd tell it all. With a smile on his face, he looked over at her. She'd just bit into her chicken when her eyes caught his. She smiled and Ezra winked.

"Hurry up and eat, I need to be inside of you," he whispered to her.

Cannon's smiling face was the beat to his heart. "I'm hurrying."

Ezra winked at her again, sealing his plan for the next day. There was no way he could go to Houston without her, she was his everything. Where he was, she would be too. That was a promise.

18

I promise

The warm water rolling down both sides of her face was really starting to become irritating. No matter how hard she'd been trying to make it stop, every time she thought about leaving Ezra, Cannon's tears started back up. Here she was for the fifty-thousandth time that month, crying! She'd been certain that she'd been preparing herself for what was to come, but clearly even the pep talks, long hugs, lovemaking, or sweet whispers Ezra rendered, was not preparation enough.

"Come on, Mama, stop that."

Danna walked up and slapped Cannon's back lightly. "Yeah, Mama, stop that shit. You act you ain't gon' never see the nigga no more."

Once again, Cannon was sniffing and wiping her face. Her tantrum resembled something like the after effect of getting a whooping. Her chest was heaving, she couldn't catch her breath, or speak any finished words. Everything that she'd tried to get out this far had only made it half way out before her sadness overwhelmed her and tears began to flow again.

"Cannon, baby, I'm only a couple of hours away. We can see each other all the time."

"Bu . . . bu . . . but we won't thoughhhhh," Cannon was back crying. "You're going to go to Houston and find somebo-ahhhh," A chopped up expression of fear revolving around Ezra dating, never finished coming out, but he and Danna both knew what Cannon had been trying to say.

Ezra walked to Cannon and hugged her tightly. "Cannon, you have to stop this, baby. I'm not going to date anybody else, because you're all I want."

"That's because you haven't met anyone else yet." She wiped away the freshly rising tears. "But you're about to be a fucking Rocket. You're going to have all the bitches."

"I don't need to meet anyone else, I already have you." Ezra pressed his forehead to hers. "Who cares about me playing for the Rockets when it comes to the matters of my heart? Huh?" He pecked her nose. "You're the only one that's got that."

Cannon lay her head on Ezra's shoulder, doing her best to calm down. Being wrapped in his embrace was the best thing she'd felt all day. Make that all her life. Ezra was such an addicting feeling that she wanted to do any and everything revolving around him.

His leaving to go to Houston had put a nagging feeling in her gut since graduation and she had yet to get over it. All she could think about was how fine he was and how many other girls were going to think the same thing. It didn't help that he was in the freaking NBA. That was about to bring a plethora of new groupies.

"Bitch, get yourself together. You act like Ezra is going to be the only nigga that's meeting new people? When we leave, there's going to be niggas everywhere in Atlanta trying to get you too. You might not even want his ass in about a month or two." Danna stood next to Ezra with a large smile on her face.

"That shit ain't happening." Ezra told her.

Cannon said nothing to object what Danna was saying because she didn't feel the need to. Her stomach hurt just thinking about not being with Ezra, so she already knew she wouldn't be entertaining any other men. She had all she wanted and needed, in him.

"Cannon."

Cannon looked up at Ezra's handsome face.

"Don't let Danna get you fucked up, okay? She on that bullshit because she's brokenhearted as fuck. You ain't. We in love, don't let her bitter ass taint that . . . aight?"

Cannon's eyes wandered over to Danna before smiling. Ezra was right about her. She was brokenhearted and had been since all that shit went down with Don. Though she'd done her best to carry on a happy façade, she'd failed miserably. She'd called Cannon plenty of nights suffering behind her heartbreak, but she was making it, and Cannon was proud of her for it.

That hadn't been an easy pill to swallow. Which was probably the main reason for her running from man to man. Every other day there was a new man taking her somewhere, or bringing her something. Cannon and Ezra weren't fans of Danna's bounce back mechanism, but whatever made her feel better. Ezra still didn't know who or what had changed Danna, but he knew it was something. Cannon did her best to detour his mind from Danna and her secret man, but any time a new man popped up, he was quickly reminded.

"I ain't listening to her. I only want you."

Ezra pecked her lips. "Good. Now stay here and be a good girl for me. If I have some time, I'll come see back and check you out before the season starts."

Cannon nodded and sniffed as hard as she could to keep her tears away.

"You got my baby situated?"

"Yeah, Karina's cool. She's a little nervous about me not being there every day, but I know she'll be fine. I'm going to prepare her as much as I can before I go."

A distant look was in Ezra's eyes as he held on to Cannon's waist. "I love you."

"I love you too."

"We forever. This li'l long distance shit ain't gon' break us."

Cannon nodded in uncertainty. Her doubts were so loud and clear she was surprised Ezra couldn't hear them.

"I got you something," Ezra stepped back and pulled something out of his back pocket.

Cannon and Danna watched him lower to his knee in front of her. Naturally, Cannon's hands covered her mouth as a small yelp came out.

"Boy, what the hell you doing?" Danna walked around him so that she could see his face.

The diamond ring was small, but it sparkled, and it was hers . . . from him. Cannon allowed Ezra to pull her hands from her mouth and slide the ring on the rightful finger.

"The first time we ever made love, you promised me that we would get married and be together forever. I'm ready to make good on your promise."

Cannon screamed excitedly jumping up and down in place. "I promise. Yes!"

"Promise me that you won't give your love away while we're apart."

"I promise," Cannon gazed down at the sincerity in Ezra's eyes.

He slid the ring on her finger before standing back to his feet. "I want you to move with me. Don't go to Atlanta, come with me."

"I will," Cannon told him with no hesitation. "When? Right now? I'll go now." Her eagerness overtook her.

"Nah, not right now. It's too sudden. Let's just go along with our original plans and when I have time to sort all of this out, I'll come and get you."

"Ezzy, what she say?" Vonetta's voice came out of nowhere.

They all turned toward the front porch where she was standing. Her hands were clasped together in front of her while her signature smile was plastered across her face. Ezra smiled even harder at his mother.

"She said yeah, ma."

Vonetta clapped happily and waved Cannon over for a hug. Cannon ran straight to her, smiling and jumping the whole way.

"I'm so happy for y'all, baby." She squeezed Cannon further into her body. Cannon closed her eyes enjoying the sincere love coming from her mother-in-law. "Don't get too settled up there in Atlanta. Go where your husband is. Absence makes the heart go yonder, sweetheart. Wherever he's at, that's where you need to be also."

"Yes ma'am."

"Vonetta, don't be up there helping your son steal my new partner in crime." Danna stomped toward them with her arms folded across her chest.

Ezra, Vonetta, and Cannon all laughed at her pretend tantrum. They were still laughing as Ezra headed for them. He kissed the side of Danna's head sloppily as he passed by her to get to Cannon.

As soon as he was next to her, Cannon jumped on Ezra with a large smile all on her face. She was beyond happy. Even though she inwardly wished she could just go with him right away, and forget all about Atlanta, she had to be logical. They all talked happily with Vonetta for a little while longer before she went back into the house. The three of them headed back toward Ezra's truck so that he could hit the road.

"I knew y'all dumb asses would get married to each other one of these days." Danna smiled happily at the two of them.

Ezra and Cannon were still holding on to one another as they smiled and laughed. The time ticked by, and before long they were parting ways. Cannon and Ezra were both sad but hopeful, while Danna on the other hand hadn't stopped smiling since she and Cannon had gotten into her car.

"You're really killing my joy," she looked at a sulking Cannon.

"Well, you're getting on my last nerve acting all happy."

"You need to be just as happy as me. We're about to have some fun!"

Cannon's eyes rolled.

"For real, Cannon. You need to stop being sad. You and Ezzy will be fine. It's natural to miss the nigga, but he ain't gon' do no shit that's gon' hurt you. Y'all will be alright. Anytime y'all start missing each other, just visit. It won't be that bad, you're just being really dramatic right now. Besides, the nigga just said y'all will only be apart until he can get things together. Probably won't even be in Atlanta a full semester before you're leaving again."

"I'm not though. I really didn't want him to leave me."

Danna's hand rested on Cannon's leg. "It'll be cool. Y'all needed this time apart to breathe a little. When it's time for y'all to be together, you both will be ready without the drama."

Honestly, Cannon's mind hadn't gone that far because all she could think about was being with him, but Danna had a point. She still wasn't about to allow her mind to travel into entertaining Ezra and other women, but she could probably take a minute for some girl time with Danna.

"I guess."

Danna smiled and clapped her hands playfully as she drove. "No, girl, don't guess. Know."

"I can't stand you."

"You're going to love me before it's all over with."

"Don scarred you. You're such a savage."

Danna quieted for only a moment before shrugging. "Niggas don't give a fuck about you, Cannon, and won't another man on this planet make me believe any different. Fuck they dog asses."

"Aww, Danna. They ain't all the same."

Danna sucked her teeth. "The hell you say."

"Ezra ain't."

"Look, I would say what I want to say, but I won't because you're too sensitive, but Cannon, listen. All niggas will do shady shit if given the right opportunity. That's just what I believe. I could be scorned, bitter, angry, or whatever justifies my feelings, but niggas ain't shit. Period. There may be some good ones, but fuck them too."

Cannon snickered as she watched Danna in empathy. She was truly ruined. "What about Quay? He was a good one right?"

Danna did her best to hold her smile in. "Yeah, Quay was cool, but I'm good on that jailhouse shit. Niggas in the pen got more time to cheat than niggas on the street. Maybe in another lifetime, but for now," Danna shook her head from side to side. "I'm popping pussy whenever I feel like it, and I ain't explaining it to nobody. Especially not no nigga."

"Jesus," Cannon sighed dramatically. "I don't know what I've gotten myself into going out of town with your mean ass."

"A whole lot of fun, bitch!" Danna screamed in excitement again.

Cannon laughed with her that time. Danna was a damn fool. Even with her being older than her, Cannon could already see she was about to have to be the big sister. Danna was already excited about moving from Columbus and getting a fresh start on life, to add that in with her being on some fuck niggas, shit, there was no telling how she was about to cut up.

"Well let's get it then, sis."

"Oh, bitch, we finna' get it so good, you gon' be like Ezra who?"

Cannon stopped smiling. "Never."

Versus saying anything, Danna just laughed and kept driving. When they finally pulled into the driveway of her little townhouse there was another car in the driveway. She and Cannon both squinted their eyes trying to see who was behind the dark tint, but neither of them were able to.

"Girl, what man you got over here waiting on you?" Cannon looked from the large black truck to the Danna.

Her face was frowned in confusion as she bit the side of her lip. Her smile was gone and she looked just as confused as Cannon.

"Chile, I don't know who that is. I've never seen that truck a day in my life." Danna told her as she pulled in behind the large truck.

"No, bitch!" Cannon pulled at the steering wheel. "Don't

park. You don't know who that is. What if it's somebody coming here to kill you?"

Danna's laughter drew some from Cannon as well. "Cannon, you're so damn sheltered. Get your hand off my steering wheel before you make me hit something."

"Okay, you think everything is funny until we're laid out in the fucking morgue. I just got proposed to, bitch. I'm trying to die as Cannon Mendoza. Kill your own damn self." Cannon sat back in the seat and crossed her arms over her chest. "I'm marrying your fucking brother. You'll die alone today. I can guarantee you that."

Danna sat smirking at Cannon, but Cannon wasn't playing. She knew Ezra and Danna's father was involved in a lot of street stuff, and she may not have known personally how things went down, but she knew enough not to be running up to unmarked cars. Danna could go right ahead, but she wouldn't be going with her.

"I'm sick of you. I am really sick of you." Danna pointed at Cannon playfully. "Sit your scary ass right here."

"Gladly." Cannon pouted her lips up and looked out of the window.

Danna was still smiling as she cut off her car and got out. With her purse thrown over her shoulder and her hand tucked down inside of it, Cannon watched her approach the vehicle slowly. Once she was finally at the driver's side window, it rolled down. Danna's body visibly relaxed and her hand came out of her purse, assumingly off of her gun. Though, she hadn't smiled or shown any form of happiness, she hadn't run off yet, so that gave Cannon the green light.

With her nerves still jittering a bit from uncertainty, Cannon slid from the car and headed toward Danna. She heard his voice before she saw his face, so she too relaxed. Don's large body took up the entire front seat of the car as he sat leaning slightly out of the window talking to Danna. His eyes were low and red, but his haircut and everything else were on point.

Cannon could even smell some sort of cologne. When he saw her coming, he paused his conversation long enough to nod his head at her. Cannon waved briefly before walking to Danna.

"Let me get your keys, I'ma go in the house."

"You don't have to go nowhere. This nigga finna' leave." She stated, matter-of-factly.

"Danna, I just told you, I ain't about to do this crazy shit with you today. I just want you to take a ride with me for a second."

Cannon waited on Danna to respond. When she didn't, she took that as her cue to reach for the keys again. If Danna wasn't going to ride with him, she would have vocalized it immediately. The way she stood there looking at Cannon as if waiting for some sort of approval let her know that she was contemplating it. Which Cannon could totally understand. Love was hard, and when you were in it, there was no telling what you would do. Danna loved Don, and no matter what had transpired between the two of them, it wasn't going to go away that fast.

"Just go with him. Hear him out, sis." Cannon encouraged her.

The last thing she wanted Danna to do was turn Don down because she felt judged by Cannon. That would surely only make things worse.

Danna sighed and looked at Don, "Where are we going?"

"Anywhere you want to go."

"I won't be gone long, Cannon."

Cannon shook her head and held her hands up. "Don't rush for me. I'm a big girl. If I get ready to go, I'll have my mama come get me."

Danna nodded and walked to the passenger side of the truck. Don's eyes followed her the entire way. He even leaned over to open the door for her. He may have been a cheating dog, but he loved her. It showed. Cannon wouldn't give him any passes for his past transgressions, but everyone deserved a chance at real love.

"Be safe." She waved and headed into Danna's front door.

She waited until they'd pulled off before closing and locking the door. Maybe the time Danna spent with Don would change her mind about niggas. It was a long shot, but Cannon had faith. If it didn't, she was in for a wild ride with Danna and her heartbreak recovery methods.

19

Now or never

Don sped down the highway, headed toward the small hotel he'd gotten on the outskirts of town. He'd finally made up his mind about his plan, so there was no need for him to go to his house. The last thing he needed while trying to win Danna back was for Totiana to pop up with her drama, which he was sure would be soon. He hadn't talked to her since the day he'd left her house in pursuit of Danna.

True enough, it was wrong for him to leave her there like that, but it had been just as wrong for Danna to have to see him there with her when he was supposed to still be in jail. If he had never known how much he'd loved Danna before, he knew that day. To see her crying and falling apart like that tore him up and solidified his deepest desires all at once.

"Why you so quiet?" Don's hand went across his console and rested on top of hers.

Danna's back was turned to him as she looked out of the window. He couldn't see all of her face, but the side that he could see was enough. Her smooth chocolate skin, the thickness of her well defined lips, and the long locs that waved and swayed every time she turned her head, had him all riled up. He wanted so badly to just grab her and make love to her right there in his rental truck, but he knew that wasn't happening. She was barely speaking to him, so he was sure sex was the last thing on her mind.

"I don't have anything to say."

"Why not?"

She shrugged. "Said it all before."

"I'm really sorry, Danna, and I promise nothing will ever come between us again."

Danna said nothing, but she did nod her head. That was enough to give Don some hope. Hope that she could and would still love him, even after her father was found dead. He'd been watching Vonetta's house for the past four nights and Echo was there every one of them, at the same time. Tonight would be his final visit.

The previous night would have been it for his ass, had Danna not been there. Just as he was about to pull the trigger on the gun he'd had aimed directly at Echo's head, Danna had walked in and saved him. From the driver's seat of his truck, he'd had the perfect shot, but the moment Echo had pulled Danna to him for a hug, Don lost focus. When he could do nothing else to gain another clear shot, his vengeance had gotten the best of him, and he'd gone inside.

The small going away party they'd had for Ezra had been a perfect distraction. The look on Echo's face had been priceless when he'd laid eyes on Don. The boiling hate that Don had been feeling for Echo for so long had damn near spilled over in the middle of dinner with his family, but because of Danna, he'd been able to reel it back in.

Every time he looked at her and how much she doted on her father, he calmed his trigger finger. Her smile, her touch, everything that involved her and Echo had sent Don's blood pressure through the roof, but he'd had to fight to contain it. Danna's continuous banter about hating him was also a major help. The way she expressed her dislike for him had deterred his mind just enough to keep him from breaking Echo's neck after dessert.

"Where are we going?" Danna turned to face him.

"Riding."

"For what? I don't feel like driving around for no reason."

Don held his open hand out to her. "What do you want to do? Tell me, so we can do that."

Danna looked at his hand as if it were on fire. "I want to get the fuck away from you," she sneered. "I want to go back to my house and get into my bed, so I can finish crying over your dog ass." She looked at him. "That's what I want to do."

"Danna," Don sighed. "I'm sorry, baby. How many times do you want me to say that?"

"I don't care how many times you say it, I'm still not going to believe you, so it doesn't matter."

"Well, tell me how I can make it better."

Don took the exit toward the hotel and stopped at the light. Danna's body was now facing the front of the truck and she was looking at him.

"I'll do anything," he told her.

The truck was quiet as he waited for her to tell him the cure to her pain. He'd do it. Whatever it was, he'd do it, because she was who he planned to be with. After finding out her father was dead, she would need comfort, and he'd be right there to provide it. Echo's death would be the perfect reason for them to get out of town. She'd been telling him for months how she was ready to leave the city and get a fresh start; he was down if she was.

"I want to get married and have kids, Don. I want to go on dates and be happy. I want people to see us together. Posting pictures, and making cute videos and shit. That's what I want, but you can't give that to me." Her eyes watered. "And I'm tired of trying to make you. What we have may be real, but it'll never work."

"Why it can't? I can do all that shit you just named."

Danna turned to face him. "What about my daddy?"

Don's body got hot. If anybody kept them from being together, it wouldn't be Echo, and that was on his life.

"Fuck your crybaby ass daddy."

Shock covered Danna's face before she started laughing. "Don't talk about my daddy."

"I couldn't say shit if he hadn't been sitting there with water in his eyes last night. I couldn't even eat my damn food for waiting on that nigga to go ahead and cry us a fucking river."

Don could see her trying her best to hold in her laughter, but she couldn't. Danna's smile lit up his car. He'd definitely kill to see that every day. Fuck anybody that tried to get in the way.

"What about Totiana and your kids?" Danna's voice was softer that time.

Don's mind drifted off momentarily. "Fuck them."

"Fuck the kids?" Danna asked in disbelief.

Don's tone was serious when he looked her way. "We can have more."

Danna's eyes remained on him as he drove and parked. He'd pulled into the parking lot of the hotel and was parking, so he couldn't make eye contact, but he could definitely feel her eyes on him. The remark about the kids had probably thrown her for a loop, but that was just how much he loved her.

Her ignoring his calls and running away from him had opened his eyes to her, and he had no plans of ever closing them again. At least, not without closing hers as well. If she decided not to be with him, he was going to kill her as well. He'd never loved a woman the way he loved Danna and if she thought he was going to let her ride off into the sunset with another nigga, she was sadly mistaken.

"Why are we at a hotel? Why couldn't we just go to your house?"

"I wanted us to be alone with no distractions."

Danna nodded and was gathering her things to get out of the car, but stopped and spun around to face him.

"Distractions? What kind of distractions would we have at your house?"

Don huffed and got out of the car. He already knew what she was getting at. "Come on now, Danna, damn. I'm trying."

"Whatever. You just don't want Totiana showing up there acting a fool."

Don stopped in front of the truck so that they were facing each other. "That's exactly why. Now, can we go inside?"

Defiance was in every step she took toward the hotel, but as long as she was with him, he could handle the rest. He could see right then what she needed, and he'd been waiting to give it to her. Being that he'd already checked in and gotten his key for the room, they were on the elevator and headed for their room as soon as they entered.

"You should have told me we were coming to a hotel, I could have grabbed me some clothes or something."

"You don't need clothes." Don walked up to her and pulled her to him. "Take these off." Don pulled at the shirt and pants she was wearing.

"No. I don't know where your dick been. You probably fucked Tot before you came and got me. You need to go take a shower before you touch me."

Don's head fell back in laughter as he listened to her talk to him like she was bad. Her stance was combative and she was scowling. Clearly, she knew she ran shit, because nobody else in their right mind would talk to him as crazy as she always did.

When he was finally able to stop laughing, Don smiled and pulled his shirt over his head. Danna's eyes went straight to his bare chest. The lust for him was all over her face as she stood back on one of her legs with her arms crossed over her chest. Her gaze hadn't left his body yet, and had recently traveled to his growing erection.

"You want it, don't you?" he asked her while holding his dick in his hand.

Danna licked her lips and smiled seductively. "Not with it dirty like that." She winked before walking away from him and making herself comfortable on the bed. "Clean it, first."

"I got you." Don stripped out of the rest of his clothes.

Danna's eyes hadn't left his body again until he walked into the bathroom. He hit the shower water and made sure it was extra hot before stepping in. He'd been waiting to be back with his baby, and it was finally happening. With a smile on his face, Don cleaned himself the best he could with the hotel soap and wash-cloth. He washed a couple of times to make sure he was clean before just relaxing beneath the water.

He needed to get his mind together for the night he had planned. He was going to need all the energy he could muster before getting it started.

"Ahhh," he exhaled as he thought about finally ending Echo's life.

He was positive that he wouldn't be going back to Vonetta's house since he'd seen him there the night before. That would be something a fool would do, and in the profession Echo was in, he couldn't afford to be that, but neither could Don. Which was why he'd camped outside of Vonetta's house until he'd snuck out of her window in the wee hours of the morning. Don had followed him directly to the hotel they were at right then, and would be making his way up the stairs the moment he put Danna to sleep.

Don smiled. His troubles were finally about to be over. He had his freedom and his girl, he'd figure the rest of the shit out once it hit the fan.

20

The hood's finest hour

Why am I here with this nigga? Danna lay on her back staring up at the ceiling. She had been asking herself the same question for the past ten minutes since he'd been in the shower. It was a fact that she loved Don, but she'd never played the fool for any man, and didn't plan to start with him. He'd caught her slipping a few times because she hadn't known what was going on, but now she did.

Staying with him after knowing he was dogging her out was a totally different level of stupid, and she didn't like it. The more she thought about it, the madder she got. Before long, she was sitting up and grabbing her things. He was taking her home when he got finished showering. He was probably going to be through the roof angry, but she didn't care. He'd get over it.

Her vibrating phone drew her out of her thoughts. When she saw the same number that Quay always called from, she silenced it. She couldn't talk to him right then. Quay was too domineering. After getting on to her about screening his calls, he would surely give her a hard time when it was time to hang up, and she couldn't chance that with Don being around her.

She'd just opened her social media account when her phone vibrated again. He was calling back. Danna sighed because she

wanted to talk to him too. She stared at the screen for a few seconds before going against her better judgement and answering.

"Yooo, Danna, what's good, baby? Why you ignoring me?" his
tone was calm as usual, totally surprising her.

"I'm sorry. I've just been trying to get back to me, ya know?"

"I guess," He paused. "Aye, Dan, where you at?"

What in the world? Did he know?

Danna's eyebrows scrunched up as she tried to think about
whether or not she needed to lie. Quay was in jail, so he couldn't
possibly know where she was right then or who she was with, but
why else would he ask that?

"Out, why what's up? You need something?" She made her
dismissal sound as sweet as possible.

"Yeah, I do actually."

Danna looked over her shoulder when she heard the shower
cutting off. "What you need?"

"I need you to come outside. Don't make a scene, just come
out here."

Danna pressed her phone further into her ear. "Huh?"

"I'm in the parking lot next to Don's rental truck. Come get in
this red car with me."

"What the fuck?" Danna asked more to herself than anything.

"Now, Danna. You have to come now, baby."

Danna's head was spinning as she ran to the window to see if
she could actually see him. When she saw the red car, her heart
nearly stopped. What in the hell was going on?

"What are you doing here?"

"Danna, bring your ass out of the hotel room right now. I'm
not telling you again."

"Quay?" She asked skeptically.

"Fucking now, Danna!" His voice raised and got her moving.
"You have to." His tone went down a notch and he sighed. "Come
now, baby. Please."

Danna waited no more. With her purse still hanging from her

shoulder, and no other belongings, Danna hurried out of the room and to the elevators. Her heart was beating a mile a minute as she looked between the hotel room and the blinking lights above the elevator. The moment it dinged, she heard the locks to Don's room click. Danna hopped onto the elevator pressing the buttons frantically. When the doors closed, she breathed a sigh of relief.

"Danna, you good?" Quay's calm voice reminded her he was on the phone.

"I'm scared. What's going on?"

"You don't have to be scared, baby. I'll protect you. Just come to me."

Danna nodded her head as she ran out of the lobby doors. When she got outside, she spotted Quay instantly. He'd pulled to the front of the building so she could hop into the car. As soon as she was in, he peeled out of the parking lot. Danna looked from him to the road, waiting for him to explain what was going on.

"Quay?"

"Just chill, I'll tell you in a minute. Just put your seatbelt on."

Danna sat back and did as she was told, but as soon as it was on, she was back to her questions. "How'd you know I was here?"

"I got connections." Quay looked at her with his nose turned up. "Your ass ain't have no business over here, no fucking way."

Out of her normal element, Danna didn't know what to say to Quay. Normally, she would have had something smart to fire back at him, but right then her mind was all over the place. Though the situation wasn't an extremely messy one, it wasn't normal, and she had no idea what to make of it. She'd been waiting for him to say something to her regarding what was happening, but he still hadn't yet and she was getting more and more anxious by the second.

"Did you follow me?" Danna looked from the road to Quay. "And when did you get out of jail?" She asked as if she'd just noticed. "Why you ain't call and tell me you were out?"

Danna sat back in her seat and allowed her attitude to take

control. "I guess that's what all of y'all do, huh? Lay up in your cells and tell me lies, but the moment they let you out, you go running to your real girlfriend." Danna shook her head in dismay. "I'm tired of this shit. I'm done playing second for you niggas. Just take me to my house. Forget you and Don."

Danna was seething with anger as she continued to let her thoughts get the best of her. Quay still hadn't said anything to appease her, and it was driving her crazy. He needed to at least deny her accusations, and he wasn't. He'd been driving as if she hadn't said a word.

"I thought you were different than Don, and you're not. You don't give a fuck about me just like he doesn't. You could have just left me there with him. You're not better."

Quay's hair moved across his shoulders when he looked over at her. The slits of his eyes showed as he side-eyed her with his face balled up.

"I wish you would say some stupid shit like that to me again."

"What makes you different?" Danna could feel herself getting emotional as she looked at him.

Quay was supposed to be different. He had been different, and now her hopes were crushed. Why couldn't she just get one person that wanted to treat her right? She'd acted hard long enough. She wanted to love and be loved the way a woman deserved, and she continued to get inconsiderate men.

"I don't know what you sitting over there looking sad for. You talking all that shit, but I've been calling you for weeks and you've been dodging every one. Then I get a call and find out you're over here laid up in a hotel with this dude." Quay turned his nose up at her and sucked his teeth.

"I just told you I've been trying to get myself together," Danna yelled in her defense.

"Let me guess, being with Don was going to help you do that?" Quay looked at her before looking back at the road. "I see you ain't been running away from that nigga."

Danna sat quietly playing with one of her locs. "He just popped up on me. I wasn't talking to him either. He's just persistent."

"No, that muthafucka is just crazy."

"At least he cares enough to keep trying!" Danna screamed exasperatedly. "You call two or three times and just give up on me. I swear I'm tired of y'all using me."

"What?" Quay yelled before sitting back in his seat and pushing some of his hair from his face. He took a few deep breaths before saying anything else. "You think I gave up on you? Ain't no fuckin way, Danna. Ain't no fucking way. Just like you've had shit going on, so did I. Your crazy ass man being one of them."

"Did he do something to you?" She hurried to ask.

"Hell nah, that nigga can't do nothing that I don't let him do, so don't worry about that."

"Well, what's wrong? Why you rolling up on me like this?" she looked at him and waited for an answer.

"It's a lot of stuff that I just can't explain to you right now, but believe me when I tell you, I didn't give up on you." Quay grabbed her hand and held it. "I've been doing everything but that."

Danna's smile showcased before she could stop it. To receive affection from Quay was indescribable, and had been since the she'd started getting it.

"It's about to be a lot of stuff happening, and it's going to happen fast, but I'ma keep you with me until I have time to explain everything. I don't want you freaking out and running off to get yourself together again."

Danna's head dropped down so that she was looking into her lap. The same smile that had been there earlier was fighting hard to surface and she didn't want it to. She had her mouth open to ask him a question when his phone rang. Her eyes went to it at the same time as his did.

"Elijah."

Elijah? Who is that? Danna watched him, hoping to gather

some insight from his conversation, but that one word was all he said before ending the call.

"Elijah? Who is that?"

Quay ran his hand over his mouth and pulled at his bottom lip. "Me, that's my last name."

Danna nodded, but said nothing.

"Who lives here?" Danna eyed the small brick house with the dark blue shutters.

It was a cute little house with well-groomed grass and even a small garden on one side. The tall wooden fence surrounding the property encased the driveway and rounded the back of the property. Danna sat wide-eyed, observing the dark blue motorcycle parked along the side of the house beneath a shed. It was so pretty and looked like it would be fun to ride if she knew how.

"Don't worry about it. Get out."

Danna looked his way but kept her mouth closed and got out. She switched around the front of the car and stopped once she was in front of him. Quay's tall frame bent slightly as he looked down at her. His eyes went from her face down her body and back up to her face before he held his hand out toward her. Danna took it and followed him up the driveway.

He pulled the small set of keys from his pocket and unlocked the door. As soon as Danna stepped inside of the home, the coolness relaxed her. The atmosphere was cozy and it smelled amazing. There was a dark blue furniture set in the middle of the living room, while a light-colored wooden table occupied the space near the kitchen.

Danna had just released his hand to walk over to the pictures decorating the large entertainment center, but Quay stopped her when he grabbed her from behind. His arms circled her waist and spun her around so that she was facing him. The pad of his thumb rubbed along the side of her face as he stared at her.

"You know I've been trying to think of a reason not to like you. Anything, it didn't have to be big or small, just something that would give me a reason to keep my personal and business life separate but every time you're around me I can never find one."

Danna's hands came up and circled his back. "Why would you do that? What's wrong with liking me?"

Quay's forehead pressed against hers as he closed his eyes. "It'll be too much like mixing business with pleasure and I don't do that."

"You don't have to worry about my daddy. I can handle him."

"It's not your dad."

"Well, what is it?"

Quay pulled away from her and smiled. The gold in his mouth shining in her face. "It's you Danna. It's fucking you." His laughter alarmed her because she wasn't exactly sure how'd he'd flipped from being serious so fast. "I can't have you being my girlfriend in the middle of the situation we're in right now."

Fed up with trying to piece together his statements, Danna removed her purse and threw it onto the sofa before sitting down as well.

"Tell me what is up, because you're talking in circles. First you follow me, kidnap me, and now you're talking about mixing business with pleasure. I'm lost. If you don't want me with Don, then cool, because I don't want me with him either, but you need to be a little more direct than what you're being. I can't take all this back and forth stuff. If you can't be stra—"

Quay removed his shirt, stopping her mid-sentence. He'd been sexy as hell ever since she'd known him, but that body was sick. He was so ripped up with muscles and she hadn't had any sex in so long, she could barely sit still. Her legs started jumping and everything.

"Don't stop, keep talking all that noise." Quay taunted her with that million-dollar smile.

The moment he opened his mouth her mind went back to the night they'd had phone sex. Danna could hardly breathe. Quay had literally taken her breath away. She'd sat back and closed her eyes and everything. She was busy trying to take some deep breaths when she felt the bottom half of her body being pulled from the sofa. Danna's eyes popped open and landed directly on Quay.

He was kneeling between her legs, shirtless. His shoulder length locs swayed around his face as his head bent slightly. With intent focus, he unfastened the buttons on her jean shorts.

"You'll know what I want you to know." Quay lifted the bottom of her body and pulled her shorts off. "Until then, you just do what I say." Quay leaned over and pulled her shirt from her head. "See, your problem is you think you run everything when you don't. I do." Quay leaned over and kissed up the front of her exposed stomach.

Danna shivered the moment his lips touched her skin.

"It's not your fault though, all the men in your life let you boss them around, but I'm not them. I'm a grown man, and you're going to respect me." More kisses were placed on her stomach as his fingers found the band of her panties. "As a matter of fact, stand up."

Quay sat back on the floor and leaned against the sofa. Danna didn't know why she felt so shy all of a sudden, but it took her forever to pull herself from the sofa and stand in front of him. With her love directly in his face, Quay gripped the back of her thighs and pulled her closer to his face.

"You got some big sexy ass legs, Danna. Damn." He sighed as he placed kisses up the front of her thighs. "You know how in love I am with your thickness? It's my favorite."

A bashful smile covered her face as she ran her hands through his hair.

"I'm for real. I love this shit," He squeezed her legs again. "Sit right here." He pulled her down onto his lap.

Danna lowered herself until she was straddling him. Her arms found their way around his neck the moment she was comfortable. Face to face with him once again, Danna smiled. Quay did as well, but his was followed by kisses. He kissed away every single thought and apprehension Danna had. With slow, precise strokes of his tongue, he warmed her mouth and neck with affectionate tongue play.

"You want me to make love to you?"

Danna nodded.

"Say it."

"Whose house is this?"

"Mine. Now answer my question."

"Quay, I want to get in your bed. I don't want to do it out here on the floor like this."

Quay's gold seeped between his juicy lips as he cracked a smile at her. "Aight, but I need you tell me something first."

Danna raised her eyebrow.

"What happened to you marrying me when I got out?"

"You brought me here."

"So, had I taken you to the courthouse to marry me, you would have done it?"

Danna nodded again, with no hesitation.

"Why?" Quay's large hands massaged the dark skin of Danna's back. He maintained eye contact with her the entire time.

Danna sat pondering her answer for a few seconds, trying to make sure she articulated herself well enough to make him understand her without thinking she was crazy.

"You don't have to be scared to tell me."

"I'm not, I just don't know how to say it."

"Just say it however you want me to hear it."

"What if it doesn't come out right?" The short loc hanging in Quay's face caught her attention until she grabbed it to ease her nerves.

While she sat in his lap playing with his hair, Quay sat patiently waiting for her to open up to him. Danna could tell by how relaxed he was that he was prepared to wait there until she'd told him what he wanted to hear. Nervous out of her mind, and afraid that it all might blow up in her face, Danna began to bounce her leg. Quay stopped her with an open palm to her thigh.

"If I'm your man Danna, you can't be afraid to talk to me."

"But you're not my man though."

"I ain't?" Quay's voice was calm, but Danna felt the weight of his question.

"I mean, yeah, I guess you can be."

"Just tell me why you would have married me, we'll get back to me being your man after I find out why I'm good enough to be your husband."

Danna snickered at the irony of his statement.

"I would marry you because I know you would take care of me. It's like ever since we've known each other, you've always been straight up with me. You never lie, you never rush me, and you never demand more out of me than I can give you. You're patient with me. The way you study me, and the way you handle me, lets me know that you care about the person that I am. I like that." She finally released his hair and looked at him. "I need attention because I'm suffering from abandonment issues terribly because of Echo, so I fight men off instead of letting them close to me. Then to add Don onto the pile of insecurities I deal with because of Echo, I can barely believe you like me." Danna's hands found the band of Quay's pants and tugged at it. "I like that you see me, and if you can see me like this when we haven't even been together, then I can only imagine how you'll look at me when I'm your wife."

"So, you trust me, basically?"

"If you want to dumb it down to just that, then yes."

Quay hugged her to him playfully. "I'm not dumbing it down, baby. I'm just trying to get you to see that our love can be just that simple. We don't have to complicate it with no bullshit, no lies, or no other people. Just us two." With her neck held tightly between his two hands, Quay kissed her lips. "So, we getting married or what?"

"I guess. Even though I like Danna Mendoza better than Danna Elijah."

Quay's laughter interrupted their intimacy, but she was happy it had because he looked so amazing when he laughed. Just beautiful for no reason at all.

"Danna Elijah sounds fucking amazing. You tripping."

Danna was still smiling when she leaned forward and grabbed his bottom lip. "Can we have sex now?"

"Yeah, there's just one more thing I have to tell you."

"Tell me after you put it in," Danna's voice was low and sultry as she fondled with the weighty piece of him that she couldn't wait to feel. "I'll listen to you then, right now I'm not listening."

"Bet," with one arm around her back and the other pushing himself from the floor, Quay stood to his feet and carried Danna to his bedroom.

The long dark hallway finally ended when he pushed them into his bedroom. Danna's eyes wanted to roam over everything he'd used as decoration, but couldn't due to the fact that just the smell of him had her fiending. The entire room smelled like Quay and it was making her fall apart.

"We gon' get married for real?" Quay asked as he placed Danna softly on the bed and removed the rest of his clothing.

Danna eyed Quay's nude body before screaming dramatically. "Hell yes I'm marrying you. With dick like that," Danna rolled her eyes, "just let me have it, Quay. I don't think I can wait no longer."

His throaty chuckle vibrated her chest as he laid on top of her. Danna's legs fell completely open, surrendering to him. With no words spoken, Quay removed the rest of her clothing and tossed them carelessly to the floor. Danna's body was growing more and more impatient by the second. When she felt Quay at her opening she pushed forward in a hurry to feel him deeper.

"Ah, shit, wait, Danna. Let me get a condom."

"Married people don't use condoms."

"We ain't married." He looked at her with the same sexy look she'd been doting over since meeting him.

"And I'm not waiting. So, what's it going to be?"

Quay looked at her for a little too long for Danna's liking and it pissed her off. She was all for safe sex, but he was acting like she was nasty, and before she allowed him to insult her, she'd keep her goodies to herself.

Danna sat up on the bed and pushed past him. "Move out my fucking way."

"Girl, you better lay your ass back down."

"Nigga no." Danna fumbled with her panties. "You just tried me."

Quay snatched Danna to him forcefully before placing a sloppy kiss on her lips. "Ain't nobody trying your ass, I was just trying to make sure I didn't get you pregnant, but fuck it. You want a baby by me, then I'll give your ass one."

Danna was back on the bed with Quay between her legs within seconds. This time, he didn't even give her time to change her mind before pushing his way inside. Two loud gasps sounded throughout the room as they connected. Danna's eyes fluttered while his closed. Yeah, he was her husband. She could feel it. All in the sex. Everything about that immediate connection foretold the rest of her life.

"Fucking Danna!" He grunted loudly.

"Baby," she moaned as she wrapped her legs around him.

"You ready to listen?"

"Yeah," Danna barely got out between ragged breathing.

Quay leaned back just enough to look in her eyes. Danna stared back up at him lovingly, even pushing some of his hair from his face.

"I love you," she whispered.

"I'm a Fed."

Say what? Danna's smile disappeared. *What in the fuck did he just say?*

21

The truth behind your lies

Danna sat holding her head in her hands as people swarmed around her in a rush. The room was buzzing with an array of conversations while she did her best to maintain the little bit of sanity she had left. It had been a long day, and from the looks of things, was only going to get longer. It had been a little over an hour since she'd heard the first lie, which led to the second, and the third, and so on.

For the life of her, she couldn't fathom the amount of betrayal she felt in that moment. The feeling had been so overwhelming that she could hardly believe it was happening. She'd been in the same spot for the past twenty minutes trying, with no success.

"Miss Mendoza," the redheaded agent called her name.

Danna raised her head, but said nothing.

"I know this may be a lot for you right now, but your cooperation would really help."

"My cooperation?" Danna scoffed. "What y'all need my cooperation for? It looks to me that you all have been doing just fine without me all of this time, who needs my help all of a sudden?" Danna's sarcasm gave way to the officer's discomfort.

She could tell by the way she cleared her throat and fluffed her collar before speaking again. "Don," she paused and Danna's eyes closed. "We need you to call him."

"Call him? You've got to be fucking kidding me."

"Dan," Quay's hypnotizing voice captured her attention.

His locs were pulled back into a neat ponytail at the back of his neck while the gold grill that she loved the most was nowhere in sight. A set of perfectly white teeth rested in their place as his thick lips covered them slightly. His eyes were sympathetic as he reached his hand out to her. Danna's eyes shrank as she squinted them at him in anger.

"Danna." She corrected him curtly.

Quay licked his lips and Danna rolled her eyes. That sexy bastard. He was the reason she'd been caught slipping and ended up in the mess she was in right then. If she could help it, she would have never allowed the police to corner her.

"Can I speak with you for a second?" Quay asked her properly.

"Oh, you don't even talk like you're from the hood anymore." Danna smacked her lips sarcastically. "Isn't that something? Different element, different Quay huh? Oh wait, Federal Agent Elijah, right?"

Quay's chest heaved as his nostrils flared. Danna could tell by the heavy breath he'd just released that he was angry, but she didn't care at all. She was angry too and would slap the taste from his mouth if she felt it would serve some sort of purpose.

"Excuse us for a minute." Quay told the redhead before snatching Danna from the sofa by her arm.

Danna fought against him pointlessly because he didn't release his hold on her arm, nor did he slow his stride. They were outside in his backyard before he stopped moving. The moment she was steady on her feet, Danna snatched her arm away from him and began walking away. Quay caught up with her immediately, grabbing her from behind.

"Get off me, Agent Elijah!"

Before she could utter another word, Quay spun her around so that they were face-to-face. His eyebrows were scrunched together and his face held a scowl.

"Stop this fucking shit. Right now. Just quit it." He shook her roughly. "I know you're mad, but you know me better than to think I'm about to let you talk to me any kind of way. Now I'ma give you some time to be angry, but you better get that attitude in check." Quay shook her once more before letting her go.

The moment he did, Danna's hand came down hard across the side of his face. "Don't you dare tell me how to fucking act. All this time I've been thinking you were one thing when you're really another. You've been around my family, you know all of our business and shit, I can't believe you would do this." Danna cleared her throat to hold back the tears she felt rising.

Quay was so handsome, and she'd really been feeling him. So, to be standing there with him looking the way he looked, smelling the way he smelled, and him not being the person she was used to seeing, was taking her some time to comprehend.

"I'm trying to see who you are right now, Quay. I mean damn! All this shit you've been to me and it's all be a lie. Everything you said, everything we were," her words trailed off and she had to hold her head down to prevent him from seeing what he'd done to her.

If it was one thing she was tired of, it was niggas lying to her and making her cry. She'd cried enough for ten women and she was over it.

"Danna, everything we were was real to me." Quay was back in her space and holding her by both of her arms. "My profession was the only lie. Everything else was real, I swear on me it was real." Quay leaned down some so that he could see her face. "You are real to me. I wasn't playing about my feelings for you. It's fucked up on my part because I never meant to fall for you the way I did, but fuck that shit now. I love you and we're still getting married. You're not getting away from me this easy."

Soft sniffles could be heard as Danna did her best to keep

quiet. She'd been trying to hide her tears from Quay but he wouldn't let her. His face was only inches away from hers and he was directly in her space. So close that she could feel his breath on her face.

"The person I was to you, that's me. All this other shit is just how I make a living. You're my girl, and that's what you're going to stay." Quay pecked her forehead before leaning back some so that he could wipe her tears away. "We may have met in some crazy ass circumstances, but we met and that's all that matters to me."

"Not to me. You lied then, and you're probably lying now." Danna tried to pull away but was pulled right back. "You're flaw, Quay. You're a liar and I don't want to do any of this with you anymore."

"Danna,"

"Don't call my name, Quay," Danna stepped back while shaking her head. "You're just like Don, you just want to use me up for your selfish reasons, not giving a fuck about how I might feel. I'm done. For real this time, I'm done with all of y'all."

"Don't say that to me, Danna." Quay stepped to her and she held her hand up to keep him away. "You can't do that shit to me."

"Watch me." Danna swiped her tears away and nodded her head trying to reassure herself. "I'ma get past this mess with you the same way I got past it with Don."

There was silence for a while and it almost alarmed Danna, but she forced herself not to care about him or what he thought about her and their situation. It took her a few more moments to stop herself from crying, before she finally lifted her head. When she was able to make eye contact, her chest constricted. Quay was staring at her with glossy eyes.

His bottom lip was tucked between his teeth and he had pulled his hair free of the ponytail. The dark brown eyes that she'd fallen victim to so many times before glared at her.

"So, you're standing here telling me that we're not going to be together?" Quay's arm dropped from his face and fell to his side.

"After all of the shit I've said to you? You're really going say that to me?"

"Yes, Quay!" Danna screamed to the top of her lungs. "Look at this shit we're in. Just look at it."

"I don't give a fuck about this, this is nothing." Quay snatched her to him forcefully and held her tight. "But you," He grabbed her chin and made her look at him. "You are fucking everything. Now listen, we're about to go in this house, I'ma put all of them out of here, and it's just going to be you and me, okay?" Quay kissed her chin, then her nose, both eyes followed. "Let me make this right before you leave me. Just let me do that."

As always, Danna's defenses weakened at the first sign of affection. She was doing her best to stand firm but everything in her was making her want to open her heart to Quay. Though his words sounded truthful, that wasn't enough. They'd sounded that way before.

"I promise, I can make this right. I am who I am. I just have a job that you don't like, but that's it. The person I've been to you doesn't change."

"You're a snitch." Danna quipped.

Quay smirked, as did she.

"No, I'm not. I protect snitches."

Danna rolled her eyes and gave way to her smile. "You're going to make them leave right now?"

Quay nodded. "Under two conditions."

"What?"

"One, you have to call Don. It's important, and two, you have to agree to still marry me."

"You're pushing it now." Danna shook her head. "I'll call Don, but that marriage part is out of the question. I don't know what I even think of you right now."

Quay grabbed her mouth and kissed her sensually. Danna eagerly obliged. They stood kissing for a while, until Quay finally pulled away and smiled at her.

"You gon' call Don?"

Danna nodded. "Call him for what? You never told me what's going on."

When Quay stepped back, Danna got a tad bit nervous. He was rubbing his chin and looking at the ground as if trying to think of what to do next. She waited in anticipation of what was going to come next. When she couldn't hold it anymore, she walked over to him and touched his arm softly.

"Is it that bad? I mean I can kind of tell that it's something because you're the police, and all of your police friends want me to call him." Danna licked her lips and ran her hand through her hair. "Then you scooped me from the hotel out of nowhere, so clearly y'all are watching him or something. What's up?"

"I'm trying to think of an easy way to say this."

"Just say it. At this point, I don't see anything surprising me."

Quay shook his head and some of his hair fell over his shoulder. "Your father is in witness protection."

Danna's eyebrows raised in confusion. "Say what now?"

"Your father has been a confidential informant for years now."

"You're lying. My daddy isn't a snitch."

"He is."

Her head shook adamantly as she took a seat on the small wooden swing next to her. Quay followed her and pushed the swing some once he sat so that they were rocking back and forth.

"Echo used to be big time in the streets, but once we caught up with his ass, he flipped. It was either do jail time, or make other niggas do it for him, and what do you think he chose?"

The breath left Danna's body as she sat forward holding her head in her hands. This wasn't true. It couldn't be. Her father dealt dope, he didn't snitch. That wasn't for people like him. Echo was street through and through. There was no way he was turning on his own people.

Quay's hand to her back provided enough comfort for her to raise her head again. "I know what you must be thinking, but from what I was told, it wasn't easy for him. The only reason he agreed to it was to protect and provide for y'all."

Danna's misty eyes came to him as she waited with hope.

"Being an informant allows him to carry his name in the streets without ever being found out, while still being with you all sometimes." Quay shrugged. "I can understand why he did it."

"I can't believe this." Danna sat back and lay her head on Quay's shoulder. "So, how does Don come into all of this? He's a snitch too?"

Quay tickled Danna and she fell over in laughter. "Stop saying snitch like that." His laughter brought about more of hers. They laughed until he stopped tickling her.

Danna wiped her face and turned so that she was facing Quay. "Tell me about Don."

"I wasn't on this particular case in the beginning, but from my understanding, Don and your father were really good friends and your father flipped on him. Apparently, Don is the first person to ever realize Echo was the truth behind all his lies, and planned to get him back. He's been plotting to kill all of y'all for a while now, but—"

"All of us? He was going to kill me?"

"No, I don't think so. That's where the problem came in. He had every intention of doing that, but I guess after falling in love with you, he couldn't." Quay kissed her forehead. "I guess you have that effect on people."

Danna smiled bashfully and looked away from him for a minute.

"This is crazy."

Quay stood to his feet and pulled her with him. "Yeah, it is. We've got it under control though. We've had people in place to watch your family from the time he was released. Echo couldn't come around much, so it bought us some time, but the moment him and your father ended up at Ezra's dinner together, we figured it was time to move."

Speechless was a good word to describe Danna right then. None of the things she was hearing made any sense to her. She'd thought her life with Quay had all been a lie, but hearing the things Quay was telling her was downright devastating.

Danna palmed her forehead. "Lord, I can't take this."

"Yes, you can. It'll all be over soon."

"So, you were one of the people here to watch me?"

Quay nodded. "Myself and Agent Collier."

"Collier, who's that?"

"Cannon's mom."

The hell you say! Danna's knees got weak. She couldn't take anymore.

"Just take me in the house. I need to lie down, I can't even think straight right now."

As always, Quay's hands were on her. Once she was secure in his arms, he looked down at her and rested his forehead against hers.

"Forget all of this, I'll handle it . . . what I can't believe is that I was seriously out here about to cry over your ass."

"I can. Most polices are bitches." Danna's laughter mixed with his once he realized she was joking. The lighter note was appreciated.

"We'll see who is crying when I get done with you."

Danna looked him up and down once before heading into the house. Quay followed close behind. As soon as she laid eyes on all the agents circulating through his house, all bets were off. Danna spun on her heels preparing to go back outside, but bumped into Quay's chest instead.

"For me, please. I promise it's almost over."

Danna pouted, but rejoined him back in the house. "You owe me for this shit."

"I know I do, and I'm sorry." He wrapped one arm around her shoulder and pulled her back to his chest. With a kiss to her ear, he made it all better. "I'll spend forever paying you back."

22

I should have known better

The loud noise coming from the front room of Danna's home startled Cannon awake. Her eyes popped open as she looked around the bedroom wildly. It was black dark like it had been before she'd fallen asleep, only now she could tell that she wasn't alone. The weird feeling of another person's presence stirred up her uneasiness.

"Danna?" she called out.

"Nah, baby girl, try again." Ezra's voice had Cannon jumping from her spot on the bed, even knocking the bedside lamp over in the process.

She'd been at Danna's house all day waiting on her to come back and had obviously fallen asleep in the process. Her hands went to her eyes quickly, trying to rub the sleep from them.

"Ezzy!" She squealed in excitement.

Cannon was on her feet and straining her eyes the best she could trying to find him. With her arms stretched out in front of her, she felt around the darkness for her man's body.

"Come to me, Ezra. Flip the light on or something. I can't see you."

"Danna's house is always dark like this." Ezra spoke again.

"I know. Hit the light. The switch is by the door."

Cannon stood in place waiting for Ezra to turn the light on. She could feel and hear his movement, but it was still dark.

"Ezra, what are you doing?" she grew impatient.

"Getting you ready to see me."

Cannon smiled at his voice. She was so in love. "I'm not supposed to be seeing you. You should be in Texas by now."

"I couldn't leave without you. I came back to take you with me."

Finally! The lights flipped on and she could see her baby.

A loud scream pierced the silence of the room before Cannon's hands landed over her open mouth. Her eyes were wide as saucers as she stared at the large silver gun resting against the back of Ezra's head. His long hair was down and covering his face slightly as he stood, noticeably affected by the situation.

"Calm down, mama. I'm good."

Still in a state of shock, Cannon shook her head while still covering her mouth. In her heart she wanted to believe that Ezra was "good," but from what she could see that was most definitely not the case.

"Don," Cannon cleared her throat. "What are you doing? Why do you have a gun to his head?"

The crazed look on his face while holding Ezra at gunpoint was enough to kill Cannon by itself, but she had to hold it together. *I knew this nigga was crazy*, Cannon thought as she finally lowered her hands from her face and looked Don in the eye.

He was sweating profusely and his breathing was rapid as if he were in some sort of hurry. His eye darted all around the room as his hand tightened on the fabric of Ezra's shirt.

"Where's Danna?" his eyes went from Cannon to Danna's bed before returning to Cannon.

"I don't know. The last time I saw her was when she left with you earlier. She hasn't been back since." Cannon swallowed hard. "Why, what's wrong?"

"She's fucking with me." Don growled lowly before growling a little louder. "Somebody's going to tell me something." Cannon gasped when Don removed the gun from Ezra's head and pointed at her. "Call her, call her right fucking now."

Cannon ran to grab her phone but Ezra stopped her. "No, Cannon! Don't call her. He's going to kill her."

Don's scowl deepened at the same time as he slapped Ezra across the top of his head with the gun. "Shut your punk ass up!" He then pointed his finger at Cannon. "You fucking call her right now! Call her before I kill every fucking body!"

Cannon's body shook with fear as she looked at Ezra's bleeding head before running to grab her phone. Although she didn't want Danna hurt, she didn't want her or Ezra to get hurt either. At least with Danna around, she had some leverage. Don loved her, and not regular love. That nigga was downright crazy in love with her. Maybe she could talk some sense into him and they could all live.

"Cannon, don't you fucking call her," Ezra told her weakly.

Cannon looked to him with pleading eyes as she held her cellphone in her hand. "I have to, Ezra. He's not going to hurt her. Are you Don?" Cannon nodded her head at him.

In a daze, Don nodded his along with her. "I love her."

"The fuck?" Ezra spun around. "The fuck you mean you in love with her? Nigga, you're old as shit."

Cannon hurried to intervene, because Ezra clearly didn't care. "They're in love, Ezzy. I saw it myself. It's beautiful."

Don's hand released Ezra's shirt as he walked toward Cannon nodding his head. "It is, and it's real. She's just mad right now. I can't let her leave me, Cannon. Call her, please."

"I will, but you have to promise not to hurt her. Danna loves you."

"But she left!" Don stood from the bed and began pacing the floor back and forth. "She fucking left me." He said again before hitting himself in the head with his fist.

Cannon and Ezra both looked on in uncertainty. Ezra took this opportunity to get closer to her. Once his body was a shield between Don and Cannon, Cannon called out to Don.

"Calm down, I'm about to call her."

Don stopped walking and looked at Cannon. He was still breathing hard, and his eyes still held a crazed look, but he wasn't pointing the gun anymore, so that was a good sign. Before calling Danna, Cannon said a quick prayer in her head that she would answer. The phone rang and rang and just before the call went to voicemail, Danna's voice came over the line.

"Hey, Cannon, let me call you back sis. I'm in the middle of something."

"No!" Cannon yelped without thinking. "I mean, hold on. I have someone that wants to talk to you really quick."

"What? Who?" Danna had an attitude for reasons unknown to Cannon, but oh well. She was about to talk to Don whether she wanted to or not. "Tell whoever it is, I'll talk to them another day."

"Look, Danna, it's Don."

Don's eyes widened when he heard his name. Cannon gave him a soothing smile before extending the phone toward him. Before taking it, Don just looked at it for a moment, but eventually grabbed it.

"Oh," Danna's voice lowered. "Put him on."

"I'm here already . . . why'd you leave?" Don's voice had taken on a totally different tone that before.

He'd been yelling and threatening to Cannon and Ezra, but his voice was soft and almost sweet as he spoke with her.

"I'm sorry, I just wasn't sure how I felt about being there after the whole Totiana thing."

Cannon watched as Ezra's face frowned in confusion. He looked to her with questioning eyes, but Cannon just shook her head slightly. It was a time and place for everything and right then wasn't it. She would have to fill him in on everything at a later date. Right then, her sole focus was on staying alive, something he obviously knew nothing about.

"Danna, I told you about that. Fuck her. Fuck the kids, fuck everything except for you." Don began pacing again. "I can't live without you."

There was a long pause before Danna began talking again. "Don, it's not that simple."

"Yes it is." He fumed. "You're the one making it hard." Don flopped on the bed and sighed heavily. "Where you at? Just let me come see you, please. I just need to see you."

"I don't know, Don, you're saying all of that now, but things could change."

"No the fuck they won't!" he stood back to his feet yelling.

"Don, let me talk to her for you," Cannon reached for the phone.

Don looked like he wanted to object, but held the phone out to her anyway. "You better not fuck up."

"Danna, girl, Don loves you. You need to stop acting up on him. He popped up over your house with Ezra and everything trying to get you back. Everybody makes mistakes, he said he's not worrying about that girl and those kids, then neither should you."

"That's easy for you to say." Danna sucked her teeth. "You're not the one in love with him."

The way Don's chest sank and his head fell forward displayed his obvious defeat. Cannon reached to pat his shoulder so he wouldn't lose hope before she could get her and Ezra out safely.

"Danna,"

"Don, just give me a few minutes and I'll be there. Are you still at my house?"

"Yes."

"Stay there. I'm on the way."

After Cannon was sure their conversation was over, she pulled the phone away and sat next to Don on the opposite side of the bed from Ezra. He was bent over holding a shirt that had been on Danna's bed, on his head. His face was stoic and Cannon could only guess why. Ezra was a very no nonsense type of person, so she was more than sure that he was over the whole situation.

"You think she's coming for real?" Don asked Cannon.

"I know she is. Danna loves you just as much as you love her. Y'all just going through some stuff right now. All relationships have their ups and downs. You just have to be strong."

Don didn't say anything but she could tell that he was listening, so she continued. "Me and Ezra are at each other's throat ninety percent of the time, but you see how good we are together."

Don's head turned slightly in her direction before a small smile appeared. "Yeah, I saw y'all the other night at the little dinner, it was cool."

Cannon smiled. "See, it's not all bad." She was about to say something more but her phone rang. "Do you mind if I answer the phone for my mom?"

A quick shake of his head was his reply.

"Hey Ma, what's going on? Everything okay?"

"No, listen to me, Cannon. Don is a very dangerous man. Are you and Ezra okay?"

Cannon's mind went from zero to one hundred because of that one question. How in the hell did Karina know anything about what was going on right then, furthermore how in the world did she know Don was dangerous? Cannon's forehead frowned momentarily, but she got herself back together quickly.

"Yes, we're good. Just sitting at Danna's house waiting for her to get back."

"Danna is on her way, but she's coming with the police. When she gets there, I want you and Ezra to walk out of the front door."

"But Mama, I don't want to leave her here by herself. I told her I would spend the night." Cannon did her best to play it off.

Don was staring at her with an unreadable look. It wasn't threatening, but it wasn't the friendliest either. Cannon gave him a small smile to keep him calm as she finished her conversation.

"She's going to be fine, you all just need to be out of there. Do you understand me?"

"Yes ma'am."

"I'll be there shortly. Call me if something goes wrong before I get there."

"Yes ma'am." Cannon ended the call and tossed her phone onto the bed.

The situation was such a stressful one, she wanted to do everything she could to ensure she remained calm and normal. Don may have been chilling right then, but he'd still walked Ezra into the house at gunpoint. Not to mention the ferocious way he knocked him across his head as well.

"Call Danna again," Ezra told Cannon.

The shirt on his head was soaked with blood as he lay backward on the bed. One of his legs was also resting on the bed while the other one hung off.

"Yeah, call her again." Don co-signed.

"She's on the way y'all."

Don spun around to her and pointed in her face with the gun. "Do what the fuck I just said, and you," He pointed toward Ezra, "you come with me."

"Where y'all going? You don't want to be here when I call her?" Cannon rushed out as she hopped from the bed and grabbed Don's arm.

He looked at her like she'd lost her mind before snatching away and pushing her backward. Ezra immediately pushed between them and stood in front of Cannon.

"Keep your fucking hands off my girl. I don't give a fuck what you do to me, but you ain't about to be putting your hands on her like I'm not standing here."

Don and Ezra participated in a small stare off before the scowl on his face softened and his top lip curled into a smile.

"Nigga, I fucking like you. Bring your young ass on." Don began walking out of the room. "Got more heart than your pussy ass daddy."

Cannon and Ezra shared a confused look before Ezra continued out of the door behind Don. Cannon followed. She still hadn't called Danna yet, but that wasn't her biggest concern at the moment. Don and what he planned to do with Ezra was.

Cannon stood back watching as Don pushed Ezra out of the door in front of him. The way Ezra continued to scuffle with Don even with his head bleeding profusely was really starting to worry Cannon. Although she knew this would never happen, she wished Ezra would just go with the flow and stop fighting Don every step of the way.

"Call Danna!" Don spun around and yelled at her from where he was standing. He and Ezra were now standing along the side of Danna's street near the back of his pickup truck.

Cannon snapped out of her trance rapidly and pecked her fingers across her phone screen to call Danna. When she answered, Cannon wasted no time.

"Bitch, where the fuck you at? This crazy ass nigga over here has me and Ezra at gunpoint. You need to get your ass here," she whispered quickly.

"What?! I'm about to pull up. I'm like two seconds away, but girl, I got Quay with me."

Cannon's head began to spin. "Why, Danna? Why the fuck would you bring that nigga over here? Don is acting crazy as hell."

"It's a long ass story, but he's the damn police, girl," Danna sighed. "Him and your fucking mama. Apparently, my daddy is in witness protection or some shit and they've been around here spying on our ass this whole time."

"Get the fuck out of here." Cannon's open palm went to her forehead.

"Girl, they've been trying to save us from Don."

Cannon's eyes went to Don and Ezra. Don was snatching

something from the back of his truck, while holding on to Ezra. Every time Don moved, he snatched Ezra's lean body with him.

"Help me get this shit!" Don screamed at Ezra, making Cannon's heart drop in the process.

"Oh my god! Ezra, just help him," Cannon yelped in a panic. "Danna, get your ass here."

"What he do to Ezzy? I'm pulling in now."

Cannon could hear the panic in Danna's tone, but she was settled quickly by who Cannon assumed to be Quay. All she knew was the voice was deep and it was close. Her stomach was twisted into knots as she watched Ezra struggle to pull the large bag over the back of the truck. When it finally hit the ground and Ezra was able to stand back to his full height, Cannon breathed a sigh of relief. He was moving slowly and looked like he was about to pass out, but leaned over the back of the truck instead.

The bright headlights of the car shone into Cannon's eyes as the dark truck turned into the driveway. Seconds later, Danna was out of the passenger seat and headed towards Don. He didn't miss a beat as he marched toward the truck she'd just exited.

"What nigga this is?" Don yelled at her as he passed by her, headed for the truck.

Danna moved quickly to grab Don's arm. He stopped as soon as she grabbed him. "That don't matter. What matters is why you're at my house with a gun? What's the problem?" Her hand went to the side of his face.

Cannon watched as Don leaned into the palm of Danna's hand and stepped closer to her. Minutes passed with the two of them staring at each other, before his hands circled her waist. Danna's body went willingly.

"You left?"

"I already told you why." She rubbed her hands from his face down over both of his arms. "Why are you here with a gun?"

"I had something to show you."

Cannon, Danna, and Ezra were all ears as they watched Don

pull away from Danna and walk toward his car. Ezra moved away the moment Don got too close.

"Ezra, come help me with this shit," he mumbled.

"Hell, nah. My fucking head hurt. I can hardly stand up," Ezra mumbled as he walked toward Cannon.

Don looked over his shoulder and raised his gun toward Ezra but Danna's flailing arms stopped him. "Don, no! What are you doing? You would really shoot my brother?"

"I would shoot anybody as long as it got me you." Don stared at her for a minute before his eyes drifted behind her toward the truck.

Cannon followed his gaze and felt the weight in his statement. Cannon could hear his threat loud and clear. This was getting to be too much. With a deep sigh, Cannon met Ezra in the middle of the grass and helped him to the door.

"Call the ambulance." She pushed him and her phone toward the door, but the loud sound of a gun being fired paused all of them.

Ezra's body was in front of Cannon pushing her back into the house at the same time Quay emerged from the truck. A brief uproar of screams circulated throughout the yard as everyone tried to figure out what was happening.

"Don!" Danna yelled while walking to him.

Still holding the gun, Don stood with his face frowned and heavy breathing. The look on his face as he stared at Quay was of sheer anger. Cannon was so afraid of what would happen next that she could barely breathe.

"Why the fuck do you keep playing with me Danna? Huh? Why the fuck do you think I'm some type of game? You think I didn't recognize this nigga?" Don screamed into her face while pointed his gun at Quay.

"I'm not playing with you. You're just acting crazy," Danna answered weakly. "You're being irrational for nothing. You've come to my house with ill intent but you want me to run away with you?" Danna's voice cracked. "I'm scared Don, I'm really scared of you right now."

"I would never hurt you and you know it."

"I don't know anything. Look at what you're doing."

Don looked around the yard as if thinking about what she was saying. His gaze landed on a silent Quay and he grew angry all over again.

"I'ma kill this nigga."

Quay held his hands up in surrender. "I just wanted to make sure Danna was good."

It was as if the sound of Quay's voice infuriated Don, because the moment he began talking Don began moving. He was in Quay's face with his gun resting on his cheek in no time. Danna and Cannon both yelped in fear.

"Just good, nigga. Anytime she's with me she's good."

"It doesn't look like it. She's back there about to fall the fuck out with all that crying, and look at you. You're right here."

The way Quay taunted Don had Cannon clutching the side of Ezra's arm. Fear gripped every fiber of her being as she anticipated what was to come.

A sly smirk crossed Don's face. "Oh, you think you real hard, don't you?" Don nodded. "Yeah, you do, but I got something for you. I'll show you hard." Don snatched away and walked to the back door of his truck.

Everybody watched to see what he had. It took him a minute, but the moment Echo emerged from the car, battered and bruised, Danna broke down. Ezra moved to go toward him, but Cannon stopped him. Don had Echo's hands and feet bound with rope while blood leaked from different parts of his face and neck. Bruises were everywhere, and one of his eyes were swollen shut. It was sickening to say the least.

"Yo, nigga. What the fuck?" Quay asked while shaking his head in disdain.

Don smiled widely as he pushed Echo toward him. Echo stumbled and fell right into Danna, who had been waiting to grab him. Her sorrowful cries filled the yard as she sat holding his barely breathing body.

"Yeah, nigga. I did that shit! That's what you call hard." Don sneered at Quay.

"No, this is what you call stupid. Why would you hurt him like this?" Danna was the only one that could find her voice.

The dark night and calm air surrounding them took over as Don watched her in deep thought. Cannon and Ezra were both seated in the doorway trying their best to make sense of the situation. The lone tear running down the side of Ezra's face broke Cannon's heart. She hoped it would all be over soon.

"He ruined my life. I was just about to make it, and he stole it all!" Don's yells were boisterous and intimidating as he ran over and kicked Echo's body.

Small gurgling noises came from him as Danna shifted so that she could use her body as a shield. Don watched her try to cover her father's frame and laughed.

"Get the fuck up, Danna, this nigga is finna' die. You can either die with him, or get your ass out of my way."

"No!" Danna yelled.

Don chuckled when he pointed the gun at Danna. "Your choice." The possessed-looking smirk on his face detoured Cannon from even breathing, let alone moving to help.

"Danna, move!" Ezra jumped up and ran toward them.

The sight of him trying to pull Danna away was petrifying and heartbreaking all at once. Cannon could hardly take it.

"Danna, get up, baby." Quay spoke and sent Don into a bullet-firing frenzy.

The next couple of seconds of that night would never leave Cannon's mind again. The blur of anger and rage flooded the atmosphere, killing everything in its path . . . and leaving Cannon with nothing.

Epilogue

"I don't know how I let you talk me into this." Danna paced the floor back and forth while holding her head.

Cannon's tears slid down her cheeks as she fought back the earth shattering scream she wanted to release.

"It's the best thing for you to do, Danna. You need to get it together." Cannon walked to her and grabbed both of her shoulders. "Ezra would be happy as hell if he would have been here to see this." More tears cascaded down Cannon's face.

"Aw, Cannon, I'm sorry."

Cannon waved Danna away and forced a smile out. "It's fine, I'm fine. It's just the baby." Cannon dabbed at her eyes again.

Danna felt so sorry for Cannon. It had been a hell of a ride for her over the past month, and every day was just as bad if not worse than the one before. Danna had been trying her best to be there for her in every way possible, but there was only so much she could do.

Cannon loved Ezra, and only wanted him. There was nothing or nobody that could change that. It didn't matter who Cannon was around, if she thought about Ezra she'd be right back crying. She loved to blame it on his baby that she was carrying, but

Danna knew better. She could recognize a broken heart anywhere.

"Just finish getting ready so we can get out there. If I sit back here with you any longer I'm going to cry myself a river."

Danna held Cannon's forehead to hers and closed her eyes. "I'm sorry about all of this. I feel like it's my fault."

"It's not though, it was Don and Echo's. Echo knew the kind of stuff he was in, he could have at least told somebody." Cannon exhaled softly. "Karina too. I can't believe she had me around here thinking she worked for an insurance company."

"Right! Her and Quay. I don't know which one of them is worse. The insurance worker or the fake drug dealer."

The girls laughed before embracing tightly. "We're going to get through this. Don't worry about a thing. It's hard, but we're strong."

Cannon nodded and pulled away. The two of them busied themselves for the next few minutes making sure their makeup was still in place before walking out of the bathroom. There were people everywhere waiting, but only a few of them mattered to them.

"I thought you were in there changing your mind." Quay smiled down at Danna before hugging her with one arm.

The dark blue sling holding his other arm prohibited a full embrace. "I don't think I could if I tried."

"Aww," Cannon cooed, just as Vonetta and a host of other relatives walked up.

Cannon hugged Vonetta and a few others before going back to Danna. As soon as she was close Danna grabbed her hand and squeezed it.

"You ready?" Danna asked Cannon.

"What I need to be ready for? You're the one getting married."

"You need to be ready because I'm about to marry your ass too." Ezra's voice came from behind the girls.

Danna and Cannon both spun around with shocked expressions

on their faces. They both ran to hug him, but Danna was held back by Quay so that Cannon could get to him first. Danna punched Quay playfully before she marveled at her brother and his soon-to-be bride. He was dressed casually in slacks and a button up, just as Quay was, while holding a small bouquet of flowers.

"I should kill you. Why didn't you tell me you were coming?"

Ezra smiled at Cannon. "It was a surprise, now let's get this shit over with before I fall out. I've been sweating my whole plane ride here."

Laughter serenaded the hallways of the small courthouse.

"I already don't know how I let Quay's ass talk me into coming here anyway. Y'all know how I feel about courthouses." Ezra wiped the small trickles of sweat from his forehead.

"I know right," Danna mumbled.

The area around them went quiet for a minute, all of them rec-ollecting the last time they were in a courthouse. It had been one of the hardest days of Danna's life. To see the man she loved being sentenced to life in prison for killing her father had done some-thing to her.

It had taken her forever to get past that type of hurt, but she'd done it. The betrayal and pain she felt behind being in love with her enemy was indescribable, but with Quay's help she'd done it. He had been there every step of the way with her and hadn't let her fall victim to any parts of the trial that seemed unbearable.

"Get out of your feelings, you didn't love him like you think you did."

Danna looked up into Quay's handsome face. He was always doing his best to make light of the situation, but it never got easier.

"I don't even see why you want to marry me after that."

Quay pushed some of his locs from his face. "I wanted to marry you before that remember?"

"I remember, even if she doesn't." Cannon butted into their conversation.

Danna pushed her away playfully before looping her arm through Quay's. "It's crazy how just when I was ready to give up on love, you showed up and stopped me."

"I had always been here, just waiting on you." Quay stopped and pecked Danna's waiting lips. "Now are you going to marry me today or what?"

"Bruh, you sound like me. I've been telling Cannon she was going to be my wife since I met her, and she ain't believe me." Ezra wrapped his arm around Cannon's neck. "Now look at her. About to marry me and have my baby."

"Lord, don't remind me." Karina's voice grabbed all of their attention as she and Yara walked up.

"Mommy!" Cannon squealed while grabbing Karina's neck. "What are you doing here?"

Karina looked at Cannon as if she should have known better while passing Yara to Ezra. "You think I would miss you getting married?"

Cannon's eyes watered all over again as she looked around at all her family. She was too outdone to even speak.

"Come on crybaby, let's go get married so I can get back to Houston. I have a game tonight." Ezra moved Yara from the arm he had her in, so that he could hold Cannon with the other one.

"So, who's going first? Us or Y'all?" Danna asked Cannon.

"We're going together." Quay informed them.

Danna and Cannon looked at each other and smiled before the tears resurfaced. After all the trials and hard times they'd had, they'd finally found the love they deserved. Not only in themselves, but in each other, and in the God-sent men that had chosen them as their wives.

"Here's to us," Danna looked around at everybody.

"Here's to us . . . and our happily ever afters." Cannon added, as they all made their way into the beginning of their forever.

DON'T MISS

The Black Market by Kiki Swinson

Kiki Swinson's bestselling novels burn with extraordinary characters, triple-down twists—and a raw portrait of Southern life only she can deliver. Now she turns up the heat as a young woman cashes in on a sure thing—only to find some addictions are always killer . . .

Triple Threat by Camryn King

A tenacious reporter. A billionaire philanthropist. And all-access secrets that won't leave anyone safe fuel Camryn King's relentless new thriller . . .

Street Rap by Shaun Sinclair

They risked it all for the love of the dough, then wrote chart-topping songs about it. But can this crew escape their past?

ON SALE NOW!

Turn the page for an excerpt from these thrilling novels . . .

1

MISTY

I'd been in this world too long to just now be finding my way. But here I was, feeling grateful and shit about being healthy and having a roof over my head, thanks to the steady pay from my latest employer.

For the last five and a half months, I'd been collecting a check working as a pharmacy tech. The job was easy and my boss, Dr. Sanjay Malik, was a dream to work with. Not only was he a nice guy, he was very generous with the monthly bonuses he paid me and he would occasionally let me get off work early. The bonuses were for the extra work I did delivering prescriptions to senior citizens who weren't mobile or couldn't pick up their medication. Sanjay would have me deliver their meds to them, and after I completed the deliveries, he usually told me to take off work for the rest of the day, which I found awesome.

But three weeks ago, I noticed that Sanjay had me delivering meds to dark and questionable neighborhoods. I never said anything to him about it because who was I? And what was I going to get out of questioning him? He owned this place, which meant that he could fire my ass on the spot. So, I left well enough alone and minded my own damn business.

Sanjay wasn't aware of this, but I'd taken a few pills here and there for my cousin Jillian. Jillian got into a bad car accident over a year ago and hadn't fully recovered from it. Her doctor cut off her prescription meds six months ago, so I stepped in and threw a few pills at her when I was able to get my hands on some.

The first time, I stole two Percocet pills and two Vicodin pills. Each time I stole from the pharmacy, I took a few more pills. My nerves used to be on edge for about a day after each time I pocketed those pills, but since cops never showed up to cuff me, I knew Sanjay hadn't figured out I'd been stealing from him. I hoped he never would.

As soon as I walked into the pharmacy, I noticed that there were only three customers waiting for their prescriptions. I said good morning to everyone waiting as I walked behind the counter, clocked in, and went to work.

It didn't take long for Sanjay and I to ready those customers' prescriptions and get them on their way. After ringing up the last customer, I turned to Sanjay. "We got any deliveries?" I asked him while I searched through our online refill requests.

"I think we have six or maybe seven," he replied, before turning to answer the phone.

Sanjay was a handsome man. He resembled Janet Jackson's billionaire ex-husband. But unlike Janet Jackson's ex, Sanjay wasn't wealthy, at least to my knowledge. He owned this little pharmacy on the city limits of Virginia Beach, near Pembroke Mall. There was nothing fancy about the place, just your basic small business. But I often wondered why this doctor, who was doing well enough to own this place and have employees like me, wasn't married? From time to time I'd jokingly tell him that I was going to set him up with one of my friends. And his response would always be, "Oh, no. Believe me, I am fine. Women require too much."

Not too long after I started working here, he told me that his family was from Cairo, Egypt. From the way he talked about their homes and travel, I knew they were doing well for themselves. He also told me that education was a big deal in his country. And arranged marriages too.

"Think I could get me a man over in Cairo?" I'd teased. But his answer had no humor in it.

"You wouldn't want a husband from my country, because the men are very strict and the women they marry are disciplined. The things you say and do here in the US wouldn't be tolerated where I'm from."

Damn! "Yeah, whatever, Sanjay!" I'd chuckled.

Working at Sanjay's pharmacy was fairly easy. Time would go by fast. The first half of the day, it would be somewhat busy, and after two p.m. the traffic would die down. This was when I'd take my lunch break. If I didn't bring in my lunch from home, I'd leave the pharmacy and walk over to the food court in Pembroke Mall. This day was one of those days.

"I'm going to lunch, Sanjay. Want anything from Pembroke Mall?" I asked him.

"No, I'm fine. But thank you," he replied.

I walked over to the computer, clocked out, and then I left the building. On my way out, I ran into Sanjay's brother, Amir. As usual, he said nothing to me.

I'd always found it odd that Amir would stop by to see Sanjay during my lunch break. And if I was there when Amir walked into the pharmacy, Sanjay would send me on my lunch break or even send me home for the rest of the day. Now, I wasn't complaining because I loved when he let me leave work early, but at the same time, there aren't any coincidences. Something wasn't right with that guy and I knew it.

Sanjay had spoken to me about his brother, but I didn't know much. He lived close by and was married with three children. And just like Sanjay, Amir was also very handsome. But Amir never said a word to me. If I hadn't heard Amir greet Sanjay, I'd wonder if he could speak at all. He'd wave at me when he'd come and go, but that was it. I never asked Sanjay how old his brother was because you could clearly see that Amir was younger. He was never flashy. He always wore a pair of casual pants and a regular button-down shirt. He had the look of a car salesman.

I grabbed some Chinese food from the food court in the mall and then I took a seat at one of the tables near one of the mall's exits. While I was eating, I got a call from my cousin Jillian. Her father and my mother are siblings. My uncle committed suicide when we were kids, so she lived with her mother until she turned eighteen. From there she'd been back and forth from having her own apartment to sleeping under our grandmother's roof. Jillian was a pretty, twenty-six-year-old, full-figured woman. She wasn't the brightest when it came to picking the men in her life, but she had a good heart and that's all that mattered to me.

She'd barely said hello before she asked, "Think you can bring me a couple of Percocets on your way home?"

"Jillian, not today," I griped.

"You're acting like I'm asking you to bring me a pill bottle of 'em," Jillian protested. "And besides, you know I don't ask you unless I really need them."

I let out a long sigh and said, "I'm gonna bring you only two. And that's it."

"Thank you," Jillian said with excitement.

"Yeah, whatever. You're such a spoiled brat," I told her.

"So. What are you doing?"

"Sitting in the food court of Pembroke Mall, eating some Chinese food."

"What time do you get off today?"

"I think I'm gonna leave at about seven since it's Saturday."

"Has it been busy today?"

"Kinda . . . sorta," I replied between each chew.

"So, what are you doing after work?"

"Terrell has been harassing me, talking about he wants to see me," I told her. Terrell was my on-and-off-again boyfriend.

"That sounds so boring."

"What do you want me to do, sit around all day like you and get high off prescription drugs?" I said sarcastically.

"Oh, Misty, that was a low blow. You know I don't do this shit for fun. If I don't take those drugs I'm going to be in serious pain."

"Look, I know you need 'em, so I'm going to get off your back. But from time to time, you do ask me for more than you should have."

"That's because I be trying to make a few dollars here and there. Oh, and speaking of which, I got a business proposition for you."

"What is it now?"

"I got a homeboy that will pay top dollar for twenty to twenty-five Vicodin pills."

"Jillian, are you freaking crazy?! There's no way in hell that I'm going to be able to get that many pills at one time."

"He's paying four hundred dollars. But I'm gonna have to get my cut off the top, which would be a hundred."

I sighed. "Jillian, I'm not doing it."

"Come on, Misty, stop being paranoid. You can do it," Jillian whined.

"Do you want me to lose my job?"

"Of course not. But you're acting like you've never taken drugs from your job before."

"Look, I'm not doing it. Case closed."

"Just think about it." Jillian pressed the issue, but I ignored her. I changed the subject. "Is Grandma home?"

"She's in the laundry room folding clothes."

"Did she say she was cooking dinner?"

"Yeah, she's got a pot roast in the oven."

"Save some for me," I told Jillian.

"You know I will."

I changed the subject again. "You still talking to Edmund?"

"I just got off the phone with his frugal ass!"

I chuckled. "What has he refused to pay for now?"

"I asked him to order me a pizza online and he told me that he ain't have any money."

"Doesn't he own and operate a janitorial business?"

"Yep."

"Then he shouldn't be broke," I said. "Look, just leave that fool alone. You give him too much pussy for him to not feed you."

"I know, right!" she agreed. But I read her like a book because as soon as we got off the phone with one another, I knew she'd call that selfish-ass nigga and act like her stomach wasn't growling.

She and I talked for another ten minutes or so about her finding another job instead of sitting on her ass all day, crying about how much pain she's in. It seemed like my grandmother let her ride with that lame-ass excuse, but I knew better. My grandmother knew exactly what was going on, but looked the other way because she enjoyed Jillian's company and she didn't want to be alone in that big house. Jillian had a free ride anyway you looked at it.

"Don't forget to put some of that pot roast aside," I reminded her.

"I won't," she said, and right before I hung up, I heard her add, "Don't forget my meds either."

My only response to that was a head shake.

1

A year ago today, Mallory Knight's world had changed. She found her best friend dead, sprawled on top of a comforter. The one Leigh had excitedly shown Mallory just days before, another extravagant gift from her friend's secret, obviously rich lover, the cost of which, Mallory had pointed out, could have housed a thousand homeless for a week. Or fed them for two. Leigh had shrugged, laughed, lain back against the ultra-soft fabric. Her deep cocoa skin beautifully contrasted against golden raw silk.

That day, when the earth shifted on its axis, Leigh had lain there again. Putrid. Naked. Grotesquely displayed. Left uncovered to not disturb potential evidence, investigators told her. Contaminate the scene. *With what, decency?* She had ignored them, had wrenched a towel from the en suite bath and placed it over her friend and colleague's private parts. Her glare at the four men in the room was an unspoken dare for them to remove it. That would happen only over her dead body.

She'd steeled herself. She looked again, at the bed and around the room. Whoever had killed Leigh had wanted her shamed. The way the body was positioned left no doubt about that. For Mallory, the cause of death wasn't in doubt, either. Murder. Not suicide, as the coroner claimed. But his findings matched what the detectives believed, what the scant evidence showed so . . . case closed. Even though the half-empty bottle of high-dose opioids found on Leigh's nightstand weren't hers. Even though forensics found a second set of prints on one of two wineglasses next to the pills. Even though Mallory told investigators her friend preferred white wine to red and abhorred drugs of any kind. She suffered through headaches and saw an acupuncturist for menstrual cramps. Even though for Leigh Jackson image was everything. She'd never announce to the world she'd killed herself by leaving the pill bottle out on the table, get buck naked to do the deed, then drift into forever sleep with her legs gaping open. Details like those wouldn't have gotten past a female detective. They didn't get by Mallory, either. Beautiful women like Leigh tended to be self-conscious. What did Mallory see in that god-awful crime scene? Not even a porn star would have chosen that pose for their last close-up.

The adrenaline ran high that fateful morning, Mallory remembered. Early January. As bitterly cold as hell was hot. Back-to-back storms in the forecast. This time last year, New York had been in the grips of a record-breaking winter. Almost a foot of snow had been dumped on the city the night before. Mallory had bundled up in the usual multiple layers of cashmere and wool. She had pulled on knee-high, insulated riding boots and laughed out loud at the sound of Leigh's voice in her head, a replay of the conversation after showing Leigh what she'd bought.

"Those are by far the ugliest boots I've ever seen."

"Warm, though," Mallory had retorted. "I'm going for substance, not style."

"They'd be fine for Iceland. Or Antarctica. Or Alaska. Not Anchorage, though. Too many people. One of those outback places with more bears than humans. Reachable only by boat or plane."

Mallory had offered a side-eye. "So what you're saying is this was a great choice for a record cold winter."

"Absolutely . . . if you lived in an igloo. You live in an apartment in Brooklyn, next door to Manhattan. The fucking fashion capitol of the world, hello?"

Mallory had laughed so hard she snorted, which caused Leigh's lips to tremble until she couldn't hold back and joined her friend in an all-out guffaw. Complete opposites, those ladies. One practicality and comfort, stretch jeans and tees. The other back-breaking stilettos and designer everything. They'd met at an IRE conference, an annual event for investigative reporters and editors, and bonded over the shared position of feeling like family outcasts who used work to fill the void. Leigh was the self-proclaimed heathen in a family of Jehovah's Witnesses while second marriages and much younger siblings had made Mallory feel like a third wheel in both parents' households. To Mallory, Leigh felt like the little sister she'd imagined having before her parents divorced.

That morning a year ago she'd stopped at the coffee shop for her usual extra-large with an espresso shot, two creams, and three sugars. She crossed the street and headed down into the subway to take the R from her roomy two-bed, two-bath walkup in Brooklyn to a cramped shared office in midtown Manhattan, a five-minute walk from Penn Station in a foot of snow that felt more like fifteen. She'd just grabbed a cab when her phone rang. An informant with a tip. Another single, successful, beautiful female found dead. One of many tips she'd received since beginning the series for which she'd just won a prestigious award. "Why They Disappear. Why They Die." Why did they? Mysteriously. Suspiciously. Most cases remained unsolved. Heart racing, Mallory had redirected the cabbie away from her office down to Water Street and a tony building across from the South Street Seaport. The building where Leigh lived. Where they'd joked and laughed just days before. She'd shut down her thoughts then. Refused to believe it could be her best friend. There were nine other residences in that building. She'd go to any of the condominiums, all of them, except number 10. But that very apartment is where she'd been directed. The apartment teeming with police, marked with crime tape.

"Knight."

Jolted back into the present, Mallory sucked in a breath, turned her eyes away from the memory, and looked at her boss. "Hey, Charlie."

"What are you doing here? It's Friday. I thought I told you to take the rest of the day off and start your weekend early."

"I am."

"Yeah, I see how off you are." He walked over to her corner of the office, moved a stack of books and papers off a chair, and plopped down. He shuffled an ever-present electronic cigarette from one side of his mouth to the other with his tongue. "That wasn't a suggestion. It was an order. Get out of here."

He sounded brusque, but Charlie's frown was worse than his fist. It had taken her almost three years to figure that out. When she started working at *New York News* just over four years ago he was intimidating, forceful, and Mallory didn't shrink easily. Six foot five with a shock of thick salt-and-pepper hair and a paunch that suggested too many hoagies, not enough salad, and no exercise, he'd pushed Mallory to her limit more than once. She'd pushed back. Worked harder. Won his respect.

"I know it's a hard day for you." His voice was softer, gentler now.

"Yep." One she didn't want to talk about. She powered down her laptop, reached for the bag.

"She'd have been proud of you for that."

"What?" He nodded toward her inbox. "Oh, that."

"'Oh, that,'" he mimicked. "That, Knight, is what investigative journalists work all of their lives for and hope to achieve. Helluva lot of work you put in to get the Prober's Pen. Great work. Exceptional work. Congrats again."

It was true. In this specialized circle of journalism, the Prober's Pen, most often simply called the Pen, was right up there with the Pulitzer for distinctive honor.

"Thanks, Charlie. A lot of work, but not enough. We still don't know who killed her." A lump, sudden and unexpected, clogged her throat. Eyes burned. Mallory yanked the power cord from the wall, stood and shoved it into the computer bag along with her laptop. She reached for her purse. No way would she cry around Charlie. Investigative reporters had no time for tears.

She was two seconds from a clean escape before his big paw clamped her shoulder and halted her gait. She looked back, not at him, in his direction, but not in his eyes. One look at those compassion-filled baby blues and she'd be toast.

"What, Callahan?" Terse. Impatient. A tone you could get away with in New York. Even with your boss. Especially one like Charlie.

"Your column helped solve several cases. You deserved that award. Appreciate it. Appreciate life . . . for Leigh."

"Yeah, yeah, yeah. Out of my way, softie." Mallory pushed past him the way she wished she could push past the pain.

"Got a new assignment when you come back, Knight!"

She waved without turning around.

Later that evening Mallory went for counseling. Her therapists? Friends and colleagues Ava and Sam. The prescription? Alcohol. Lots of it. And laughter. No tears. At first, she'd declined, but they insisted. Had they remembered the anniversary, too? One drink was all she'd promised them. Then home she'd go to mourn her friend and lament her failed attempts to get at the truth. After that she'd go to visit her bestie. Take flowers. Maybe even shed a tear or two. If she dared.

Mallory left her apartment, tightened her scarf against the late-January chill, and walked three short blocks to Newsroom, an aptly named bar and restaurant in Brooklyn, opened by the daughter of a famous national news anchor, frequented by journalists and other creative types. Stiff drinks. Good food. Reasonable prices. Not everyone made six figures like Mallory Knight. In America's priciest city, even a hundred thousand dollars was no guarantee of champagne kisses and caviar dreams.

Bowing her head against the wind, she hurried toward the restaurant door. One yank and a blast of heat greeted her, followed by the drone of conversation and the smell of grilled onions. Her mouth watered. An intestinal growl followed, the clear reminder she hadn't had lunch. She unwrapped the scarf from around her head and neck, tightened the band struggling to hold back a mop of unruly curls, and looked for her friends.

"In the back." The hostess smiled and pointed toward the dining room.

"Thanks."

"Heard you won the Pen. Way to go."

"Gosh, word gets around."

"It's one of the highest honors a reporter can receive, Mallory so, yeah, a few people know."

She turned into the dining room and was met by applause. Those knowing people the hostess described were all standing and cheering. After picking her jaw off the floor, Mallory's narrowed eyes searched the room for her partners in crime. A shock of red hair ducked behind . . . Gary? Special correspondent for NBC? Indeed. And other familiar faces, too. The *Post*, *Times*, *Daily News*, the *Brooklyn Eagle*, *Amsterdam News*, and other local and national news outlets were represented. Highly embarrassed and deeply moved, Mallory made her way across the room, through good-natured barbs, hugs, and high fives, over to Gary, who gave her a hug, inches from the dynamic duo who'd undoubtedly planned the surprise.

"You two." Mallory jabbed an accusatory finger into a still shrinking Sam's shoulder while eyeing Ava, who smiled broadly. "When did you guys have time to do all this?"

"Calm down, girl." Ava shooed the question away. "Group text. Took five seconds."

Ava. Her girl. Keep-it-real Holyfield. "Thanks for making me feel special."

"You're welcome." Ava munched on a fry. "Always happy to help."

Just when Mallory thought she couldn't be shocked further, a voice caused her to whip her head clean around.

"Can I have everyone's attention, please?"

There stood Charlie, red-faced and grinning, holding up a shot glass as two tray-carrying waiters gave a glass to everyone in the room. Her boss was in on it, too? All that insistence that she get out of the office? Damn, he was trying hard to make her cry.

"She doesn't like the spotlight, so next week I'll pay for this. But I was thrilled to learn that a celebration was being planned for one of the best reporters I've ever had the pleasure of working with, Mallory Knight." He paused for claps and cheers. "Most of you know this, though some may not. The hard work done on the Why series has resulted in three women being found and reunited with their families and two arrests, one of which a cold case that had remained unsolved for fifteen years. Good job, kiddo."

Mallory accepted his hug. "Thanks, Charlie."

"Speech! Speech!" echoed around the room.

"As most of you know, I'm a much better writer than I am a speaker. At least without a lot more of these, so . . ." Mallory held up a shot glass holding pricey liquor. "Hear, hear."

She downed the drink, swallowed the liquid along with the burn that accompanied its journey down the hatch. Holding up a hand quieted the crowd.

"Okay, I . . . um . . . thank you guys for coming. The Pen means a lot. But your support means a lot more. Um . . . that first toast was for me. Let's do one more for another IR, Leigh Jackson. Everybody here who knew her knew she was . . . pretty amazing."

Mallory blinked back tears. "She was the inspiration behind the series and why I have this award." She held up a second shot glass. "To Leigh!"

For the next half hour Mallory accepted congrats and well wishes from her colleagues, accompanied by a medium-rare steak dinner and more vodka. The crowd thinned. Mallory grew quieter.

Sam squeezed her shoulder. "You okay?"

Seconds passed as she pondered the question. A slow nod followed. "As of a few seconds ago, I feel a lot better."

"Why?" Ava asked.

"I just made a decision." Mallory looked from Ava to Sam. "I know I said I'd let it go. But I can't. Whoever killed Leigh is not going to get away with it. I'm going to find out who did it, and make sure they pay for her murder."

Sam's expression morphed into one of true concern. "Oh, no, Mal. Not that again."

"You think a cold-blooded murderer should walk around free?"

"You know what she means." Ava's response was unbowed by Mallory's clear displeasure. "Or have you forgotten those first couple months after she died, when you were so bent on proving Leigh's suicide was murder that you almost worked yourself into a grave?"

"But I didn't die, did I? Instead, I got the Pen." Mallory's voice calmed as she slumped against her chair. "I'd much rather get Leigh's killer."

"I know you loved Leigh," Ava said, her voice now as soft as the look in her eyes. "And while Sam and I didn't know her as well as you did, we both liked her a lot and respected the hell out of her work as a journalist. You did everything you could right after it happened. Let the police continue to handle it from here on out."

"That's just it. They think it's already handled. The death was ruled a suicide. Case closed."

There wasn't a comeback for that harsh truth. Mallory held up a finger for another shot. Ava's brow arched in amazement.

"How many of those can you hold, Mal? You're taller than me, but I've got you by at least thirty pounds."

Mallory looked up to see Charlie wave and head to the door. Ignoring Ava, she called out to him. "Charlie!"

He waited by the hostess stand, the area now cold and crowded from the rush of dinner guests and a constantly opening door.

"What is it, kiddo?"

"Can't believe you knew about this and didn't tell me."

"Had you known, you wouldn't have shown up."

"That's probably true. I appreciate what you said up there. Thanks."

"Think nothing of it." He looked at his watch. "I gotta run. See you next week."

"One more thing. The new assignment you mentioned earlier. What's it about?"

Charlie hesitated.

Mallory's eyes narrowed. "Charlie . . ."

"Change of pace. You're going to love it."

"What's the topic?"

"Basketball."

"You want me to cover sports?" Incredulity raised Mallory's voice an octave.

"Told you that you'd love it," Charlie threw over his shoulder as he caught the door a customer just opened and hurried out.

"Charlie!"

Mallory frowned as she watched her boss's hurried steps, his head bowed against the wind and swirling snow. His answer to her question only raised several more. *Why would Charlie want an investigative reporter on a sports story? Why wasn't the sports editor handling it? Freelance writers clamored for free tickets to sports events. Why couldn't he give the assignment to one of them?* She wanted to continue doing stories that mattered, like those on missing women and unsolved murders that had won her the Pen. And Charlie wanted her to write about grown men playing games? Her mood darkening and shivering at the blast of cold wind accompanying the next customer through the front door, Mallory walked back to the table, hugged her friends goodbye, and began the short walk home. She lived less than ten minutes from the restaurant, and, although the temperature had dropped and snow was falling, she barely noticed. Mallory's thoughts were on her dead best friend, the botched closed case, and how to regenerate interest in catching a killer. Because whether officially or not, for work or not, Mallory would never stop trying to find out who killed Leigh Jackson. Never. Ever. No fucking way.

1

The black Tahoe crept onto the rooftop of the parking garage overlooking downtown Fayetteville and stopped. The driver lumbered his hefty frame out of the truck and stood to his full six-foot-seven-inch height. He flipped the collar up on his heavy mink coat, readjusted the sawed-off shotgun tucked beneath his arm, and scanned his surroundings for danger. Satisfied that the area was clear, he tapped on the passenger window of the truck. The tinted window eased down halfway, and a cloud of smoke was released into the air.

"It's clear," the giant reported.

"Good. Now go post up over there so you can see the street, make sure no funny biz popping off," the man in the truck instructed.

The giant hesitated a moment. "You sure about this? I mean, I don't trust these dudes like that," he said.

The man smiled. "You worry too much, Samson. Nobody would dare violate this thing of ours again. Look around you, it's just us and them. This is crew business, and this shit has gone on long enough. Tonight, it ends, one way or another."

The window glided up, and the giant assumed his position near the edge of the parking garage.

Behind the dark glass of the Tahoe, two men sat in the back seat sharing a blunt while a brooding hip-hop track thumped through the speakers. The men casually passed the blunt and enjoyed the music as if they were at a party, and not on the precipice of a drug war for control of the city's lucrative narcotics trade. Although partners, each of the men was a boss in his own right. Their leadership styles were different—one was fire, the other was ice—but it was the balance that made their team so strong.

In the back seat of the Tahoe sat Qwess and Reece, leaders of the notorious Crescent Crew.

"Yo, that beat is bananas, son!" Reece remarked to Qwess. "You did that?"

Qwess nodded. "You knowww it," he sang.

"Word. You already wrote to it?"

"I'm writing to it right now," he replied. He pointed to his temple. "Right here."

"I hear ya, Jay-Z," Reece joked. "So, anyway, how you want to handle this when these niggas get here?"

Qwess nodded. "Let me talk some sense into them, let them know they violated."

"Son, they know they violated."

"Still, let me handle it, because you know how you can be."

Reece scowled. "How I can be? Fuck is that supposed to mean?"

"You know how you can be," Qwess insisted.

"What? Efficient?"

"If you want to call it that."

Headlights bent around the corner and a dark gray H2 Hummer came into view. The Hummer drove to the edge of the garage and stopped inches in front of Samson. He spun around to face the truck. The giant, clad in a full-length mink, resembled King Kong in the glow of the xenon headlamps.

Inside the truck, Qwess craned his head over the seat to confirm their guests. "That's them," he noted as he passed Reece the blunt. He climbed from the back of the truck and tossed his partner a smirk. "Stay here, I got it."

Qwess joined Samson while men poured out of the Hummer. When the men stood before Qwess, someone very important was absent.

Qwess raised his palm. "Whoa, whoa, someone's missing from this little shindig," he observed, scanning the faces. "Where is Black Vic?"

One of the minions stepped forward. He wore a bald head and a scowl. "Black Vic couldn't be here tonight. He sends his regards." The man thumbed his chest with authority. "He sent me in his place."

Qwess frowned. "He sent you in his place? Are you kidding me? We asked for a meeting with the boss of your crew, and he sends you?"

The man nodded. "Yep."

Qwess shook his head. "Yo, get Black Vic on the phone and tell him to get his ass down here now."

The minion chuckled. "I see you got things confused, dawg. You run shit over there, not over here. Now are we talking or what?"

Samson took a step forward. The other three men took two steps back. Qwess gently placed a hand on Samson's arm. The giant stood down.

"I need to talk to the man in charge," Qwess insisted. "Because we only going to have this conversation one time."

"Word?"

"Word!"

Suddenly, the back door to the Tahoe was flung open, and all eyes shifted in that direction. Reece stepped out into the night and flung his dreads wildly. Time seemed to slow down as he diddy-bopped over to them, his Cuban link and heavy medallion swinging around his neck. He pulled back the lapels on his jacket and placed his hands on his waist, revealing his Gucci belt and his two .45s.

"Yo, where Victor at?" Reece asked.

Qwess scoffed. "He ain't here. He sent *these* niggas."

Reece looked at each man, slowly nodding his head. "So Victor doesn't respect us enough to show his face and address his violation? He took two kis from my little man, beat him down. My li'l homie from Skibo hit him with consignment, and he decided to keep shit. Now, we trying to resolve this shit 'cause war is bad for business—for everybody, and he wanna say, 'fuck us'?"

"Black Vic said that you said 'fuck us' when you wouldn't show us no flex on the prices," the minion countered.

"Oh, yeah? That what he said?" Reece asked. He shook his head and mocked, "*He said, she said, we said* . . . See, that's that bitch shit. That's why Victor should've came himself. But he sent you to speak for him, right?"

The bald-headed minion puffed out his bird chest. "That's right."

"Okay." Reece nodded his head and looked around the rooftop of the garage. "Well, tell Victor this!"

SMACK!

Without warning, Reece lit the minion's jaws up with an open palm slap. Samson lunged forward and wrapped his huge mittens around the neck of one of the other minions, who wore a skully pulled low over his eyes. Qwess drew his pistol and aimed it at the other minion in a hoodie, while the soldier in the passenger seat of the Tahoe popped out of the roof holding an AK-47.

"Y'all thought it was sweet?" Reece taunted. He smacked the bald-headed minion again, and he crumpled to the floor semiconscious. "I got a message for Victor's ass, though."

Reece dragged the man over to the Hummer and pitched his body to the ground in front of the pulley attached to the front of the truck. He reached inside the Hummer to release the lever for the pulley, then returned to the front of the Hummer. While the spectators watched in horror, Reece pulled bundles of metal rope from the pulley and wrapped it around the man's neck. Qwess came over to help, and when they were done, the two of them hoisted the man up onto the railing.

"Wait, man! Please don't do this!" the minion pleaded. He was fully conscious now, and scrapping for his life. Qwess cracked him in the jaw and knocked the fight right out of him.

Reece fixed him with a cold gaze. "*We* not doing this to you, homie. Your man, Victor, is," he explained. "His ass should've showed up. Now, of course, this means war."

Reece and Qwess flipped the man over the railing. His body sailed through the air, and the pulley whirred to life, guiding his descent. His banshee-like wail echoed through the quiet night as he desperately tugged at the rope around his neck. Then suddenly, the pulley ran out of rope and caught, snapping his neck like a chicken. Both Qwess and Reece spared a look over the edge and saw his lifeless body dangling against the side of the building.

Reece turned to face the others. Slowly, he slid his thumb across his naked throat, and the AK-47 sparked three times. All head shots.

This was crew business.

Connect with U s

Visit us online at
KensingtonBooks.com
to read more from your favorite authors, see books
by series, view reading group guides, and more.

for sneak peeks, chances to win books and prize packs,
and to share your thoughts with other readers.

facebook.com/kensingtonpublishing
twitter.com/kensingtonbooks

Tell us what you think!

To share your thoughts, submit a review,
or sign up for our eNewsletters, please visit:
KensingtonBooks.com/TellUs.